The secret of the king

John Miller

CHAPTER 1

Anna

Anya slammed the book and put it in its usual place - on the writing desk, to the left of the ink device. How long is she still destined to keep her favorite book on her desk? It was a collection of young poet Nikolai Gumilyov, published five years ago, whose verses were either not noticed or scolded.

But Anya, once having opened a book with the mannered name "Pearls", which had long been gathering dust on the shelf, was amazed at the word music and quickly got used to read two or three Gumilev's poems every day, which, oddly enough, helped to soothe emotional pain.

What did this person write about in his book - "screaming, roughened and perfumed", in the words of one vicious literary critic? About conquistadors, pirates, giraffes and parrots? What is the business of the young widow of a Russian officer, who has not yet cried a burning sorrow, to giraffes and Lake Chad?

But from the words of Gumilev, and indeed strung together like pearls in a necklace, for some reason it became a little easier to breathe, like spells from withers.

Repeating to myself: "And my heart aches and knocks, sadly smacking the fatal ...", Anna wandered around the apartment that was empty before her eyes. So the piano was taken away, and yesterday she packed the porcelain sets herself, and now the gloomy sideboard silently reproaches her with ruined dusty shelves ...

Moving from room to room, Anya stopped by a large mirror in the front. From the bronze frame, a sad face framed in black lace widow tattoo looked at her. The woman in mourning clothes, who was reflected in the mirror, seemed unfamiliar to her, although Anya had become accustomed to seeing this face in the mirror for more than twenty years of her life. But now there, behind mirror glass, there was some other Anna, without a smile, pale, with deep melancholy in the eyes, swollen with tears, with hair pulled back under a mourning tattoo ...

Anna's husband, Lieutenant Chigarev, who fought in the army of General Brusilov, died in battle during the Carpathian operation and was buried, singed by the regimental priest, somewhere in Galicia, in a hastily dug front grave. It is unlikely that an unfortunate widow will ever be able to find this grave to cry over the mound and put flowers on it. And it will be abandoned, no one in a foreign land needs a grave mound to crumble, crumble until it is equal to the ground ...

What remains of her life now? Loneliness and longing. And the pain of loss, almost physical pain, from which it is difficult to breathe.

She is only twenty-one ... How old is Anna ahead? Perhaps a lot more. Many, many years filled with this pain, loneliness and longing ...

All of her relatives went into another world, leaving Anya completely alone in this world to pull a hateful life. Mama died when Anya was still a girl, then her father passed away, the elder sister Nina died of tuberculosis a year ago. And now they killed Alyosha ...

It seems that quite recently, radiant Anya was standing in a white wedding dress next to her fiance at the lectern, and how much joy life promised her! And so the war, the bitter farewell of her husband in the army, the long wait for front-line letters, giving hope that joy will come back and you just have to wait patiently and patiently ...

Anna got used to go to church every morning and ask the Mother of God to save Alexey's life - she no longer had anyone to ask for help.

But her prayers were not heard - too many women throughout Russia asked for their loved ones, apparently, every single voice was indistinguishable. Anna received a notice that her husband, Lieutenant Chigarev, was killed in battle.

After his death, it turned out that the money affairs of the Chigarevs were not in the best condition. And why do such things always turn out after someone's death and always unexpectedly? Two estates that belonged to her husband were mortgaged and re-mortgaged. It turned out to be easier to put them up for auction than to clear them of debts. The money from Anino's bank account was spent by the newlyweds on the arrangement of their family home and on the military equipment of her husband who went to the front. Alexey enthusiastically prepared to fight - ordered smart chrome boots from an expensive shoemaker, a tailored overcoat, indispensable for trench life, and a few extra uniforms (because at the front everything quickly becomes useless, it will be difficult to wash and iron uniforms!), He bought a new a checker and five pieces of revolvers of different brands, not trusting the government service weapon ...

They said that, having arranged a farewell dinner for friends, Aleksey finally decided to play around with cards and lost big. But Anya did not attach any importance to these conversations - even if he did, he is going to fight, when will he still have a carefree time of fun?

But anyway, it suddenly turned out that the bank account, from where it was always possible to withdraw money, was almost empty. There was nothing to pay for renting a rich Moscow apartment to a young widow, and, hiding her tears, had to give up the family nest that Anya arranged with such love after the wedding. Tastefully selected carpets, curtains, antique chairs and vases had to be sold for pennies. There was a war, and the furnishings sharply depreciated - everyone was no longer up to the interiors ...

However, it was becoming more and more difficult to live in Moscow anyway - since the beginning of the war, food prices in large cities have increased significantly, and the cook, returning from the market, did nothing to complain about the high cost of living. It's a joke to say, for a pound of beef, which before the war the red price was a dime, now they asked for half a pound ... Even the bread went up too!

Anya thought and thought and decided that the best thing for her would be to leave for the old grandfather's estate Privolnoe, inherited after the death of her parents. Thank God, this estate was not mortgaged, but in the village you can live quite comfortably on a small widow's pension. Alexey, as soon as he got into difficult financial circumstances, every time he persuaded Anya to lay or sell Privolnoe, but with all her love for her husband she could not do it - her grandfather and grandmother were buried in the manor park. It was impossible to sell along with the estate the graves of loved ones?

Fortunately, the husband eventually realized that she could not part with Privolny, and not only stopped insisting on selling, but even leaving for the front, asked her to save her old grandfather's house at any cost.

And now, Ani has her own corner where she can find peace. In Moscow, none of my acquaintances wanted to understand her longing - she was forced to take part in some charitable committees, be on duty at the hospital, collect parcels for the front ... It was considered that it was extremely useful for widows to load themselves with social activities. Her friends came to her to read letters from the army from her husbands and grooms, showed pictures of handsome men pulled into military belts ...

The handsome military men in their messages to relatives in every possible way praised their front-line exploits and were sometimes so carried away that they blurted out too much, and their letters, falling on the way home into the hands of military censorship, were covered with a lot of black blots hiding dangerous words. But these boasters, supposedly almost single-handedly capturing the shelves of the Germans, were alive and well and continued to delight their relatives with their bikes.

And her Alyosha was no longer in the world! Only one thing could be worse than such letters - when those familiar with feigned dismal faces looked into Anna's eyes and said: "Honey, we are so sorry for you! Wow - Alyosha was killed! And who would have thought! Such a blooming man, almost a boy - and here you are! But you seem to be recovering slowly? Make an effort, dear. You are still so young, and time is the best doctor. "

No, to leave, to leave from this annoying Moscow rush, from tactless people, from sympathetic inquiries, concealing obnoxious curiosity to someone else's misfortune ... And to hide from everyone the pain.

Privolnoe was located at the very border of the Moscow province, in a remote place where the centuries-old Vladimir forests were wedged. From the nearest train station to the manor, it was necessary to go another twelve miles away on horseback.

The old nanny, who had lived her life in Privolnoye after Nina and Annie grew up, met her pet at the station, having contracted a chariot.

Anya came out of the car and inhaled with delight with a full chest - the local air, filled with the scent of herbs, needles and wild flowers swaying along the railway tracks, was so different from the summer air of Moscow, saturated with cement dust and the heat of stones and tin roofs that were hot in the sun ... slightly spinning.

"Oh, my dear little child," the nanny rushed off with tears to Anna. - Unhappy you are my orphan! Oh, they killed our falcon, a handsome man written! Oh, woe ... Here it is, the war is damned! Nemchura damn it that has done! Vdova my krovinochka left in twenty years! To their wives aspid so widow! So they all gone, damn seed! To burn them with heavenly fire, so that they swelled with hunger ...

- Nanny, stop, please wail! - Anya said, kissing the nurse in the wet with tears cheek. - My heart is already so heavy. Do not tear my heart. Let's go home.

The driver set up the women in a tarantass, placed the luggage and touched the horse. The nanny, who had time to wipe away the tears, rumbled all the way, telling local news about some forgotten, or even not at all, familiar to Anna people. Anya listened absently, looking around. Vast fields, interspersed with coppices, were soon left behind, and on the sides of the road, two tall, jagged walls of old firs grew.

Four miles remained before Privolnoye, when the driver suddenly dragged the reins and, shouting, "Damn it, damn!" Stopped his leisurely horse.

- What happened? - Anya asked him.

"Do not ask, darling, on the road ahead of the funeral." Omen bad. And to meet the coffin galloping is not good, and passing by is bad. We turn from sin into the forest. Leskom something else faster, come, we'll get.

The driver moved the horse from a well-groomed road to two loose ruts going into the thicket. The nurse, stretching out her neck, glanced toward a rather crowded funeral procession. It was already possible to discern that a simple wooden coffin was being carried on simple hearse, followed by a whole crowd. Having crossed over, the nurse whispered:

- God rest, O Lord, your new servant, the innocently slain.

- Hey, Makarovna, who is buried? Go, Pelageya, Kuznetsov daughter? - asked the driver with a goat. - People, look, prorva gathered. No other way, Pelagia was taken to the churchyard.

"Her, her, poor thing, let her rest in peace ..."

Anna was finally distracted from her own sad thoughts and asked:

"Nanny, why is the funeral so crowded?" This Pelageya was probably loved by everyone here.

- And why not love her? - responded nurse. - The girl was good, kind, modest. Yes, and she died like ... Oh, Nytochka, I didn't want to talk to you before the time, but it was the same. Not the first girl dies in our places - the nurse looked around cautiously and went into a whisper. - Already the fourth in the forest with a cut throat is found. First, Matreshu, that in the tavern at Sysoev, served as a servant, they found the dead, and the throat, they say, spread from ear to ear, protect the Lord. Then popovnu, the father's daughter from the Church of Grayev stabbed to death. Batyushka came down with grief, he could not serve for ten days, but when he recovered, he came to matins, we look, and he is all gray. There was something, while the daughter was alive, with gray, salt and pepper, as they say. And then white became like an harrier. Here is something that makes goryushka!

The nanny sighed heavily and shook her head, expressing sympathy for the unfortunate priest.

- The girls would be careful not to stick their nose out of the house until such things happen, so no, they all run around the forest until the murderer gets into his hands. A young teacher from the parish school was slaughtered next to her, such a pretty young lady was white, merry ... Everything was busy with the kids ... And now they bury Pelagia. And who to think - we do not know. People completely without a cross has become. In the forests, they say, fugitive deserters are hiding, they have gotten into a crowd, damned, sometimes, they are robbing on the roads. They, go, and for the murder began ... Who else?

- Yes it is, come, not deserters, - the driver intervened. - You sin on them, Makarovna. Deserters, our boys, simple, baptized, will not take such a sin. Another thing is to rob someone on the road with hunger, this is understandable, hunger is not an aunt. You want to eat, so willy-nilly you will reach out to someone else. And in order to cut the throats of the girls in the woods - we have never had such a spawn. I'll tell you what, madam, you are mine ... At the sawmill, the captured Turks are working ...

- Turks? - Anya asked in surprise. - At the sawmill?

"Well, maybe not the Turks, the dog knows them, but they look like Turks," the driver continued. - This is their bashurman grip - to chick with a knife on the throat, mark my word, theirs. You, madam, also have a caution, don't wander around in the woods for nothing. Now that we have done. Oh, all the war is cursed! From it and in people's heads, clouding occurs.

As soon as the tarantas drove up to the manor and stopped at the main entrance, rather gloomy in appearance, though the marble steps were decorated with a portico with columns and two old vases with dancing nymphs, Anya jumped off the seat and, without entering the house, headed to the part of the park where among the neglected beds stood a large granite monument.

"Well, hello, grandmother and grandfather," she said, brushing litter and small branches from the gravestones that attacked from the birch trees. - I'm your granddaughter Anna. I will live here in Privolny. My dear, I was widowed and came to you, I have nowhere else to go. Only your house and stayed to shelter. - Anya felt tears running down her cheeks, and continued, sobbing: - Granny, if you meet my husband Alexei there, tell him how I yearn ...

Behind Anya, footsteps and crackling bushes sounded. Towarding her with wild skirts against her skirts, the nanny hurried.

- Nytochka, my darling child, let's go away. The place is not good, everyone will tell you. What is there to stand long? Bowed to the dead and okay. Come on, let's go, honey, you have to wash your face from the road, change clothes, eat ... I give you some warm water, we wash tears from your face!

And the nurse, embracing the crying Anna by the shoulders like a little one, led her into the house.

At night, Anya could not sleep, all the time there were some sounds, rustles, creaks ... It seemed that the old house was breathing and tossing and turning.

"It's all nerves, just nerves," Anya reassured herself. - In the morning, when the sun rises, everything here seems more fun.

I'll get used to this house, settle down here, get settled. Everything will be alright. This is my family nest, who am I afraid of? Although what the nanny told about the murders in the district ... This is terrible. But the killer will not climb into the house where there are people? He attacks his victims in a deep forest ... "

In order to distract herself, she took Gumilev's correct volume, but, before plunging into reading, she decided to tell fortunes by old habit. What awaits her?

Opening the book at random, Anya, with closed eyes, jabbed a finger at the page, and then looked at the lines on which her pink fingernail had hit.
I dreamed: we both died, We lay with a soothing look. Two white, white coffins Supplied next ...
- read Anya, feeling the heart poured melancholy.

Why did she get these particular lines? Suddenly in them the ominous true sense is hidden? "We both died ..." Maybe it is Alyosha calling her out of nothingness? And what if death comes now, without pain and suffering, and will take Anna from the earthly vale to other worlds, where there is no war and grief, where she will reunite with her husband ...

And then she clearly heard footsteps above her head. It was no longer the crackling of cracked floorboards and not a murmur rustle. These were the usual heavy steps, most likely masculine. Upstairs someone walked, stamping their boots ...

CHAPTER 2

Helena

Since the war began, I should limit myself in the addiction to read newspapers at breakfast. Anyway, the press today is no longer the same as in former times of peace. Now in the newspapers there are only military reports and the bickering of the leaders of political parties accusing each other of lack of patriotism, and the few news are too often unpleasant. Our troops surrendered Lviv, Lublin, near Warsaw things were also bad.

And the bad news received in the morning, as you know, sets a negative tone for the whole day.

But nevertheless, the incomprehensible desire to quickly find out the last sad military news (I still can't send back troops to help the front, no matter how much I read the lines of the newspaper!) And selfishly overwhelmed the selfish desire for spiritual comfort. A newspaper sheet pulled to itself, like a drug, and I, like an inveterate cocaine, first thing every morning, grabbed hold of a fresh press.

Moreover, I not only eagerly swallowed up the official military chronicles and reports of front-line correspondents, but also looked through the lists of the dead, published in the newspapers, each time praying to myself, so as not to meet familiar surnames.

But, alas, familiar names in mournful lists were encountered more and more often. So, the relatives of the victims need help and support. By help and support, I mean not so much a bouquet of flowers and a note of condolences handed over to the widow as real practical matters - to collect papers for an inheritance, to patrol about orphaned children in educational institutions for public account, to find a new poor cheap apartment ...

I often had to take such chores for myself, not being distracted by unnecessary sentiments, which made me finally deserve a woman's callousness and not inclined to compassion, especially among those who preferred to ponder a little, hugging a widow, and then return to their own business, completely forgetting about another misfortune.

I don't know why my manner of acting, being conformed only with my own conscience, acts so depressingly on many people ...

This time, being in a particularly melancholy mood, I did not even bother to get acquainted with other news by opening the newsletter right away on the mournful lists.

Name columns with a petit in the "Russian Word" were especially extensive today - the Carpathian operation led, alas, to great losses. It is no wonder that in society more and more often they began to repeat that the British had sworn to fight the Germans to the last drop of Russian blood ... Probably, this is a joke, but very sad.

The wounded, the dead, the missing - the three newspaper columns were simply enormous because of the grief that contained them. Reaching almost the end of the alphabet in the list of those who fell on the field of glory, I suddenly stumbled upon the name of Lieutenant Chigarev, which seemed familiar to me.

- Elena Sergeyevna, serve coffee? - looked at the door of the dining room my maid Shura.

"Wait, Shurochka, not before that," I answered absently, looking at the newspaper line.

- Yes, how can I go? - offended Shura. - Everything cools, you yourself will not drink cold coffee. A newspaper and after you can read ...

But my attention was focused on the fine print of the newspaper line. Chigarev ... Chigarev ... My God! This is, after all, the young officer, whom Anya, the younger sister of Nina, of my gymnasium girlfriend, married. Well, of course, Alexey Chigarev, then he was still a second lieutenant ... I even had them at the wedding.

Wow, Anya was a widow. And at such a young age! She is only twenty-one. I, too, had once been widowed, being only half a year older than she is now, and I understood perfectly well what a young woman who just got married and immediately lost her beloved husband could feel. And how hard it was then for me to understand that life was not over, that many, many more happiness and sorrow were measured for me by fate ...

But on bitter days, ineradicable vitality helped me, but Nina and Anya had never been particularly optimistic about life. However, in terms of tragic experiences, the older sister, who was in constant melancholy, ran all the same in their home.

Maybe that's why Nina and I once came together so closely that we were completely different and, at first glance, her eternal melancholy and my unbridled smeshiness did not fit well together. But others were difficult with Nina, and I was not at all. After all, as you know, a wave and a stone, poems and prose, ice and fire ... and so on, according to the text of Alexander Sergeevich, in other words, the unity of opposites may well form the basis of strong friendship.

Who knows why people start to be friends? Friendship is an ancient need that has developed among people even in those times when they had to shoulder to shoulder from the predatory pterodactyls, shoulder to shoulder, closing the back of a friend. Pterodactyls have since died, but the need to lean on the shoulder of a friend remains.

Green-eyed, forever thoughtful and sad Nina was considered the most poetic girl in our gymnasium, she was even nicknamed Undine. But when, after visiting her home, I met Nina's younger sister, it became clear that Anya, still very young, went to her sister in matters of a melancholic attitude to life.

- Who is this with you, bear? - I asked a pretty girl who came to us with a toy in her hands.

"Yes," she replied sadly, looking at me with the same dreary green eyes that Nina had, "and his paw hurts a lot. Poor man, he is suffering so much ...

I had to quickly build a bandage from a handkerchief to help the plush sufferer and at least a little cheer up his little mistress. I knew that my sisters had recently died mother, and felt sorry for them ...

The last time I saw was Nina in Sokolniki, in a new, newly built private sanatorium for tuberculosis patients, where I came to visit her.

Nina always had poor health, but for some reason it didn't even occur to me that she was dying.

Nina sat on an open veranda in a comfortable wicker chair and wrapped herself in a shawl, although the day was rather warm. We chatted about this and that, about relatives, about mutual acquaintances and even a little bit about politics, as usual between intelligent people.

Suddenly, Nina was silent, did not answer a trivial question, lost in thought (this happened to her before), and suddenly asked me:

- Lelia, please promise me one thing!

- Of course, everything that will be in my power! You know, a woman can do a lot, but in our country she is not always allowed to turn around.

I, like an inveterate feminist, prepared to sit on my skate, but Nina interrupted me.

- Do not be shy. You are one of those women who can easily cope with drought, fire, flood, hurricane and bubonic plague combined, and only if they let you turn around ...

Good God, why, Nina is joking! For her, a joke is such a rare and unusual manifestation that it can be safely said that this is no accident. I held my breath.

"Lelia, I am very worried about Anyuta," my friend continued, again becoming quite serious. - She is, in fact, still quite a child, although she managed to jump out of marriage and turned into a young lady. But Anya is absolutely not adapted to life ... I mean everyday life and adversity. If she alone happens to meet this grief ... Do you understand what I'm saying? Grief can break and destroy it, like a fragile blade of grass.

I decided to slightly bring down the tragic pathos of this speech:

- Darling, why should we expect in advance that Ani's life will be filled with grief, hardship and adversity? Let her expect only bright holidays and cloudless happiness!

"I don't mind cloudless happiness," Nina smiled. "But you promise me anyway — if something happens to me, I mean ... the worst thing is, you won't leave my sister." Promise, Lelia, that in grief you will be next to her, I have no one else to ask for.

It would be a sin to refuse! Of course, I promised, to myself, thinking that people, finding themselves in a tuberculosis hospital, immediately become so suspicious ...

However, in the best of times, Nina preferred to see only the dark side in everything. Honestly, she could not be called an optimist. What a hunt for a young blooming woman to imagine that she was on her deathbed and drawn the latest testaments to her neighbors? Nina looked great - she lost weight, reaching an unusual, downright ballet grace, playing a bright blush on her cheeks, eyes that had become particularly large and bottomless, glowed with some sort of unearthly light ...

Alas, I did not understand then what a terrible thing - consumption, and even my vaunted inner voice was silent, not finding it necessary to tell me that I would not see Nina alive again ...

Three weeks later she died, leaving me with my promise to take care of Anyuta.

But easy to say - take care! Annie just half a year got married, enjoyed her new role as a loving spouse, and she was absolutely not up to me.

Have you ever had a chance to make visits to the house of newlyweds, quite satisfied with each other's company, and give them confusing explanations about the purpose of these visits (so, they say, you happened to be in your place and looked in to see how you were here ...), labeling yourself shamelessly curious person? Believe me, the business is not a pleasant one.

Besides (sadly now to recall this), it seemed to me that the husband of Anyuta, Mr. Chigarev, is a so-so young man.

I will not speak badly about the deceased, God rest his soul, let him sleep in peace, but a woman with rich everyday experience is hard to beat. In addition, miracles of insight were not required - Alexey did not particularly hide his passion for immoderate spending and gambling, and I even slightly feared whether he was going to leave the poor girl as soon as her dowry was scattered in the wind ...

However, Anya looked so in love and happy that any intervention in her life seemed completely irrelevant at that moment. I quietly stepped aside, keeping my conclusions with me ...

If, over time, she was destined to get rid of some illusory ideas, then let a similar lesson be presented by fate, and not friends — the lovers will never believe friends anyway.

And now the name of Alexei Chigarev is printed in the lists of those who fell on the field of glory. It is simply impossible not to react to such news with my character, one has only to imagine what is happening with the poor young widow ... Yes, the grief did not take long to wait! It seems the time has come to fulfill the promise given to Nina.

CHAPTER 3

Anna

Anya froze in horror, listening to the sounds in the attic. These were steps, no doubt, steps ... Someone walked through the attic, stomping and creaking boots.

In the house except for Anna there was only a nanny. A cook and a young girl from a nearby village, invited as a maid, were considered to be a visiting servant (it was cheaper for me) and went to sleep at night.

In any case, for some reason even for the servants to stay in Privolnoye, hardly any of them rose deeply into the attic in the pitch darkness and would wander there, rattling and stomping ... Maybe these steps overhead are all did they make up? It is a shame to be such a coward and to be afraid of every sound in your own home.

Anya lit a kerosene lamp, threw a shawl over her shoulders and went from the bedroom to the end of the corridor, where a narrow wooden staircase rose under the roof, into the attic, which had long been uninhabited and crammed with all sorts of unnecessary rubbish.

- Hey, who is here? - Anya shouted in the direction of the attic door, rising to the first step. - Is anyone here?

No one answered her.

She climbed the stairs and opened a heavy oak door that never locked, because there was no treasure except for the forgotten junk. It was quiet in the attic, dark, and it smelled of dust and mice. The attic, even without any strangers, in itself seemed ominous. Crossing the threshold was scary.

- Who is there? - repeated Anya is not so loud. - Is there anybody here? Answer!

The attic was silent.

"These are nerves," Anya told herself, and, picking up the hem of a long nightgown, began to go down the steps. And why does she wander around the house at night, scaring mice? Rather, get to bed, take shelter warmer, and sleep will come. There is nothing to be afraid of!

But as soon as Anya was in bed, she again thought that heavy footsteps were rattling upstairs, then the window frame slammed somewhere.

"Nerves, nerves," Anya repeated again, and covering her head with a pillow so as not to hear anything, she read to herself "Our Father".

"Nanny," Anna asked at breakfast, "did someone go around the house at night?" It seemed to me that I heard footsteps in the attic.

- What are you, killer whale, who is here to run hither and even in the attic? Try on. Although in this house, God forgive me, there are all kinds of miracles. The old days have gone so far. Such a place ... I myself sometimes get something ...

Anya just got ready to ask what kind of miracles from old times happen in her house, as the nanny has already transferred the conversation to another, reporting news about unfamiliar to Anna or long-forgotten neighbors on the estate. As it turned out, life in this quiet forest corner does not stand still.

Someone from the landowners' neighbors sold the estate, someone went bankrupt and cleaned up the house with a hammer, someone got married for a long time and got the kids, and someone, on the contrary, was widowed and wasting away from depression, drinking homemade tea alone.

It is strange that the nanny, without ever leaving the estate, knew so well all the details about the life of the landlords who lived almost twenty miles from Privolnoye and had never been a guest here. But if there was something to tell about the distant neighbors, then everything that happened in the houses of our neighbors was known to a curious old woman without reserve.

Well, I wouldn't even know what is happening, by the way, in Gireyevo, the closest to Privolnoye manor, if the nanny goes three miles to the Gireevsky church and talks after the service with the local girls.

So she told Anyuta that the lonely old colonel, the former owner of Gireev, already died a year later, leaving the estate to the adult grandchildren of the deceased brother, but his cousins, who also had views on the Gray manor, had bypassed. This colonel's maid wanted to sue the new owners, but then he decided that the case was hopeless, it would be difficult to challenge the will, waved his hand and withdrew.

Anya of the old colonel remembered very vaguely, and his heirs, including the unlucky maidens, were not at all interested in her, but they did not succeed in stopping the talkative nanny and had to, willy-nilly, find out all the details about the current Gireev landowners.

Colonel heirs - young people, unmarried, were students before the war, now both are in the army, fighting on the German front, and their mother, the respectable widow, handles the affairs of the estate. She thought up to arrange something like a charity hospital for the wounded in the gireyevsky manor house. There are a lot of young officers recovering from injuries sustained at the front.

"You, Anyuttochka, would go to Gireyevo, would pay a visit to the new mistress in a neighborly way, make acquaintance, and offer some help on the charity part," the nurse advised. - She is a widowed woman, you too ... You look and get off.

- Well, what are you saying, nanny? There was not enough to drive around with visits to the homes of neighbors! I am not looking for new acquaintances and do not want to see anyone at all. I came here to find peace. Solitude and peace, do you understand?

- That's the way it is, peace is a good thing, but only ... Mrs. Zdravomyslova had lodged in the house, all the same society. And your case is a widow, "her nanny bent. "Where are some decent men now?" All on the fronts, help them Lord, the war is coming. But these are crippled, but convalescent already. Maybe they are not so badly hurt ... What did a nun in your age for you? I'm not saying that there is a husband to look for, a friend of the heart or what ... But it's necessary to stay in public so as not to fade away from melancholy. Not everyone is sitting here in Privolnoye, as in a forest skete, until you completely finish it. You listen to the old woman, I will not give you the bad.

- Nanny, you say some nonsense. I'm sorry, but I don't want to listen to anything else.

Anna threw off the napkin and left the table, knocking her chair irritably.

"Well, stupidity," the nanny murmured after her. - No nonsense. The case is a widow, a young one. And there are good gentlemen, noble ones, even from nobles. Here and acquaintance to reduce in a neighborly way. Grooms something now on the street is not lying. The war of all povybet. You would, Nyutochka, do not get lost! Yes, I see the goryushko not otbelela yet ...

The next morning, Anya went for a walk through the estate park, freely spread out on many of the land tithes. She walked around an overgrown, covered with green duckweed pond with a sculpture of Venus that had fallen into the ground near the bank, sat on a shaky, rotten bench in the gazebo, looked into the cracked fountain that had long been deprived of water, sneaked through the thicket of feral jasmine, stood at the gravestone of the grandfather, and went to the gravestone of the grandfather, and her grandfather, and her grandfather, and her grandfather, and her grandfather, and her grandfather, and her grandfather, and her grandfather, and her grandfather, and her grandfather and her grandfather, and sat down at went deep into the lime linden alley. The path between the old lindens is completely overgrown with grass, it seems that no one has walked here for a long time.

"So now my life will look like this fading park," thought Anya. - In solitude and longing you can find your bitter charm. Walking alone along unmarked paths so that no one bothers to indulge in memories ... After all, memories are the only thing I have left. "

But the nanny led her out of a state of poetic sadness, almost running down the avenue, picking up her skirts.

- Nytochka, baby, I found you. Oh, Bozhechka, out of breath ... A guest came to us, a killer whale. Asks you. Take him, dear. And I will order the snack and the samovar.

- What is the guest, nanny? I do not want to see anyone! Tell him that I am unwell today and generally do not accept anyone.

- What are you, how can you! The officer gave us a visit to us, the honorable man did you honor, asks you to accept. And you - I do not want! This is not human!

- I do not want. I have already said. I will not accept anyone.

"Nytochka, listen ..." Mr. Officer asked me to convey that with Lieutenant Chigarev, with your Alesha your deceased, he fought together, in the same regiment. And the whole wounded himself, his face is scarred, there is no place for the living. To look and it is a pity. Surely you are a colleague of her husband, a hero who shed blood for the fatherland, you cannot tell the door to tell the door? As you wish, not in a human way, Anya.

But Anna was no longer listening. Co-worker husband! He will tell her something about Alyosha, about his last days. God, she was stupid, she almost refused this man from home, she could hurt him, push him away ...

- Nanny, where is he?

- Well, where should he be - sitting in the lower living room on the couch. The rooms are not all right; the clean rooms are one-two-time, and you can give them a hand, where else can you call, "the nurse muttered. - Dispose of even the ceremonial chambers clean, Nyutochka, here will be where to take guests. There, in a hall, and a dance party can be arranged, especially in summer, while it is warm. In winter, in such a mansion ovens you will not get lost ...

"Okay, more on that later." You take care of guest food.

Leaving the nanny, Anya hurried to the house.

In the living room on the corner sofa sat the captain, whose face was disfigured by several deep scars. Seeing Anna, he jumped up from the couch. Judging by the impetuousness of his movements, he was much younger than he could have been concluded on his face.

- Hello, madam. Please forgive me for breaking your privacy. Thank you for accepting me. Allow me to introduce myself - Valentin Petrovich Saltykov, fellow soldier lieutenant Chigarev. Being in the neighborhood of your estate, in the gireevsky hospital, he considered it his duty to pay homage.

- Very nice. Anna Afanasyevna Chigareva, - Anya ceremoniously presented herself in turn. - Glad to meet you. Please sit down.

"Honestly, you and I have known each other for a long time," the staff captain said, smiling, from which the scars on his face twisted ugly, "although you probably never remember me, Madame."

Anna looked up at the captain with great surprise. "Have you known each other for a long time? What is he talking about? "

"Being a completely green, barefoot cadet, I tried to take care of your sister Nina and was received at your home," Saltykov explained. - It even seemed to me that your father was very close to me. Or maybe I was just indulging myself with that hope. You were then a lovely baby of eight years old. At the risk of appearing banal, I'll say that you have changed a lot since then. For the better.

Anya gazed involuntarily at the scarred face, trying to find familiar features in it. She perfectly remembered the young cadet Valechka from the Aleksandrovsky military school on Znamenka.

Shining with polished ammunition, a rosy cheeked cadet came to their house with a bouquet of violets for Nina and chocolate bunnies for Ani. With his tender face he looked like a wax angel from the Christmas tree ... Is this headquarters captain with his scars , wrinkles and the first streaking at the temples and that young cadet Valechka?

It seemed that his face had been carved out of a piece of granite with a rough incisor, peppered with deep grooves and made as impenetrable as an ancient sphinx ...

"I understand that now it's almost impossible to recognize me," said the officer sadly, catching Ani's gaze. "You see how ugly I have become after extensive fragmental wounds ... Such persons as mine can be found only in the photographs in the manual on military surgery."

In order to console Saltykov, Anya gathered in her turn to tell him something commonplace, like the well-known maxim that scars adorn a man, but, on reflection, abstained.

This would not only be inappropriate, but even extremely tactless. Of course, strength and determination were read on the wounded face of the captain, however, these qualities for Anna were not the most attractive in people, so she would have to not only speak vulgarity, but also incriminate her soul.

It was possible to get out of an awkward situation, having reminded of the sister which Valentine was a fan of.

"Nina died a year ago," Anya whispered, turning her eyes away from the guest's disfigured face. - Tuberculosis ...

"Yes, such a misfortune," the officer nodded.

- I still can not believe that this could happen. Sorry to upset you, Anna Afanasyevna. I actually came to you on business. In a very sad case, I already had the honor to report that Lieutenant Chigarev was my colleague, but Alexey and I were also friends. You probably read in the newspapers about the large-scale offensive of the enemy near Gorlitsa in the Carpathians. The main blow fell on our army corps ... Before the battle, from which Alyosha did not return, we exchanged crosses with him and gave each other the word that if at least one of us survived this battle, he would find the family of the deceased, give his relatives a cross and tell about his death.

Saltykov paused, then seemed to swallow an invisible lump and spoke again impassively:

- I confess honestly, Anna Afanasyevna, we were all doomed. The Germans surpassed us in manpower two times, or even three, besides constant shelling ... Only an hour after the start of the battle, no more than a quarter of the soldiers remained from the personnel, but we did not give up our positions. And there was no connection with the command post - the Germans managed to damage our telephone cable. When we saw that the Austrians were trying to get around us from the flank and cut off from ours, I led the people into a bayonet attack to prevent the Austrians from connecting with the Germans ... There were not enough gunshot supplies, they fought almost with their bare hands, saving each cartridge. After this fight, I found Alexei among the dead.

Saltykov again paused for a long time and covered his wounded face with his hands. Anya was silent too, tears running down her cheeks. Finally, the officer continued:

- I was going to go to Moscow and look for you to fulfill the will of Alyosha. And by chance I learned that, by coincidence, you settled three versts from Gireyev ... Here is the cross that Alyosha gave me before his last battle.

The captain pulled a small package out of his pocket and unfolded it. There was a golden cross, which Anya herself once brought from the Trinity-Sergius Lavra and put it on her husband's neck before being sent to the front. She immediately remembered the last night spent with Alyosha, a cross on her husband's bare chest, a candle flame playing with reflections in the gold of the cross, and hot kisses before parting, as it turned out, eternal ...

Anna's heart sank with grief. She tried to take a deep breath to get herself together, but her breathing was interrupted, and tears spilled from her eyes with a new force.

Saltykov squeezed her hand.

"Forgive me for hurting you, Anna Afanasyevna," he said quietly. - Will you find the strength to listen to my story to the end or is it better to postpone this difficult conversation?

- No, no, say, Valentin, say, please, - Anya did not even notice that she called Saltykova just by name, as she once called her in childhood. - It hurts me, but I want to know everything. Especially since Alyosha asked you about it. Please speak.

- Good. But get ready for the heavy news.

She involuntarily thought that Alyosha's death was probably too terrible, so Saltykov does not dare to go into details, and asked:

- You want to say that he was very tormented before dying? Did he suffer unbearably? Yes?

- No, do not worry, he died immediately and most likely without much suffering. But the nature of his wounds ... It was terrible. You see, Anna Afanasyevna, your husband was shot in the back.

Anna looked at Saltykov uncomprehendingly.

"I repeat, we were going for a bayonet attack," he continued, worrying. - And if Alex fell from an enemy bullet, he would have met her breast. And he was shot in the back, and it was made by someone from his back chain. That is, I want to say, there, under Gorlitsa, on the battlefield, he was meanly killed by one of his colleagues ... Considering the circumstances, this can be called inhuman murder!

"But maybe in the heat of the attack, he turned to the soldiers to call them behind him?" - Anya asked. "And so the enemy bullet hit him in the back?"

- It is difficult to talk about it, madam, but my opinion is unequivocal - judging by the position of the body, Alexey was shot from our side. Once again, I beg your pardon for bringing you the tough news.

Anna was silent, feeling how everything went awry in her head ... Yes, it was bitter for her to think that Alexei was killed in battle when he went on the attack on the enemy's trenches, but still it is a majestic, sublime, proud death. And if he was shot at his own, treacherously, in the back? It means that this is an ordinary murder, a cruel criminal offense for which no one has been punished. And the person who doesn't understand why he took her beloved husband, happiness and the whole meaning of life is now happy that he managed to turn things around so cunningly.

The headquarters captain continued to say that he would not leave this case, that only his own serious wounds received in the very next battle forced him to postpone the investigation, but as soon as he got stronger and returned to the regiment, he immediately began to look for the killer ... Anna did not could listen more.

"Valentin Petrovich, I beg you to forgive me," she whispered with whitened lips. - I find it difficult to cope with such a blow. I ... I don't feel well.

- May I help you? - Saltykov asked worriedly. - Dispose of me, all that is in my power ...

- Thank you, everything you could have done. Please let me be alone.

The captain-captain bowed, and Anya, clutching a golden cross in her hand, wandered, staggering, to her room, where she collapsed on the bed and burst into tears. It hurts her, hurts, hurts ... Lord, what a terrible pain is tearing her heart! It was necessary for this man to come to her house to make it even more painful!

Anya cried for a long time, until, exhausted, she fell asleep.

She woke up at night, in the dark, someone, apparently the omnipresent nanny, managed to take off her shoes, unbutton her dress, remove the hairpins from her hair and wrap a blanket. Anya got up to change into her nightgown, comb her hair, wash her face and go to bed as it should be.

It is strange that she still wanted to observe all these rules and act "as expected" when her world collapsed, leaving only emptiness in her soul ...

In her hand was still clamped cross Alexis. Keeping a thin chain with a cross out of her fingers, she lit a kerosene desk lamp. It was necessary to remove the dress, stockings, unlace the corset, go to the washstand, on which stood a jug of water and a basin ...

But Anya sat down again on the bed and began looking at the golden cross with longing. Steps rang out the door.

- Nanny, is that you? - Anna asked, but received no response. Having listened, she realized that the steps of the men are like that — the metal boots of the officer boots squeak and sound like the heels of the taps. It even seemed to her that the spurs clinked ...

Taking a lamp from the table, Anya went to the door, flung it open and looked out into the corridor, which went into the darkness. At the staircase, where the darkness especially thickened (the faint rays of the kerosene lamp could not illuminate all the space), a tall male figure flashed and melted behind the stair railing. It was evidently bad, but it seemed to Anya that the man was wearing a military uniform ...

Leaning against the doorjamb, she listened to her heart pounding wildly and blood pounding in her temples.

- Hey, listen! She cried at last, coping with the excitement. - Who you are? And what are you doing in my house?

She was not answered again. Then Anya went to the stairs and shone a lamp down to where the night guest disappeared. The staircase was empty ...

CHAPTER 4

Helena

Alas, my willingness to rush to the aid of widowed Anechka Chigareva came across an unexpected barrier - after the death of her husband, Anya moved from a Moscow apartment somewhere to a village, to an old grandfather's estate. I had to interview all my acquaintances to find out where this lonely place is located.

It turned out not so far - just a few hours drive from Moscow. I was about to go to see Anna, see how she got settled, how she was doing, and offer her help and support in case of need (after all, I can safely consider myself an authority on the question of widowhood), but at the last moment resist the temptation to go in such a simple way. The simple way is not always the right one.

It may be that Anya took refuge in a quiet forest estate from people, in order to stand alone in grief, and the arrival of an uninvited guest would prove defiantly inappropriate.

And then I remembered my husband's great aunt, Varvara Filippovna Zdravomyslova, on whose invaluable help I had repeatedly relied.

I recognized her in difficult times, when Varvara Filippovna, a widow who had two sons, was in very constrained circumstances, trying to put her boys on their feet. The venerable widow struggled in the grip of poverty, and every penny she could manage to postpone, borrow or beg, left to give her sons a good education. Then several large inheritances fell on the heads of the Zdravomyslov family, one after another, Barbara Filippovna's affairs got better, and she was able to direct all her energy to raise money to the field of social and charitable activities, having quite succeeded in the new field.

Now she was fascinated by the new project - a device in the recently inherited estate of the sanatorium for recovering front-line soldiers.

The wounded from the front arrived in such numbers that the rear military hospitals could not cope with the flow of mutilated people, and a patriotic movement was unfolding among Muscovites to set up charity hospitals and clinics.

Private clubs, boarding houses, residential mansions, assembly and sports halls in educational institutions used to give chambers for the wounded ... Not a single wealthy entrepreneur could assure his creditworthiness of partners if he did not organize a couple of hospitals with his own care. Even low-income residents of the free Solodovnikov apartments used all the halls and lobbies in their homes to accommodate the wounded.

But Varvara Filippovna went even further - she set up a boarding house for front-line soldiers in a forest estate, where fresh air, healing springs, fresh milk, natural food, and medical assistance from an experienced rural doctor were at the service of convalescents.

Realization of such a noble plan required titanic efforts, and these efforts had to be exerted mainly in the offices of the authorities, seeking permits and approvals - Zemstvo authorities in many places opposed the design of private military sanatoriums, fearing that front-line soldiers would start committing outrage and rural areas far away in boredom from the garrison guardhouse on them there.

Prince Trubetskoy, for example, who dreamed of arranging a sanatorium in his own Kaluga estate, where up to one hundred convalescents could be accommodated, received a waiver upon his application, where it was announced: "It is too dangerous to leave a large, idle crowd of people in the village without a discipline".

The prince quickly surrendered, but such an initiative lady as Mrs. Zdravomyslova, one refusal from the path was not to turn away - she again and again filed petitions, sought an audience with the high chiefs, persuaded and persuaded, scandals and prayed and managed to achieve her own.

"Not every wounded person can, for one reason or another, use his vacation leave to go on an amendment to his family's home," said Barbara Filippovna. "There are lonely unsettled people among the military, orphans, widowers, residents of the occupied provinces, finally ... And our duty is to help such people who honestly fought and shed blood for the fatherland, to get up after being wounded on their feet! After all, there is no one to take care of them!

The venerable widow was more than indifferent to the needs of the front-line soldiers - both of her sons were in the active army. (However, more recently, I began to suspect in the extensive charitable activities of Varvara Filippovna a fair bit of egoism, oddly enough it sounds. Of course, she did people a lot of good, but not self-serving - she always needed gratitude. And the hotter the gratitude better. The venerable widow did not allow anyone to forget how he was blessed with good luck ...)

Spreading out a huge detailed map of the Moscow province on the living room floor, I crawled to the northeast on all fours and found out without difficulty that Gireyevo, where our dear aunt works in the field of helping others, and Privolnoe, where the young widow indulges in grief, is only a few versts apart.

Well, for starters, I will offer my help to Varvara Filippovna, she will be superfluous to her. And it is where, where, and in Gireyev I will definitely not be denied hospitality. And from there, in a neighborly way, it will be easier to pay a light-hearted visit to Privolnoye and see on the spot how Anya Chigareva lives, how she copes with her grief, and whether the first seeds of madness have fallen on her mind, which is already prone to depression and despondency.

My dearest spouse was just going to another long trip to the places of deployment of our troops (for health not recruited, Michael, like a real man, did not want to stay away from the war, joined the Union of Cities, transformed over time into some mysterious paramilitary "Zemgor", engaged in military supplies and constantly disappeared somewhere near the front line, breaking my heart).

I was always on the nerves, imagining how my beloved spouse, suddenly being in the midst of the battle, spontaneously enter into battle with the erupted parts of the Germans and begin to fend off the enemy in hand-to-hand combat, risking their own lives.

Fearing to lose him, I, praying for intercession from the Lord, was even going to give some vow, but nothing suitable came to mind, and I managed to do without empty promises, trusting in the power of prayers and the disinterested kindness of the Almighty.

Perhaps a trip to Gireyevo with the good goal of helping others will distract me from unnecessary anxiety and help to relax a little. Yes, and urgent matters, because of which I could not leave the Mother See, I now did not have.

Even my favorite brainchild - a perfume factory, built a few years ago, could well now do without the master's attention. The production of perfumes, colognes and eau de toilette had to be steadily reduced - since the beginning of the war alcohol had become a burning deficit, aromatic oils and other components of perfumery products purchased abroad, because of widespread hostilities, got into Russia in a roundabout way, irregularly and in small quantities, good chemists were drafted into the army and were setting up military toxic chemicals at military plants ...

I managed to keep my factory afloat only due to the increase in the output of simple soap supplied for the needs of the army and rear hospitals. But the process of soap making, in contrast to the process of creating a new perfumery fragrance, is so devoid of all romance, so prosaic that it never occurred to me to spend the night and spend the night in a factory watching boiling boilers with soap.

For this there is a manager on a good salary. And for me, life is more than just the pursuit of money.

Having signed off with Varvara Filippovna, I, as I expected, received an enthusiastic invitation from her - God himself sends me to Gireyevo, for the honorable widow needs to leave on urgent business, and she was just going to beg me to look after a week or two behind the house, but the main thing is for the hospital for the front-line soldiers, because such a thing cannot be abandoned to its fate ...

I will not say that the coming weeks promised me a lot of pleasure, but a sense of duty called me on the road.

The next day, in the late afternoon, I drove along a forest road to the Gireyevsky estate. Varvara Filippovna, who met me at the station, already in the crew began to give various economic instructions:

- Lelia, dear, I am so glad that you responded to my request for help, because you can safely rely on everything. Please ensure that the wounded menus include more dairy foods and vegetables, they need healthy food. The doctor visits us once every two or three days, and if he prescribes any medications, immediately send the coachman with prescriptions to the city, to the pharmacy. The coachman is with me lazy, he needs to be reminded about everything five times, otherwise the wounded will be left without medications ... Two qualified sisters of mercy deal with current medical affairs, but they also have to be watched for. Mainly, in order not to allow yourself excessive liberties with patients, well, you understand me ... There is no place for amorous intrigues. Discipline first! Girls should be trained so as not to bloom too much.

I sighed a little. No, I will not take on a similar mission. Varvara Filippovna, meanwhile, continued:

- We now have a lot of laundry, but please, my dear, don't take it up by handing the laundry to the sweaters, make an inventory, and then take your laundry one by one, especially small items - towels, shirts, napkins. Laundresses always lose and confuse everything, be sure to miss something.

In tune with her requests, the honorable widow nodded her head so vigorously that it seemed that the feathers from her hat were about to fly apart. The head of Varvara Filippovna was decorated with one of those intricate "crow nests" that usually cost a lot of money.

In general, the appearance of my aunt has undergone a number of significant changes since our acquaintance. Varvara Filippovna did her best to give herself more respectability. The rings glittered on the fingers, an intricate hairstyle required at least three hair rollers. The chic fit of her silk dress was clearly intended to hide some excesses in the waist area, although, I am afraid, here the efforts of a nice aunt were in vain.

And yet I was heartily glad that those times when Varvara Filippovna suffered from noble poverty and had to wear blouses of the color of yesterday's oatmeal, adorned with darn art, were irrevocably ...

"There are a lot of lower ranks, noncoms and privates among our patients, they live in common wards arranged in a large outhouse," she said. "There are only nine officers, and I have taken rooms for them in a big house." They need special attention - you know, men become so suspicious and capricious when they fall ill. Just like kids! Lelya, if possible, try to talk more with each of them. The boys are a little bit harsh from the front-line life, indulged in despondency, and the women's society is so beneficial ... Only women's participation can instill in them a brighter view of the world. I treat the officers in a maternal way, and they respond to my sons with devotion, even tell their little secrets.

Perhaps, my dear Barbara Filippovna, as always, is inclined to cross all reasonable limits in her demands. I must admit that I didn't have a special need to elicit little secrets from each officer, it's another thing to make sure that they get the medicine ordered on time, give them fresh milk and don't lose their shirts when washing.

And let the officers keep the secrets with them (in my heart I was sure that they could take care of their secrets themselves).

However, our aunt belonged to the breed of people who love to make life plans not only for themselves, but also for those around them, not expecting to meet with any objections ...

"Feel at home here, my dear," Varvara Filippovna completed the stream of instructions with this ritual phrase.

God knows, I was not sure that I could feel at home in someone else's estate, crowded with front-line soldiers languishing in boredom ...

The officers, who were introduced to me in the estate, at first seemed indistinguishable from each other and merged into some single khaki-colored creature tied with belt belts, but gradually the faces of the Girey patients began to acquire their own features, and the general mosaic disintegrated into components.

First of all, the captain with a scarred face that seemed dimly familiar to me attracted the attention. But I was never able to recognize him, but I had a closer look at the advice — he could have misinterpreted my curiosity. People who have suffered such injuries are often so suspicious.

The young lieutenant, visibly limping, was also not like the others. If nature has rewarded you with a round, snub-nosed and cheerful face, it is not easy to seem a painful creature, but he succeeded. I even thought that he was trying to look a little weaker than he really was, just to make others feel sorry for himself, the unfortunate ...

I suppose the boy likes being pitying, he just got a taste, and the wound healed too quickly, not allowing him to fully enjoy the pity of others.

His friend, another lieutenant, with a face (yes, yes, with a face!) Was like the gentlest of Christ's apostles. But, despite the icon-painting appearance, he behaved rather boldly. Rather, it was a mixture of boldness and embarrassment, typical of young nihilists, who had not forgotten their mother's strict notations. The lieutenant's finger was decorated with a massive ring with a skull, symbolizing, probably, the free-thinking of the owner.

Actually, I never trusted such a written beautiful woman - young men of this type look too much at the noble poisoners who served in the henchmen of the Borgia family.

For some reason, these two young officers immediately made me wary - it seems that each of them came to the general philosophical rejection of the world and now nursed a nascent misanthropy.

If I didn't know that front-line soldiers were healing the wounds, I would have thought that this couple had robbed a bank, shot five people along the way, or had committed a major terrorist act and is now hiding from the police in a remote rural place.

(Forgive me, Lord, for evil thoughts, young officers most likely did not deserve such suspicions. But on the other hand, what can you do if I didn't like both lieutenants at first sight - the first impression is often the most persistent.)

After dinner, everyone gathered in the living room, where for the beginning I shouldered the heavy duty of pouring tea for the heroes. Gentlemen, who missed Gireyevo without society, seemed to be glad to see a new person in my face and bombarded me with questions about Moscow life.

I talked in detail about everything that interested them (Moscow really changed a lot during the war), but I thought to myself that it was necessary to write out all the major newspapers here, for it was cruel to leave the wounded without fresh news. This is a clear omission of Varvara Filippovna. Apparently, she wanted to conceal bad reports from the front from the officers in this way, but in wartime it would still be better to have all the information.

After a thorough conversation, I considered myself entitled, referring to fatigue, to be the first to leave society and retire to my room. Varvara Filippovna went to accompany me, telling me some details on the life of each officer. The venerable widow never missed the opportunity to share spicy information from the life of others. However, this lack of her nature was balanced by other, very numerous advantages.

Putting my hand on my heart, we can say that my aunt has already fully deserved a nimbus the size of a dinner plate for her good deeds ...

"By the way, Lelechka, I will have another request for you," she suddenly remembered. - A young widow settled nearby, in the nearby estate Privolnoe. So young, quite a girl. Parents are no longer alive. My husband died at the front. God, what makes this inhuman war! I understand why the poor thing left the big city - came here to look for peace. Could you try to make acquaintance with her? After all, you always knew how to easily converge with people. I would like to involve the poor thing in charity work - it cannot be left alone, it is fraught with bad consequences ... And helping others usually helps to cope with their own grief, I know from myself. Yes, and be useful in public. Visit the poor thing, she will be mired in complete despair ...

I already understood that this was Ana Chigareva, but I overcame the temptation to admit that I have known the young widow for a long time. When she learned that Anya was the sister of my high-school girlfriend, Varvara Filippovna would certainly have tried to pull out all the neighbors on the estate from me.

Of course, it would have been impossible to tell anything to disgrace Anyuta, but I still didn't want to feed on the insatiable imagination of the venerable matron.

But, if you don't show your own awareness, it's not difficult to keep your mouth shut in the presence of Varvara Filippovna - she knows how to speak, practically without stopping. While I was getting ready for bed, I had to listen to the tragic saga about another young widow who had laid hands on herself from grief.

"I myself know how important friendly signs of attention are, especially when a person is ill and he is alone. It remains only to reproach ourselves that in time they did not extend a helping hand to the poor girl, the venerable matron summed up. - After all, we could help her, do not be so busy with their own personalities.

Even during this experienced monologue, she did not change her usual manner - to hold her head proudly high, in a manner that appeared to Barbara Filippovna after receiving the first major inheritance. Of course, for the owner of two powerful chins, the pose is very advantageous ...

Unfortunately, God returned to this lady a high social position and the opportunity to be visible just when irrevocably took her youth and beauty.

But after all, a woman always wants to be attractive, communicating with people, and this is not at all vain, as strict moralists of the male assert, but a vital necessity, pushing the ladies to the excusable tricks. I do not think that because of these innocent tricks, Barbara Filippovna can be called a deceitful person who leads a double life ...

Finally left alone, I first thought about how dark places are here. And it's not just the sullen spruce forests surrounding the local estates - everyone around does what they remember the dead and talk about death. From the covenant of the ancient Romans - memento mori (remember death!) - just do not go anywhere. None other than the souls of the dead soar in the dark forests and disturb the living ...

Night hours dragged out without sleep, but I still had nothing left but to indulge in gloomy thoughts — the mosquitoes that had flown into my bedroom predatoryly itched over my ear and how vampires strove to get drunk on my blood. It was simply impossible to fall asleep in such conditions.

CHAPTER 5

Anna

In the morning, Anya was not herself. Night vision again and again appeared before her — a barely distinguishable male figure in the darkness on the steps of the stairs. Who was that? There is not a single man in the house ... Vision? For some reason, she remembered yesterday's visit of the staff captain Saltykov and his story about the death of Alexei.

What if? .. It is terrible to imagine, but suddenly this spirit of Alexei appeared in her house to tell his wife something. If Alyosha was indeed killed the way Valentine says, then the soul of the unfortunate clearly cannot find eternal peace ...

From this guess, Ani's heart sank, and her temples squeezed like an iron hoop. She did not faint, but she lost her ability to move completely. It seemed that it was simply impossible to move a hand or a foot - each finger was filled with a leaden weight.

Meanwhile, the nurse, pouring tea into cups, said something:

- This is the horror just what is being done. Savvishna, the thrush that brings us milk, said, have mercy, Lord, that Pelageya, Kuznetsov's daughter, the women at the ravine saw ... She was dead, they killed her, her throat was cut. After all, they buried her for days. With the funeral, honor to honor. And then the women are watching - in the evening Pelageya is walking past the ravine as if it were alive. Eyes on the women zyrknula and disappeared in the fog. They already died down. And then they looked - where it passed, the grass is not taken!

It was too similar to the fairy tales that the nurse told Anyuta as a child: "The prince rode up, threw the lid off the coffin, and the princess, the beauty written, lay in the coffin as if alive. For nothing that a year has passed. He leaned over the coffin, but she opened her eyes and the hand of his DAC! "Once, little Annie's heart stopped breathing from these tales and caught her breath. But now it was, really, not at all. What kind of princesses and Kuznetsov daughters, when with what happens in their own house, you will not understand.

The nanny quickly crossed herself and continued:

- The whole village is pounding like a fever. So, after death, darling does not find her peace of mind ... Beginning! The men had just wanted to dig the grave of Pelageya and drive an aspen stake, but the blacksmith did not allow it. "Whoever comes to the grave of the daughter, he himself's aspen stake from me," he says. He, a blacksmith, characteristic painful, wild, afraid of him in the village. Moreover, as he buried his daughter, he drinks without drying out ... But now in the evenings, as it gets dark, not a single dog from the nose of the hut appears. Scary. We haven't had such a long time since our Count, your grandfather, Nyutochka, God rest his soul, calmed down ...

Anya, lost in her own thoughts, woke up with the last words of the nanny.

- calmed down? What are you talking about, nanny?

Before answering, the nanny again struck herself with a triple sign of the cross.

"The late singer, too, has long been ... appeared," she said in a whisper. - Calm could not find, hearty.

Anya again felt her heart squeeze with icy cold. And the nanny kept whispering:

- Barin far away from the house lay down his head - he went to the Balkans somewhere went to fight with the Turks. For the freedom of fellow Slavs, they said. At that time I was still young, single, I went to girls. I remember how His Excellency was escorting something to the war ... And your grandmother, a young countess, says: "I wish my husband to accompany me on a long hike! I do not have the strength to part with him in a moment of danger. " I brought my son, boy, your father, to my relatives, and she herself went there too, to the Balkans for these. Yes, only three months later he returned, all in black, and after her on the cart, the men in the closed coffin were being brought in — that is, the Turks of the count were killed. Well, the lady did not leave him on someone else's side, she brought him to her homeland for burial. The near church with a cemetery in Gireyevo, kind of like how to bury there. And your grandmother in any.

"I don't want to part with my beloved husband, bury him here in the park by the house." No matter how they admonished her, both her relatives and father, the rector of the church in Gray, asked the body of the count to be offered to the earth in the cemetery, so no one could do anything about it. "Bury here" - and the whole story. "The time will come," he says, "and I'll lie down next to my husband. In the meantime, I will not part with him! "They said that the countess seemed to be clouded by reason after her husband's death. Not so much that it turned into a fool, but it still became slightly insane. In those days I, in my youth, didn't take pains to figure out who was in his head and who was out of his mind, but the older ones explained it to me. Well, Nyutochka, they buried the deceased gentleman, your grandfather, in the park, put a granite stone over the grave, put all the honor in honor. The countess remained in the estate to live, every morning, to the gravestone, was hacking, as a service,

The nanny interrupted her story, got up from the table and began to be baptized into icons. Apparently, the very touch in talking to such topics did not seem to the old woman a godly deed. Anya was holding her breath, - for the first time she heard vague family legends in such a presentation, and suddenly realized that in the fate of her grandmother, much resembles her own. The nanny's silence dragged on and had to distract her from the icons with a question:

- Nanny, and what happened next?

- Yes, that was, that was ... Became the owner to appear. They worried him darling ... That's what happened!

The nanny lowered her voice to a barely audible whisper.

- That, happens, will appear in park at night. Will be at the pond, and stands on the house. Then the trees had not yet grown so much as now, the gardeners had cut them, observing regularity, and the view from the windows was already on the other side of the pond, especially from the second floor. Sometimes you look out the window at night, and there the officer's uniform turns white ... And then the fog thickens - it looks like there is no one else. Oh, we have suffered fear, Nyhochka, do not pass. And even around the house, it happened, the owner used it. Well, there's really even carry the saints. Sometimes, suddenly, it would blow like cold from the grave, and the steps - top-top-top, and even spurs - tink-tink-tink! Either the door will lock itself, or as if someone's hand will touch you, and no one is around ...

The nanny for a long time talked about all the mysterious and terrible cases, and Anya again deep in thought. Now it seemed to her quite obvious that the night visitor came to her home from another world. But who was it - Alyosha or the late grandfather? Since the count grandfather was in the old days, then maybe his ghost is wandering around the house now. What a pity that she could not see the face of the ghost, and in general did not see much and understood with fear ...

Pushing the cup back, Anya came out of the dining room, went down the steps of the porch to the park and ran to the gravestone.

- Grandpa, do you hear me? Help me! I don't know who was in the house at night. If you come to the house at night, then give me some sign, and I will not be afraid. I believe that you will not harm me. And if it was Alyosha, explain to him how painful it was to me that he passed by and did not notice me ... If he came for me, let him take me to his place, I have nothing to lose in this world!

A sharp gust of wind hit Anya's face, and suddenly she was chill. Maybe this was the very sign?

Chapter 6

The next morning, Varvara Filippovna went on her business trip, promising to return no later than two weeks later, and I stayed at the Gireyev estate on the farm.

The breakfast menu served by the wounded was fine with me, even fresh sour cream and fresh milk were in the diet; after talking with the cook, it became clear that there would be no problems with lunch.

The doctor's visit on this day was not expected, therefore, there will be no new appointments and prescriptions and there's no need to drive the coachman to the city.

I had only one important thing - the reception according to the inventory of the washed linen at a careless laundress. Honestly, it is difficult to call the officer pants for the identification of a possible shortage a pleasant thing, but what can you do if the owner of the estate left me such a delicate assignment? In the end, I always boasted that I did not suffer from prejudice ...

But I did not have time to embark on my responsible mission, as one of the Gireevsky patients approached me, the same staff captain, whose face was riddled with deep scars from shrapnel wounds.

- Excuse me, madam, you did not recognize me? He asked, looking into my eyes.

When someone looks into his eyes so intently, it's not easy to prevaricate, and I honestly confessed that I could not recognize the unfortunate staff captain.

"Yes, now it is not easy to recognize me," he sighed bitterly. - But we were acquainted, Elena Sergeevna. Remember, in former times, still a high school student, you lived in the summer at a dacha near Moscow, on the Khimka River, along the St. Petersburg path. And your friend Nina was staying with you ... And nearby, outside the village of Vsekhsvyatsky, they stood in the camps of the junker of the Alexander Military School. And the two cadets were yours with Nina standing gentlemen in the dacha dance circle ... Remember? You then danced a great waltz.

I looked more attentively at the wounded face of the captain. And suddenly from under the scars looked out, like in magical pictures, a completely different physiognomy — boyish, with delicate peach skin, the first gun above the lip and surprised naive eyes.

- My God, Valentine! Sorry, I didn't recognize you. However, we after all were on "you". I see no reason to refuse the friendly simplicity in circulation ... Hello, Valechka! Hello, my dear! Good to see you.

In memory, as cinema shots, pictures flashed — our wooden cottage with a spacious veranda; Apple orchard; pine forest with springs in sandy ravines; a military brass band extracting Strauss waltzes from shiny copper pipes; two young sons of Mars in summer field uniform; long bright evenings, benches under lilac bushes, kisses and furious mosquitoes, which had to be brushed off with a branch ...

And in the ears the old army song sounded very silly, but damn popular among the junkers:
Hello, summer residents, Hello, summer women! Summer maneuvers have already begun a long time ago. My favorite song, Beloved, Boule-Boule-Boule, Baclazer, my marching…
Valentine was considered a fan of Nina, and my friend Ivan Malashevich was my cavalier, and we were all young, in love and happy ... And then the summer ended, noisy Moscow spun us on business, the cadets rarely happened, and our meetings somehow lost summer romance and became not so interesting ...

However, having terminated for various reasons three engagements with other suitors, a few years later I still married the faithful Ivan Malashevich, who had become a lieutenant by that time. And it was not my fault that a year later he found it necessary to shoot himself, losing state money to cards, and I had to sell the Khimki dacha received as a dowry in order to pay off his debts and clear the name of her late husband from shameful stigma.

Alas, what is usually called the vicissitudes of fate is familiar to me to the full ... (Lord, why are there those who always remember those who are no longer among us!)

Mourning Ivan and paying off his debts, I soon met my second husband. And Valentine Saltykov, after parting with Nina, got lost in some kind of dusty provincial garrison ... But I still counted him among my friends and, I confess, I remembered with such tenderness a little ... Sweet, nice, in love boy! And now Valentine, who has matured, has changed beyond recognition, is now standing before me.

To be honest, I was surprised that he is still the staff captain. It was time for him to become, if not a lieutenant colonel, then at least a captain. Especially in wartime, when the ranks are caught on the fly and army careers are distinguished by dizzying takeoffs. After all, Valentine never looked like a man completely devoid of ambition ...

But I had to bite on a language in which the tactless question of a career was already spinning - most likely the poor fellow had to endure some kind of official troubles related to demotion in the ranks, and it is not at all necessary to recall this. Moreover, being afraid of hurting him, I didn't even hint that Nina was dead. Suddenly he doesn't know about it yet?

"Helen, I was surprised to hear that you are an active member of the League of Struggle for Women's Equality, the most radical of all feminist organizations," said Valentin, meanwhile. - Your photos are often flashed in newspaper reports on the actions of feminists, which are now called "our conscious public." Only your photos for some reason "Mrs. Croatia" are signed. I thought all the time - is it really you?

- Sorry, but what really? Is a feminist or is it really Mrs. Croatia? Both are true. I was really fascinated by the struggle for the rights of women, and now, really, by my husband, I wear the name of Croatia. Or are you one of those friends who would like to see me all my life as a quiet inconsolable widow of Lieutenant Malashevich?

- No, no, that you! I didn't want to say something, Valentin mingled.

- Okay, my friend, forget. May I, in the course of a radical struggle for my rights, put some of my responsibilities on your shoulders?

"At your service, madam," Valentine bowled gallantly.

"Now the laundress will come with your laundry, be so kind, take everything from her in the inventory," I asked with friendly ease, as if it was a question of some trifling service. - Varvara Filippovna attaches special importance to the counting of linen. Maybe she is afraid that the German agents will recruit the laundress and start paying extra from operational sums for damage to the property of Russian officers. But to me, by golly, not too long to shake up every little thing.

I do not know whether the captain managed to understand the depth of the hidden prayer that sounded in my voice, but he was moved and promised to assist me. Probably, thanks to the general memories of youth, a kind of spiritual connection arose between us, which was already bearing some fruits ... I exclaimed with relief:

- God, how nice to meet an old friend who is ready to put his shoulder in a difficult moment!

Having blessed Valentina with this beaten phrase, I handed him an inventory of linen and, with a clear conscience, retired to change my clothes, having considered my charitable mission as of today exhausted. I had to do an important job, for which I arrived in these dark places, to pay a visit to the unfortunate widowed Anya.

However, before I had time to leave the Grayev manor, I still had a chance to go through several difficult and in every sense ambiguous moments.

- Listen, Valentine, and you seem to be well acquainted with Mrs. Croatian? - it came to me because of the locked door of my bedroom. The voice belonged to the angellike lieutenant, who had already drawn my unfavorable attention to himself. Such a lazy voice with light ironic intonations, it would be difficult to confuse it with others.

And how clearly every word is heard! Amazing acoustic effects occur in old wooden houses, however, gentlemen officers were talking in the corridor, right at the door of my room, believing it was likely that I had already left the manor back home and could not hear them.

My first impulse was to make it clear that I am here and I hear everything perfectly, since we are talking about me. But curiosity, as always, did not allow me to discover myself.

In the end, I don't overhear, secretly sneaking up on someone else's door, but simply choose a hat while in my own room. At ease, to the gentlemen of the officers, shouting to the whole house, not making secrets from their conversation ...

"Yes, once Elena Sergeevna was very friendly," Saltykov replied restrained, meanwhile.

- Interesting lady! - the lieutenant in reply with some unpleasant intonation. - Extravagant such. I am not familiar with her, but we, like most Muscovites, have common friends, and I have very, very much heard about her person. Like all ladies applying for social activities, she is always in sight, gives rise to gossip, and not without reason. Mrs. Croatia is a business woman and has managed to change four husbands in her life. The first husband, as far as I know, was a big mistake, but he quite prudently and promptly laid hands on himself. However, his two followers also moved into another world. I don't presume to say that Madame contributed to this matter, which I don't know, I don't try to judge, but when chance turns into a regularity, this leads to certain thoughts. However, the manufacturer Likhoveev, spouse number 2,

I hid behind my door like a mouse under a broom, feeling the blood rush to my cheeks. Valentin, too, was silent for some reason, but the lieutenant's speech flowed like a full-flowing river:

- Now, my dear Elena Sergeevna is in her fourth marriage, and I would suggest that he was finally concluded for pleasure and everyday joy, because they say that Mr. Horvath is a man with charming manners and a great love for everything beautiful. But his face, unfortunately, was horribly disfigured by a rare form of some terrible tropical smallpox ... Probably, the lady has somewhat perverted tastes, if she was fascinated by this Quasimodo. True, I heard that a certain St. Petersburg professor, the luminary of plastic surgery (there is such a new direction in medicine that came to us from America, by the way, bear in mind!) Literally fashioned a new face for Mr. Croatoff. But still, all the scars and scars could not be hidden ...

At that moment, the lieutenant suddenly fell silent so abruptly, as if he was choking on his own tongue, and from behind the door came the crackle of thick cloth - it seems that someone was grabbed by the breast, and I even knew who it was ...

"Listen, Krivitsky, I advise you to remember the following well," said Saltykov's quiet voice, which nevertheless clearly contained restrained rage. - First, that first husband of Yelena Sergeyevna, whom you consider her a big mistake, was my close friend, and I advise you not to forget about it, and secondly, I will not allow anyone to dismiss dirty gossip about a respected woman, so we will assume that you did not say anything, but I did not hear anything. But if you intend to continue the discussion of similar topics with me or someone else, I will have to shoot to stop it. I, you know, very scrupulous in matters of honor. You can send me your seconds.

- Well, what are you, Valentine, calm down! - The lieutenant was healed. - I take all my words back. And what did I say that? I just remembered some idle tales to which there is nothing to pay attention to. I did not want to offend anyone, let alone offend the ladies 'honor. You see…

After that, the voices in the corridor subsided, apparently, the gentlemen officers went to continue the conversation in another place. And I remained in my bedroom with a hat box in my hands and in total confusion of feelings. Well, I wanted to satisfy my curiosity - that's the result! Get it, madam!

No, I am not so dependent on someone else's opinion, especially from the opinion of some army farmer, but still ... Hearing this about myself, no one would come to a joyful mood. Probably a weak, vulnerable woman, brought up in ladies' novels, could feel that her heart was broken.

However, my heart, tempered in everyday troubles, has a special endurance and it is not so easy to break it. It is pleasant to think that the power of my spirit is like a granite rock, and when it hits it, gossip and malicious insinuations crumble.

And this lieutenant Krivitsky is just a darling! Cheerful such, cheerful, not alien to curiosity, he would have turned out to be an excellent robber from the main road. I don't know what he is being treated for here, in Gireyevo ... In my opinion, he is incurably sick with soulfulness, and has been in a bad way since childhood, and now the process has turned into a chronic form.

However, God bless him, duties are waiting for me - it's time to visit Anna Chigareva and see how things are going in her cloister of grief ...

To cut my way, I walked straight to Privolnoye, through the forest. I do not so often manage to wander through the forest paths and breathe the coniferous air. For the townspeople, this is a great luxury. But all doctors say that walking in the fresh air is extremely beneficial to health. So I need to extract at least some benefit from this trip for myself!

It turned out that Anya was walking in the manor park. A lovely old woman who looked like a nanny who had taken root in the house explained to me how to get there. Having walked around a vast overgrown pond, I saw a huge granite tombstone from a distance (quite a rare decoration for parks near Moscow). Near a stone in a pose of a cemetery marble cherub a young widow froze.

- Hello, Anya, - I called out - Forgive me for violating your solitude ...

Anya turned her face to me, and I stopped talking because a lump rose in my throat. Of course, the widow should be mourning and gentle, but, by God, a twenty-year-old beauty with a faded look, a face swollen from constant tears, and also dressed in deep mourning and simply personifies a walking monument to the dead - this is a blasphemous spectacle. In addition, she attracted attention with her frank restlessness, and this was very striking. Just a dried blade, which is about to be blown away ...

Not without difficulty, coped with the excitement, I wanted to say that, being in these places in the case, I decided to visit Anya next door ... well, and everything else that could give my unwelcome visit ritual decency, but Anyuta rushed to my chest and burst into tears, repeating that God himself sent me.

- Lelia, what a blessing that you came! You have always been like a sister to me, and now I am glad to you just as never before. I feel so bad, I think I'm going crazy! You will live with me? Just a little, huh? I can no longer bear this loneliness and fear. I was disturbed by visions ...

At first I did not attach any special significance to her words about ghosts - Anya clearly suffered from deep depression, and during depressions people often see things. Who hears voices, and who is disturbed by fantastic visions.

But I did come here to help! I will try to distract her somehow and adjust her to lighter thoughts. If only I could find the necessary fine line between sympathy and vitality ...

When she learned that I was temporarily settled in nearby Gireyevo, where, in the absence of the hostess, I observed order in the sanatorium for wounded front-line soldiers, Anya with a new force began to persuade me to move to Privolnoe.

- Lelechka, you should agree, because you will be much more comfortable here than in Gireyevo. How can a woman feel crammed inside the house? It's like a barracks. Any lady will definitely feel discomfort in such conditions! But you can follow the order in the sanatorium from here, from Privolnoye. You will go to your Gireyevo in the morning, go to the sanatorium, and come back for dinner ... And I can also help you with everything. True true! Just please stay with me. I am afraid to stay here alone, - Anya paused, looked around and continued in a very quiet, barely audible whisper: - Although the fact of the matter is that I am not alone here - some creatures live in my house.

Apparently, these creatures were Ana in her visions. It seems that the poor thing seriously believes that she has the ability to communicate with the other world ...

Some couple of days ago, having heard this, I would laugh, remembering the instructive story from a children's book about a gang of evil house-dwellers who lived in the basement of a poor old woman (where harmful creatures were probably cleverly disguised as potato tubers), and would draw amusing parallels with Anya story. Connivance in dealing with malicious spirits can not be allowed. It is not harmful for aliens from the world to make it clear who is the master of the house ... But now I no longer ventured to joke on such a delicate topic — by God, I myself in these places often had the feeling of someone's invisible presence. As if someone is standing behind his back and drilling the back of your head with a glance, and you turn around - a void, only invisible shadows are melting in the haze ...

By evening, I moved my things to the gloomy house of Anna Chigareva. In the windows of the dining room, where we sat down for a samovar, looked at the trees of the park. With an indulgent evening light, a park overgrown with weeds with a dirty pond no longer seemed so neglected.

Before going to sleep, Anyuta and I were passing the time for a conversation, the topic of which would have seemed interesting to fans of demonology, spiritists, mystics, and members of theosophical societies, as well as to neurotic rhymes.

The most amazing thing in her stories was that Anya personally saw a ghost in the form of a young man in military uniform who was walking down the stairs from the attic. She swore that it was a holy truth, and only found it difficult to say exactly who appeared to her - the late grandfather, whose spirit, according to her, had a restless temper and in former times often allowed himself to stroll through the estate, or her husband, who was recently killed in Galicia.

The circumstances of the death of Alexei Chigarev, who became recently known to Anna (shot in the back from their own at the time of the bayonet attack - vile and mysterious murder, the motives of which, like the name of the murderer, remained undisclosed), suggested that the lieutenant's soul had no peace . However, in all known literary works, mere mortals are precisely the innocently ruined and unrequited souls of deceased relatives. Take even the shadow of Hamlet's father ...

"You know, I am dying of fear at the mere recollection of these phenomena," said Anya. - But for all that, if it really was Alex, I ... I would like to see him again. Let it be a glimpse of a light shadow ... I miss him so much. And even you will not believe, with a sinking heart, I expect him to appear again. Only ... He stayed in Galicia. I do not know whether it is possible for him to appear here in the Moscow province? Perhaps it was still a grandfather buried in the manor park.

I was sure that the deceased Alexei is now in places far more distant than Galicia, and you can't get him out of there in any way ... Yes, and grandfather, peace be upon him, most likely there is a company to his grand-son-in-law. But do not talk about this with inconsolable Anna.

"Can I ask you a couple of practical questions?" - I asked. - Tell me, what color was the ghost on the ghost, if it appeared to you in military uniform?

- Single coat? - Anya asked puzzled. - By God, I do not remember, I simply did not pay attention. Lelia, I was neither alive nor dead from fear, I almost lost consciousness, and you ask about the tunic. Another would be stars on epaulets inquired! What is the color of the jacket?

- Very big. If you were a grandfather, he should have been in the form of the times of the war in the Balkans and most likely in a white tunic. Well, in the extreme case, in the dress uniform of those times. And if the uniform was khaki, then this ghost is modern. Only during the Japanese war, our command thought that on the field of military operations the protective color of the jacket was much more practical than the snow-white one, which served as a good target for enemy shooters. Nowadays, the military were wearing khaki almost without exception, but for the first time a protective uniform appeared in the Russian army only in 1907. As for your grandfather, God rest his soul, then I think that for all the restless nature he would not have changed his outfit according to the current military order.

- Lelia, what is your clear mind after all! I would not have thought of that. Grandfather really should be in his old-fashioned uniform!

But I was not up to compliments. It was necessary to clarify in detail one more important thing, which Anyuta, who was immersed in romantic fantasies, also did not think of.

If we assume for a moment that the ghost that appeared on the stairs is not a ghost at all, but an ordinary living person of flesh and blood, who needs something in Anna's house (and life experience persistently prompted me to this version, although I also fell under the spell of mystical secrets), how does this person pass through locked doors?

He got the keys to the door, or someone lets him into the house, or, deftly using the stairs and cornices, he gets through some dormer window?

That's what I tried to find out from Ani.

"Spirits don't need keys," she said sadly. "Although there were never any problems with keys in our house, they are full of them here ..."

- What do you mean? - I was surprised. "They are full here" can be said about mushrooms in the forest, and even then only in the mushroom summer, and there are usually strictly limited quantities of house keys.

- You see, in this manor often happened all sorts of strange things. For example, the doors unexpectedly slammed and locked by themselves ... The nanny thinks that this is also related to otherworldly phenomena, even to the spirit of the late grandfather he sins, that this is his trick. They say that my father, in his early childhood, experienced a strong nervous fit after he was locked up for half a day in a dark, stuffy closet. He then had bouts of claustrophobia. Similar stories happened with the servants, and even with the mistress, my grandmother ... So she ordered that a spare key should be hidden near each door and the victim of the evil spirits could always unlock the lock. All you need to do is look under the rug, behind the lintel, on the shelf of the nearby shelf, on a stud in a dark corner by the door there will certainly be a spare key.

Anya sighed and switched to a mysterious whisper:

- Have you seen two large pot with dancing nymphs on the steps at the entrance? In the right of them is hidden a spare key from the front door. But why is it necessary for the incorporeal spirits ... They are not a physical substance!

- Anya, I'm not talking about perfume. If you can find a spare key from it near each door, it means that it is easy for anyone to travel around your house, and there seems to be no constipation ...

- No, not to anyone, but only to those who know about the keys. But who needs it? We are not in Moscow, here, in our backwoods, there are no and have never been swindlers sneaking into someone else's dwelling to steal spoons. Before, it never occurred to me to lock the doors for the night, it was the war that made me so nervous and shy ... These are all new trends. They say that now some deserters are robbed on the roads of passers-by, but will it not occur to them to take by storm my house? I have not heard about this.

Well, everything became clear to me. Suppose the robbers, deserters do not dare to break into the house (and maybe take a risk, who knows, the criminal world progresses rapidly in troubled wartime), but the fact that every person curious enough to look at the decorative pot at the entrance can to take a key from there and, at a convenient time for oneself, to walk about Anina's estate, is absolutely obvious.

Even if Annie doesn't talk about all the keys that were laid out under each door, we have enough inquisitive people to figure out this secret on our own.

"You said the spirit was coming down the stairs from the attic." Is there anything interesting or valuable hidden there? - I decided to clarify.

- Well, what are you? Just some old furniture, junk, and any unnecessary junk. I myself really do not know what is there. In our attic for a hundred years the human foot has not stepped. Well, maybe not a hundred, but twenty years for sure. They say that in ancient times someone hanged himself there, and it is terrible to go there. I personally would not go there for anything. When I first heard the noise there, it occurred to me to look behind the attic door, and that was so creepy ...

We were silent for a moment. I, frankly, ran down the back chill from the thought that in this terrible attic, it may happen that someone is still hanging, but I immediately dismissed this thought as completely absurd.

- Well, perhaps we should go to sleep? - finally asked Anya. "I absolutely screwed you up, but tomorrow is a new day ... You have so much trouble with the gymnasium hospital, you need rest." We'll talk again tomorrow.

Her face hardened with an expression that reminded me of the sad Vasnetsov Alyonushka, who was pondering over a quiet backwater, should she not drown for company with her brother. So, the very fact that Anya, who has turned into the personification of human grief and the walking monument to deceased relatives, is making at least some plans for tomorrow, I was pleased.

We went up to the second floor, where Anina was the bedroom, and where we prepared a room for me.

"Listen, if the spirits come to bother you again at night, wake me up immediately," I said to Anya in farewell. "I may not hear their sinister footsteps, but if you wake me up in time, I will deal with them."

- And you are not afraid at all? - Anya was surprised.

- While I am not familiar with them and did not see firsthand what they are capable of ... Why be afraid in advance? It may be that during a personal meeting they will manage to intimidate me, but generally I don't suffer from excessive impressionability.

For the night I was given a spacious room, furnished in the old-fashioned and pompous style. Anya called her "grandma's French boudoir."

The stagnant air gave away dust, mothballs and family secrets, and the situation, apparently, did not change since the sweet grand-mother went from here to her Balkan campaign.

Gold plated cupids on the frame of the clouded mirror; couch Napoleon Empire; a huge bed under a canopy, mounted on twisted columns with heraldic rosettes; the walls are covered with fabric with bouquets in a royalist style and decorated with paired tapestries with images of Pierrot and Columbine; drapes with lush folds wherever you look ...

But all over here lay the seal of desolation and slow extinction ... And the cupids went in small cracks, and the legs at the couch loosened, and the bouquets poved and the drapey rose ... Even the firewood that was burning out in the fireplace cracked somehow grieving, old-fashioned.

The situation in nearby Gireyevo, where I stopped at first, was much more cheerful — no artistic excesses like cupids and canopies. The furniture, unpretentious but good-quality, was cut down for some sixty years ago by some fortress joiner, and embroidery and lace tablecloths were obviously made at the same time by needlewomen from the maiden.

A lot of masterly houses preserve such items. Since the serfs got the will and it turned out that you need to pay money for embroidery and bookshelves, most middle-class landowners have lost their taste for changing the situation.

Well, it was time to get ready for bed. I cannot say that the bed under the canopy looked very hospitable, but I still have to spend the next nights on it. I hope only that it is not too rassokhlos from time to time and will be able to serve its intended purpose even at least a week.

I don't know how to whom, but in my new place I don't always sleep very well. And then there were all the sounds and smells of someone else's house supplemented by the thought of some uninvited guests who used to roam here at night ...

No matter how I invigorated my conversation with Anya, still the thought of ghosts engendered a feeling of anxiety, which did not contribute to a peaceful sleep. It was necessary to urgently do something.

For a start, I opened my case and found a thing that was absolutely necessary for our time to travel. It was a Browning system pistol from the collection of small arms, which the late lieutenant Malashevich left. As an officer, he had a real passion for pistols and revolvers and collected about thirty copies of military firearms of various modifications.

Until 1906 it was easy to collect such collections - the weapon was sold freely and was inexpensive. A good revolver or Browning cost no more than twenty rubles, and it was possible to pick up a model for fifteen, moreover, the gun shop sellers used to give discounts to regular customers.

It was only in December 1905, when people armed with these browings and Nagans climbed onto the barricades to shoot at government troops, and at the same time at random passersby in the firing line, the Ministry of the Interior thought about their omissions and demanded that everyone the buyer of the weapon presented a personal permit for the purchase, issued to him by the head of the local police.

Lieutenant Malashevich, as an officer, would probably have no problems with resolution, but he still did not have time to feel any inconvenience from the new system of selling weapons. In 1906, taking one of the collection pistols, Ivan put a bullet in the forehead ...

I experienced a difficult time in every sense - not only did I have to bury my husband and pay him incredibly huge debts, but society also turned away from me, accusing him of dying.

Of course, the fact that the lieutenant lost the state money to the cards and decided to remove the shame from suicide knew a very narrow circle of people, and his poor widow was visible and accessible to any gossip and malicious attacks.

I was just starting to live completely independently, and not as an attachment to my spouse, and all my feelings, crushed by marriage, literally blossomed, which was seen in our circle as a brazen challenge to society.

"Surprisingly, this person needed only a year to bring to the grave of a strong, healthy, handsome young man, a clever girl, before whom a brilliant career opened ... That's what an unwary marriage means," said moralists.

It was precisely at that time that they gave me the nickname Angel of Death, which finally consolidated on the day when my second husband, a wealthy entrepreneur Likhoveev, received a deadly knife wound from a jealous gypsy at a merchant banquet ...

Yes, my life experience cannot be called mediocre, too often I have seen men with a disadvantageous side for them. However, it is time to stop indulging in the hopeless recollections of the deceased husbands (peace be upon them) and think about pressing practical matters.

And yet it is surprising why in these places the dead constantly remind of themselves?

I hid Browning under the pillow and prepared a book of Shakespeare, which I was going to re-read at leisure in the village, believing that in the evenings I would have nothing to do here and nothing would prevent me from indulging in intellectual pleasures. But alas, it was a rash decision. Shakespeare's tragedies, where all the characters have the habit of dying in the finals, of course, harmoniously harmonized with these places, making their gloomy contribution to the general tone, but I would now prefer something lively.

With disgust, throwing a thick volume of a great classic of English literature on a bedside table (at the very least, Shakespeare can serve the cause of self-defense, because a blow with such a book on the head would be quite noticeable!), I went to sleep, but remembered the spare key, which, according to Ani , idly lying in a flowerpot on the steps of the porch.

To tell you the truth, to scatter the keys to the door wherever you are - a uniform idiocy (let the former mistress forgive me, not be remembered). However, in this house in general there is something abnormal. Well, is it possible to fall asleep without even knowing whether the key to the front door is in place or not?

Throwing on a dressing gown, I went downstairs, went out onto the porch, and lowered my hand in a large pot, girded with a relief image of the nymphs.

The key in the pot was not. Which, however, did not seem surprising to me.

CHAPTER 7

Anna

The arrival of Elena Sergeevna Krovatova turned to Anya with great joy. She herself did not expect that she had not forgotten how to rejoice to such a degree.

In fact, Anya always loved Lelia, the most cheerful and naughty of her older sister's friends ... But when Nina died, it was hard for Anya to continue to maintain relationships with her friends. The thought involuntarily arose that Nina and Lelia were the same age, they grew up together, studied in a gymnasium and should have lived the same long life.

But Nina is no more, she is so cruelly and irrevocably torn out of life, leaving Anya alone in the whole world, and Mrs. Croatia, still as beautiful, blooming, healthy and cheerful, continues to live and enjoy all the charms of earthly existence ...

In this very thought there was something bad, humiliating for Ani. It was a shame to think so. She tried to drive away this dark thought, but as soon as she saw Lelya, for some reason, despising herself, she returned to the same reasoning.

Because of this internal struggle, in which it was impossible for anyone to confess, every meeting with Madame Hvatovánova turned into torture for Ani.

But now, tormented in her manor from loneliness and anguish, seasoned with the same fear, Anya was ready to cry with grateful tears, realizing that Lelia does not hold her evil. The very presence of such a cheerful and sensible person in an old mansion seemed to break down the spellbound spell that invisibly entangled an abandoned house filled with the shadows of the dead.

Probably, such a sense of security arises in a frightened child, when someone adult, intelligent and strong appears next to him. For the first time in recent years, Anya fell asleep quietly, knowing that behind the wall in the "French bedroom" - Lelya and no longer need to relive all fears alone.

And the dreams seemed somehow pleasantly pleasant - little Anya in a lace dress, dad, still alive, cheerful, sparkling with pince-nez glasses in a gold frame, young Nina in the form of a schoolgirl and Lelia, also in a white uniform apron, with a bow in curly hair, tells something funny ... Everyone laughs around, even Nina, hiding the sadness in the depths of her green eyes, smiles with her mysterious smile, which papa calls the Mona Lisa smile. Suddenly, someone nearby starts screaming ... No, the scream comes from far away. But from where? Anya hardly opens her eyes, emerging from the depths of sleep.

The dark bedroom, painted with silver moonlight, was so peaceful, and everyone didn't want to let Anya sleep, but her anxiety grew and grew. What awakened her? Scream? Was it a dream or a reality? And who shouted?

And here again a horrible, desperate feminine cry, breaking the silence of the night, flew to the windows of the old manor. God, God, what is it?

Jumping up, Anya tried to find with her feet the slippers that stood on the rug beside the bed, but when she got to sleep, she could not find them and ran into the corridor barefoot. Lelya ran out of her bedroom in a silk robe with dragons and with a gun in her hand.

- Lelia, are you all right? What a blessing it wasn't you screaming! - Anya rushed to the guest. - But what is this happening? It is not known where the heart-rending cries are heard ... Are the ghosts from another world again?

- Ghosts? "I don't think," answered Lelya with concern. - Too much these screams look like a living being's voice. By the way, your ghosts dragged from the pot a spare key from the front door, I discovered this before going to bed. They allow themselves too much. And I do not like it.

"My God," Anya whispered, "and what should we do?"

"You'll go back to your room and shut yourself up just in case." And I'll go see what happened and who screamed. Maybe someone needs help.

- Lelia, will you go alone? I am afraid for you! Let's go together!

"Honestly, I would be more comfortable thinking that you are hiding in the house, safe." Do not worry, I have a weapon. I grabbed the Browning in case of emergency, and if this is not the same case, then I don't know what can be considered as an absolute necessity here.

- What nonsense! From the evil forces from the world of another gun will not protect you, as they will not cover me at home walls. Let's go together, for God's sake, do not leave me alone! Together, all the same is not so scary! I just need to put on shoes, I'm barefoot ...

"Okay, consider that you persuaded me," the guest agreed, not without some internal resistance. - But please, rather!

They almost ran down the stairs. In the anteroom at the entrance, the nanny, who had thrown a motley shawl over her shirt, was rushing around and muttering:

- Lord, have mercy on us sinners! But what is it done? The cries of such a manor, as if cutting someone, defend, the Creator! And in fact there is not a single peasant in the house, there is no one to intercede, even though we can all be cut here

When she saw that Anya and her guest were about to leave the house, the old woman wailed:

- Batiushki-holy, my girls, so where are you going? At night! To the grip of the hands? At the mercy of? I won't let you go! Cut me though! On the threshold lie down, but do not comin!

Leaving Anya to explain to the old woman, Lelia jumped out onto the porch. The screams had already fallen silent, but she managed to understand that they were coming from the side of the park, from its far outskirts, and maybe from the edge of the forest that was pulling over the park. Running in home shoes without backs on the overgrown, neglected alleys is not easy, besides, the floor of the robe clung to the branches of the bushes all the time. The air was cool and humid from a hazy mist that enveloped the park and was thickened by white veil near the pond and stream. It seemed that this heavy substance interferes with breathing ...

- Lelia, where are you? Wait for me! I am with you, - Anna screamed out of the hands of the nanny, trying to catch up with the guest.

But judging by the heavy steps and lamentations, the nanny also could not stay in the house and decided to join the general pursuit of an unknown intruder.

At the far exit from the park, where the rusty, leaning and for a long time unlocked gates crowned the half-destroyed fence, there was a small manor's lodge. There was a faint light in her window that looked like a candle flame.

Lelia herself noted that later she had to go to the inhabitants of the gatehouse - ask if they had noticed anything. In the meantime, having run out of the gate onto an old grassy road, she looked around in bewilderment - neither the victim who made wild cries in the night, nor the potential intruder with the bloody dagger in her hand was nowhere to be seen. And it was even strange to imagine that in this quiet, deserted town, shrouded in the night mist, someone could scream and call for help.

Anya caught up with her guest already outside the gates and, breathing hard from the fast run, whispered:

- You see, no one. I told you - this is another phenomenon of intangible origin. Screams of ghosts ...

"You mean that the same general auditory hallucination struck us all?" - asked Mrs. Croatian , peering with interest into the darkness.

- No, no, this is not a hallucination. I wanted to say, - began Anya, but Elena Sergeyevna suddenly with a shout: "Stop! Stop or I will shoot! "- pulled off the place and rushed to the forest edge.

At the edge of the forest, behind the bushes, a certain creature was dawning, poorly discernible in the dark, but the crackling of the branches came from there quite distinctly.

Lelya, who managed to reach the high trees that protrude beyond the edge of the forest, seemed to dissolve into the air at some point. There, where she rushed, between the trunks flashed a bright spot, like, if you look closely, at the silhouette of a man ...

Anya, feeling her heart break in terror, leaned her back against the fence and held her breath.

- Holy, holy, holy, - whispered, finely baptized, the nurse came in time. - As if the unclean Elena, our Sergeevna in our wilderness did not start ...

Without answering anything, Anya tried to breathe evenly and deeply, which, as is known, acts soothingly, although the peace was far from her at that moment as never before. She did not feel such wild horror even when she saw a mysterious man in a military uniform on the stairs of her own house.

Whom does her guest chase through the forest? What a bright spot flashes among the trees? Who is there luring Lelia in the bowl? None other than the ghost appeared ... Lord, do not leave!

From the forest, Elena Sergeevna's powerful cry was heard: "Stop! Stay, you bastard! "- after which a shot slammed, scattering in the misty air with a distant echo. Anya realized that her legs did not obey, and sank on the grass by the fence.

And then, through the bars of the lattice, two curved horns stretched almost to her very face, and then dark eyes looked out and the smell of foul breath came from the grinning mouth ...

Making a wild cry, Anya fell unconscious.

CHAPTER 8

Helena

Honestly, running at night through the forest with Browning in hand is not a pleasant pleasure. But you can safely admit that you live a full life, and on your deathbed you will have something to remember.

Even in the park, I had the feeling that someone was hiding nearby, away from the path along which we ran, but still beside us. And when I noticed how at the edge of the forest behind the bushes someone's obscure shadow was sweeping, a chill of horror passed over my back. But the excitement of the chase had already seized me, and I could not stop.

"Stop! Stop or I will shoot! "I shouted without much hope that someone would listen to my words. If it is a beast, then the scream will simply frighten him away, and if the person ... Alas, not everyone will be afraid of the order shouted out in a female voice, even if you decorate the voice modulations with metallic notes.

Meanwhile, I rushed into the forest, ominously blackened in the dark, and I ventured to shoot into the air to frighten an unknown enemy. A rustle in the bushes was becoming clearer, it seemed, just about someone, breaking branches, would fall out to meet me ...

But then the sounds began to be deleted. As I expected, my order: "Stand!" Was ignored. I walked quickly, and then ran for the receding noise, breaking through the bushes. The fact that branches scratch my face and hands, did not have to pay attention. Anyone who knows the feeling of a hunter at the moment of a dangerous chase for a game could understand me. This sense of ancient predatory excitement beyond reason leads you farther and farther away, persecution turns into a fascinating and, perhaps, deadly game, the blood in your veins boils, and just like that suddenly stop, to go away with nothing, it is simply impossible.

And then I saw the object of my pursuit - a human figure that quickly flickered among the trees, disappearing for a while in the shadow, where the darkness was gathering, and again, for a split second, arising on the moonlit places ...

The figure seemed strange. It seems that the man ran a measured trot, but in his run there was something abnormal. One thing could be said with certainty: he did not float over the grass, as it is supposed to spirits, namely, he ran, walking heavily on the sinful earth, smashing through the shrubs on the move, leaving sharp fragments of branches that scratched me to the blood.

It means that I had no reason to suspect this being of incorporeality and immateriality. That's it! This is not an alien from the other world, but an ordinary person! The ghost would surely seep through the bushes like a cloud, or melt like the same cloud before my eyes, leaving me with a nose.

Indulging in such comforting reflections, I did not notice the powerful fir root sticking out of the ground, stumbled and fell with a sweep, hitting my head against the stump.

The pain from the blow was so strong that I could not immediately rise. And the rustling that had disappeared, to the sound of which I was rushing like a hound, calmed far away in the distance. It did not make sense to continue the pursuit - it became absolutely incomprehensible where to go further.

Damn it The bastard managed to hide from me ...

Having suffered a shameful fiasco, I got up and shook the pale needles and pieces of moss off my dressing gown with annoyance. I had to go back to the gates of the manor park with nothing. I found the road out of the forest in the dark, not without some difficulty - in the heat of the chase it would not occur to anyone to notice the milestones on the way, and I was no exception. But still, despite the darkness, I managed to get in the right direction.

At the entrance to the park, I found Anya lying on the grass under the fence and a nurse desperately sobbing over her. Bringing a whim from a crooked goat with a piece of string around its neck watched this picture with interest, pinching leaves from the nearest bush of overgrown and run wild jasmine.

Well, maybe, for Anya, everything turned out not so bad - in a critical situation it is better to faint than to go crazy, which sometimes happens to ladies endowed with too much imagination.

Unfortunately, I didn't have any smelling salt, nor ammonia, nor vinegar, and I had to revive Anyuta in the old, tried and tested way - slapping her cheeks.

- What, what was it? She whispered, waking up and finally opening her eyes and lips.

- I do not know. Probably, some spirit from those that are found in abundance, tried to lure me into the forest, - I replied, not showing proper seriousness. "But I stopped the persecution on time, and he got out of the way."

"And this foul devilish face with horns that looked out from behind the fence?" - Anya asked.

I looked around for someone to fit this description, and I looked at the goat.

- You do not mean it?

Annie stared at the goat with such horror, as if it really was the embodiment of an unclean spirit.

- Lelia, what do you think, but the devil could not turn into a goat to confuse us? She finally muttered, crossing herself.

Nothing more stupid in these circumstances and it was impossible to invent. But what to do, one must tolerate the delusional ideas of the poor thing, whose psyche is constantly worried about all the new and new upheavals.

"We'll check now," I promised, throwing a pebble toward the goat. - Well, go out!

Offended by glueing, the satanic offspring left the gnawed jasmine alone and trotted across the grass along the fence somewhere into the misty distance.

"You see, the most common goat," I reassured Anyuta. - Admit it, the devil would not have simply given up and would not allow himself to be put to shame. Are you able to rise? Let's go to the house. I honestly hit my head hard and would like to apply a cold to the bruise until the lump is too big. Such ornaments as bumps, I, in my opinion, not to face.

Hearing my words, Anya was frightened again.

- Lelia, do not be frivolous! Head injuries are a serious matter. Bruises to the cranial area can be very dangerous! If you feel dizzy, go to bed immediately!

- What a blessing that at the beginning of the war you managed to finish the courses of sisters of mercy! Now there will be someone to give me qualified help! Well, so, Anya, let's go to the house or lie down for half an hour here, by the road?

We moved along the dark alleys to the porch of the manor, accompanied by a nanny, who was loudly crying and wanted an unknown enemy who had hidden in the night more often, various misfortunes. The wishes were so ingenious that they would undoubtedly be of interest to folklorists. Count Uvarov and his comrades would greatly rejoice, adding to the ethnographic collections, but, alas, there was no scholarly graph among us.

I was personally struck by the phrase: "So that he, as an adversary of the accursed, an internal worm ate from now on until the century!"

Strongly said. And the sight of a good old woman is not bloodthirsty at all ...

We had not had time to go deep into the park, as someone hailed us from the gate. The voice was normal, without satanic notes and not even without affection, but after the current events, the male baritone that sounded suddenly in the dark seemed so scary to me that I shuddered, releasing the hem of my robe, already wet from the night dew. True, it did not take me long to pull myself together.

Having recovered from the fright, I involuntarily came to the conclusion that a couple more weeks of serene rest in this wonderful forest place — and we could all be accommodated in the wards of the yellow house ...

However, now there are no vacant places there - contusive men who have lost their memory and gone mad in gas attacks of the military are being brought from the front lines.

- Elena Sergeyevna, is that you? - He continued to ask the passer-by at night, who turned out to be one of the patients of the Girayevo hospital, thereby the iconic lieutenant, whose ring was decorated with a dead head. - I was walking nearby, I heard screams, and then a shot ... I rushed to the sound of firing as a front-line habit. What happened here and who shot?

- I shot. To the air. To frighten an unknown enemy. And what happened, we confess, and do not really know. Anna Afanasyevna and I were also alarmed by the shouts, I ran in the dark with a weapon to the sound, but I didn't catch anyone, I didn't find anything and, unfortunately, I cannot tell you anything specific.

Despite the drama of the situation, during my short monologue I involuntarily looked down and looked at how decent my toilet looks after the chase. A bathrobe with deceit, generally characteristic of such clothing, often strove to swing open at the wrong moment, but I did not want to appear before an unfamiliar man in complete negligee. It seems that this time my clothes behaved decently, and I cheered up.

"Let me introduce you to the ladies," I said to the officer in a secular tone that was not very relevant at the moment. - Lieutenant Krivitsky, Boris Vladimirovich. And this is Anna Afanasyevna Chigareva, the widow of Lieutenant Chigareva, the mistress of the estate Privolnoe. And Anfisa Makarovna, the housekeeper and the right hand of the hostess ...

Having heard the name of the mistress of the house, the lieutenant was stunned. I could not understand the reasons for his confusion (in my opinion, a bit of a scandal), until he stammered out, turning to Anna:

- Ma'am, are you the widow of Lieutenant Chigarev? Alexey Chigarev? I served in the same regiment with your husband.

Anya, who had not yet recovered from fainting and was in a state of inhibition, was not very pleasantly impressed by the words of lieutenant Krivitsky. And, it seems, I understood why. Indeed, since it became known that Alexey was shot in the back by one of his own, each of her husband's colleagues was on suspicion.

But, being a well-bred lady, she kept her emotions in check and replied to the lieutenant with some polite banality. However, if Krivitsky was going with the help of this magical confession to make a closer acquaintance with a young widow of a colleague (relatives usually cordially welcome their fellow soldiers), then he did not succeed in these plans.

The lieutenant, as befits a noble man, led us through the alleys of the park to the porch of the house, assured that he would be at our service at any time and in any situation, and politely bowed. Maybe I was somewhat hurried to conclude about his bad manners?

Finding ourselves under the roof of the manor, we would have to disperse into bedrooms without exhaustive conversations, fall down exhausted from fatigue and fall asleep without a break.

After a night chase for an unknown villain and all accompanying disturbances, I really wanted to sleep, so much so that even the prospect of hearing the steps of visiting a ghost house or turning into a late dinner for a flock of hungry mosquitoes now did not seem so terrifying to me. Doctors do not for nothing argue that it is necessary to treat such like. After experiencing a strong fear, small fears and inconveniences seem so insignificant ...

But from sleep, as always, distracted some affairs. For a long time I cherished my lump, putting a napkin soaked in cold water to it, in order to minimize the unpleasant decoration. Fortunately, the injury was not as painful as it seemed in the forest.

However, in order to fully restore mental comfort, something was missing ...

"I hope you won't be surprised, but now I wouldn't refuse a glass of brandy," I admitted to Anya. - As a preventive measure against insanity, a small dose of alcohol would be extremely helpful in the circumstances. What a pity that with the beginning of the war, the government imposed a ban on the sale of alcohol. This is a terrible, just the same fatal mistake! Firstly, in the time of adversity, the authorities deprived their people of a proven tonic and sedative, secondly, under the state monopoly on the trade in vodka, they lose a lot of money, so necessary to the front, and thirdly, our ministers do not take into account their native Russian specifics . The government, which decided to take away the strong drinks from its people, will not last long at the helm of power. I'm afraid Goremykin's cabinet is already doomed.

Anya looked up at me with her sad mermaid eyes and calmly, as if something ordinary, said:

- Lelechka, if you want to drink a sip of brandy or wine, this is not a problem. Under the house there is a wine cellar, where many old stocks are stored. Only now the nanny has already gone to her and, probably, laid down. I, forgive, do not want to disturb her with requests to go for wine. Go down to the cellar, please, choose what you like.

- And you will not make me a company in the expedition to the life-giving springs? I cautiously asked (I must admit that I don't like to manage among other people's supplies, especially those that are scarce in modern times!).

- Oh, Lelia, for God's sake, dismiss! The cellar is dark and scary, but since childhood I can not tolerate dark corners. All the time it seems that some vile creature will jump out of the darkness at me. Please, if it's not difficult for you, go away by yourself, "Anya said imploringly.

- Listen, but you can not be afraid of what is unknown! - I tried to persuade the agitated hostess. - After all, before you get scared, you have to see this nasty creature. And she, maybe, will not jump out at all or it will turn out to be not at all terrible ...

- See? - Anya trembled even more. - Yes, I just will not survive such a spectacle. The very thought of the inevitable approaching of a vile creature terribly scares me, and even face it face to face ... When you go down into the cellar, it seems that out of all the dark corners someone's eyes are looking at you! If you insist that I go down to the wine cellar at night, then promise that you will bury me next to my grandfather and grandmother, because I was not destined to return from there.

A conscience slumbering woke up in me.

"Okay, give me the keys, coward." I will go myself - hunting more than bondage.

"I, to my shame, do not remember where the key to the wine cellar is," Anya sighed, "but in my house, as I have already said, there is no shortage of keys. Here, take this bundle with the economic keys, maybe one of them will go to the lock. Check on the spot everything. I think the key to the cellar should be here, among others ...

Anya handed me a heavy steel ring, on which twenty antique keys of various shapes and sizes were strung on pieces.

What to do? Grabbing a candle in a bronze shandal, I went down to the wine cellar all alone and began alternately trying the keys with Anina ligament.

At first, no key would fit the lock (and some did not even fit into the keyhole), then the massive key of the yellow metal with an intricate twisted head not only ideally fell into the lock grooves, but also turned easily.

With some difficulty I opened the door, which creaked with rusty hinges, and stepped over the threshold. Eyes slowly got used to the darkness, which my pathetic candle candle could not disperse.

It seemed to be surrounded by some gray, silent, dead space. But gradually separate objects began to appear in it. Along the wall I could see the silhouettes of huge barrels with copper taps, and right in front of me, there were whole batteries of wine bottles placed on a special wooden rack with stands.

Everything was covered with moss, a thick layer of dust, slightly fluctuating from the strong drafts caused by the door wide open. Involuntarily there was a terrible feeling that the bottles and barrels were moving.

Yes, this space is not as dead as it seemed to me at the beginning. And it seems that someone's shadows lurk in the depths, and the darkness is threateningly approaching ...

With an effort of will, throwing this burden off me, I stepped over to the shelf and took the first bottle from it. Blowing away enough dust from the label to read the inscription, I disassembled that I caught Armagnac.

Well, in these circumstances, this noble drink, which generally can not be considered ladies, is quite suitable. Today, nothing seems too strong. Grabbing my booty, I turned to the door ...

And then something terrible happened.

From the blast of a draft, the door slammed shut, right in front of my nose, and I almost heard two more sounds at the same time — first, the lock that clicked closed by itself, and secondly, the keychain dropped from the outside doors from a sharp blow.

Oh dear, I was bricked up in this basement, where any claustrophobia should strike a normal person! No one except Anya will come to my aid, and she will struggle for a long time with fear before she decides to go downstairs!

And besides, during this time, Anyuta could have time to doze off from fatigue and experienced anxieties and now she will quietly sleep until morning. It will take more than one hour until she realizes that I went to the cellar for the wine and did not return back ...

I felt how my legs from obedient servants turn into bulky, poorly managed structures, which still strive to bend down and knock over their mistress. The world is painted in the most bleak tone.

A candle stub will soon burn out, and in the pitch darkness I will be sticking up in the morning, struggling with weakness, in this eerie basement, where hungry rats will surely run hither and where there is even nothing to sit on except on a cold floor covered with a thick carpet of dust compressed ...

And in my soul it will be imperceptibly stirring the thought that this kind of nasty creature that lives in Anina Manor, has arranged for me such meanness, and now giggles soundlessly in the dark, invisible and imperceptible, enjoying its victory!

CHAPTER 9

Anna

And Nyuta sat alone in the dining room for a long time, waiting for Lelya to return, but that was not and never was.

I was terribly sleepy, because there was a deep night, and the experienced excitement, a strange chase, it is not known who, fear, a swoon — everything made itself felt.

At first Anya thought that Lelia had been busy in the wine cellar for too long, choosing something unusual for her exquisite taste ... And she could hurry too!

But then anxiety replaced the annoyance - what if Lele became ill there in the cellar? Suddenly she also had a faint? And she without feelings lies on the cold floor among the bottles? After all, Lelia hit her head in the forest very hard when she tried to catch up with the mysterious creature. The consequences of such blows are fraught with loss of consciousness and could already have the most deplorable effect ... We'll have to hurry to help her!

Going downstairs was unbearably scary, but Anya gathered all her will and headed for the door leading to the wine cellar. Leaving Lely to the mercy of fate will simply be shameless, you need to overcome yourself ... Suddenly it is already a question of life and death? After lighting up the gloomy basement corridor and the door of the wine cellar, Anya saw that the door lock was locked, Lelya was nowhere to be found, and a bunch of keys was lying on the floor ...

- My God, my God! What is it? - Anya whispered dead lips.

After all, Lelya did not go upstairs! So where is she? Where could disappear? Did the ghosts of the old manor take her to the unknown distances? Or is it the crafty pranks Anya, forcing to see is not what it really is?

It seems that the nanny said that there is a special old prayer for the expulsion of evil spirits from man. But what saint is supposed to pray in such a case? Nicholas of Myra Oh no, the great martyr Nikita ... We need to remember the words of the prayer, because the nanny once taught Anna!

"O great martyr of Christ and the miracle-worker, the great-martyr Nikito, who adheres to your holy and miraculous image, does your deeds and wonders and much your compassion for people praisingly, we pray you diligently: bring me with humble and sinful power, I am deceased, I have come to you, I come to you, I am a weaker, I am deceitful of you, I am a weaker, I pray you. in memory of the words of the ancient prayer, heard in childhood ...

An old oak door, covered with stripes of wrought iron, swung open, creaking nastyly, and Lelya, smeared with dust, with a bottle in her hand, appeared on the threshold.

- Good God! - shouted Anya. - You were in the cellar! And I thought - a misfortune happened to you ...

- Indeed, almost happened. "The door to the cellar slammed shut by itself, immuring me inside," Lelia answered quite coolly.

- By herself? - Anin's voice treacherously trembled. What nonsense! Such things do not happen by themselves. Surely there was not without otherworldly intervention, even if the pragmatic Lelia would deny it. - And what? How did you get out?

- Fortunately, you managed to tell about the habit of your late grandmother to hide the spare keys to the door everywhere. I began to look for a spare key until the candle burned out. And the truth is, from the inside of the cellar, on a small nail at the very door there was a key. Here he is. I will hang him in his place; perhaps he will more than once allow unfortunate prisoners to break free from the wine cellar.

- Lelia, are you sure that the ghosts living in the house did not have a hand on this occasion? - asked Anya, who wanted to stick to the mysterious interpretation of the incident. "Do you think they could not turn the key in the door?" Or not, rather - to make him turn under the influence of some non-material force?

"Well, if these are ghostly tricks, they will regret their imprudent behavior," Mrs. Croatianova promised ominously. - We'll have to teach them a lesson of good manners and prove that it is impossible to behave with ladies with such unceremoniousness! Let's go and have a drink on the glass. By God, we deserved it today.

A glass of alcohol not only drove drowsiness, but also gave women courage.

Washed, disguised as a clean peignoir, Elena Sergeevna again applied a compress to the bruise, and Anna, who was slightly tipsy from the strong drink she was not used to, got into the chair with her legs and slowly reasoned:

- Listen, Lelya, maybe, the spirits inhabiting the estate are not at all evil. Just such restless souls. I admit that in life they could have done something unseemly that does not allow them to find eternal peace now ... But now, in order to atone for their sins, they provide protection to the people living here.

Anya took another sip from her glass and continued in a desperate tone:

- For example, today it seemed to me that the silhouette of a man in white (maybe just my grandfather in the uniform of the war in the Balkans) was guarding you in the forest when you rushed for an unknown criminal. The fugitive could have been armed, would have started shooting back and shot you ... And then what? You after all insanely risked, and the ghost seemed to protect you with yourself. Well, you know, like Mons angels ...

Mrs. Croatian looked in surprise out of her compress:

"Angels of Mons?" What is it? What are you talking about, Anya?

- Well Lola, do not you remember? Angels Mons - the most famous supernatural phenomenon of our days, about him already a year soon as they write in all the newspapers, and you ask, what is it? At the very beginning of the war, in August 1914, there was a terrible battle in Belgium near Mons. German artillery spared no shells and brought real fiery rain to the positions of the British and French. Those did not have reliable shelters, so fifteen thousand people immediately died, and the survivors were forced to retreat under heavy German fire ...

"I remember that." The Allied armies suffered greatly in Mons. It was one of the first major defeats of the Entente. But what have the angels? When fifteen thousand people die in one day, there can be nothing sacred in this matter.

- You are mistaken, Lelya! You, as always, read only military reports, and most importantly, you missed ... Retreating soldiers were escorted by some spirits who protected them from enemy shells. Many people said almost the same thing - ghostly warriors in old clothes put a barrier between the retreating allies and the Germans who were chasing them. Even the sisters of mercy, in whose hands the soldiers wounded in the battle of Mons, were dying unanimously spoke of the extraordinary exaltation of dying and strange visions that had troubled them before dying. This supernatural phenomenon and received the name "Angels of Mons." It may well be that it was thanks to the otherworldly intercession that at least one of the Entente soldiers was able to escape. English front-line journalist Arthur Machen was in those days in positions and witnessed mystical events. He wrote the story "The Archers", suggesting that the defense of the defeated armies of the Entente rose soldiers who fell in the XV century in the battle of Azhinkure near Mons. Rather, their souls rose. So to say, distant ancestors helped their descendants ... In September, this story was published in the London Evening News and almost immediately translated from English into other languages. He caused an extraordinary interest in the whole world ... I had somewhere the story "Archers" translated into Russian, I will find and let you read.

- Thank you, Anya, but you told this story in such detail that I already have enough idea about her. Such literature is not necessary to study on primary sources.

"So, I think that the repentant soul of one of my ancestors may be the ghost of these places." Therefore, he protects us in order to atone for his life-long transgressions.

"The idea is not new," Elena Sergeevna replied. - Even the ancient Romans believed that they were helped by the Lars - the spirits of dead ancestors, providing protection to their descendants. They were revered on a par with penates, homemade spirits. Some Lars were guarded not only by families living in the house, but also entire cities and even areas. Similar beliefs were among the ancient Slavs, who believed that each person and his house, and sometimes the whole race protects the spirit of the ancestor - schur or chur. Hence, the word ancestor, and the expression "chur me!" As a request for help when meeting with the supernatural ...

- So, maybe this is just the schur of our kind and is in the house? - Anna suggested. - It would be nice to know why he cannot find peace and whether he needs help ... I should have figured it out somehow!

Elena Sergeevna slowly pulled the head from her head. She seemed to have no desire to get to know the ghost-schur closer to find out his secrets.

And Anya had already reasoned that an experienced medium would be able to establish contact with a ghost and find out what was so unfortunate of the unfortunate and why he could not find peace and fall asleep forever. You can invite any knowledgeable person from the Moscow spiritualistic society to Privolnoe, because this case is certainly of great interest to spiritualists ...

"Anyuta, for God's sake, just no seances," Mrs. Kvatovova interrupted her. - I have nothing against such a sweet and caring ghost, who is also related to you ... But looking for him for a closer acquaintance - no, please. And in general, immediately stop talking about ghosts, otherwise they would dream of me. It is even scary to think in what image they will appear in my dream. Maybe in the image of vampires? Something about life here already looks a lot like a gothic romance ... Let's go, my dear, in our own rooms and try to get some rest. Soon it will start to get light, but we didn't even close our eyes ...

"So do you advise you to forget about the ghost that is in my house?" Do not pay him any attention and be done with the end? - Anya was indignant.

- Well, what are you? I don't like to give advice at all. This is a very opposing and completely useless exercise, "Elena Sergeevna replied, waving a little soul, heading for her bedroom.

Anya was not found with the answer. And what could have been the answer to such an indisputable statement? Besides, it's really time to get some sleep ...

CHAPTER 10

Helena

Taking a sleeping pill in the form of a pair of glasses of aged Armagnac, I fell asleep as soon as I climbed under my pompous canopy and touched my head with a pillow.

But the evil ghosts, despite my contempt for them today, still decided not to give me rest. Well, they would still run hither and around the house, echoing their footsteps and groaning ... A tired person might not have heard them, and they could have let themselves romp in their leisure time without interference.

But moving the furniture over my head at night, interrupting the long-awaited, so clearly not starting a dream, was more than shameless of the spirits. The local schur could show more hospitality to the lady who was forced to live under the roof of his gloomy house!

I woke up in great irritation, listened to incomprehensible sounds and again suspected that the whole mysterious noise was most likely not of metaphysical origin. I am afraid that this is exactly the case, and restless schur has nothing to do with it ...

I remembered again that the pot, in which the spare house key was to roll, is empty (an urgent need to buy a new lock in the nearest hardware store and invite some locksmith to insert it).

But, on the other hand, this noise at the top suggests some thoughts ... What is the practical purpose of the secret visitor? What is he doing up there? Moves furniture to become more comfortable? To penetrate under a cover of night into someone else's house in order to restore order in the attic is, by God, somehow unnatural. But what can a living person need at night among the old junk? What did he lose there?

Hoping to preserve the remnants of healthy skepticism, I again pulled the faithful Browning out from under the pillow and, moving as silently as possible, crept to the end of the corridor towards the stairs. Mille tonnerress! Annie did not lie to me!

A manly figure, indistinctly without light, descended the stairs and melted below in the darkness of the hall. A minute later, the front door slammed.

Leaning on the railing and looking to where the night guest had disappeared, I froze in amazement. The most incredible thoughts frantically jumped in my head. What should be done in such extraordinary circumstances? Faint? It is stupid, and it is dangerous - look at it, spill over the railing of the stairs and roll down ... So it won't be long to be crippled.

In the end, I matured for an inhuman cry and had already gained more air into my lungs, but then a very rational thought came to me: would it make sense? Well, I will outrun the whole house (the whole house is Anya and the nanny, to disturb which would be the height of egoism!), But why? Can they help me with something? In vain I will only frighten ...

In addition, I did not feel any particular horror, to wail in the night, rather, a strong surprise. Maybe because the limit of nervous shocks was exhausted today (after all, everything should be a measure, otherwise I should have gone to a psychiatrist a long time ago!). And maybe because the phenomenon of the ghost was not accompanied by effects typical of aliens from the other world, and I could not help but notice. There was no grave chill, chilling fear of the soul did not squeeze my heart, unearthly radiance did not spread around the house, and inhuman voices did not sound ...

And although the male figure just flashed before me in the dark for a moment, I would not undertake to assert that this is some kind of ephemeral substance. So who is this?

Damn it If I had bothered to get out of bed a little earlier, as soon as I heard a noise, I would be able to wait for the mysterious visitor and meet him on the steps of the stairs face to face.

Yes, precisely face to face! The inner voice told me that he has a normal human face, and not a skull with failed eye sockets, or that guests from the world of the dead still wear the face ...

Of course, it would be possible to shoot a night alien from browning. A ghost shot does not hurt, but an earthly attacker falls dead. At least it will immediately become clear whether this is a spirit or a person. After all, such a thing can not be left to chance.

Yes, it would be possible to shoot, but ... but I somehow am not ready to commit a murder ... And who, in fact, will be easier if the next morning in Anna's house they find a corpse, the police arrive, and they arrest me, put them in shackles and throw them into the torture chambers? No, thank you, I will not deliver such joy to my enemies!

I stood still a bit on the stairs, peering into the gloom around me, and then a brilliant (yes, brilliant, I'm not afraid of this word!) Idea came to me in its simplicity. Shoot need not from Browning, but from a slingshot! Precisely that of a slingshot! The stone put by the mark with the hand is harmless again for the ghost, and for the person it is very tangible, although it will not kill him.

As a child, I have often played with boys who have dedicated me to all the details of slingshots. And I could well recall the lessons learned from them, only high-quality tires should get somewhere ...

Returning to my room, I plunged into dreams, pondering every detail of my plan. So, perhaps, it is necessary to sacrifice a new rubber heater, purchased at the Ferrein pharmacy on Nikolskaya, - in war as in war, sometimes you lose something dear to your heart.

The next time, armed with a slingshot, I will set an ambush against an annoying spirit and shine a stone between my shoulder blades. Let's see how our night guest will react to my attack ...

It may not be possible to behave with such unceremoniousness with real spirits, but it seems to me that it is all the same to them, you cannot cause pain to an incorporeal shell.

So, if a stone, without meeting an obstacle, passes through a mysterious visitor and flies farther away, therefore, you can't do anything about it - it's a vision and a vision.

But if a certain gentleman quite earthly denounced us, oh, his leprosy will cost him dearly. A stone in the back is a deserved punishment, and there is nothing to stand on ceremony. Not for that I left all the business in Moscow to endure such jokes here.

I managed to doze off in the morning, when clear dawn rays filled the room. But I was very pleased with my plan and mentally drew myself a magnificent nut slingshot with red factory tires. How will I put a pebble in it, but how I will stretch it ...

Still, whatever you say, but I managed to keep the charm of youth and unbridled cheerfulness. (Sometimes you have to say compliments to yourself, since you will never hear them again from anyone! However, one should not allow the demon of pride and boasting to capture my soul into their tenacious paws.)

The next morning we all woke up quite late, which, however, is quite understandable by circumstances. The night was unusually stormy, and I felt completely overwhelmed. It seems that it was about this state that Nekrasov said: "There is no bone not broken, there is no vein not drawn ..."

But most importantly, now, in the bright light of the sun, I had absolutely no confidence that everything that had happened the day before either had a dream or a dream. Perhaps all this crazy night leapfrog was just a series of delusional visions?

Suppose the question of whether I was running through the woods with Browning, chasing in the dark for someone unknown or not, you can clarify with Ani - if she dreamed the same thing, then it wasn't a dream.

But the figure of the ghost that flashed on the dark staircase could well have been my personal dream, a fad of a weary brain ... I'll ask you to start strong coffee, maybe it will bring me back to life and it will clear up in my poor head!

Some incredibly fatty pancakes were just added to the table, seasoned with sour cream. Probably, the nanny was going to restore our strength, acting in her own mind. I decided that you should not abuse such dishes, you can limit yourself to a cup of coffee. In addition, there was absolutely no desire, probably, on nerves.

Rejected pancakes offended drooped on a plate. God, what a strange house after all - even inanimate objects behave here as if they have a character ...

Nanny at first did not want to talk at breakfast about yesterday. She tried to conduct an abstract conversation, apologizing to me, as a guest, for the current state of the park (as if the night before we had gone there just to walk and admire its beauty!).

"Desolation, desolation," the old woman lamented. "Look at that, in the alleys you will stumble on the root or stray into the nettle ... First of all, there was no such thing, the park, having experienced how the picture looked. Under the Countess, blessed memory of Grandmother Nyutochkina, five gardeners were kept in the house ... Yes. In the old years, the estate was filled as it should be ... It was immediately obvious that these gentlemen lived here! And now? Servants something, read, and did not remain. House in desolation. And who is to deal with the park? And there is no one at all! Well, I, an old stalk, dug up a little in the back of the piece of land, smashed a vegetable garden, parsley there, onions or cucumbers to grow to the table ... And what? Only silushki and enough, that weed the heels of ridges from the weed, and then the day can not bend back, and aches, and aches, damn! And so in the park, as in former times,

The young mistress and I were absent-mindedly listening, but, admittedly, we were altogether different. God is with them, with the leftists ... After an extremely unsuccessful attempt to detain an unknown villain and all subsequent events, I felt unable to indulge in light-hearted conversations about the good old days.

Anna, also not responding to the words of the nanny, spoke to me about night adventures, and her memories so much coincided with my own that there was no doubt - at night we didn't feel anything, we really heard shouts and rushed from the house to help an unknown victim, but on my return I was bricked up in a wine cellar ... It was not a dream, but a cruel reality!

At this point, the nanny also joined in the conversation and reportedly conspiratorially that, returning to the house at night, she didn't sleep almost until the morning, got out of bed, walked through the rooms, and "got a crunch" about her.

Listening to her, I guessed beforehand that it was the "old lady" who "clambered" - a male figure on the stairs leading to the hallway ... I, after all, saw the night-time guest descending from the attic in the dark.

The nanny, on the other hand, was bent for a long time before she decided to admit that she had seen a man coming down from above.

I am afraid that life experience has maliciously prompted the old woman that the unknown gentleman was heading for the entrance doors not from the attic, but from the second floor where the master and guest bedrooms were located. But, on the other hand, she liked more to regard the stranger as a ghost, rather than as a living person, returning from a romantic date with one of the ladies living in the house ...

"Well, I think to myself," she explained, "this cannot be the case for men in our house to run so easily!" If they are kasatiks, where they are taken at night, they are not here. We have a white afternoon, read it, there are no male guests ... So it means that I got a crunch ...

The nanny paused, pushed the cup away from herself and whispered conspiratorially:

"As if it is not this ... not Grandfather Annochkin, the old master." His spirit happened to be in a mess at home. Earl in the old days, as from the Turkish war, he was brought to the grave, was ... used to go around the rooms ... So how would he not take up the old again. This is not good, oh not good, if the dead person is seen ... It is necessary to sprinkle holy water in the corners, and then Grandma Sychuha should be called to reprimand the little room. If the doors in the house are conspired, so the evil spirits in them will not get through ...

Anya and I immediately became interested in what kind of Sychiha was such that she easily controlled with evil spirits.

It turned out to be a local landmark, someone like a rural healer or a witch, Melanya Sycheva. The deceased mother of Melania and even her grandmother were suspected of witchcraft, so the inhabitants of the surrounding villages had bypassed women of this kind for more than a decade.

In her youth, Melania was distinguished by her rare beauty, she left the house early, moved to the estate, where she served as a maid at the lady's house, Privolnoye's mistress (it's about Anna's grandmother, who was young Malasha and served as a servant). The countess called her noble Mila, dressed in fashion and taught to read French novels. Mila-Malasha was one of the most trusted servants and was almost inseparable from the mistress.

When the countess was widowed, clouded with grief and began to spend days and nights trying to evoke the spirit of her deceased husband, Melania helped her in these dangerous affairs, and then suddenly left the aristocratic mansions, abandoned both novels and fashion hats, returned to the witch's shack and She took from her Vedov's secrets. After that, the mother soon died (they say how the sorceress will give her skill, so she should emit the spirit soon - on earth nothing more holds her), and Melanya somehow at once turned from a young beauty into an old woman, began to avoid people and spend days gathering herbs and roots and a brew of magical potions ...

In the village, she was greatly feared, but the gentlemen, you see, by old memory treated the healer well. When her shack had completely collapsed, Anna's father allowed Melanier Sycheva to move into a gatehouse on the outskirts of the estate park, where she has since been living, almost without seeing people.

But those rare brave souls who ventured to ask her for help, said that Grandma Malasha does not refuse anyone, helps and does not take money, unless she accepts the little egg or heels of eggs from the petitioner, but nobody was angry with her.

"I'll go to Melania," the nanny decided, "I'll take the varenitsa to her and say:" Do not seek it, mother, that I am disturbing, but only the young mistress, your mistress's granddaughter, the damned tortured me. Help the poor widow, mother, do not refuse! "Perhaps he will come and speak the house!"

Listening to the nanny, I could not get rid of the feeling that I was in a fairy tale, only this tale is a bit scary.

Sitting in Moscow in my apartment on the Arbat and enjoying all the benefits of civilization, I could not imagine that it was worth driving a few hundred miles away, and something ancient would surround me, giving away a deep Middle Ages. Directly Berendeyev kingdom!

Wow, the second decade of the 20th century is coming, after some eighty-five years the new millennium will begin, and here, by candlelight, we will wedge the old manor by conspiracy to prevent the undead from entering our vaults!

Oh, we must get to practical matters as soon as possible, until I finally moved to a certain astral world. Domestic problems are usually well distract from the supernatural. And Anya should not be left alone in this "enchanted" place. It would also be better to divert her to mundane topics ...

"Anya, you wanted to help me in the affairs of the gymnasium," I recalled. - Let's go together in Gireyevo, let's see if everything goes right there. I promised Barbara Filippovna to keep order in her sanatorium. Take a walk along the same time, breathe the forest air ...

"Do you want to walk through the forest?" - Anya asked with incomprehensible horror in her voice.

- Why? It's straight to Gireyevo, very close, and the weather is wonderful today.

- Lelia, for God's sake, but not along a forest road, I beg you! It is better to ride a horse around the bolshak - at least there are no people there and there are still not so scary. I will never go on foot in the forest!

I did not object to anything - life in Privolnoy even spoils my nerves, it is not surprising that Anya has become so fearful.

An ancient stroller was found in the carriage shed (surely remembering the late Slavophil count as a curly boy), an equally old mare, a real bedding bed that had long dreamed of peace, was harnessed to this kolymagu, and with great difficulty rose up on high goats.

While the crew was preparing for us, I decided to take another small and non-binding undertaking - put my hand in the pot that adorned the porch again to see if there was anything new in it.

It was strange to hope that, for example, the missing key from the door would return by itself, but still ... Still ... You never mind!

And I managed to find in the pot with nymphs something other than dried leaves and small litter.

- Lelya, what do you want to find there? - Anya asked. - Is there anything interesting?

- Yes, it is interesting. And, it seems, has already found. Here, look!

An expensive cigarette with a gold stripe across the mouthpiece was clamped in my fingers.

- Ugh, how disgusting! - Anya grimaced.

- Disgusting, of course. But the paper is completely fresh, not yellowed and not damp. I can tell you one thing - when last night I checked whether a spare key for the front door was in place or not, this nastiness was not here yet.

"Well, maybe the officer who offered us assistance at night threw a cigarette butt here," suggested Anya. "He took us to the house and stood by the porch." But littering at another's threshold is not very noble.

"No doubt," I agreed. "But only Mr. Lieutenant did not smoke when he walked us from the old gate to the porch (it would be just as ignoble for the ladies to breathe in the face). And after saying good-bye, he immediately went home and left your house away. So, the stub threw someone else here ...

- And who was it? - frightened asked Anya.

- I don't know yet, unfortunately. Either someone at night hung around with a cigarette around your house and even climbed onto the porch, or this is our milestone ghost that slipped through the door, pampered at last with tobacco and left a real trail of his stay. I don't like both options at all, "I summed up, sitting down in a pram. - Especially for a ghost smoking - too extravagant habit.

A gray-haired driver touched the reins, and we drove along a broken country road with two deep bumpy ruts. We were immediately followed by a pack of stray dogs, dumbfounded with happiness, that there was such a wonderful object for barking. With this ecstatic escort, we moved from the park near Privolinska towards the carriageway.

CHAPTER 11

Anna

The dogs finally fell behind, silence reigned around, the horse slowly trotted along the long road towards Gireyevo, and the women sitting in the carriage just as slowly were talking.

"You know, among other things, I don't understand why this ghost hurries to the attic endlessly, and also moves heavy things. I wonder what he lost there? - Elena Sergeevna inquired when Privolnoe, who remained far behind, disappeared behind the edge of the forest.

- I vaguely remember that in the attic, among other old things, chests belonged to the late grandfather. Maybe this is still the ghost of the grandfather looking for some of his records, or a nominal weapon, or a lost medallion with a portrait of his beloved, or something else like that? - Anya suggested. - Such cases are known. For example, in the patrimonial castle of the English earls of Norfolk in Sussex, the ghost of a man in a blue caftan is often seen. He was called the Blue Man. So, he always comes to the county library and sorts through the books, and sometimes in irritation throws them off the shelves. It is believed that this is one of the ancestors of the current owner of the castle is looking for an old book with secret records belonging to him ...

- What are you saying! I thought that such bibliomans are found only among modern privat-docents, - Lelya could not resist.

Anna did not notice the irony in her voice.

"No, no, this is an ancient ghost," she explained very seriously. - For the first time, the Blue Man appeared in the castle of the count in the 17th century, during the time of Charles II, but since then he has not found his manuscript and has not found peace. The current Earl of Norfolk is interested in mystical secrets and regularly publishes in the English press all new and new messages about the phenomena of the Sussex ghost.

Elena Sergeevna wanted to argue that the British graphs with their ancestral ghosts were not decreed for us - it is so accepted in Great Britain that every decent lord who claims to be true aristocratic would have a couple of ghosts in his castle, otherwise the price is worthless and the castle, and most lord, but abstained, so as not to upset Anna.

Let yourself be fond of romantic stories, since they bring her comfort ...

"Well, well," Elena Sergeevna agreed, "suppose the ghost of the late count can search in the attic among her own old things for something memorable for him." Let's say. And if this is a living person? What do you think? Could an ordinary live person for some reason be interested in your attic?

"I don't know what could be interesting for ordinary living people," Anya shrugged. - Is that for some junk ... I told you, for many years no one went to the attic. Nothing but old stuff you will not find there, but it is very scary to climb there.

"I hope you will allow me to somehow make a pilgrimage to your attic in order to take a closer look at this rubbish of bygone times?"

"Whenever it pleases you," Anya agreed. - Only for God's sake, be careful, the attic is some kind of mysterious and dangerous place. It seems there once was someone who hanged himself. But I do not remember the details.

In the hospital, everything was almost okay. Almost, with the exception of a small but very unpleasant incident - one of the sisters of mercy, invited by Mrs. Zdravomislova to care for the wounded, slowly escaped from the estate. She had already complained for a long time to her partner that the service here is heavy, there are too many patients, the hostess is strict and picky and, in general, the wilderness is fed up to death ...

On the eve, the girl dressed up and left the estate, allegedly for a walk, but then did not return - she probably reached the railroad herself and went home to Moscow.

Before leaving, Varvara Filippovna inadvertently gave all staff a salary, so the nurse's money was there, and nothing particularly held her in Gireevo (except for a sense of duty - a subject that seemed to many too burdensome in today's difficult times).

The second sister who remained at his post complained bitterly that she needed to do fifteen dressings now, and even injections and other procedures prescribed by the doctor ... At least break apart! Real hard labor! That's always, some consider themselves entitled to walk and have fun, while others should overstrain and lay down their bones because of this. There is no justice in life!

Mrs. Croatian had to roll up their sleeves and also get down to business. Yes, and Anya attract. "In the end, it will only benefit the young widow," Elena Sergeevna decided, "because nothing distracts from her own grief as helping her neighbor."

"You studied nursing at the beginning of the war, which means you can cope with dressings," she told Anya. "If the empress Alexandra Fyodorovna, along with the older princesses, is caring for the wounded in a military hospital, why should not we take part in such a noble cause? The Christian soul must be merciful.

What will you object to? Anya meekly went along with Elena Sergeyevna to the outhouse where the lower ranks were located, and took up the dressings. She was tired of being used to death, but she was not left with a pleasant feeling that she was finally doing something important, not for herself, but for people.

Having rendered all possible help to the suffering, the ladies returned to the big house and decided to drink tea. The company they made up the entire officers of the patients of the hospital.

Among gentlemen officers, the appearance of two beautiful women created a real sensation. Everybody was eager to serve the ladies and engage them in conversation. True, the topic of conversation is constantly concerned with something unpleasant. But what else could have been the subject of a secular conversation in a country that was mired, like in a swamp, in endless war (if, moreover, the population of this unfortunate country prefers to engage exclusively in antigovernment activities and disobedience to the authorities)?

The officers excelled in bitter sarcasm, trying, even in such a bleak situation, to impress the ladies with their wits.

Especially zealous lieutenant Krivitsky, throwing from time to time heavy byronic glances at the young widow. He walked wickedly at each of the representatives of the highest state power and satirically described the foreign and domestic policy of Russia, its recent past and immediate prospects.

- Alas, now for many political intrigue has become a commercial affair. And brings good dividends, I dare say. However, our politicians have always loved to arrange a slaughter, and then spend time at banquets in honor of the sons of the fatherland, whose immortal memory will forever remain in the hearts of grateful fellow citizens. Is not it? - the lieutenant asked a rhetorical question.

(During his passionate monologue, decorated with some freedom-loving delicacies, Krivitsky, oddly enough, managed to never turn his head - his face was all the time in relation to the ladies in a romantic position three-quarter full, so beloved by provincial photographers ...)

No doubt, many now recalled with bitterness the beginning of the war, accompanied by pompous parades, as well as patriotic expressions of enthusiasm and loyal feelings, were ashamed of these feelings and would like to renounce them.

And yet, the last tirade of Krivitsky, full of bilious gloating, seemed to Anna Afanasyevna, who had lost among her sons of the fatherland's husband, completely irrelevant. Of course, she was not spoiled by such exquisite eloquence, but the lieutenant should not forget that he was talking to the officer's widow ...

"Perhaps your Krivitsky is some kind of anarchist," Anya whispered in Elena Sergeevna's ear. - All these gentlemen love beautiful poses and long anti-government conversations, and patriotism for such is an empty sound ...

Meanwhile, the lieutenant Krivitsky, who took the attention of the young widow for approval, tried to consolidate the success. He reached for his guitar and saddened the ears of those present with the performance of a romance, the words of which were extremely far from everything he had just said.

- The time will come, it may be, Love will creep into your heart, you will stop laughing, And passion will fill your blood. Consciousness of your tears, I will redeem my torments ... I wish you the same torment, But I still love you,
- he deduced in a pleasant, but somewhat sweet voice, which was in good harmony, however, with his icon-painting face.

In any case, love poems about passion, torment and torment much better fit with his mannered way than cynical political speeches ...

"What a pity that Eugene's sister ran away," remarked Staff Captain Saltykov, when the lieutenant's voice dropped. - We were left without our angel of mercy. Krivitsky and Zhenya sang a duet beautifully. Alas, there is no perfection in the world, and angels are also bothered by virtue ...

- Are you sure that Sister Eugene escaped, Mr. Captain? - suddenly gave a voice to Anya.

- What do you mean madam? - asked several voices at once.

"Couldn't some misfortune happen to her?" - Anya tried to express herself more clearly.

- Misfortune? - surprised staff captain. - In these quiet places?

"In these quiet places, Mr. Captain, four girls have been brutally murdered lately," Anna said mournfully. "Have you not heard of it?" They found the unfortunate people in the woods with their throats cut ... On the very first day after my arrival I ran into the funeral of one of the victims.

The words Anina undoubtedly impressed. Society in the dining room boomed in surprise. Strangely enough, it seems that none of the officers who lived in the closed world of the Girei estate, really did not know about the crimes that took place in the district, and if they heard something briefly, they did not realize the full horror of what was happening.

For an active Elena Sergeevna, the words of a friend also sounded a revelation.

"Anya, why didn't you tell me anything about this before?" - asked Mrs. Croatia, with some distrust. "I mean about dead girls?" About anything you said, just not about that?

- Somehow the word did not have to. Yes, and I did not want to scare you, excuse me. There is enough of everything here ... But I was totally against us walking on foot through the forest, that is why. In the forest is now too dangerous. There you can run into a killer who attacks women to cut their throats ...

- Oh my God! - Elena Sergeevna cried suddenly. - Gentlemen! At night we were woken up in Privolnoye by terrible screams coming from the side of the forest. Screaming woman. Anna Afanasyevna and I even jumped out of the house, believing that someone needed help, but, alas, we didn't find anyone in the dark. And now it turns out that one of the nurses is missing. How I did not immediately compare these facts! I must have found an eclipse ... It was a misfortune that could happen to your Zhenya, gentlemen!

Staff captain Saltykov jumped up and straightened his tunic.

- Gentlemen! - He turned to the officers. - I believe, long conversations are unnecessary. It is necessary to comb the square in which the screams were heard. Elena Sergeevna and Anna Afanasyevna will show us the place. I will go to the outhouse and assemble a team of lower ranks. I hope that everyone who is able to walk a long distance due to his health will take part in the search. Gathering in the yard in a quarter of an hour.

The officers were blown out of the canteen as if blown away, and after a few minutes, the first members of the search group began to gather in the courtyard under the windows of the estate.

"You know, Lelya, but there is something in this headquarters," Anna said thoughtfully, looking through the lace curtain into the courtyard. - something truly masculine, noble ...

"Oh yes, a real classic Valentine," Elena Sergeevna replied with a smile.

- Classic Valentine? - Anya did not understand.

- That's it. Just such a Valentine public applauds hotly in the fourth act of "Faust", recognizing it as a model of nobility. Brother, avenging the honor of his sister. Our Valentine is also one of those who are always ready to stand up for someone's honor. And this, in contrast to the picture of muscle flexing, is a true manifestation of masculinity.

"Yes," Anya agreed. "You'll tell me right away that Valentine is a real man." What a pity that his face was so badly disfigured by the scars ... However, his smile is very pleasant.

"The scars of a real man cannot be disfigured," Elena Sergeevna snapped. "And all these angel-like lieutenants with rings on fingers next to him look like boys from the church choir." And in general, noble men in our time have become an endangered individual, they are no longer counted in thousands. And this should be remembered! With the current universal savagery, every surviving copy of a decent, well-educated person should be appreciated.

CHAPTER 12

I found it necessary to join the team of the military in their search - it was necessary to show them the place from where the terrible screams came and where I ingloriously tried to fight an unknown intruder. Dead for horror, Anna, I found it good to leave in Gireyev.

The captain and lieutenant Krivitsky and I took advantage of the crew, while the rest of the search expedition had to walk through the forest on foot and catch us on the edge of Privolnoye.

To be honest, I have long wanted to speak frankly with Valentin about the latest events in the Privolinska manor and on the old friendship to consult about something, but somebody was disturbing us all the time.

And now it was impossible to confide in the Krivitsky company - for obvious reasons I didn't trust this cherub much.

To the place from which the screams were heard at night, we reached quickly, and in half an hour we were joined by other soldiers who came by a short forest road.

I showed Saltykov the old park gates, through which we ran out at night in search of the villain, the forest edge, where dim shadows flickered behind the bushes and trees, drew his attention to the broken branches and my own tracks left during the night chase ...

In the bright sun, the surrounding landscape looked extremely peaceful and poetic, and if it were not for the grassed grass and broken branches of bushes in those places where I was chasing an unknown enemy, it would be a completely pastoral corner of rural nature.

The soldiers stretched into a chain and plunged into the forest, combing every square fathom. I wanted to sit on the grass at the park gates in anticipation of the search results, but natural curiosity took over.

True, it is not very convenient to comb the forest with ladies' shoes with heels, but I could not stay away from such an important matter. If I make up the company to Valentin Saltykov, who has assumed the duties of a senior teammate, then I will be in the very epicenter of what is happening. And there will be so many valiant warriors around that one of them will surely carry me out of the forest, if I break my leg, stumbling over the roots ...

Jumping over snags sticking out of the ground, I jumped behind the military, ready for any turn of events.

Meanwhile, the weather suddenly began to deteriorate. Thick clouds gathered in the sky, right before our eyes turning into dark clouds, and a strong wind, flew from nowhere, ominously rustling with tree branches, tightened the sky with marmara. The sun tried to resist the clouds and the wind, but it was clear that it would not last long.

A wonderful day suddenly turned into its wrong side ... Soon it began to rain, becoming more and more powerful.

- Simchenko, Leshakov, - noncommissioned officers called out to ordinary soldiers, - well, report back - you discovered what?

- No, your honor! Pobeda all clean. There were no extraneous bodies around the dead vole, "the rank and file responded cheerfully, who considered, despite the rain, their sally as something of a general jaunt. - A mouse, even dead, for the corpse can not be considered ...

But all the fun ended at that moment, when one of the soldiers, a young freckled guy with protruding pink ears and a hand on a sling, shouted in his own voice, pushing the branches of the wild hazel.

On the empty patch between the bushes of hazel lay the dead sister of mercy from the Giraevsk hospital.

For some reason I expected to see her in her usual outfit - in a sisterly kerchief with a red cross and white linen robe or apron. But the little sister dressed up before her death. The girl had a fashionable shanzhan silk fabric jacket (thoroughly drenched in blood), and on her unnaturally pale face with traces of smeared lipstick, a beautiful straw hat with a blue ribbon and a scattering of forget-me-nots slipped.

I was surprised by a completely absurd in its irrelevance phrase:

- Lord, this can not be!

The rain had already started running with might and main, and the deceased spilling water over the jacket merged into large wet spots. Under the pressure of the rain spurts, the hat, which was crookedly held on the sisters' forehead, moved and a wide-open, dead eye looked out from under the straw fields ...

Out of fear, I squeezed my eyes shut and crossed myself three times. Yes, now there is no doubt that this poor thing was screaming in the woods at night. Oh god, I see how she runs, driven by horror, and the killer, armed with a knife, chases her by leaps and bounds. It was enough to imagine how the pictures flashed before my eyes one more terrible than the other.

Lord Almighty, what is happening in this quiet corner of the forest? And why should I always end up somewhere near the bloodthirsty murderers, with whom you have to fight or not?

Even if nothing happens to me personally, then some monstrous event takes place side by side, and my character never let me stand aside. Meanwhile, the scene of the incident was instantly surrounded by a crowd of soldiers, who were running from all sides to the ill-fated Hazel, and without a corpse who did not look very merry.

- Mother honest! You look at her throat - there is no place for the living! We are somehow in a bayonet attack with Hans on the positions being finished, and then there - on the girl an unfortunate hand has risen from some kind of viper! - Eh-ma, sister, sister - a beautiful, young, would you live and live, but what are you ... Goreto what! - I suppose her mother is still alive - she will receive news about her daughter ... - God forbid! I wish you at least at the front of a bullet or a shell there ... And then in the deep rear, in Moscow gubernia, it was possible to accept death. - Quite the people got mad! - the crowd of soldiers was buzzing with different voices, adding some front-line epithets, without which, as they say, it can be difficult to do in the trenches.

- Get away from the body! - ordered frustrated Valentine. - Do not crowd, come all traces have already trampled the devils. Leshakov, Krutikov, will remain for protection near the corpse. Two more - to protect the road, not allowing strangers here. Sub-lieutenant Lushin, take the crew of Elena Sergeevna and take a living spirit to the village after the police officer. Explain it to him, what's the matter, and deliver here to the place. The rest are free. Thank you for the service, brothers! And I ask the village not to talk about what happened.

I am afraid that the last request turned out to be late - on the edge of the hazel bushes the first spectators from the local inhabitants were already gathering together, as if with a wave of an eye found in the forest.

The gawkers were not stopped by rain, wind, or the sky, tightly overcast. Of course, for a poor country life, killing is an extraordinary phenomenon, which the local aborigines will remember for years and tell legends to their grandchildren ...

The village public, ignoring the bad weather, arrived and arrived in the hope of seeing with their own eyes the climax — the appearance of a contractor, and then the removal of the body covered with a sheet. For some reason, such representations to many to taste. People even agree to get wet in the rain, catch a cold and fall down with pneumonia, just to look at someone's body.

But our wounded, trampling nearby, despite the order to disperse, perhaps still should not increase the crowd, it is better to rest and dry out somewhere in a quiet place.

- Mister Staff Captain! - In the presence of subordinates, I decided to turn to Saltykov strictly officially, so as not to subject him to compromise. - Allow the soldiers and officers to wait out the rain here, next door, in the estate Privolnoe? To Gireyevo, even by a forest, on a short road, is not less than two versts, people will get wet under such heavy rain. But not all is still well recovered from injuries.

"I don't mind," Valentine answered laconically. - I hope, madam, to me your kind invitation also applies?

- You can not doubt, the captain! Your hand!

We went through the park to the house. Weather with might and main showed its disgusting character. Neither the rain nor the wind subsided for a minute. But in the end, no just cause can never do without suffering and suffering. This is how the martyrdom crowns are mined.

The wet skirt slapped me hard on the legs, demanding that we hurry to the shelter, and I hurried to fulfill her wish.

The following hours were filled with some utterly tiresome bustle.

My appearance in Privolnoye without Anna Afanasyevna, but at the head of the detachment of the military plunged the nurse into complete disarray. And the news of the female corpse, found in the woods behind the manor park, finally brought it out of itself.

I had to take the old woman to her room, where she fell on the bed, sobbing and lamenting. I dribbled the poor Valerian woman and returned to the guests.

I decided to invite the soldier to the large dining room, where, at my request, they lit a fire in the fireplace in order to dry out.

Taking with them a promise not to spit on the floor and not to scatter "goat legs" around the cigarette butts, I went to the kitchen to persuade the cook to cook something hot for the military.

She tried to resist, citing lack of adequate supplies. But I, appealing to the mercy of a kind woman, agreed to something unpretentious like a pot of porridge or vegetable soup, if only the dish was hot and would be enough for everyone ...

On top of my murderous (oh, how wrong now this definition!) Arguments I described the cook in bright colors as war veterans suffering from wounds, all as one, not to say a word, got up and went in search of the missing girl; they walked along a country road for several miles on injured legs; in the rain, in the cold wind, we combed the forest and finally came upon the dead body of our beloved sister of mercy, brutally killed and thrown in the bushes ... How they stood over the girl's body, brushing rain from chapped faces ... It was a sin not to support the soldiers in such a difficult moment at least a bowl of hot soup! We are not beasts!

Struck by my eloquence, the cook, wiping the end of her apron with a reverent expression on her face, who had become rude from eternal standing at the stove, promised to do everything she could for front-line soldiers, especially if a couple of soldiers come to her kitchen and help with cleaning vegetables.

Honestly, I was still going to go with a basket to the wine cellar and give wine to the sodden military in a glass of wine, but at the last moment I changed my mind. And not so much because it is indecently so shamelessly to dispose of other people's supplies, - I am sure that in these deplorable circumstances, Anuta would easily forgive me for this arbitrariness.

Simply, I was most vulgarly afraid to reveal to the bored front-line soldiers the secret of the place where innumerable stocks of alcohol are stored, for fear that the valiant soldiers would decide the next night, scaring all the ghosts, take Privolnoe along with the wine cellar by the rules of military fortification, and a few garrison of the estate Anna, nanny and I will be swept away by a mighty hurricane ...

Let concealment of secret and not too merciful in relation to the fighters soaked in the rain, but more than prudent for the inhabitants of Privolnoye.

The conspirator did not have everything, and the members of the search team, meanwhile, were already supported by hot food — a vegetable stew and millet kulesh, seasoned with onions and lard. And in the kitchen, a double-bucket samovar delivered by the cook reached and jars of jam were taken out of the pantry.

Yes, when Varvara Filippovna asked me to follow the sanatorium menu, I'm afraid she meant some other food, more dietary. But who at that time could have guessed such a tragic development of events for this quiet corner?

Valentin Saltykov and I, on a general basis, also received a bowl of kulesh (who would have thought it was so tasty?) And retired to the small side lounge for a heart-to-heart talk.

The small living room was not used by the hostess for its intended purpose for a long time and was surprised at its firstness with gloomy lifelessness: sofas and armchairs wrapped in linen, a chandelier in gauze, muddy glass in the window, pieces of web in the corners, everywhere a noticeable layer of dust, not like in the cellar, but still quite impressive ...

However, today we had more important things, except for examining the situation of a neglected estate. However, Valentine still could not resist the comments:

- Gloomy house. Beautiful, but gloomy. And all over the seal of corruption ...

- Oh, you have no idea what kind of seal! - I interrupted him. - There are more places where the spirit of an ultra-modern civilization has not penetrated. With what, and with corruption here everything is in order. Style "vampire". Even ghosts around the house hang around and bother us at night.

Valentine looked at me with a long, strange look.

- Ghosts? Helen, what are you talking about? - finally he asked.

Oh, if I myself could so unequivocally formulate - about what ... The devil knows what, frankly.

- I would not like you to think ... Well, in the sense ... You understand ... I want to say ...

Usually I was not accustomed to crawling after a word in my pocket, but now my speech didn't want to form beautiful, smooth phrases, because the words jumped in my head like mad grasshoppers. Waving my hand to the conventions, I hurried to admit this strange weakness, and it became easier to speak immediately.

- It seems that eloquence has completely refused me, and that is why. At night, I almost did not close my eyes and now I feel like a snoot fish. You see, here, in Privolnoye, there are some mysterious phenomena ... You do not think, I myself usually do not believe in ghosts, in the materialized souls of former owners, wandering through old houses, in vampires coming to life at night and so on ... And even if the spirits are deceased they will drag me to hell, on my grave you can write as an epitaph: "She did not believe in ghosts ...". But not believing does not meanyat obvious. You know, I am not one of those who shudder at every rustle and shy away from every shadow, but only at night I could hear with my own ears sounds that should not be in this house. It is possible to assume that the ghosts decided to move a couple of old chests in the attic, just for fun.

Valentin smiled incredulously, apparently considering my words as some sort of strange joke. Of course, such an utterance makes a strange impression on an unprepared listener. But I could not stop and continued to say:

- Moreover, I saw with my own eyes the vague silhouette of a man walking up the dark in the stairs ... It was such a strange phenomenon. I did not even fully understand - it was a ghost or a human being. I had an idea to make a slingshot and shoot another time an uninvited guest with small pebbles. A ghost of this would not have felt, for it is an incorporeal spirit, and a living person would have betrayed himself from pain and surprise. Of course, you can count all this hallucinations - auditory and visual. But we have suffered in such a Privolnoye ...

Here I touched in more detail all my vivid impressions, as well as what I knew from the words of Ani. At the same time, I stubbornly, though unsuccessfully, tried to reason logically.

"So, if we assume that this is not a ghost, it means that a person who enters the house with inexplicable intentions, perhaps criminal ... Especially, the key to the front door is gone," I sadly summed up my words.

- The key is gone? - Valentine was surprised.

And again I had to talk about the key, completely disappeared from the pot with nymphs, about the cigarette butt that appeared in its place and other riddles of the old manor.

"Why didn't you let me know earlier?" - worried Valentine. Skeptical smile from his face flew without a trace.

- I, as you know, did not come here for a long time to immediately realize the scale of the rampage of otherworldly forces in this house. And then, easy nonchalance is generally one of the main features of my character. And that, oddly enough, more than once rescued me from difficult situations. No need to rush headlong solve every problem immediately after its occurrence. Problems are often resolved by themselves without our participation, and this way of resolving them is very practical, isn't it?

Saltykov laughed again, but quite sympathetically, and I added:

"Would you be delighted if at night you received a note from me with a messenger about the atrocities of ghosts in Privolny?" Do not rush to complain about annoying ghosts, because it is not known how other people will perceive your words. Suddenly such statements seem paranoid delusions? Most people, especially men, do not believe in such devilry. But I would not like to be considered a neurotic, suffering persecution mania and ready to take any shadow for a ghost ... You must also laugh at me in the soul. Before such stories and I amused, but now a sense of humor begins to change me.

"I can calm you down, Lenochka," people who know you very well will never be mistaken for a person suffering from neurasthenia. And please save your unparalleled sense of humor - you need to bring something life-giving into this damned life. I also do not believe in ghosts, or rather, in what people ignorantly call "ghosts," but I firmly believe that there is much more evil in the world than we would like. I do not exclude that someone, by evil will, decided to intimidate weak women living in such a lonely place. If you allow me, I will move to you in Privolnoe and deal with this shadow of Hamlet's father.

- Valentine, please do not remember in vain Shakespeare, in the plays of which for the final almost all the characters become deceased. I would not like to be directly involved in the embodiment of such a story. If someone conceived of playing a Shakespearean show here, then I will try to force him to restrain his creative impulses. And then, sorry, dear friend, but from your words it blows outrageous male chauvinism! Do you really think that women are so weak that they cannot stand up for themselves? Let me remind you that I have the honor to belong to the leadership of the Moscow branch of the League of Struggle for Women's Equality, and I find such statements offensive. I have given too much strength to the struggle for the rights and freedoms of women to accept your position. A woman is not always a weak and defenseless creature.

- Slingshot? - Saltykov sarcastically inquired, making innocent eyes. - This is a terrible weapon, especially in female hands. All the ghosts are already trembling in their dark alleys.

"Inappropriate irony," I finally felt offended. - Besides the slingshot, I can also find browning. And if you call for help, it is only to ensure the superiority over the enemy in manpower and firepower. Still, in a critical situation, two browning is better than one. Or do you have an official officer's revolver? Well, nothing, and Nagan come. I will always be glad to see you here, but only before you receive an invitation to move to Privolnoe, you need to ask for permission from the mistress of the estate. Ghosts are ghosts, and do not forget about propriety.

"Just do not think, Lenochka, that I impose my society on you," Valentine began to worry.

- Well, you, this is out of the question. After all, I tried to lure you to visit Anna's estate in the hope of your help. In addition, you probably own hand-to-hand combat techniques, and I would dearly give this imaginary ghost to claw at you in the event of exposure. I, as soon as I can, will talk with Anna Afanasyevna about your move to Privolnoe. I think she will be glad if you do us a similar service.

"Anya has become so much like her sister," Valentine said suddenly neither to the village nor to the city, and his face turned completely, in my opinion, out of place with dreamy thoughtfulness.

CHAPTER 13

Anna

Left alone, without Lely, in a strange, unfamiliar house, Anna felt uncomfortable, despite all the attempts of Lieutenant Stepanchikov to somehow entertain the guest.

The snub-noble lieutenant was the only one of the Gireevsky officers, who, citing the pain in his leg, did not go along with others in search of the missing sister of mercy. Nevertheless, to invite Anna for a walk in the vicinity of the estate, the injured leg did not prevent the lieutenant, and as a matter of courtesy, she just oozed out of Stepanchikov like sticky syrup.

However, Anna was absolutely not to the courtesies and not to walk - she preferred to dwell in the living room of the house, and in the shower she was very sorry that she could not be here alone. Disturbed feelings require privacy.

The presence of the lieutenant caused terrible annoyance - and the sound of his voice, and some kind of sinful expression of his eyes, and even a piece of plaster, probably hiding a razor cut on his cheek, - everything in Stepanchikov was extremely unpleasant ... And in general, his face, which at first seemed even cute, on closer examination, those no longer looked. Very unsympathetic and even unpleasant face, for nothing that is young ... Rather, arrogant.

Neither Elena Sergeevna, nor the staff captain Saltykov, nor the other officers and lower ranks returned to Gireyevo for dinner, and after dinner stretched hour after hour, but the search party was not there. It became clear that something bad had happened, maybe even the worst thing, and it was scary to think about it.

On the table by the window magazines were laid out, mainly "Niva", "Alarm Clock" and some other scattered numbers of the "World Illustration".

Scrolling through a couple of magazines, Anya absently remarked:

- what are the old magazines! Even before last year come across. And the news of peacetime is little that hopelessly outdated, so now they seem so insignificant ...

"Yes, we are strongly protected from the latest news here," agreed Stepanchikov. - Probably, doctors believe that the current reports from the front lead to spiritual despondency, which does not contribute to accelerated healing of wounds. But I, you know, always ignore the advice of the doctor. I had to agree with the driver so that when he went to the station he would bring for me personally all the newspapers that he could find in this wild, god-forgotten place. For example, I already know that after the recent meeting of the Headquarters with the command of the North-Western Front, our troops again significantly retreated, letting the enemy go deep into Russian territory. They call it "straighten the front" ... Damn it! In order for us in the trenches, we fought for every sazhen of the land, so that the generals would simply withdraw the army, yielding our positions to the nemchure and the Austrians?

"And where is the front line now?" - Anna finally became interested in his stories. - The Germans are very advanced?

"But if you please," the lieutenant opened an atlas with a detailed map of Europe and ran a pencil line across Lomza, Verkhniy Narev, Brest-Litovsk and Kovel. - Maybe on the map it looks and more beautiful than the old front line, smoother in any case, but I don't see any other reason to leave the previous positions! For me, it was necessary to keep to the last!

- Lord, what a big piece of our land we have lost! - Anna was surprised, for the first time getting a visual idea of how much the situation on the fronts has changed in recent months. - Is it the border? And the front line went here? How far! They say that the whole of Moscow is filled with refugees from the western provinces ...

- Yes, - agreed Stepanchikov. - Soon we will be fighting a year, and here they are, our results. Do you want me to make you tea? Evening, but our squad with the gallant staff captain is no and no ...

Tired military team, and with it Elena Sergeevna returned after dark. They walked along the forest road - the crew of Elena Sergeevna yielded to the consignee, who went to the station to call the judicial investigator by telegraph. The missing girl was found dead in the forest and was due to start a criminal inquiry properly.

"Annie, this is some kind of nightmare," said Elena Sergeevna. - The sister of mercy was lying in a hazel with a throat cut. Those terrible screams that woke us up last night were the death screams unhappy. She was killed last night there, in the forest, not far from Privolnoye. And we were there and could not help her! I am tormented by guilt feelings. I do not know that I will explain to Varvara Filippovna and that I will write to the mother of the deceased girl. And besides, I realized that I won't get any help from the local police authorities in that case - they searched for two hours to inform him about the tragedy. And when he arrived at the place, he made a senseless bustle, tortured us all with questions, dragged the wounded people here and there for a long time and finally said that, according to the paragraph of the instruction, the constables do not have the right to independently engage in criminal investigation upon receipt of a report on a crime, he is obliged to report this to the camp bailiff, the judicial investigator and the associate prosecutor of the District Court. And only when the judicial authorities arrive, will the consignee truly join the investigation ... And how much time has already been lost! Besides, the bloody rain must have washed away all traces. I have a feeling that the weather always stands on the side of our enemies.

- Lelia, so what should we do? - Anna mumbled. - You can not leave everything as is? Already not the first girl in these places perishes! We need to take serious measures.

"That's right, the girls are being killed, the contractor throws up his hands, the investigator from the District Court arrives and, twisting himself for a couple of days, leaves, assuring that he will do everything in his power ... And so on until the new murder. - Choking with indignation, Elena Sergeyevna took a deep breath and continued: - You know, this wild carousel must finally be stopped. While we were waiting for the contractor, I got a horse in the village and sent a man to send a telegram from the station to the Moscow branch of the Detective Police with a request to send an agent here.

- And they will go to such a distance?

- Why not? Indeed, in small towns there are no departments of the Detective Police, and the county county police officer will not help us, which means that syskari are obliged to travel to complicated cases throughout the province and even along its outskirts, "explained Elena Sergeevna. "While the local authorities didn't apply to Moscow Sysk, they thought that they themselves would cope, but things went too far ... I have an acquaintance among Sysk employees, a detective agent Stukalin, an intelligent uncle, sly, burdened with uncommon life experience, gout and a large family. I hope he can come himself. I will place him here, in Gireyevo, closer to the habitat of the late girl, but if he wanders on your business for free, you will have to take him there too. Of course, you counted on peace and solitude ...

- Yes, what peace can be here! - Anya threw up her hands. - Let your detective come, even if he settled on my estate, if only he could help. You can't let the killings go on. Girls in the evenings is dangerous to leave the house.

"Anya, by the way, you and I will have to spend the night in Gireyevo," Lelya remembered, pouring water into the basin for washing. - Do not go back to Privolnoe for the night looking. The killers run hither and thither in the woods ... I really don't fear so much the killers as I am tired from my feet. I simply will not go to your house, you will have to drag me, and if the ghost will not let us sleep again, I will fall into an irresponsible state ... And then there is a quiet room and a wide, comfortable bed. And most importantly - no ghosts. I have one dream - to wash and fall asleep ... And so that there would no longer be any unusual incidents. At such moments, you are especially keenly aware of what this value is - peace ...

But before enjoying the peace, Elena Sergeevna decided to do another important thing - she went to the room of the deceased girl, collected her things and transferred them to her bedroom.

"Let this little chest and its laying be under my guard here," she explained to Anna. "Then I'll give them to the investigator or detective agent." At least so I will have the confidence that no small detail important for the investigation will disappear without a trace.

- And where can she disappear? - Anya was surprised.

- You never know - Lela shrugged. "Suddenly, the girl was well acquainted with the murderer, and at night he would dare to enter the bedroom of the unfortunate and steal letters, or a diary, or a memorable photo, or a book with a dedication, or something else that could lead to his trail ... that the criminal is not a random person, but connected with the victim, and even quite close. This version has the right to exist.

- I am amazed how you know such legal subtleties. This could have occurred only to the policeman, but even the local constable did not care at all about preserving the things of the deceased.

"Which once again proves that in our police, especially the rural ones, completely incompetent people serve," said Lelia in an uncompromising tone. - I, for example, found the diary of the murdered and allowed myself to look into it (I hope the circumstances justify such indecisiveness). Suddenly the diary will help the investigation? The girl had a love story, and, apparently, with one of the local inhabitants — she clearly writes about her romantic experiences hot on the trail, and besides our officers, conscript, deacon and telegrapher, there are not many bachelors in these places.

- Has the young lady described her novel in detail in the pages of the diary? - Anna asked with an incomprehensible excitement in her voice. - And who was her chosen one?

- The name, alas, is not named. And in general, her love adventures are somewhat similar to the works of Mrs. Charskaya, - Lela sighed. - It is so sentimental that on the third page such a reading is boring. But the investigator may be interested in individual facts. Therefore, we need to take measures so that the mysterious elect of the deceased sister of mercy would not withdraw her diary from under our noses.

- And if the offender guesses that you brought the deceased's belongings here, and at night he will attack us in order to pick up the papers compromising him? - scared Anya.

- Well, in order to get into our room, he will have to break the door - here, in Gireyevo, the spare keys do not roll anywhere. And before he can do it, I will raise wild turmoil and shooting, and it is in the house, crowded with military! It will twist in two minutes. No, he will never decide to attack, unless, of course, our little dude is not a complete idiot, but, alas, everything says the opposite. He is cunning and cautious. So good night to you, dear. Today, I hope we can finally sleep.

The night really passed quietly. Almost calmly, except for the mosquitoes, whose constant presence in the bedroom, had simply to be ignored.

In the morning, Elena Sergeevna, cheered up with affairs, besides
the usual business hustle and bustle, which is always so much in the
hospital, it was necessary to prepare rooms for the judicial
investigator and detective agent, because they could appear in
Gireyevo from minute to minute

And Anya has already accustomed to the duties of a nurse, replacing
the dead girl. This time, she did much better with the dressings, she
herself sterilized the instrument, and even under the guidance of her
second sister, she ventured to give several injuries to the wounded.

The doctor who arrived in Gireyevo to examine the patients found
Anina's work quite satisfactory.

Strangely enough, the detective police agent Stukalin arrived from
Moscow much earlier than the judicial investigator from the nearest
county city.

The detective immediately went to the place where the body of the
unfortunate maiden was found the day before. The investigator who
appeared two hours later, on the contrary, did not express a desire to
crawl through the forest glades that were wet after the rain yesterday,
preferring to interview all patients and staff of the gymnasium in a
warm house by the fireplace and draw up detailed protocols.

Since Elena Sergeyevna and Anna Afanasyevna almost did not know
the late girl (Anya never even saw her) and the women couldn't tell
anything except about the night cries and their unsuccessful attempt
to catch the criminal, the investigator spoke shortly to them . Having
scribbled a protocol, he took the things that were killed, including
diaries and letters, and with a clear conscience he let the ladies go to
Privolnoe.

The contractor returned the ladies a long time ago to their crew, but the old horse, who had worked unusually a lot the day before, barely moved his legs and, despite all the efforts of the old driver, crawled very slowly. After yesterday's rain, it became very cold, and both women, who left home in Privolnoye on the eve of a warm sunny morning, were in light dresses. I had to grab a woolen blanket from Gireyevo, with which they wrapped themselves up so as not to freeze too much in the carriage blown by the wind.

"I don't think that there will be a big deal from the judicial investigator in this matter," said Elena Sergeevna, looking at the forest slowly sailing along the road and straightening the rug's fringe. - Too he has a static manner of investigation - he sits in the manor, talks and waits for the murderer to come to him and repent. A detective agent immediately went into the woods to inspect the scene of the murder. It feels good detective grip, such a person, no doubt, at least something, but he will find.

"Well, the investigator is also not devoid of vigor," Anna snorted. - While he was talking to me, he walked around the room endlessly from corner to corner, and he walked around, running around, loudly knocking his heels. And flashed before my eyes back and forth, back and forth, quickly speaking on the run ... Questions were falling right and now to the left, and finally it seemed to me that I was among a whole herd of distraught investigators ...

Elena Sergeyevna laughed, but then again became serious.

"You know what I thought," she said. - Here it becomes too dangerous. Not only did the ghosts torture us in Privolnoye, the murders of women in the district continue. This is not a joke at all. Due to circumstances, it would be good to invite someone from reliable people to Privolnoe. We could use some kind of security ...

- Security? You mean to invite a reliable caretaker? - asked Anna. - In the village, you can hire some old man to guard at night.

- The old man from the village will sleep safely at night on the porch of the estate under the shadow of the dancing nymphs in an embrace with a rifle. It is better if any of the officers from the highlands of the city live in your house. For example, the staff captain Saltykov. After all, he is our good friend ...

- Lelia, just please do not tell me how he held me in his arms and brought me chocolates when I was little. That was too long ago. Honestly, now I find it difficult to perceive him as a close friend. Moreover, he served with my husband, and Alyosha died allegedly at the hands of one of his colleagues, "Anya replied with incomprehensible irritation.

- Do you suspect Valentine? - Elena was surprised. - He himself came to you and told the truth about the death of Alexei. Without it, you wouldn't know about anything.

"Who knows what his goals were?" I don't believe anyone else but you. And then, you yourself have always argued that there are no such cases that women could not cope on their own without the help of men.

- Yes, but there are some things that are easier for a military front-line officer to handle than peaceful people. And it's not about discrimination against women. At times of danger, the reaction of the military is faster, and, you see, they have better weapons and hand-to-hand combat techniques. At least by virtue of her experience, "Elena replied. - I just do not have the habit of jumping up in alarm and fleeing the enemy with a weapon at the ready. In a critical situation, I can lose a couple of precious minutes ...

"You're right about that," Anya didn't argue. "Okay, I will think about it and, maybe, I will invite Saltykov to Privolnoe, although, you see, the presence of an outsider in the house will hamper us." But today I don't want to solve anything. Let's first recover after yesterday's shock.

When the crew drove up to the porch of the Privolinsky house, it turned out that an old woman in a black headscarf was standing at the door next to the nanny and sprinkling around herself with water from a bottle, muttering darkly:

- Bleach the unclean spirit from our house, from all places, crevices, doors and corners, back streets and ceilings, from all, from all places. We have the Lord's Cross, the Holy Spirit is with us, all the saints are with us ...

The nurse, turning to those who arrived, made terrible eyes and showed signs that they did not interfere. Apparently, she managed to still call the famous Sychiha to read her magic spells. A huge black cat was spinning near the sorceress. Anna was holding out a hand to stroke him, but the cat quite clearly made it clear that he would not allow his local inhabitants.

Having finished the spell, the black old woman turned and, ignoring the presence of Elena Sergeyevna, glared at Anna's face. She blanched and fluttered, like a birch leaf, under her black eyes gushing. Sychiha pulled out a piece of wax from the folds of her shapeless clothes and, not taking her eyes off Anna, sternly said:

- Well, hello, God's servant Anna. Is there a cross on you?

"Yes," Anya murmured with disobedient lips.

"Show me," the healer demanded.

Anya pulled out a golden cross on a chain from under the collar.

"Welcome," Sychiha nodded and whispered to the wax, "sign here, servant of God, Anna, with a life-giving cross, at the right of hand and oshuyu. The cross is upon you, God's servant Anna, the cross is in front of you, the cross is behind you, the cross of the devil and all the enemies are victorious. Let the demon run away, all the power of the enemy from you, the servants of God Anna, who saw like lightning, scorching the power of the cross ...

Having read this spell-prayer, which ended with a triple "amen", Sychiha stuck a wad of wax crumpled in her fingers onto Anna's cross and said in a completely different, calm, melodious and kind voice:

- Everything, child, henceforth the evil spirit is not terrible for you - it will not be able to cause evil. Do not be afraid of spirits, people are afraid, evil can come from a dashing person. And you, an orca, - she suddenly turned to Elena Sergeyevna, - accept this water ...

As if by magic, another flask appeared in the hands of Sychiha.

- On, take it, pour it into the cup, cover it with a handkerchief and place it near the image of the Virgin Mary. Let it cost three days. Mother Theotokos in all troubles intercessor, will send all the help. And if someone next to you says that it is bad for him, sprinkle it with water three times.

With these words, Sychiha descended from the porch and walked along the path, but suddenly looked back and as intently as Anna, looking into Elena Sergeevna's eyes, said:

"You are secretly worried about your husband." Do not worry, killer whale, he is alive and healthy. See you soon. Be patient a week or two.

And the old woman hobbled away again. Kotyara, reaching out, jumped off the steps and trudged behind his mistress.

Three women silently watched the healer after. Elena Sergeevna was the first who came to her senses:

"And your Melania creates the spell with God's name," she said thoughtfully to the nanny.

- And then! - confirmed that. - I would lure her to the house, if she were engaged in demonic witchcraft. And in God's name there is no sin. We all ask the Lord for help, but only not all skillfully ... It would be necessary to order a requiem prayer service in the church - for the souls of the murdered soldiers of Alexei da Peter, Nyutochkin's grandfather. You look, the peace at our house and descend ... Here's just the father of the church in Greece, he is all sick - like his daughter, he was young, he was killed, he will not recover in any way. It happens that for three days the service can not serve ...

"God, I suddenly wanted to sleep," Anya whispered. - I'm right off my feet.

- And you go, child, lay down in bed and sleep, - advised the nurse. - This conspiracy Sychiha comes into action. Apostle talking to her all in a dream and throws. And then you wake up and the strength seems to be doubled. I also pine for an hour. It is impossible for me to preserve anything anyway, and it is no wonder - it seems to me that the girl with a slit throat around the house wanders and gazes through the windows, look at that, throw, Lord, save! And now the wraith will leave, but only the last ones will pull out, leaving. One thing remains - to pray and sleep, give yourself a rest. And you, Elena Sergeevna, would rest after all the troubles ...

Chapter 14

Helena

Soon there was complete silence in the house. Apparently, Anna and the nanny really slept soundly. But communication with the sorceress didn't have any hypnotic effect on me, perhaps because I slept quietly at night in the Girevskoy mansion last night, or maybe because Sychiha mentioned my husband, giving rise to some vague anxiety in my soul.

And how did she know that Mikhail went to the army and I worry so much for him? I'm trying not to talk about it with anyone. Surprisingly insightful grandmother!

I decided to write a letter to Mikhail. Of course, I was not about to write about any ghosts, much less murders. It was not enough that, where it was dangerous, where the Germans could break through the front line once again, Misha would have filled his head with my problems. Let him think that I am fine ...

"I am invited by Varvara Filippovna to visit her in Gireyev and in the nearby estate Privolnoe, where one of my friends lives. I believe that a couple of weeks spent in the village will benefit me. There is marvelous forest air, fresh milk, and the society has been extremely pleasant, so this place is quite suitable to hide from the bustle of Moscow life. I enjoy peace and I must say - idleness has a great effect on the nervous system ... "

Having written these lines, I was distracted. Something was obviously happening in the house. I thought of some kind of barely audible, slurred sounds, and the desire to constantly be on the alert began to become a habit for me.

Grabbing Browning, I made a detour around the early asleep manor. Now it was light, not at night, and the uninvited guests could be properly considered.

Wise woman Melania promised that we no longer need to fear evil, only dashing people (and for some reason we wanted to believe this strange woman). However, I do not know who is capable of bringing more evil - a disembodied ghost or a mysterious stranger (maybe the same dashing person and even a terrible killer!) Visiting the old manor house with incomprehensible regularity.

Bypassing the first and second floors, I did not find anything suspicious, but the feeling of anxiety did not leave me.

Yes, idyllic pictures of rural life do not often manage to impart such a sharp element of drama. If only Mikhail knew what this holiday in the village would result in - insatiable mosquitoes, feral dogs, bloodthirsty murderers, ghosts, rural healers - and that's not all!

Those who believe that rural life differs only in tranquility and regularity are deeply mistaken. And in the wilderness, you can find a lot of adventures, just need to know where to look ... No, I really want to go back to civilization, I'm sick of the wondrous forest air.

Returning to the unfinished letter, I absently finished writing it, twisting my thoughts somewhere far away ... So, I checked both residential floors, but did not visit the attic, which I had been pulling for a long time. After all, our ghost often looks right there, stomping there, knocking, moving heavy things ... Maybe he is now hiding somewhere under the roof. It is necessary to find out what he wants there? I'm afraid it's not my fate to spend the rest of the day in idleness and idleness ...

Anya, I remember, said that the key to the attic had been lost for a long time, which means that the door is most likely open and the entrance to the attic is free from time immemorial ... I will go up the stairs of the ghost to his secret abode.

"We have the Lord's Cross, the Holy Spirit is with us, and all the saints are with us," I repeated the words I heard from Sychiha, and taking the weapon just in case, I went up the stairs along the cracked steps.

The door to the attic, as I expected, was ajar. I carefully checked to see if someone was hiding behind her, but I didn't find anyone.

The attic, thoroughly clogged with old junk, in fact, was not an attic. Once it was a residential attic, or, as they say in Russian landlord homes, mezzanine. Probably, in those days, when a lot of people lived in the house and every free room was on the bill, a very cozy bedroom was set up for some governess or a poor relative, who agreed to the place under the roof.

Since then, faded faded wallpaper has been preserved on the walls of the attic, and an ancient silk curtain soaked in dust hung on a small semicircular window. Over the years, as I understand it, the manor was thoroughly deserted, there was no shortage of vacant premises, and the room under the roof was turned into a closet for unnecessary things.

Among the antediluvian cabinets, chest of drawers and upturned chairs with protruding legs were some chests and worn wardrobe cases, hat boxes, empty baguettes and dim mirrors. A plaster Apollo peeking out of the corner, shyly covering itself with a fig leaf. A layer of dust lay on everything, even Apollo's broken nose turned a dark gray shade, but unlike the dust of a wine cellar, it was difficult to call the local dust untouched.

Here and there on the dusty objects could be seen traces of varying degrees of freshness. Here on the cover of the coffer someone's fingers imprinted. Here, on the mirror, is a band left by the edge of someone's clothes, as if, passing by, a man carelessly touched a mirror glass hollow and brushed away some of the dust.

Yes, Anya was clearly mistaken when she assured me that in recent decades a person's foot had not stepped here. Not only stepped, but not too carefully ...

Looking closer, wax stains could be found everywhere, dripping from someone else's candles (so that it was the spirits that burned candles here, I will never believe in my life!). The drawers of the dresser are pushed unevenly, as if someone was rummaging through them, and then closed them somehow. Some thing was covered with thick canvas, lifted from one side. By golly, this is someone's hand carelessly threw back the canvas when a curious nose got under it.

Well, and it is not a sin for me to be curious that this is hidden there.

I picked up a canvas cover and saw under it an old fine work cradle of a walnut tree with carved angels at the head ... Before my eyes, like a ribbon in cinema, pictures of family happiness that prevailed in Privolnoye at that time, when in the cradle I sniffed sweetly, ran kid…

Being so impatient, I did not immediately realize that something disturbing had got into the field of my side view — a black human silhouette was being drawn over my shoulder ...

Turning sharply, I threw out my hand with a pistol and... laid down the old tailor's dummy on one leg, modestly lurking near the twisted bookcase. Having overturned, the mannequin hooked also the bookcase, and she dragged the ironing board leaning against her ...

All this was supposed to collapse with a deafening noise, but long before me someone had thrown on the floor paper, notebooks, folders and small boxes, which were probably on the shelves of the bookcase before. This pile of paper muffled the blow.

Pulling out a pair of notebooks from the general heap, I found in them exercises on grammar and dictations, written, according to calligraphy, with an unfaithful child's hand forty or fifty years ago.

Behind a bookcase, a dummy and an ironing board, as it turned out, there was a voluminous road chest, the lock from which was mercilessly knocked down and idly dangled from the side on half-torn loops.

In the footsteps left around the chest and on the lid, it was possible to assume that he had recently been moved, opened, and then disguised with small objects like a mannequin and whatnot so as not to catch the eye. Naturally, I also could not resist, so as not to open the lid.

The things lying in the chest were completely unceremoniously dug up, turned over and turned into a single disordered pile, but the very first thing that caught my eye turned out to be a uniform military suit of the old model. Once white, the tunic slightly yellowed, and the gilding of the epaulettes dimmed. It was probably the uniform of Anya's grandfather who fought the Turks for the freedom of Slavic brothers in the last century.

My next find was a case with antediluvim single-shot pistols. Duel set of a nobleman. The fabric that the case was wrapped in from the inside was mercilessly ripped with a knife.

Consequently, someone who had rummaged in this chest was looking for some small object, one of those that could be hidden under the cover of the weapon case. An object or document — rather, a document — after all, a paper would easily fit in here, and not even one.

Well, it is quite likely that our ghost needed the papers with some records (if you had to know what was written in them!). And of course, it was not the souls of the departed who were strangled by other people's possessions, but someone quite tangible ... It's just unknown if he succeeded in his quest.

Before closing the chest, I mechanically (probably from the usual female desire for harmony) began to put in order the gutted things - each uniform had to be shaken off the dust and neatly folded according to the rules of road laying so that the shoulder line would not hesitate and not break the shoulder straps.

Shaking up another jacket, I felt that there was something in my inner pocket. Unfastening the button of the valve, I found a golden locket there. Such medallions usually store the memory of lovers - a portrait or a curl - and are revealed by pressing an invisible button.

The lock of the medallion was quickly managed to cope with, and the oval miniatures hidden inside were revealed — portraits of an officer with a noble-willed face and a young woman resembling Nina and Anna.

No doubt, these were portraits of Anya's grandparents, although it was difficult to call these very young and beautiful young people so beautiful. Anya, by the way, mentioned some lost medallion with a portrait of her beloved, belonging to her grandfather ... Surely that very thing. It is strange that it did not occur to anyone how to inspect the pockets of the county's clothing.

However, losing a loved one, it is psychologically very difficult to disassemble his things, reminiscent of the habits of the deceased and keeping his smell ... It seemed to me that the old uniforms still smell of strong pipe tobacco, old-fashioned cologne and road dust, as if yesterday the owner was wearing them on his shoulders. Probably, Anina's grandmother, widowed, was simply unable to open the lid of this chest.

- Hello, gentlemen! - I greeted the former owners of the manor, who looked at me with portraits with interest. - Glad to see you. I am visiting in your house to help your granddaughter and heiress Anna. She is the only one of your kind who is still alive. Do not leave her with your patronage!

Having spoken my heartfelt speech (because if this manor has a Genius loci, like a dialect or ancients, that is, a kind genius, the guardian spirit of this place, then surely Anin is a grandfather, and it is him who should ask for intercession), I apologize to the owner , grabbed military field glasses from his trunk. Fighters with an unknown evil should not forget about the proper equipment. I hope grandfather will understand this and will not be offended for arbitrariness.

Now it would be possible to go downstairs, and if Anya woke up, hand her my find - a medallion with portraits of ancestors. But before I could slam the lid of the chest, another clap rang out behind my back - the attic door closed. And suddenly the key in the door turned, locking the lock from the outside!

That long-lost key not only ended up in the lock, but was also turned by someone's hand, locking me in the attic, and then removed from the lock ...

I felt that I was becoming ill. They say everything in life repeats itself, but this incident, by its mystery, far surpassed the history of the wine cellar. Still, the incident could have been somehow explained without mysticism, using ordinary logical deductions - there was a strong draft in the cellar, so the door slammed shut; the key remained outside in the lock, it fell out of the door strike, but when it fell, it touched some internal teeth of the lock, from which the lock worked ... As a working hypothesis, it is quite suitable.

But now the door is clearly closed and locked! But nobody was outside, I checked it myself, bypassing the house with Browning in my hand. Involuntarily remember the ghosts! And if I had not allowed myself to just so familiarly turn to the former owners! Maybe they considered this an insult and decided to teach me a lesson? But still, for the host, the manner is very strange - to constantly lock up the guest in various outbuildings. Even if this guest allows herself to stick her nose where she is not being asked, such jokes seem funny only once ...

Feeling weak in my legs, I sank into a chair that stood beside me, and immediately soared because the spring protruding from the chair dug into pleasure ... as if more elegantly put it ... in that part of my body that was accessible to it. This unfriendly action could also be regarded as the tricks of my grandfather and tremble with fear, but I, on the contrary, brightened in my brain. Anger always gave me strength.

Why do you need to endlessly blame ghosts for everything that is happening here? In the end, I have long suspected, but what I suspect there, I'm just sure that these evil machinations are a matter of human hands.

Yes, I walked around the house and did not find anyone, but an unknown villain could get in the door and go up to the attic a little later, when I was already looking at the contents of my grandfather's chest with enthusiasm. And this disgusting villain could have been dragged away a long time ago by the key to the attic door, so Anya doesn't know where this key has gone ...

I rushed to the keyhole and stuck to it first with my ear, and then with my eye (how sad it is that you cannot watch and listen at the same time through the keyhole!). But, alas, all my efforts were in vain. Of course, I so stupidly lost a few precious seconds, lost in thought, and the attacker took advantage of them and disappeared ...

Well, let him think! Believes, probably, that scared me to death. Naive! What actually happened so terrible? Getting out of the attic is a couple of trifles, at the very least, I'll open the window and call for help. Sooner or later someone will hear and let me out. But first of all it is necessary to look for a spare key from the inside - after all, I was freed from the cellar in this way. Dear old woman was Anina grandmother, prudent and caring ...

However, on this path, at first disappointment awaited me - I didn't find any small nail on which the key would hang, as in a cellar, near the door. And if the key is stored in one of the drawers of various dressers and cabinets, in abundance presented in the attic, or in countless boxes and boxes, you can search for it until the second coming!

So, calm, let's arm with logic ... At the time of the grandmother-mistress, not all cabinets and boxes were already dumped in the attic, and the key to the door is still more convenient to hide somewhere near the door ... What would I do in that case? I would have thrust the key under the sill or behind the casing if there was a suitable slot there.

A coarse carved platband with old-fashioned curls designed the door, it seems, from the time when there were living rooms here. Probably, some serf master learned to embody the complex rococo motifs in the tree, and the first, still imperfect samples, were ordered to be used not in the ceremonial chambers, but where the interiors are simpler ...

Having pulled the chair with the springs sticking out to the door, I, with some caution, climbed onto a malicious piece of furniture and ran my hand over the upper platband, where wooden curls rose like a kokoshnik, leaving behind a deep slit.

The logic did not deceive me - there really was a key covered with dust and cobwebs, but before I managed to find it, I discovered another object, much more cumbersome.

It was an old leather-bound notebook with a copper clasp. Truly my expedition to the attic was fraught with many surprises ...

Winning the desire to immediately delve into the reading of an old manuscript (if there were grammar exercises written by a careless student in the seventeenth century, it would be very disappointing!), I first of all tried whether the key was suitable for the lock.

With no effort on my part and a wild rattle from the side of the castle, the door still opened. The exit was free, you can safely descend the stairs at will, but before that I opened my notebook and eagerly dug into the half-faded lines ...

Yes, the records were not perfectly preserved, in some places the pages were washed away with moisture, touched with mold, gnawed by mice, thoroughly attached to the leather cover, and at the same time not disdained and text. But it was still possible to read a lot, but the records turned out to be such that my heart simply sank at the touch of a burning mystery. It is necessary to immediately show Anuta's old notebook, she, like no one, should be interested in revealing family secrets.

I grabbed a notebook, Browning and a medallion with portraits and hung binoculars borrowed from the heroic grandfather-count around my neck, and I almost slid down the stairs head over heels. If, nevertheless, it is assumed that it was the spirit of the grandfather who locked me in the attic, then thanks a lot to him for that — he probably wanted to help me find the handwritten treasure in leather binding.

I had already reached the second floor and was just about to turn from the stairs into the corridor, as a wild cry stopped me ... From surprise, I dropped the Browning, and he jumped down the steps. Lord, what is happening in this house?

Anna screamed, standing in the wall by the stairs ...

Chapter 15

Anna

After talking with the healer, Anna felt such a weakness that she barely got to the bed, fell on her exhausted and did not notice how she fell asleep. The dream was very deep, dreamless, like a dip into a dark abyss.

And even when she was awakened by the noise and knock, Anya was not immediately able to finally wake up and was still half asleep for a long time. But gradually her mind came to the meaning of what was happening, and sleep was already gone. Again it seemed that in the attic, right above his head, someone was walking, moving things, banging something heavy on the floor ... No spells of the old healer helped!

But after all, Sychiha spoke to her cross and declared that now the ghosts could not do harm ... The cross on her, therefore ... Anya got out of bed and went down the hall to the stairs to the attic. You need to finally find out what is happening there! The conspiracy man has nothing to fear.

She had already reached the stairs, but stopped near the railing. She suddenly became unbearably frightened - the clearly audible sounds of someone else's stay swept from above. They moved something, rustled it, then grated the key in a long-locked lock ... Well, how the cross will not help?

Anya felt her back feel cold and goosebumps. Soon, the steps of the stairs creaked and some cautious steps were heard.

"We have the Lord's Cross," Anne mumbled the words of Grandma Melania, pulling a chain with a cross from her bosom. Surely the healer fooled? But the cross itself is a defense ...

A woman in white came down from above, with a dark rope dangling around her neck ... They also said that in ancient times someone had hanged herself in the attic!

- Aaaa! - Anya was unable to cope with horror, feeling that her legs were bending and she was about to fall ...

The ghost dropped something heavy, rumbling through the steps, gasped and ... turned around Leleu. The fact that Anya took the rope turned out to be a leather cord from a case with field binoculars that hung at Lelya's neck.

- God, how you scared me! - in one voice said the women, reproachfully looking at each other.

"Did the ghosts wake you too?" - finally asked Anya, a little breath. "They thundered in the attic again."

"These are not ghosts, I thundered there," answered Lelya guiltily. - Forgive, Annie, I did not think that you would be so scared. By the way, someone locked me in there again, but I found the second key and opened the lock. And one more thing I found, now I'll show you, just go down after Browning. I do not like it when the weapon is lying wherever it is.

Quickly having run down the stairs, she picked up her gun and again rushed upstairs to Anna.

- Look what was behind the carved platband in the attic. I found the notes of one of your ancestors! - Lelia showed an old notebook with a copper lock. - Judging by the handwriting and style - the end of the eighteenth century. Let's go read more.

- Lelya, this is not urgent! Let's drink some tea first. The notes have been safely lying here since the last century, so let them lie down for a while, "Anya suggested, but in the eyes of her guest the hunting excitement burned, like a greyhound who took the game's trail.

- Annie, tea will not go away! - in the heat of the moment cried Lelia. - The inner voice tells me that we will now open a certain secret. Do not you want to be on the other side of the past, alone with your ancestor? Do you have a magnifying glass? Bring more soon!

The women entered Anna's room, laid out a notebook by the window on the writing table, and began to make out the intricate handwriting of the unknown author of the notes.

This book is written in Sli .... under the death penalty ...

... to store in the hitherto secret place and not to disclose his writings to anyone.

- What does it mean - written under the death penalty? - Anya asked.

"Apparently, in anticipation of the imminent death penalty," explained Elena. - Old Russian momentum is not always possible to translate into a modern adverb literally. We usually need a lot more words than our ancestors, although it is considered that the literary Russian has since become much more beautiful. But what was going on .... Damn mice damaged the page so that nothing can be read!

"Well, that's just that simple." In Shli .... ty means - in the Shlisselburg fortress, I suppose. In the annals of our kind there is a story connected with Shlisselburg. One of my ancestors, the grandfather of my grandfather, was, under the decree of Emperor Paul, imprisoned in a fortress and even sentenced to death, but Alexander's accession saved him. Presumably, these are the notes of that great-great-great-grandfather who was imprisoned while awaiting execution. Well, read on ...

The angel of the Lord pours out cups of calamity, so that people may come to mind, and faith commands us to obey when God's hand punishes us to suffer, without complaining, in order to atone for our sins, voluntary and involuntary.

A person has different properties: one seeks fame and honor, another loves of love, the third is not only unwilling, but does not think of the like, but few who would avoid it will be presented to him by the Fortuna Occasion ...

- That's right! - Lela noticed. - No one rejects the gifts of Fortune, there will be an opportunity. In the common sense of life your ancestor can not refuse.

The Lord let the great skills of me, that I could barely bear them ...

But a good man is tempted by those skills, like gold in the furnace, and shines with virtue, and who is weak in virtues, will acquire only a secret, not able to be expressed to anyone grief.

"It seems that your great-great-grandfather believed that the imprisonment in the fortress was sent to him as a punishment for sins," Lelia continued to comment on the reading.

"The reasons for his imprisonment in our house have always been talked about in a dull way," answered Anna. - It seems that under Empress Catherine he was in great favor at the court, and under Paul he suddenly fell into disgrace, lost everything and found himself on the Secret Expedition ...

- In those days, this happened often, - Lelya sighed and continued reading: - Ekaterina Alekseevna, our most gracious Empress ... Well, everything, on this page it is impossible to read anything else. You know, you need to consult with a detective agent who arrived from Moscow. They say criminologists have developed such methods of photographing spoiled papers that words that are not visible with the naked eye, easily appear on the film. I do not know how true this is ...

"Okay, for now let's read what we can make out," Anya grabbed a notebook and carefully turned over the old page.

It responds to this: whatever the Empress doesn't act before you, no matter how far her courtesy in the argument of love comforts comes, you just have to keep silent and smile, for all people, from young to old, are not saved by any fortresses from the sweetest arrows of the mischievous god love, Cupid named ...

From this ... voluptuous pictures were born in my inflamed brain, which I shouldn't dare to imagine in my position ...

Having disdained conjugal debt and profaning the pure name of my beloved wife ...

- God, how disgusting! - screamed Anna, who suddenly didn't want to read the notebook to the end. - Lelia, I do not want to read about these shameful secrets of my ancestor. Just think, he twisted tricks with the aging empress! He cheated on my unfortunate great-grandmother, "desecrating her pure name"! And I think, disinterested! Pathetic Alfonso!

- Take it easy! We are all imperfect. After all, isn't the ability to forgive constitute the basic commandment of a Christian? We did not live at that time and cannot understand all the circumstances that pushed people to this or that act! More than a hundred years have passed, life has changed completely, "Lelya reasonedly began to say," and then, your great-grandfather repented and redeemed his guilt with the throes of imprisonment ...

- It is better to have no guilt to be atoned for, much less such a shameful one! - Anna answered passionately.

Grasping the notebook with both hands, she tried to break it in half. But, despite the sharp jerk, the binding work of the old masters endured, the cover only cracked a little.

- Stop! Shouted Elena Sergeevna. - Think again, Anya! You commit an act of vandalism! This is not the intimate secrets of your relatives, this is a valuable historical document. You can not go to the extent of their feelings. So inquisitors burned everything that seemed godless to them, as a result leaving humanity without great works of art and scientific discoveries. What is it rattling? Is the cover torn?

"No, the cover is intact, it just peels off a bit," answered Anna, confused. - Lelia, there is something there! You see, there is paper between the skin of the binding and the inner sheet.

With the help of a penknife and a crochet hook, the women managed to extract what was hidden under the cover of the notebook of the ancestor.

The plan, drawn on thick paper, clearly belonged to a later time than writing in a notebook, and was accompanied by a small handwritten commentary.

Putting aside for a short time the new find, Elena Sergeyevna persuaded Anya to finish reading the old notes, especially since the next two pages were hopelessly spoiled by dampness (they could not even be untied) and the text remained quite a bit.

Thoughts with the precious family of mine, my wife and children, who, in my eternal absence, are orphaned in abying ...

... being displeased with this, I thought nightly, as if to fulfill my good intention to leave St. Petersburg and secretly get into my suburban, where my children and household ...

Having myself only a great casket, in which all imperial presents without seizure were preserved: gold, stones, diamonds, sapphires, Indian emarads, and everything else that could be used to help my family in the hour of inevitable disasters brought on their innocent heads are nothing more than just one of my insanity ...

"You see, your ancestor was not deprived of a certain decency," commented Lelia. - Yes, I have sinned by force of circumstances, I misled the demon or simply did not give him any choice, I did not have to joke with the empress ... But I was executed for my own disorder and took care of the family! At what time was he in the court service and was in favor with the empress?

Anya thought.

- I don't remember the exact date, but I suppose, in the 1780s. Perhaps in the second half, or rather even towards the end of the eighties ...

- Oh, it was a turbulent period in the life of Mother Catherine. After her favorite Lanskoy died in 1784, she longed for almost a year, and then decided to dispel sadness, changing the favorites one by one - first Alexander Yermolov, then guardsman Dmitriev-Mamonov, soon made by the sovereign in earls, then Platon Zubov who turned into 22 years from captain-seconds seconds immediately to colonels and adjutants ...

- My ancestor, apparently, wedged between Mamonov and Zubov. And I am afraid that the count dignity and my ancestors received it then, because the family did not like to remember our title. I, having married a non-titled nobleman, now for my husband I am considered just a noblewoman ... And my father did not like his title. And no wonder!

(To admit, Anya looked so aristocratic that it seemed incredible that her family's birth title got only some 125 years ago, in the last years of Catherine's reign. Looking at a beautiful purebred face with refined features, one could swear that Anna's distant ancestors with their retinues they called Prince Vladimir Krasno Sun on the battlefield, challenging the Kiev throne in him, and maybe they ruled the Varyags' rook, paving the way for Ryurik ...)

Anna, meanwhile, frowning aristocratic sable eyebrows, continued to complain:

- Just think, the great-great-great-great-great grandfather deserved shame in love joys ... Standing behind his title in line for Dmitriev-Mamonov!

- But, Anya, apparently, he was not such a bad person, except a little frivolous! Yes, he is a child of his courtly age. But at the same time he was a soul mate for loved ones and, realizing how unreliable the fate of the royal leader was, he tried to ensure the future of the family ...

- Why are you comforting me! - Anna gave up. - Secure the future? Than? What earned in the bed of the Empress?

- Annie, in the Holy Scripture it is said - do not judge, but you will not be judged! The Bible is a very wise book ... And what is this near Moscow to which your great-great-grandfather dragged his great casket with the gifts of the king? Whether it is Privolnoe?

"Most likely it is Privolnoe," Anya confirmed. - This is an ancient patrimony of our ancestors. You know, in my childhood I heard some stories about a treasure that my great-great-grandfather, the first earl, hid somewhere before the imprisonment in the fortress, but it seemed to me just a funny family legend, and it never even occurred to me that the treasure is real. to be somewhere here ... And he himself, it must be supposed, considered his treasure to be very valuable - "juveniles, Indian emeralds" ...

- Yeah, that's all - gifts to the empress, and Catherine did not have the habit of small things in such matters. Presumably, the newly minted graph in the literal sense of the word.

Elena Sergeevna thought for a moment.

- Annie, how much is a wide circle of people devoted to your family secrets? Even if it never occurred to you that the ancestor's treasure is a reality, then it is quite possible that it came to someone else who learned about the great casket ... It is possible that information about the gifts of the Empress to your great-grandfather remained in some historical annals and caught the eye of strangers? Could it be that there have never been any ghosts here? But just connoisseurs of ancient legends, driven by greed, are looking for the treasure of the king's favorite?

"Logical," Anya agreed. - But why only women die around our manor? How to combine the treasure hunt and the killed girls? This fact really can not be applied to the picture drawn by you. No motives.

"If we do not know the motives for the killings, this does not mean that they are not there," answered Lelya. - Okay, let's read the notes to the end. Here again two pages stuck together, turn over ...

Their Imperial Majesty Our sovereign were angry with these bold words of mine and ordered me to shackle ...

... under torture, he admitted that he had composed deceptions from pride and imaginary praise from people, more than that, he dared to say bold and offensive words relating to the blessed memory of the person of Her Imperial Majesty, who died in Boz Mother Catherine ...

Former with me I recognize the action of an unclean spirit, an enemy of mankind that embarrasses people and seduces them, for those daring words, which would be best kept secret, are one and all true and not bald ... A weak person.

... aza this audacity and outrage, allegedly an insult of the highest authority, is guilty of the death penalty.

... and prepared himself for many guilt not only to torture, but also to death.

But their Imperial Majesty, facilitating the severity of legal regulations, indicated deigns instead of deserved punishment to put me in the Shlisselburg fortress with orders to keep me under strict guards so that I did not communicate with anyone, nor had any conversations ...

I write these things and trust in the Lord that He will allow me not to divulge this penitential work to anyone except my beloved wife, who is heavily and immensely guilty, and heirs, who are now in childhood, but as soon as they come to age, to my father's work they will appeal, for they will desire it ...

I pray to my heirs: accept all that I leave to you, for I have redeemed my guilt gravely, and my riches have been purified. And the secret place in which this treasure abides, my wife knows ...

"I wonder if your great-great-grandmother used the treasure, since her place of preservation was known to her?" - Elena asked.

"Perhaps she disdained," Anya suggested skeptically. - I would not want to use such a handwriting in her place. In any case, family legends have not preserved any legends about finding and using the treasure by any of my ancestors. But in the place of this miserable great-great-grandmother I would even think disgusted about such an inheritance.

- And on your own? - the practical Elena Sergeevna immediately asked.

- On your own? - Asked the heir to the treasure. - I do not know, I somehow did not think.

"And by the way, this phrase:" I pray to my heirs: accept all that I leave to you, for I have redeemed my guilt, and my riches have been cleansed, "has a direct bearing on you. For now you are the only direct heir to your courtly ancestor who cared so much for the welfare of the family. And after years of age, you can give up on the somewhat dubious origin of the treasure. In the end, in the world practice this is exactly the accepted. I can immediately call you a dozen of the richest families in Europe and America, whose hereditary wealth was obtained by sea pirates or robbers from the main road who became the founders of noble families. And no one hides these facts, considering only an amusing historical curiosity. And it is simply indecent to reproach the descendants of the royal favorites - strangers cannot understand the affairs of the heart ...

- So you think that I have the right to great-great-grandfather's treasures? - Anya asked, considering a new turn.

"Without a doubt," Lelia confirmed. "Unless, of course, you manage to find them." As soon as the jewels are a gift of the Empress, therefore, we now have the right to perceive them, for example, as an aid from the reigning house to the widow of a valiant defender of the throne and the fatherland. Why not? For all the will of God. "Accept all that I leave to you ..." - asked your ancestor. And this, presumably, is a great treasure. Happiness, of course, is not about money, but they greatly ease the burden of adversity in life. You are in a difficult situation, and such a legacy from your ancestors would be just a gift of fate. By the way, let's see what the plan was hidden under the cover ...

The plan, drawn on a sheet of thick paper with monograms, depicted a certain rectangle, on three sides of which circles were drawn and a cross was put on one of these circles.

Under these mysterious geometric figures there was a postscript:

"So, the fateful day is coming. Soon I am going to fight in the Balkans, because I can no longer blithely indulge in love and the feeling of my happiness ... My heart, shocked by recent impressions, cannot find peace, my Slavic blood boils at the thought of the suffering of our brothers in blood and faith. I am called for debt.

My beloved spouse Anna Vasilyevna gathered to accompany me to the place of hostilities. I cannot approve of this, but I also have no obstacle. But we will surrender into the hands of God, only He is the master of our destinies and all His will. And before leaving I believe this important secret paper.

The grandfather's treasure, so well-known in the traditions of our family, was found by me after much work and was hidden from someone else's eyes in a secret place known to my spouse.

Details about the search for treasures, worthy of the current adventure novels, are written by me for posterity and can be found by them among other records in the papers stored in the Petersburg house.

Here is also a plan for finding a treasure for a case, if, besides aspirations, neither I nor my spouse can retrieve it from the cache, which I arranged in my grandfather's near Moscow estate, Privolnoe. Let then my grown-up son, Athanasius, now still a foolish child, or his descendants, my grandchildren, will take the treasure of their ancestors from a hiding place and use it for their own benefit.

I remain in the hope that this paper, which I wrote with my own hands and hidden under the cover of my grandfather's notes, will be found by our posterity. "

Under the calligraphically derived lines, there was a sweeping old-fashioned autograph, completely unreadable, but even without it seemed clear that there was a letter from Anny grandpa, a Balkan hero entrusting the treasure of the royal leader to his son and grandchildren.

"Well, you see," Elena Sergeevna said, "your grandfather managed to inherit the jewels and passes them on to his descendants, the children of the son of Athanasius, that is, to you!" The question of the moral side of such inheritance can be immediately removed. This is not a gift from the reigning dynasty, but a gift from your grandfather, a hero of the Balkan war. He knew that his granddaughter was facing hard times, and seemed to help me find these records to support you. I think we should treat the situation this way. And then, there is a certain pattern - your grandfather found his grandfather's jewels, and now his granddaughter will find them ... The treasure can be considered as hereditary property, traditionally transferred to your family through a generation. It is quite aristocratic and not without an adventurous charm. By the way, I found a medallion in the attic with a portrait of your grandfather. Here look.

Anya immediately seized the medallion and looked at the portraits for a long time, brushing tears from her eyes.

"I knew, I knew that they would not leave me with their care," she whispered, stroking the portraits with her finger.

- It remains the most perfect trifle, - summed up Lelya, - to guess exactly what place your grandfather depicted on his plan. It seemed to him simply obvious, since he did not provide the picture with comments. Apparently, the men from your family were good husbands - both indicate that the place of the treasure cache is known to their beloved wives. And this led in one and in another case only to the fact that many years later the grandchildren must search at the cost of considerable work for valuables, carefully hidden where it is not known where ...

But no assumptions about the grandfather's cache of the ladies did not have time to push. The evening of discoveries and guesswork was interrupted at the most interesting place.

- To you, gentlemen, officers from Gireyev have come! - announced the nanny who has risen to the second floor.

"For now, not a word about our findings to any of the outsiders," warned Elena Sergeevna.

Anna was going to immediately go downstairs, but Lelya prudently asked her to hide the old notebook and paper with her grandfather's plan in the drawer and lock the drawer with a key.

- Hide the key in some box, but do not forget where you put it. It is possible that this is a very great value, - she warned. - Anya, and now, if it is not difficult for you, go down to the guests and receive them yourself. I have to clean up after traveling to the attic. I'll go to the living room later.

CHAPTER 16

Helena

As it turned out, the staff captain Saltykov, frightened by my story about the one who had disappeared to the key to the door of the Privolinsky house, decided to take care of the widow of his late colleague. He went to the village, bought the most reliable lock of those that were there in the hardware store, and brought a young ensign who had technical skills in a peaceful life, so that he slammed the lock into the door of the manor.

The ensign was very young, thin and short, in a civilian dress, he would look like a boy. But since his early years, short stature and insignificant rank were compensated for by a magnificent, smart-looking uniform sewn from a good tailor, the boy was full of his own dignity, and he worked with dexterity worked out by long practice.

It seems that before the war he studied at the Higher Technical School and at the same time ran his affairs in the mechanical workshops of his father, then went to the front as a volunteer as a volunteer and now, having received his first little rank, dreamed of an officer's career.

When I quickly pulled out the cobwebs from my hair and splashed cold water from a jug in the basin to wash off the dust (alas, you can live in a luxurious house without any comfort) and went downstairs to the guests, the installation of the lock was in full swing. But there was no one on the porch except for the young man who worked with the chisel.

Anna and Valentin have gone somewhere ...

I have noticed before the sparks of mutual interest, involuntarily flickering between the young widow and the staff captain. Less than anything in the world, I wanted to disturb the nascent feeling, and I did not search for them.

Soon it began to get dark, and it was necessary to light a kerosene lamp to the ensign, who had not had time to finish the work before the sun went down. The boy should have been helped, especially since the prospect of spending this night in a securely locked house, all the keys to which will be at the disposal of the owner of the estate and no one else, seemed to me very rosy. How nice it will be to leave nosy ghosts with your nose!

Anna and Saltykov, fascinated by the conversation, left the dark alley of the park just when the work was completed and I was going, taking upon myself the responsibility of the hostess, to give tea to the young ensign who was left in my care.

I must say, the appearance of this pair was furnished with an inimitable taste - neither give nor take the scene from the Chekhov's play. Oh my garden, ah poor my garden!

Valentine very praised the beauty of the old park. The day before, having appeared in Privolnoye together with the search team, when all attention was focused on the dead body of the unhappy sister found in the forest, he did not have time to properly consider all the peculiarities of this poetic corner. (Interestingly, did the park really appear in the twilight before the inquisitive staff captain in all its glory or was Valentine just dummizing what he did not see?)

"Oh yes, the park is very beautiful and original," I grumbled back in a secular tone, sipping a sip of tea primly, as if this topic was quite natural and very important. "If I could even invite a gardener to break flower beds, prune bushes and mow lawns ... However, there is a charm in neglected corners."

The officers did not stay away for a visit - the time was already late. Having drank a glass of tea and exchanged a couple of phrases with us, they bowed out - they still had to walk two miles to Gireyevo with woods ... Unlike us, they were not afraid of night walks to attack armed forces in the forest, risking getting a bullet out of the gun surely no murderer will dare.

We, having said goodbye to the guests, also scattered about the rooms - today, like all previous ones, was too densely filled with events, and after all, a tired person needs at least a good rest. I personally felt a certain discomfort from chronic lack of sleep and constant nervous tension.

Lord, when I return from this quiet forest corner to military Moscow, I first of all will go to sleep and sleep all day long without getting up.

Without briefly indulging in such sweet dreams, I immediately began to think about two very important, though less pleasant questions - tomorrow's conversation with the detective agent who had arrived from Moscow, whom I was going to tell you in detail about the events taking place in the estate, so that he himself could select the facts, important for the investigation, and the mysterious plan of the Slavophil grandfather (go ahead guess what is depicted there?).

Since these questions did not touch each other in any way, I had to jump my thoughts back and forth - from the investigator to the grandfather's plan and back, and the thinking process did not go as smoothly as it might seem from the outside.

Who knows what miracles of insight I would demonstrate and what heights of logic I got on this difficult path, but I was overwhelmed by a dream — fatigue took its toll.

Lord, only when you are in extraordinary circumstances, when a full sleep becomes an inaccessible luxury for you, you begin to truly appreciate it. And how bitter was my awakening, when in the middle of the night I heard a fuss, cries and crackling of boughs under the windows! Looks like someone was beaten up there.

Alas, if I fueled hope how to rest, then this hope turned out to be groundless ... I understand that in every corner of immense Mother Russia there are their own traditions, but the Prolynin tradition does not regularly allow people to sleep, it is impossible to approve. Moreover, I declare with all responsibility that I am categorically against such customs!

Well, it is necessary to intervene in an incomprehensible fight, which took place near the house, especially I didn't expect much to meet the spirits. Brawl obviously wore a completely ordinary material character.

My hand stretched itself towards the forgotten Shakespeare volume on the nightstand - if used skillfully, it could turn into a terrible weapon. But, perhaps, I now prefer firearms to all types of weapons. Grabbing Browning, with which I rarely managed to part in these lovely places, and mentally preparing for the fact that you can finally shoot everyone with a clear conscience, I ran into the yard.

I didn't manage to get out of the house right away - when I woke up, I forgot that the door was now locked to a new lock. To open it, I had to go upstairs again after the key.

"No, there was still a lot of practical sense in the spare keys hidden near each lintel," I reflected, stomping back up the steps. "It's a pity that anyone except the owners could use them."

Events under the windows of the house continued in the meantime to develop in their own way without me. Running up and down the stairs, I missed the most interesting part.

The fight, the noise of which woke me up, was already completed, the heavy sounds of blows and the wicked jerky interjections subsided, but from the side of the park came the sound of chases and a sharp male voice shouting inarticulate damnations.

Someone in darkness ran away along the alleys, and someone pursued him, demanding to stop immediately, and the vocabulary of these demands was very far from literary norms.

I probably should have joined the chase, but lately I have accumulated such fatigue ... Lack of sleep and eternal hassle have killed my will to fight.

I decided to sit on the steps of the porch and see from here what will happen next and how events will unfold without my direct participation! Even the volume of Shakespeare, which could be given to someone on the head, in order to put into this head an importance for the beauty of the literary language, was not at my fingertips.

However, the noise of the fight woke not only me ...

- What happened? Lelia, is that you? What is happening there? - Anya screamed, appearing on the balcony of her bedroom. "Why did they shout so much under the window?" There was a fight, yes? Did someone get killed again?

- Pip your tongue! - I answered not too politely, but the circumstances partly excused my rudeness. "It seems that no one has been killed yet, in any case there were no shots, and someone quite alive and healthy is fleeing from here at full speed, as if half a dozen furious ghosts are chasing him. Anya, please listen to my request - do not pretend to be Juliet on the balcony, do not lean on the railing. They are quite dilapidated, rusted to the ground and can break through. And in general, it is better to leave the balcony, I will be calmer!

"Wait, I'm coming down to you now," Anya replied, leaving her vantage point.

But before she could appear in the courtyard, a nanny crawled out on the porch, moaning and lamenting. I must say that involuntary insomnia especially acutely affected the character of the old woman, who was already prone to grumpy grumbling ...

I haven't heard such sophisticated curses to an unknown enemy who has allowed himself the excesses under the windows of the house. Especially colorful phrase turned out: "To him, damned, in the next world in a frying pan with boiling oil to sit!"

Having tried to imagine the cursed enemy cooked by the devils in deep fat, I could only call the visual image of pancakes served here for breakfast ...

These comforting reflections slightly reconciled me with life - because if you take everything seriously, you can go crazy. Already very monotonous, I spend time here. No, there are variations, of course - at night there are screams, now fights, now ghosts; they will lock me in the cellar, or else in the attic; then I pursue someone, wildly cursing, but it's not I, but others; killing again is not every day ...

However, a certain uniformity in these adventures is observed and already begins to bother me. If this drama has an author, then his creative style does not hold water.

When our entire female garrison was assembled, we heard footsteps and heavy breathing as the man approached the house. Despite all attempts to cheer up, my mood, for obvious reasons, was of a somewhat melancholic and nervous nature, which always pushes on rash actions. I picked up a revolver and prepared to shoot, using a pot with nymphs as a shelter (I'm afraid, not very reliable), but none other than Valentin Saltykov, trying to catch his breath after a run, left the park.

Valentin responded to the threat posed by me in a very relaxed manner.

- Helen, do not kill me! He joked, raising his hands. "To top it off, all you had to do was fall from your bullet on Mrs. Chigareva's porch ..."

I lowered the weapon.

- I hope you will explain something to us? - The question had to be asked with neutral intonation - it was still unclear what the role of Valentine in the new act of our drama was, and it was not worth rushing with warm friendly notes.

- Helen, the inherent spirit of adventurism has infected me too. I not only changed the lock at your door, dear ladies, to leave an uninvited night visitor with a nose, but also slowly returned and set up an ambush under your windows, "Valentin repented of repentance. - Please forgive, if when you try to detain the attacker violated your peace. What a pity that my grip was not the same. Alas, I missed the scoundrel. Never ask myself that.

- Detain the attacker? - stammering, repeated Anya. - Oh my God! And who is he?

"I suppose that was your ghost," Saltykov replied. - So-called. Left without a house key, he decided to climb up the stairs to the attic ...

As it turned out, a large wooden staircase was attached to the roof in the place where it was easy to climb out the mezzanine window, which usually hung on the wall of the shed in the far economic yard.

Valentin, who was sitting in an ambush near the house, saw a man coming up the stairs, rushed towards him, knocked him down the steps into the bushes growing under the windows, and tried to twist him.

But the villain was not timid, moreover, is very strong. A fight ensued. Distorted, the uninvited guest with a mighty blow threw off our defender and rushed to run. Making his way right through the jasmine bushes that grew under the windows (the terrible crackling of fragile jasmine branches lifted us all to its feet), the bastard managed to reach the lime alley, jump out of the park gates and hide.

The unfortunate captain after his injury was not in the best shape, and he simply did not have enough breath to catch up with the evader.

Worst of all, Valentin didn't see how the intruder's face was in darkness and general turmoil, and now it was completely unclear who we should fear and suspect in a daring attempt to penetrate into the possession of a lonely widow under cover of the night ... However, the boot on the foot of the villain was a military model, Saltykov assured us swornly - he got acquainted with the boot most closely when he dragged the unknown villain by the foot from the ladder, and again when he received a blow to the stomach with this boot.

"I don't know what intentions the subject was guided by, but it's clear that his intentions were unkind," Valentine noted thoughtfully, summing up the nightly incident.

Since I learned about the great-great-great treasure with the gifts of the empress, I had some insights about the intentions of the night visitor, but for the time being I thought it best to keep them to myself.

We brought lanterns and kerosene lamps and the four of us went around the house, trying to find something. There must be evidence at the crime scene! True, nothing interesting was found so far, since we ourselves didn't know what we were looking for.

In addition to the stairs that remained near the wall of the house and the broken jasmine bushes under it, nothing stopped the sight. Perhaps, by crawling in the grass, we could find some trifle lost by the villain — a ring, a button, a penknife out of our pocket (and even better — a lost letter with his name, that would be luck!), But, alas, for there was clearly not enough detailed search for light from greasy cinder in the lanterns.

In the end, we returned to the house, inviting Saltykov to the living room. He playfully fought back, saying that his appearance was not suitable for late visits to the ladies. And in fact, after a fight with the unknown, he was covered in mud, and his nifty uniform was a rather pitiful sight.

But questions of secular propriety worried us with Anya now, far less than our gratitude to a man who is ready to defend two women as a guardian angel, standing on the clock under their windows.

As far as possible, we cleaned Saltykov's tunic, gave the captain's glass a glass of hot drink (an opened bottle of Armagnac and stood, carefully wiped from dust, on the shelf of the buffet from the time I went to the cellar) and placed a sofa in the living room for the night - do not send the same person back in the dead of night after all the unrest.

Valentin crumbled in gratitude, and I felt that I was tired from my feet in the most direct sense.

"And now, gentlemen, one of two things — either they will give me some sleep, or the hour of my eternal sleep will rapidly approach, and you will soon have to mourn my cold body," I said, retiring to my bedroom.

Everything, no one else can interfere with my sleep - neither a herd of starving mosquitoes, nor the ghosts of grandfathers and great-grandfathers, nor an unknown burglar rattling the stairs under the window. I don't want to know anymore! Sleep, sleep, spa ...

CHAPTER 17

Anna

The next morning, Valentin Saltykov first went to Gireyevo, immediately after breakfast. Elena Sergeevna approved such prudence - if the staff captain appeared in the hospital together with the ladies from Privolnoe, all the Gireev inhabitants would have completely unequivocal suspicions about where he had spent that night, and there would be no end to playful questions.

Gossip and leisure speculation always entertain a bored society, but to become the object of such a distraction is not a pleasant thing. As for the reputation of the ladies, as well as for the general peace of mind, the staff captain Saltykov had better appear in Gireyev alone.

However, after the night of the incident, Anna began to lean toward the idea that it was still necessary to invite Valentine to live in Privolnoye, and therefore, gossip would be inevitable anyway. In such circumstances, it is better to immediately state your plans to all who are interested in honestly and unambiguously than to give rise to all kinds of ridiculous rumors.

Going to go to the hospital in order to resume the duties of the sister of mercy there, Anya went into Elena Sergeevna's room. She in ecstasy spun in front of the mirror, trying on outfits taken out of the suitcase. Several fashionable dresses were laid out on the bed, and two hats were carefully placed on the under-the-mirror mirror.

- This suit looks good, but the skirt is very wrinkled and requires iron. Now you will not leave it in the house, "Elena Sergeevna thoughtfully said, looking at herself from all sides. - And yesterday was too busy to see ...

- Lelia, do you really want to dress up after all our nightmarish events? - Anya was surprised.

- Exactly. After all our events, you just want to dress up like never before. A woman must always remain a woman. You know, if I have serious troubles or too many problems, I extract all the best from my wardrobe to decorate my person, dress up and go to people. With this, I bring myself into a harmonious emotional balance and reinforce the shaky sense of self-respect.

Regretfully, Lelya took off her fashionable light gray suit and got into simpler clothes - a sports sweater and a tweed skirt, putting on something like an anther or a raincoat of monophonic fabric.

"Of course, rural life doesn't provide so many opportunities to showcase outfits, but the current cooling will still allow me to upgrade one of the latest acquisitions. Pay attention - the novelty of this season's Parisian fashion, light aviaty women's overcoat. The cut resembles the clothes of the aeronauts. Since the beginning of the war, women's clothing has also begun to actively use the "military" style. Perhaps it is not so feminine, but elegant and meets modern trends. As additions I use a light sports sweater with a "golf" collar, covering the neck, and a silk scarf.

The scarf removed from the suitcase was tied up in the most intricate way to the head, adding to the owner of that same femininity, a small part of which was taken by an aviatic coat.

"You see, and in the rustic simplicity there is its own charm," continued Elena Sergeevna. - Where in Moscow could go in a sweater? Is that in a skating-ring or on the court, play a game of lawn tennis. If I had declared myself in a tight-fitting sweater to the theater or to a public lecture, they would have pointed a finger at me. And in the village in a sweater you can go almost anywhere. It fits well with military-style clothing and is not at all fatal, allowing you to hide a browning holster under a hollow coat. It is a suitable outfit for a lady who has embarked on the path of fighting an unknown evil.

"Yes, very elegant," Anya confirmed. - And so unusual. Amazon XX century. You probably spend crazy money on clothes?

- Nothing out of the ordinary. I have always been proud of my practicality and ability to look decent, without getting into debt. Although looking with someone to compare. You know, I somehow, even before the war, caught the eye of an interesting article in Ogonyok. It cited data on how much money the European queens spend on clothes. After all, representatives of the ruling houses for many are the benchmark in terms of fashion and good taste. Moreover, the correspondent very kindly transferred all sums of money to the ruble equivalent - the sum in some lires, guilders or pounds sterling, for example, would not have said anything to me. So, some monarchs, as it turned out, are fighting on the verge of complete poverty. The Dutch queen Wilhelmina, poor thing, can afford to spend an amount of only ten thousand rubles on clothes. Can you imagine? At the level of the Moscow shopkeeper mediocre. In second place by the stinginess, the English Queen Mary and the German Queen Augustus Victoria — they spend twenty thousand rubles on their dresses. The Italian queen Elena spends thirty thousand a year, and the Spanish queen Victoria looks like a crochet against the general background, spending as much as forty eight thousand rubles. So, if we talk about my own spending, measuring them in royal terms, then I'm probably not happy about the Spanish queen - too much luxury sucks, but I don't allow myself to dress as poor as the Dutch queen. I will dwell on the level of my namesake, Queen Helena - for thirty thousand people, you can dress quite elegantly and without a vulgar pump. In second place by the stinginess, the English Queen Mary and the German Queen Augustus Victoria — they spend twenty thousand rubles on their dresses. The Italian queen Elena spends thirty thousand a year, and the Spanish queen Victoria looks like a crochet against the general background, spending as much as forty eight thousand rubles. So, if we talk about my own spending, measuring them in royal terms, then I'm probably not happy about the Spanish queen - too much luxury sucks, but I don't allow myself to dress as poor as the Dutch queen. I will dwell on the level of my namesake, Queen Helena - for thirty thousand people, you can dress quite elegantly and without a vulgar pump. In second place by the stinginess, the English Queen Mary and the German Queen Augustus Victoria — they spend twenty thousand rubles on their dresses. The Italian queen Elena spends thirty thousand a year, and the Spanish queen Victoria looks like a crochet against the general background, spending as much as forty eight thousand rubles. So, if we talk about my own spending, measuring them in royal terms, then I'm probably not happy about the Spanish queen - too much luxury sucks, but I don't allow myself to dress as poor as the Dutch queen. I will dwell on the level of my namesake, Queen Helena - for thirty thousand people, you can dress quite elegantly and without a vulgar pump. spending as much as forty eight thousand rubles. So, if we talk about my own spending, measuring them in royal terms, then I'm probably not happy about the Spanish queen - too much luxury sucks, but I don't allow myself to dress as poor as the Dutch queen. I will dwell on the level of my namesake, Queen Helena - for thirty thousand people, you can dress quite elegantly and without a vulgar pump. spending as much as forty eight thousand rubles. So, if we talk about my own spending, measuring them in royal terms, then I'm probably not happy about the Spanish queen - too much luxury sucks, but I don't allow myself to dress as poor as the Dutch queen. I will dwell on the level of my namesake, Queen Helena - for thirty thousand people, you can dress quite elegantly and without a vulgar pump.

Anya sighed a little. She, with the widow's pension, alas, is not enough to reach the level of Wilhelmina. Yes, modest mourning is in every sense salvation for a widowed woman ...

But Lelia, as if reading the thoughts of a young widow, completed her monologue in a completely unexpected way:

- As soon as we cope with all the local problems, we will go to Moscow and walk through fashionable salons. Despite the war, fashionable life in the First Throne is just beating the key. Models in the salons work like damned, throwing out for sale more and more new models - and oddly enough, they are bought up instantly. Many have managed to cash in on the war and now waste money. So, I want to order for you a new wardrobe to lift your spirit. You will see, as soon as you dress in a fashionable dress of French silk, you will immediately feel how the world is changing rapidly.

"Yes, but money ... I must confess that I was in such cramped circumstances that I cannot afford the extra expenses," Anna sighed bitterly.

- Oh, my dear, do not think about money. A handful of grains will always be sent to the bird of God. The Lord is merciful, will he really give the poor widow such a smallness as a few dresses and a pair of hats? For example, I will gladly pay your bills from the moderator, considering it to be a small contribution to the benefit of the widows of the defenders of our fatherland.

- Oh, what are you? I would be embarrassed! - Anya objected. - Better donate money to the needs of the front.

- To their commissaries plundered? No, dudki! It is much more pleasant to help a friend's widow than to plump money in a bottomless barrel of anonymous charity, Lela did not agree. "What are we talking about?" Maybe, not today or tomorrow, the treasure of your ancestor will be found and you will become rich like Madame Dupont and Madame Rothschild together! And by the way, don't you want to try on something now?

And she reached for the hat box.

- But I'm in mourning! - Anya brought the last killer argument.

- So what? Just try on a fashionable thing from pure academic interest, in order to make sure whether it is face-to-face or not, and widows are not forbidden, "Lelya retorted. - Look, what a hat! A real masterpiece. By the way, it is black. Just for the inconsolable widow ...

"Did you bring new hats with you to the village?" - Anya was surprised, trying on the aforesaid moderator's masterpiece. - God, how beautiful!

- I take a couple of new hats with me on any trip, otherwise the trip will not be a joy. A hat box will not pull it away, but how much joy is hidden in it! Anya, this style suits you very much! As if it was created specifically for your face. Listen, do not take off your hat from your head, you will go to Gireyevo right in it. And in general, wear it always! You just changed. If I had decorated my hat like that, I would have slept in it ...

"But the style of the hat is so ... piquant," Anya hesitated. - Is he suitable for a widow? Not too defiant? And will such a fashionable hat be combined with mourning?

"And who said that a widow should resemble a weeping willow?" - Lelia asked a rhetorical question, adjusting a black veil on Anya.

Anya realized that she did not have the strength to give up this beautiful thing - after all, in a fashionable hat, the forgotten sense of self of a beautiful woman returned to her ...

Dear, while the old horse, slowly crossing her legs, was dragging the stroller in Gireevo, Elena Sergeevna returned to her concern.

"Anyuta, maybe after a nightly incident with a fight and a chase, I should have been distracted from our discovery of yesterday, but I'm still madly interested in your grandfather's plan." Where did he hide the treasure? I am puzzled that he depicted the area with circles on the drawing, and I can't think of anything. But this is something simple, everyday, that his relatives should immediately recognize ... He, it seems, did not even doubt that his plan was obvious to the heirs. Maybe in your park or in the near forest there is some kind of glade covered with trees or bushes along the perimeter?

- And under one of them buried a treasure chest of Catherine's favorite?

- Why not? Treasures are sometimes buried in such places, and they can lie underground for a long time. I read somewhere that two years ago in the Caucasus, in Svaneti, in a remote mountain village, an absolutely incredible ancient treasure was found. And found by chance. One peasant decided to make a talk on the waste ground behind his house for the threshing of bread. To do this, it was necessary to clear the ground from large stones and level the ground - highlands, where to go. The largest stone was not given. The stubborn Svan called for help from his neighbors. When it turned out that several strong healthy men were unable to cope with the damned stone, they led the horses ... In the end, with a horse-drawn ingrown stone, they managed to budge, and a deep hole was opened under it, in which an old clay vessel was kept. The peasants broke it, and a huge pile of gold coins woke to the ground. As it turned out, these were staters - the main monetary unit of Alexander the Great's empire ... Now it remains only to guess who buried the treasure under a stone in the mountains in those ancient times and why he could not take his treasure, leaving it to distant descendants ... And you would not like to leave your treasure in the earth for ages. Descendants are descendants, but for you it is not superfluous.

"Well, well," Anya thought. - In a free minute, you can walk through the park and look for a place with trees or bushes, reminiscent of a grandfather's picture. I'm afraid to go to the forest, the killer is wandering there ...

"We'll grab a Browning and a reliable guide for a meeting with a possible killer," Lelya promised, referring to probably the staff captain Saltykov.

"Look, look," Anya shouted suddenly, pointing to a clearing surrounded by bushes, past which the horse slowly trod their horses. - Here, for example, is the right place. Need to count the bushes. Do you remember how many laps were on the plan?

"I'm afraid that at the time of your grandfather this bush was not yet, it is too young," Elena Sergeevna sadly remarked. -

And in general, if the grandfather had in mind some natural corner, we, even passing by, can not recognize this place. Over the past decades everything has changed a lot - some trees have dried up and fallen, others have been cut down, bushes have grown ... Well, we'll think about it later, and now I will mentally prepare myself for a conversation with a detective agent. I need to focus so that I don't miss anything important with him.

And Lelya was silent, looking at ate sailing along the road ...

Upon arrival in Gireyevo, she retired to the hostess's office with a detective, who seemed to be just waiting for this moment, and Anya started dressing the injured and thought for the first time that the work, initially forced and not very pleasant, began to bring her some satisfaction.

And there is really nothing to sit around, withdrawing in his grief, as if in a sink — one has to be with people ...

Having done all the dressings and completed other medical affairs, tired Anya sat down to rest in the gazebo in the garden. Leli was still out - as it turned out, the investigator joined her negotiations with the detective agent and the three-way confidential conversation was very long.

But Ana did not manage to be alone - the lieutenant was broken by the lieutenant Stepanchikov, who tracked down the young widow with the aim to make her company and entertain with funny talk.

"Think of it, our kind Elena Sergeevna fell into the clutches of this boring police agent," he said in a tone that seemed to be important news. "But a good detective is like a ghoul, if he catches a person, he doesn't get off a living person." Yes, Elena Sergeevna, poor thing, you will not envy. A conversation with a detective agent is a most unpleasant affair. Oh, you should know how I hate the police! Since my student days ... I was a student before the war and did not even think about an officer's career. And I have my old scores with the police. Do not believe it, today at breakfast I could not eat a piece - the mere presence of a police agent at the table was detrimental to appetite.

While the lieutenant, smiling cheerfully, carried some utter nonsense, considered suitable for the entertainment of the ladies, Anna could not take her eyes off his face - Stepanchikov had her cheekbone broken, not counting several more abrasions and small bruises.

"It's embarrassing to look at his bruises so closely, you need to turn away," Anya mentally told herself, not listening to the words of the lieutenant, but nodding back to him, like a Chinese dummy. - And yet, why does Stepanchikov face so much broken? Did he fight with someone? At night, the captain fairly poured in an unknown person who was trying to enter the house along the ladder ...

Our uninvited visitor should also have bruises on his face, Saltykov did not show any particular delicacy. Maybe it was just Lieutenant Stepanchikov in the dark who ran into the fist of the staff captain? Is the lieutenant sneaking into my house at night? What could he need there? "

Stepanchikov, catching Anna's strange look, was embarrassed and decided to explain himself:

- I see, madam, you are worried about my appearance. Do not worry, nothing terrible. Traces of the vulgar brawl. Yesterday in the evening I went on business to the village, and the local guys, young mutts, decided to God only tell you why you need to protect the village beauties from me. I had to show the local dolphins what it means to attack an officer ... I guess I managed to teach this company a lot ...

"Probably lying," thought Anya, feeling that a small tremor was starting to beat her. It's hard to sit next to a possible criminal without giving out your suspicions.

It would be necessary to transfer the conversation to another topic, having touched some other, far-off matters with secular ease ... But for some reason, nothing secular to Anna hadn't occurred to her, and her silence was indecently delayed.

- Oh, Krivitsky! - Stepanchikov nodded to another lieutenant who approached the arbor. "You didn't come out for breakfast today." I do not get sick? Or did not want to share the meal with a police snoop? I took the risk and, I confess, the food in such a company did not go to the future. Here, I am complaining to Anna Afanasyevna about a spoiled appetite. Bah, look and you mark on the face? Our ranks are expanding ...

Anya turned her eyes to Krivitsky. A noticeable bruise spread over his left eye.

"Why, such nonsense has come out," spread Krivitsky. - I usually fall asleep late and I like to walk before bedtime. Three or four miles, it happens, you will pass, so that later you can fall asleep with a rat, otherwise insomnia will torture. Oddly enough, after the front, the local silence presses, it seems alarming. And to the sound of gun-cannonade, sleeping is a sweet affair. So, yesterday, towards the night, I was returning from a walk along a deserted road and, if you please, I ran into some gangsters. Apparently, the most notorious deserters, of which everyone here speaks. A gang of drunken tramps! Well, I'm not a young lady to allow myself to just be robbed and stabbed. Entered melee and gave them pepper ...

Krivitsky continued to talk about his victory in colors, and Anya thought about it involuntarily. Maybe it is Krivitsky who lies, not Stepanchik? And there were no deserters, and there was a fight with Saltykov under the windows of Anino at home? Krivitsky suspected of criminal intentions is a snap. Indeed, on the night when the girl was killed, it was Krivitsky who appeared infrequently from where he was near the crime scene, saying that he came running to the scream and the sounds of gunfire ... These are his nightly walks around Privolnoye ... He's generally strange. And his bruise could well be the mark of the fist of the captain.

But on the other hand, the day after the murder, Stepanchikov also had scratches on the face, glued with a plaster ... For some reason, Anya then thought that he had just cut himself while shaving. This is the first thing that occurred to her. But after all, an unknown killer at night, in the dark, ran away from the armed Leli into the forest through the bushes and could scratch his face with branches and fragments of branches ...

So which of them is a criminal - Krivitsky or Stepanchikov?

- Hello, Anna Afanasyevna! Let me express the utmost admiration! - On the railing of the gazebo a young ensign was leaning, who had just inserted a new lock into the door in Privolnoye. The lieutenant's face was also adorned with fresh bruises and small bruises, which made him noticeably embarrassed. - Can you imagine what a bad luck with me came out? Yesterday I was returning from your estate straight through the forest, did not notice the spruce root in the dark, stumbled, and directly face the trunk of a Christmas tree ... With a swing! Well still the bitch did not touch the eye!

Well, also a second lieutenant with a broken face! This is just not enough! Oh, he somehow does not fit into the invented picture and only confuses Anna with her bruises. What does the Christmas tree do with it?

"Gentlemen, since I have taken upon myself the duties of a local sister of mercy, let us treat your injuries with some kind of antiseptic," Anya suggested, realizing that her head was spinning and who exactly was to suspect, she no longer knows ...

"Oh, madam, I am delighted to place every scratch at your disposal, if only to please such a charming, merciful Samaritan woman," Stepanchikov gallantly bowed.

"Lord, how long Lelya talks to this police agent," thought Anna. In the society of Stepanchikov and Krivitsky she somehow felt uncomfortable.

Chapter 18

Sending a telegram to the Investigative Police, I was asking to send agent Stukalin for nothing, and was glad that they listened to my request. The rest of the gentlemen who labored in the service in Gnezdnikovsky Lane did not cause me any confidence at all.

We met four years ago with detective agent Stukalin under very dramatic circumstances. I was a witness in the murder case of a Moscow businessman (according to my husband, I have a rare gift to get into various troubles), and my active life position inherent in me did not allow me to calmly observe how the Detective Police made one mistake after another, and from an outside observer I quickly became a direct participant in the drama played out.

In fact, against the background of a peaceful and calm pre-war life, the case of the murder of Mr. Krudner seemed overly complicated and confusing. At first, syskari did not even want to believe my intuition, which suggested that a crime had occurred, and did not believe until the body of the unfortunate entrepreneur was discovered ... But later, without taking any lessons from the incident, the police continued to be extremely painful to accept any attempt to explain them quite obvious (even in my amateurish opinion) things.

As a result, I was one-on-one with the murderers, and I almost broke my head to diminish my enthusiasm; only the small fiddles got confused in the networks of the police, and the real criminals managed to escape ... And some of them, as far as I know, have still not been caught.

However, the activities of our police, as is known, cannot serve as a benchmark in the protection of the law, rather the contrary.

And it is our happiness that as yet not every inhabitant of the Russian Empire is ready to rob and kill. But if such ideas come to mind to a large number of our citizens, the police will not only be impotent, but will most likely be swept away by this muddy wave.

The events that took place in Moscow quite recently, at the end of May, confirm this with particular clarity. I will never forget how the brutalized crowd of rioters who started the hunt for Moscow Germans rushed through the streets of my beloved, sweet, kind city ...

Apartments, shops, workshops and factories that belonged to people of German descent were crushed, and the Germans themselves were severely beaten and even killed ... Houses burned, warehouses were looted, women who were torn to pieces were rushing through the streets. Men with faces turned into a bloody mess were lying on the sidewalks near the houses. Over seven hundred objects suffered from unrest (and what a terrible meaning is embedded in the words of the object of unrest, when massacre begins in a peaceful rear town?). And the police was inactive! Pogroms lasted several days ...

And only when the troops were pulled to Moscow, the riots managed to stop by force of arms ... The press, crushed by military censorship, tried not to exaggerate the issue of pogroms, and the police authorities wrote in reports that an explosion of patriotism, unbridled, ugly, but still patriotism was observed in the city ...

It only remained bitterly ashamed of their fellow countrymen and hiding the family of Dr. Schönenberg in their own home.

But back to those distant times when the murder of a German was considered to be as terrible a crime as any other murder. The Krudner case, widely reported in newspapers, stirred up the whole of Moscow and was discussed with horror on every corner. It was then that my acquaintance with Mr. Stukalin, who was engaged in the investigation of this case, took place.

Regular verbal clashes with a detective agent eventually still led us, oddly enough, to a feeling of mutual sympathy and almost friendly relations ... But it happened already when I, due to an oversight of the police, were injured by a criminal hand, and therefore in further the actions of the police agents perceptibly showed guilt.

I didn't bother to insult my offenses and write complaints to supervisors on detective agents, reproaching them with negligence by the service ñ the adventure experienced in those days was the most exciting in my whole life, and it's worth something and the head is bandaged by no means the highest fee.

Mr. Stukalin considered this approach very noble and sometimes began to come to visit me - to visit, drink a cup of tea and tell a couple of entertaining police tales.

But now, when the detective agent was on duty again, and I again became a witness to the crime, Stukalin, who had completely forgotten about our friendly tea parties on the Arbat, suddenly started a conversation with me with a strict remark:

- Elena Sergeyevna, darling, I know your flowery fantasy well. Therefore, please strictly adhere to the facts. I repeat, facts and facts only. No speculation interests me.

The very formulation of this strange request seemed extremely offensive to me. I glanced at Stukalin with a mixed feeling of surprise and annoyance. No, that was not what I expected from his arrival in Gireyevo.

"Let me say," I said with dignity in response to the words of the detective, "that if I were you, I wouldn't say such a lady if, of course, you are interested in receiving information from her." Such statements degrade women.

It should be added that this way I will even want to talk with him altogether, but by an effort of will I restrain myself. Excessive principles in communicating with the police are also not beneficial to the cause - they, poor things, are so vulnerable ...

"Oh, Elena Sergeyevna, I remember your feminist grip," Stukalin grinned at his large, sadly drooping police mustache. "Now you saddle your skate, start with our supposed disrespect for the mind and insight of the ladies, and finish by demanding to give women electoral rights in elections to the State Duma ..."

- And this, by the way, would not hurt, - I could not resist. - The female half of the country's population is practically deprived of the possibility of free will, and for some reason the state authorities are sure that this is necessary. Whom you, men, got into the Duma, we already had the good fortune to contemplate. And let me say, it is not the first time when your deputies have been balancing on the brink of a parliamentary crisis, being unable to reach an understanding with the outside world. No wonder immediately after the declaration of war, the Duma was dissolved, as if it interfered with the common cause. And this year it was convened in January for a very short time, for three days, only to approve the budget ...

"But on the nineteenth of July, immediately after the anniversary of the outbreak of the war, the deputies were again convened," Stukalin cautiously objected.

- Yes, and immediately managed to quarrel with the Prime Minister, and with each other. Goremykin is already bothering about the next dissolution of the Duma. Maybe we, women, get political rights, everything would be better with us. And not only to choose deputies, but also to sit in the Duma themselves - women are much more practical and prudent.

"Well, let's go back to practical things, if so," suggested Stukalin. - I am amusing myself to hope that the Lord will not live up to such horrors as a woman deputy.

- What if you like it? - I could not resist. - You have not tried to live in conditions of equality!

- Yes, God bless him at all, with equal rights to it! Tea, not tomorrow women will be elected to the Duma ... Let's talk, we'd rather talk about daily life, "the detective agent dodged the discussion.

M-yes, dear man, although a bore ... Muckled up in prejudice, a policeman cracker! Well, now is not the time to campaign among representatives of the Detective Police.

- Well, about the vital, so about the vital, I do not mind, - I responded. "I summoned you to this wilderness due to the killing of a sister of mercy from a gymnasium, but apparently you already know that this is the fifth violent death of a young woman in these places." I repeat - the fifth! Agree, a little like a chain of accidents. All the dead - girls of twenty-twenty-five - were found in the forest with a throat slit. I guess the killings are related. As you say in the detective, the general handwriting is traced.

At the words "I suppose ..." in the person of Mr. Stukalin something stirred, perhaps he considered this assumption to be one of those little interesting speculations. But the agent no longer dared to interrupt the flow of my words with a new remark.

"In addition, there are a number of oddities that need to be explained, because they too can be associated with the death of girls," I continued, inspiring. "A secluded estate Privolnoe, belonging to the young widow of the officer, Anna Afanasyevna Chigareva, where I was staying, is located nearby. Ms. Chigareva lives with an old woman nanny in a huge old house. And there is no one else there. Servants in Privolnoye coming. So ...

I have just started a story that promised to become as entertaining as Mr. Stukalin said that the judicial investigator must be present at presenting all the strange facts, since it seems to me that they are relevant to the case. How can I tell such important things in the absence of the investigator?

I was sure that the investigator and the detective agent were not so sympathetic to each other, so that they would certainly fight crimes together, shoulder to shoulder. But Stukalin still went looking for his involuntary companion in the investigation of murders.

Being alone for a short time, I could think at my leisure about the vicissitudes of free will ... I can't say that in these circumstances I felt unearthly bliss and that I always wanted to be interrogated by detective agents and judicial investigators, even if as a witness. This pleasure is dubious.

In all honesty, I would have preferred to completely dispense with conversations with a judicial official, because I already had the honor of talking with him the day before, and his manner of conducting the investigation did not cause me anything but tragic irony. But is it prudent to publicly announce it now, in the circumstances in which we all find ourselves?

The murder case in itself is rather unpleasant, why aggravate the situation with unnecessary quarrels? What is the use if I explain to the investigator that I consider him to be a pompous boob? Without a doubt, we can all understand each other much better if we learn to restrain our emotions ...

Finally, the ministers of the law, and already in a pair, appeared before my eyes, sat down at the table and stared at me with a concentratedly ecstatic look, like the provincials, who for the first time saw Ivan the Great's bell tower. Apparently, the gentlemen expected some exciting entertainment from me.

I did not count on such a benefit performance and involuntarily became worried that some thoughts that I carried here from Privolny, were scattered along the way.

Yeah, nice people, these detectives. In vain they all slander.

So, under the crossfire of double skepticism, I had to embark on a story that already looked not very believable. I had to leave out some beauties like the "Angels of Mons" and the ghost of the grandfather-count, I would hardly have made an impression on the servants of the law, indulging in such romantic nonsense. And if you remove all the romance and mysticism, the rest turned out, frankly, the devil knows what.

Besides, the eloquence of today has obviously changed me. On the one hand, trying as far as possible to do without mysticism, without hints of otherworldly forces and to give all events a completely realistic interpretation, and on the other - trying to remember every little thing, I got confused, repeated every minute, went back and ran ahead ...

As I set out everything that I considered worthy of attention, the face of the investigator became more and more melancholy, and Mr. Stukalin, on the contrary, cleared up and took on a very lively expression.

When the endless jumble of mysterious strangers, missing keys, screams, gunshots, night chases, dead girls, broken bushes, unpleasant lieutenants and friendly staff captains came to an end, I allowed myself to draw some conclusions from the facts stated. Let them be considered speculation, but the facts because the servants of the law was given a lot.

- I have one hypothesis. Very strange, I would even say, incredible.

"Mrs. Croatian has a weakness to incredible assumptions," said Agent Stukalin, addressing the investigator, and it was difficult to understand whether the detective approves or condemns such a habit.

"So maybe you will share with us at least something from your incredible conjectures, Madame?" - inquired about the referee's hook with a sour, like the day before yesterday yogurt, smile. It seemed to me that his speculations were just occupied ... - Otherwise, you are all twisted around. Bolder! We do not need to explain for a long time.

"I'm not sure," I answered frankly. The investigator somehow didn't look like a man grabbing bits of information on the fly. - You, gentlemen, for example, have not yet occurred to ask Lieutenant Krivitsky what he did in the middle of the night near the estate, not far from the place where the dead girl was found the next morning? Anna Afanasyevna and I rushed to the cry, tried to catch the criminal, but in vain. A few minutes later Krivitsky himself came to us from the forest. It is strange that it does not surprise you! The lieutenant claimed that he was walking nearby (although it was already late for walks), and rushed to the cry and the sound of a shot. Nevertheless, it was he who was on the edge immediately after the alleged killer managed to escape in the forest.

I paused for a moment, thinking about what I was saying, and concluded that everything was completely convincing. Will not the servants of the law listen to my words? It is necessary that my speculation seemed even more intelligible ...

- And what if, running away from me, Krivitsky made a small detour, and then came back, pretending that he had nothing to do with it? Nevertheless, he managed to distract us from the place where the murdered young lady lay. The malice is obvious, gentlemen.

- But maybe the lieutenant suffers from insomnia and really likes to walk before going to bed? - interrupted me the investigator. - After all, he was contused at the front, and the concussed men often have certain oddities. And in general, madam, I would least like to suspect the crime of an officer, a military officer, a front-line soldier. Let me note - he would hardly have risked appearing at the scene of the crime if he really was a murderer! What is the first criminal desire? Take away the suspicion from yourself! Hide But do not climb on the rampage.

Such an assumption would be quite natural for an inexperienced person, but so that a professional lawyer so easily dismisses obvious facts only because he would not like to suspect an officer! Yes, the defenders of the fatherland are worthy of our gratitude for their feats of arms, but they are not angels at all, but people with all the vices and passions peculiar to the human race. I was outraged.

- I may not have such a rich legal experience as you, Mr. Investigator, but I also have to deal with criminals, and more than once. One should not overestimate such an audience, - I could not resist, in order not to snort with all possible contempt. "Usually the murderers think too much about themselves, otherwise they wouldn't even think that they can kill people with impunity." I am not talking about God's commandments and human duty, but the justice of the killer is considered not worth serious fear, confident in their cunning and agility. A reasonable person, even if he is the last villain, before going to kill, think of hard labor. After all, all of us are sometimes worried about the thought of how nice it would be to kill someone, but we live quietly and peacefully and keep the commandments of God.

I don't know if the investigator understood who exactly I would have finished with pleasure at the moment if I didn't consider myself a sensible woman? But, incidentally, we need to distract from these bloodthirsty visions, because Christ forbade us to sin even in our thoughts ...

"Gentlemen, I am absolutely sure that Krivitsky did not accidentally find himself at night in the forest near Privolnoye," I continued to insist on my version. "I don't know if my words can be regarded as slander, but I won't be surprised if Krivitsky turns out to be a criminal." Moreover, in my opinion, he is in first place on the list of potential killers. Krivitsky is very suitable for this role. God, forgive me if my suspicions are wrong, but the lieutenant looks like a man capable of any meanness ...

"All this is absolutely groundless reasoning, madam," the investigator said, pursing his lips in a peevish manner.

Agent Stukalin was more verbose:

- I understand that you, Elena Sergeevna, for some reason, the unfortunate lieutenant did not like. Such prejudice and led to the fact that he immediately fell under your suspicion ...

I eloquently shrugged my shoulders, but said nothing.

- You have outlined the figure of the lieutenant to the slaughter. But in order to destroy Krivitsky for sure, some irrefutable facts are required, - his detective bent. "My dear, there are actually no facts ... There is no evidence that would allow to accuse him."

I had to object, recalling the illegal entry into the house belonging to the widow Chigareva (the penetrations that had obviously criminal, although still unclear), about some material traces of the unknown man's stay in the house, about the bruises left, probably, on the face and body of the night visitor with the fists of the staff captain Saltykov (my heart tells me that Krivitsky has either a fingal under his eye, or an abrasion on his cheekbone ...).

I even tempted to give the servants of the law my main trophy - a cigarette butt, found in a flowerpot with nymphs under such mysterious circumstances.

(But you should take care of a cigarette butt until better times, so that such a trump card will not disappear in vain, but be used for sure ... But if such valuable information and material evidence does not shed a new light on this unfortunate affair, then I can be considered a round idiot!)

- You still make sure my rightness, gentlemen! - in a sinister tone, I concluded. - Just as if this lesson was not too difficult for you. As, however, for all of us! In a remote place where women are killed one by one, someone (well, let someone, and not Krivitsky at all!) Rushes into a lonely widow's house with manic persistence. Doesn't that make you think about it?

But all my efforts and exhortations, alas, did not lead to the desired result. On the contrary, the judicial investigator stated with a lean mine:

- Elena Sergeyevna, I just wonder you! We have here and really murder for murder, the situation is daunting, and you want us to deal with some nonsense nonsense. You are quite sensible woman! Judge for yourself, what is relevant to what is happening in Privolny? Someone was climbing to you, someone was smoking on the porch ... Some kind of intrusion into the house, and you allegedly saw someone on the stairs, you yourself do not know who ... There is nothing stolen in the house, and stealing, as I understand it, there is nothing special; violence with your friend also, sorry, not subjected, I'm not talking about murder ... Believe me, this is just stupid jokes of your friends or not to the best of ardent admirers. But why do you think that the District Court and the Detective Police should know what to do? We, I repeat, the murders are not disclosed, we are not up to your visitors and not to the ladies' whims.

It's amazing how people sometimes find it difficult to understand each other. However, as for me, I just saw all the hidden thoughts of the investigator as in the palm of your hand.

"I understand why you do not want to get involved in this case," I said sternly, looking into his eyes.

"Yes, the matter is too delicate," he confirmed in no way embarrassed. "Men who visit the house of a lonely widow at night are not within my competence.

- Of course, you are unlikely to be engaged in your duties with delicate zeal, preferring, as usual, to quickly leave back home with assurances of readiness to do everything in your power, but at the same time putting up with the next unsolved murder and leaving the poor widow to deal with the overcomers herself. her criminals ...

- Madam, maybe you will not be so provocative daring? - the investigator soared. - It would be rash to think that only some dummies are engaged in investigative work. Oh, I happened to reveal a lot of crimes in my lifetime, and in this matter I can safely consider myself a competent person. Therefore, your desire to teach me how to solve murders looks at least strange. Yes, there is hardly at least one person in the Moscow province, who would understand the issues of criminalistics better than me!

The judicial investigator, as they say, has suffered. He finally had the opportunity to show off his eloquence. He had long spread about the motives and motivations of the murderers, he had shown erudition about crime in general, showed himself an expert in the field of psychology, and even allowed himself to be very unflattering to respond to the Detective Police, glancing at Mr. Stukalin with a malicious smile.

Since Mr. Conan Doyle's books on Sherlock Holmes began to be widely published in Russia, many servants of the law, having confused fiction with criminalistics, have adopted the methods of the English detective and strive to be engaged in solving crimes, if possible without leaving the office (thank God, even a violin not every one of them indulges!). However, as brilliant results as Sherlock Holmes, can boast, alas, not every one of Doyle's readers and admirers.

Here, for example, our investigator, in spite of all his erudition and craving for psychological delights, hasn't had any results in the investigation yet ... And he likes to talk like that!

I was even a little afraid that I would have to listen to a lecture on the theory of criminology and criminal law until the evening, but Stukalin, wedged into a small pause, which our speaker needed to take a breath, skillfully put an end to this torrent.

"My dear sir, we admire your scientific knowledge, but we, sinners, have no time to soar in the empyrean of jurisprudence, s. We are earthly people and familiar with the matter. I had the honor to bring all the new facts to your attention. The story of Mrs. Croatian you listened. I hope your conclusions from what Elena Sergeevna reported will reveal to us the full brilliance of analytical thought. And then let me allow me, in a private conversation, to find out some little things from Mrs. Croatian. Do not ask for service.

Usually, a policeman is made so offensively polite only when he is very angry. Yes, there is clearly some kind of secret friction between the detective agent and the judicial investigator. This is not my dream. Probably the invitation of the investigator to our conversation was a subtle diplomatic move in the game that only Mr. Stukalin understood.

The investigator took his leave, and we talked with the police detective for another hour and a half. And it seemed to me that in Stukalin, at last, the familiar features of that insightful and cunning peasant, who was able to bring the most sophisticated criminal to light, flashed through. And he will surely listen to my words seriously. Suppose that as a possible killer, Krivitsky does not look very convincing yet, but he may well be in the end.

Terenty Ivanovich, of course, didn't dismiss any of my vague suspicions, but on the contrary, laid everything out. Moreover, I even received a compliment, in my opinion, very pleasant, despite its doubtfulness:

- That's why I love and appreciate you, Elena Sergeyevna, so for the fact that with all your shortcomings you are one of those women who are not afraid to stick your nose wherever you need!

What is said!

When I, tired to the limit of this endless conversation (yes, what a conversation - double interrogation with addiction!), But still satisfied with the last turn of events, left the office, Valentin Saltykov approached me.

- Lelia, how, however, your conversation dragged on. During this time, it was possible to reveal to the detective the entire background of each of the highland patients and paint their pedigrees to the seventh generation. Do you secretly work in Gnezdnikovsky Lane?

- Inappropriate jokes, - I was offended. - I was now close to making a small but very impressive scandal to the authorities. It is a pity that I kept. A good scandal can defuse the atmosphere. So far we have been talking too much and doing too little. You do not know where Anna Afanasyevna?

- Mrs. Chigareva in the gazebo, - Valentine answered and jealously added: - Surrounded by beautiful princes.

- Princes? What kind of monarchic fantasies unfashionable today? Let's better consider them knights, especially since the table in the gazebo is round. Take me to the knightly meeting, Sir Valentine!

- At your service, my lady!

CHAPTER 19

Anna

Anna was completely worn out in the officer society when, on the threshold of the arbor, Mrs. Crovatova appeared on the arm of the captain Saltykov, whose face after the night fight was decorated with abrasions.

But the fact that all other men will find similar jewelry on their faces was obviously a surprise for Elena Sergeyevna. Looking from one patient to another, she exclaimed:

- Gentlemen, are you having fun with fistfights at your leisure?

With a laugh, the officers began to retell their stories to her, and Anna, taking advantage of the general turmoil, quietly whispered with her lips:

- Lelya, let's go finally home!

Elena Sergeyevna immediately managed to gracefully interrupt the general conversation, and the ladies found it possible to bow out. Saltykov, accompanied by the envious looks of the officers, put the women in the crew, received a long-awaited invitation to Privolnoe and promised to arrive there no later than this evening to provide the inhabitants of the manor with protection and support.

A stroller, joyfully met by stray dogs, who proclaimed the surroundings with loud barking, drove along the bumpy road.

"Lelia, I am insanely tired today, although I didn't seem to do anything special," confessed Anya. - Probably, there was too much excitement. When you constantly live on nerves, you get tired as if you had to drag stones ...

"The change of classes helps a lot with this kind of fatigue," Mrs. Kvatovova said. - Something excitingly interesting ... I had one plan! You said that in the closed wing of the house there is a large ballroom with round columns along the walls. Let's take a look there and see if its device will match your grandfather's scheme. Suddenly, the circles on the plan are columns of the ballroom, and the treasure is hidden in a cache located under one of them? This is not so difficult - take out a few parquet and put the casket in the cellar. And then restore the parquet - and no one will guess about anything. Your grandfather could have done just that. Let's try to knock the floors under the columns? You look, the cache and show up. It is necessary to finally find out where the count hid the casket with jewels ...

Anya wanted to argue that it was probably dusty and dirty in the hall and it would be good to have a rest today, but it would be better to go exploring into the uninhabited wing of the house one morning, with fresh forces ... But suddenly it seemed to her that the search for treasures was really exciting. not tolerating any delay. Probably, the excitement and energy inherent in Elena Sergeevna managed to infect the young mistress of the house ...

Upon arrival in Privolnoye, the ladies immediately, armed with a grandfather's plan and a bunch of keys, set off on a journey through the old county chambers.

It was not so easy to open a high double door decorated with tarnished gilding carvings - the key turned to force in the old lock.

"Nobody opened the door for a long time," Anna stammered in an apologetic voice, opening the doors.

"But there is a hope that such a tight lock will not slam shut by itself as soon as we enter inside." Other doors in your house have a craving for such jokes. And this castle needs to be lubricated, that's all, "said Lelya, examining with interest the ceremonial chambers of the old manor.

The ballroom, very majestic, even under a layer of dust, retained the features of aristocratic decoration. Marble pillars; a parquet of rare woods (as far as it could be seen under the litter that covered it); in the piers between the windows are high mirrors that once reflected, crushing the flame of hundreds of candles with golden lights, all the splendor of the balls held here; there is a place for orchestra in the choirs ...

It seemed to Ana for a second that through the current desolation ghostly pictures of the past appear - ladies and gentlemen in dresses of the past century are spinning around the floor in dance and even the sounds of music come from somewhere far away ... She wanted to sit down and take a few deep breaths to something calm the naughty imagination.

But Elena Sergeevna, who had time to pass into the adjacent foyer, where the gallery of portraits in gilded frames was located, called Anna from behind the door and distracted herself from the visions with her questions.

- This is your ancestors, Anyuta? - She asked, looking at the portraits. - I must say, all the representatives of your family had an impressive appearance. But the manner of writing of the old masters is different in its specificity - it seems that all your great-grandfathers suffered from the most severe colds. For some reason, all the red noses and eyes seem to be watery ... What a handsome general! And the whole chest in the crosses. Who is he? Hero of the Caucasian Wars? An associate of Yermolov? Yes, apparently, the abreks had a hard time with him.

Elena Sergeevna moved to the opposite wall and stopped at a large formal portrait, performed in the style of the XVIII century.

"But this courtly handsome man in a wig and velvet jacket is surely the empress's favorite — he has a look at the call of reason, despite the painful humidity common to your kind, that Catherine did not go unnoticed. The old woman in such matters had a brilliant eye.

But Anna, frozen in the doorway, did not answer, and Elena Sergeyevna had to turn away from the portraits of the old-world nobles to face their heiress.

Holding her hand on the column, Anya, who had turned pale, pointed at the portraits and tried to say something, but her lips did not obey her well.

- God, what's wrong, dear? - Elena Sergeyevna rushed to her.

- Lelia, someone was here! - finally whispered the mistress of the house.

Mrs. Croatian, who did not forget about the practical side of things, brought a chair, shaking off and blowing it as far as possible from the dust, sat Anya and only then asked:

- What does it mean - someone was? Did the ghost scare you again?

- No, not a ghost ... Lelya, there really was someone here! These portraits ... because they were covered with canvases from dust and sunlight, and now all covers have been removed from them. Part of the frames is hanging crookedly, and two portraits are generally removed from the walls ... Look, the courtly handsome man, as you call him, for some reason is standing on the floor. And the wall on the spot where it had previously hung is broken right under the hook ... Look, look, and someone parsed the parquet in the corner. And in that far corner too. And behind the column ...

Elena Sergeyevna quickly ran along the walls, looking at every nook and cranny.

"You're right," she said, returning to Ana, who could not find the strength to stand up and was still sitting on the chair at the entrance. - Parquet here and there dismantled and plaster repulsed in places. And most importantly - I found a frozen wax, dripped from someone's candles, and several traces of men's boots. The tracks look pretty fresh. It has been rainy lately, and our secret visitor climbed into a clay puddle not far from the manor, and then brought wet clay on the soles of the house ... I suppose this is not a ghost - it's no good for ghosts to roam through the puddles in the rain!

- The nanny said that sometimes on the stairs they appear by themselves not whose traces,

- Anya responded. "But she blames it on the late grandfather's tricks."

"It seems to me that the grandfather, peace be upon him, nothing to do with it and the traces did not form by themselves ... If we look for a spare key from this door, we will most likely not find it." Someone already cleaned it ... And you are mistaken, claiming that the door to the main chambers has not been opened for a long time ... You see how everyone, it turns out, is simple - when we are disturbed by the mysterious knock that is so easily mistaken for manifestation of otherworldly forces knocks down plaster in the far wing of the house. And it's not for nothing that this one here obviously was looking for something ...

- And what could he look for? What? Does he also want to find a cache of my great-great-grandfather's jewels? - Anya exclaimed, jumping up from the chair.

"It looks like it," Elena Sergeevna replied thoughtfully. - I can't imagine how, but the secret of your ancestors became known to someone else. I hope only that he has not yet found what he is looking for, and we will be able to get ahead of him.

- Why did you decide so? What if he had already found his grandfather's treasure?

- Well, firstly, in those holes that he pierced in the walls and floor, it would hardly fit a large casket, about which your ancestor wrote. Here and a small casket can not hide. Most likely, our milestone someone knocked on the walls and punched small windows where, as it seemed to him, one could find a cavity suitable for the cache. Finding nothing, he moved further, arranging these mouse holes in the corners ... He clearly does not have a plan, and he conducts a search without any system, no matter where he gets.

"Okay, let's say," Anya agreed. - But this is - in the first place, and what is in the second?

"And secondly, if he had found the treasure, he would have tried to escape with his prey somewhere far away, and he still returns to the house and worries us, portraying a ghost ... Of course, our stranger managed to get so familiar with the spirit image that now he does not find the strength to part with a disguise darling of his heart, but the treasure would distract him. Well, my dear, give me a grandfather's drawing ...

Elena Sergeevna unfolded the paper and began to turn it in front of her eyes this way and that, trying to find in the drawing the features of the ballroom.

"No, perhaps there is some other room here," the inquisitive lady finally had to admit. - Look - at this wall six circles are drawn, and there are eight columns here. In addition, around the choir columns are in pairs, and in the drawing circles are arranged quite evenly. Yes, and with the proportions of something wrong. I'm afraid our search is again stumped. Except traces were discovered ... There is substantial evidence of the intrusion of strangers into your home. Tomorrow I'll try to lure the detective agent Stukalin to Privolnoe - maybe the traces will interest him. Whatever you may say, but Mr. Stukalin still does not dismiss my words with such ease as a puffed-up judicial investigator.

Elena Sergeevna again and so twisted the plan of the late graph.

- Listen, and maybe not a ballroom hall was drawn here, but some of the neighboring rooms? The interiors in any of them are pompous. Tomorrow we will go around them all with a plan in our hands and check whether the drawing is suitable for at least one of the premises of this wing.

"Good," Anya agreed. - And now let's go away. You are welcome. Mr. Saltykov is about to arrive, it is necessary to trace whether everything is ready for his arrival. Nanny cleaned the third bedroom to arrange the captain as it should. After all, it would be embarrassing to offer an officer a sofa in the entrance hall for a long stay. And for dinner, I had to make some additions ... Still, the man at the table, and you should not forget that he was recently wounded. He needs comfort, cleanliness and good food.

- Do not fuss you so! - Elena Sergeevna said absently, who could not find the strength to break away from the drawing. - Valentin is not a capricious person, accustomed to traveling life, but he has almost recovered from his injury ... And he would have thought on the couch wondrous, much better than in the field blindage. And again, homemade food in any case more pleasant than from an army boiler ... What am I talking about? Oh yes! Listen, is there no greenhouse in the estate?

- Greenhouses? - Anna, who concentrated all her thoughts on the arrival of Saltykov, could not understand what Lelia was talking about.

- Well, yes, greenhouses. Formerly, they were certainly settled in all the rich estates. Perhaps circles designate something like barrels with palm trees or rare greenhouse plantings, under one of which the graph buried a casket?

It turned out that there is a greenhouse - on the sunny side behind the outbuildings, but since the time of the Count-grandfather it has deteriorated a lot, in some places the glass flew up and exotic plants have long been ordered to live long. But the tireless Elena Sergeevna still went there, grabbing a drawing and a spade and giving the hostess the opportunity to meet the guest on her own.

Chapter 20

Helena

To be honest, the county orangery, on which I had placed such hopes, was in a very deplorable state and threatened to collapse on its head.

And yet, I decided to examine the greenhouse to clear my conscience - because if we assume that once there were planted barrels or pots of plants in accordance with the plan (which is more than likely!), Then the place to hide the casket seemed quite suitable and even much more convenient than under the pillars of the ballroom.

But before I carried out the trial excavations, I had to free the greenhouse from all garden trash that had accumulated over many years. Leaky watering cans and baskets, hoes with broken cuttings, plant garter pegs, hanks of twine, rusty sickles and other unnecessary junk had to be pulled out, and soon I had the feeling that the old stuff was not ending, but, on the contrary, everything was coming and coming like a horn of plenty ...

When I, as an archaeologist, took down several cultural layers, I felt almost like the Italian queen Elena (we are with her namesake after all).

The newspapers say that this enlightened empress has been engaged in archaeological excavations at the royal estate Castel Porziano near Rome for over ten years. She managed to extract a lot of valuable things from the earth - ancient sculptures, vases, weapons, household items. The Queen presents the Italian museums with her finds, and in particular the Museum of Diocletian, to which she suffers a clear weakness.

But unlike her Italian Majesty, I came across not so valuable finds. It is unlikely that anyone will be seduced by the exhibit called "The Garden Wheelbarrow (Unspecified), second half of the XIX century. Author unknown".

After freeing the bridgehead for earthworks in the greenhouse (how fortunate it is getting dark so late in the summer!), I again unfolded the plan.

Oh yes, the interior of the greenhouse could well resemble the one depicted in the grandfather's scheme. Especially if you arrange the barrels of plants in the right places. The remains of these barrels were discovered by me during the excavations, and it is very likely that I am on the right track.

Having figured out where the barrel could have stood, indicated in the drawing with a cross, I stuck a spade into the packed earth. I can not say that the earthworks were ever my strength, but still I soon managed to dig a fairly large hole in the ground and make sure that there was nothing in this place. If, of course, the treasure does not rest at a depth of three or four fathoms, which is nevertheless unlikely. They say that in the north and northeast of Moscow province there is a close occurrence of groundwater, and deep holes are immediately filled with water. Hardly Anin grandfather, hiding treasure, managed to dig up a small well and threw the precious casket into the water ...

For fidelity, I rummaged in different corners of the greenhouse (maybe the search for a secret place needed to start from another point, because the north and south are not marked on the diagram), and suddenly the spade hit the tree ... With double strength, they began to dig and pray to God My find did not turn out to be a piece of a forgotten garden tool, covered with earth in the old days, I dug a wider hole. The cover of a rather crudely knocked-up wooden casket, touched by smoldering, came out of the ground. I could not believe my eyes! In one of the old-house greenhouse's snack bars, which, strictly speaking, didn't very much correspond to the secret place marked on the grandfather's plan, the treasure was really buried!

I refused a spade and, armed with an old garden shovel, I began to carefully clean the box from the ground. Removing it from the pit was difficult, but I could already open the lid to look inside. That's just rusted hinges too tightly held her. Having thrust the scoop into the slot under the lid, I tried to use it as a lever, but, alas, I did not have time to find out what was hiding inside.

Somebody's shadow flickered behind my back, my head buzzed from a strong blow to the back of my head and everything swam before my eyes ...

... I woke up at dusk, finding myself lying on the ground in the same old greenhouse. Before me was a dug up hole, a broken, rotten casket was lying next to it, from which an impressive pile of old, green copper coins had spilled out.

The largest of them were worth in the nickle, and the total amount of the treasure, probably, would be hundreds and a half ...

But this treasure was obviously not buried by the count. The count was supposed to consist of the Empress's gifts, and she was unlikely to give the beloveds with heels and half-shells. And the year of coinage did not coincide with the time of the reign of Catherine ...

With curses, I rose to my feet and with my soul kicked the debris of the chest, because of which I almost did not suffer seriously.

Count treasure I was not given. I had to return to the house with nothing. One joy that the unknown criminal, who dared to raise a hand against a woman, didn't get anything either. He, no doubt, was counting on something more valuable than a few handfuls of coppers. I hope there were no gold bars among the penny coins, but we disdained our copper.

And I decided that I would probably not tell Anna and Saltykov about the attack, somehow embarrassingly. After all, have to look in their eyes a complete fool! Here, in Privolny, incessantly the devil knows what is happening. And what's the endless complaint to anyone? Anyuta will start to worry, to cluck ... It is painfully stupid situation, and I didn't cause much harm, except for the bumps on the back of my head.

Here is a detective agent, perhaps, and I will tell you on occasion about the next atrocity of an unknown enemy. And I will present a cone! Let him then try to say that an unknown visitor does not torture us and doesn't touch a finger at all ... Thank you for not killing you yet!

Leaving the spade at the porch, I climbed the stairs and went to the front, where I came across a pile of suitcases, trunks and field dressings that most likely belonged to our headquarters captain, who decided to move seriously to Privolnoe.

Well, with such equipment you can move anywhere, even go to the eternal settlement in Siberia.

In the dining room, a very nice and cozy picture awaited me - Anya and Saltykov were drinking tea near a samovar. The nanny was nowhere to be seen; probably the kind old woman tactfully retired to her bedroom.

I, too, would do well to show delicacy, especially since my appearance most likely made a frightening impression - after all, I had to mess around with dust, earth and cobwebs, and still have no feelings to lie down, and this does not add to the appearance of a person of freshness and attractiveness ...

But I still could not get around the dining room, without exchanging a word with the hostess and her guest. Yes, I belong to the number of women who attach importance even to such trifles as their own appearance, and I don't like to appear in front of people in the image of a chumichka; nevertheless, there are no rules without exceptions - today I was not so ashamed of my appearance. The negligence of my appearance was fully justified by the circumstances.

Anya knew what I was doing in the old greenhouse, and met me calmly, only gently offered hot water and dinner. But on the face of Valentine was read some amazement.

Well, friends have long considered me an extravagant person, I was already used to it.

"Gentlemen, I managed to find something in the greenhouse," I said, intriguing to the hostess and Valentina.

- Is it a treasure? - Anya exclaimed.

I, not giving her the opportunity to delve into the details - after all, Saltykov about her grandfather's treasures is still unknown, but the word "treasure" itself sounds quite innocent in this context, - continued:

- Imagine, yes. But he is not the only person of value. Someone, perhaps, a gardener who worked in the greenhouse, had once buried his penny savings for a rainy day. Penny in the literal sense - one copper trifle. If you want, Annie, then send a servant to collect the coppers, they are so lying in a greenhouse lying around. I already have no strength for this.

"You're right, it's probably the gardener's savings," Anya confirmed. "The nanny said that one of the gardeners at one time, while still under her grandmother, was suspected of slowly sending fruits and flowers to the bazaar to the bazaar. Here he is, his savings and hid from sin.

- Wow, how many amusing secrets keep the old manor! - Said Saltykov, it seems, has ceased to be surprised that I spend my leisure time in search of treasure ...

Anna and the staff captain found a lantern and set off for curiosity to look at the "treasure" I had found, and I grabbed a large jug of hot water and retired in my bedroom to splash around in the pelvis.

God, remembering here, amidst wild forests, my Moscow bath with sparkling copper taps, from which much hot water flows to my heart, I can get sick with the most severe nostalgia and wander around the estate, sadly repeating, like Chekhov's three sisters: "To Moscow! To Moscow!".

However, I was always proud of my condescension-philosophical attitude to the problems of being ... I remember the unforgettable neurasthenic sisters, one more idefix: "Work! Work! ", And with this I just have everything in order as never before. I put all my strength in the labor field!

Dinner, I decided to ignore. The head was still aching from the blow, and this does not contribute to the appetite.

Having smeared the cream with my hands with a shovel, I climbed under the covers and tried to focus on something fun. After such a day as I fell today, a person necessarily needs pleasant emotions, even if you have to call them artificially.

It's a pity that I don't have a single overseas roman policier or at least a domestic crime novel в in contrast to Shakespeare's bloody dramas, the same murderous stories in detective literature inspire great optimism. I can imagine what kind of candy Arthur Conan Doyle would make from Macbeth ...

Alas, in the absence of light reading, I had to concentrate on my own pleasant memories - the evening hour was just a matter of some reverie.

Lulled by my thoughts, I almost fell asleep when I was awakened by a strange sound, reminiscent of the sound of hooves on the road.

It was already quite dark outside the window, the lunar squares were scribbling the room as if for a game of "classes", and the time for riding was, apparently, completely inappropriate. Only a very good rider can ride in the dark over the overgrown paths of the manor park.

Besides, as far as I know, in the estate there was only that ancient nag, in which Anyuta and I drove in with chic to the Gireevsky porch, but this unfortunate animal wouldn't be able to gallop, not even a very good one, a horseman, so that sparks fly out from under the hoofs, and the clatter will roll all over the district.

Intrigued to the limit, I got up, went to the window, and even threw open the doors, disdaining the fear that the mosquitoes would regard my actions as a hospitable invitation for a late dinner.

From the side of the park, from the deaf thickets, a horseman was heading toward the house, which so far was not easy to see behind trees and bushes. But the dark shadow of the horsehead rushing at full speed, flickering behind the branches, was getting closer and closer. And there, where the horseman was passing, some strange, unearthly light streamed between the branches ... The picture was downright apocalyptic. "And hell followed him" ...

However, about hell you need to understand better. I remembered the field binoculars stuck from the chest of the old earl, darted to the table, rubbed the instrument eyepieces with the hem of the shirt, and set up the optics for the night guest. The rider just flew to an open place lit by the moon, and it could be properly considered.

Damn it A huge black horse with eyes spewing a terrible fire, with a flaming muzzle and burning hooves ... And on it ... Oh, God! A figure wrapped in a shapeless cloak in a cocked hat (yes, it is in a cocked hat of Catherine's times!) And with a dark spot instead of a face. Truly the black horse and the horseman of the Apocalypse!

I felt an unpleasant frost running down my back. It seems that in this manor they are accustomed to everything, but this time something new is happening, it has never been seen before! And I can not say that the surprise of the pleasant!

Have we managed to disturb the ashes of courtly ancestors? The rider in a cocked hat is not even an old-fashioned uniform, it very clearly indicates what age the person came from ... After all, the twentieth century is in the courtyard, and cocked-hat attitudes except fancy dress. And in Privolnoye for tonight the costume ball was not appointed ...

The black horseman was approaching the house when a slender male figure rushed to him from the porch with a revolver in his hand.

Wow, yes this is the staff captain Saltykov and in full military ammunition! It seems that our valiant defender did not even lay down, waiting for the enemies in ambush. Having made a warning shot in the air, he ordered the supreme one to stop, using very strange expressions indicating some emotional turmoil. A front-line habit, I suppose ... Interestingly, in the eighteenth century, gentlemen who received a refined upbringing understood this language? Probably, yes, they say, such idiomatic expressions came from the depth of ages, although their use was not encouraged throughout Russian history.

Well, the mysterious rider of the word Saltykov, one must think, will understand. But I was heartily glad that there were no children in the manor who could hear what the staff captain was thinking about all the black ghosts combined. Ladies in wartime should not be too scrupulous - there are times and situations where men do not get to seem refined and well-bred. In war as in war. I suppose now is just such a moment that one simply can't afford good manners ...

Meanwhile, the captain rushed headlong against the rider, probably intending to grab the horse by the bridle and throw the rider to the ground. The black man in a cocked hat winced and pulled the reins. A sharp movement raised the horse on its hind legs.

No, no it's not a ghost! The ghost now, without a doubt, would have to melt in the air with his hellish horse, rather than spinning, nervously spurring on a frightened animal and trying hard to keep him about.

I felt a strong desire to be with Valentin - together we would easily cope with this damn "ghost" and finally be able to look into his real face to find out who he is. But the captain was in the courtyard, and I was in the house ... I didn't jump down from the window - in the old house the second floor was very high. In the meantime, I will run through all the corridors, stairs, halls and steps, the "ghost" bastard will have time to slip away a hundred times, he is riding!

In my unhappy, broken and sore head, these thoughts jumped, I rushed around the window, not knowing what to do, and the horseman, meanwhile, sent his horse directly to Saltykov and knocked the captain down. Eh, why doesn't Valentine shoot? Shoot, Valechka, shoot, do not wait until you are trampled by hoofs!

The fallen Saltykov deftly rolled aside and armed with a spade thrown by me at the porch. As it turned out, there was no other weapon in his hand - probably the "ghost" managed to knock out a revolver from Valentine's captain or Valentine himself dropped the revolver falling under the horse's hoof ...

The rider flashed his spurs and rode away, and then Saltykov, swinging like a ancient knight with a spear, sent a spade after him. A shovel at the end caught up the horseman, hitting him thoroughly on the back and knocking off his hat. The three-cornered head rolled across the grass, and the black rider slumped in the saddle like a horse, probably in pain. Triumph, of course, was behind the captain.

Without a triangle, it immediately became noticeable that the rider's face was tied around with a dark handkerchief, the ends of which, formerly hidden under the hat, fluttered in the wind, like hare's ears. But for a long time I didn't have time to admire the back of the fleeing enemy, he disappeared into the undergrowth, and soon the sound of the hoofs subsided ...

I myself did not remember how I slid down the stairs and overcame my way into the courtyard.

Valentine was sitting on the porch, holding his side with one hand, and was breathing heavily.

- Are you okay? - I asked carefully and, seeing that Valentine was going to talk about his adventure, she added: - I saw everything out of the window through binoculars. This bastard again hangs near Privolnoye! Presumably, with bad intentions. However, remembering your fists, this time he was afraid to get into the house and decided to scare us from afar. Black ghost, you see ... I would let the dogs down on such a ghost, but sorry, Annie does not keep a kennel. You did not know who it was?

- No, he hid his face. However, a person can be recognized by habit. I have some thoughts, but this is still too early. I have to be completely sure before ... Mmm! - Valentine faltered and groaned. "Damn, he seems to have pretty badly damaged my rib ..."

- Does it hurt? Of course! Horse hooves are no joke! I will take you into the house and make a tight bandage from a long towel, they say, it helps as an emergency aid even with broken ribs. And the cold should be put on a bruise so that the hematoma does not come up. And tomorrow the doctor will examine you.

I tried to put Valentine's shoulder in the same way as the sisters of mercy pictured on the front postcards, taking the wounded soldiers from the battlefield.

But the staff captain, as should a gallant officer, rejected the support in my face.

- Do not make me laugh, Lenochka, I am still able to walk to my room without any help. But thanks for the bandage, it will be very kind of you to take care of me a little. Listen, where is Anna Afanasevna? Did she not hear anything and continue to sleep?

The absence of Anna really seemed strange ...

We found Annu as soon as we entered the house. She lay unconscious on the steps of the stairs, and the nanny fussed about in despair.

"Batyushki are holy," the old woman mumbled when she saw us. - My little child, Nyutochka, ran to the noise and stumbled ... She became completely weak - just a little, somersaults, and without feelings. Oh, I'm afraid, as if the head did not break the stage. My baby is golden ... No worse - fall on the stairs. Here is a grief! And yet fainting for fainting is not good!

Despite all my objections and reminders about the damaged rib, Valentin nevertheless picked up the insensible Anna in his arms and carefully, like a child, carried him upstairs to the bedroom.

I again had a lot of work to do - it was necessary to provide medical assistance to all those who were suffering, among whom were joined the nurse who required heart drops.

When all the bandages, rubbings, compresses, drops and mixtures were finished and the inhabitants of the house settled in their bedrooms, I, armed with a lantern and just in case browning, went down to the yard to find the three-cornered horseman. After all, she, come on, so still and lying around where he dropped her.

No matter how disgusting this masquerade was, yet the old hat is another piece of evidence ... What a piece of evidence! If not for the investigator, so to the detective agent, or at worst, she herself could have done something for me.

But the cockedheads in the courtyard did not appear ... It disappeared, as it never did.

Having made this unpleasant discovery, I turned and walked back to the house, although maybe I should have walked around the park and checked to see if he was still hiding any unpleasant surprises.

A cautious person would probably do it, but I was exhausted to the last degree and dreamed only of falling into bed. It didn't leave me feeling that in our time everything that happens is happening with the sole purpose of delivering more trouble and trouble to a person. There's no time for walks under the moon ...

The next morning I went to Gireyevo in complete solitude (Anya and Saltykov, it seemed to me, would find the strength to take care of each other without me, and you will not leave the affairs of the hospital to chance).

On this day, the local doctor just visited the wounded, and, fortunately, I did not have to search for him in all the environs in order to take him to Privolnoye to see new patients.

Hastily and with a considerable amount of formalism having remade the most necessary things in the hospital, I asked the doctor to go with me to our victims. The damaged rib of Valentina disturbed me greatly, and Ani's fainting too often happens, which, however, is completely explainable by the circumstances. I didn't even remember about my own lump on the back of my head ...

The doctor promised to put himself at my complete disposal as soon as he completed the examination of the Giree patients. I have time to find the detective agent and tell him about the phenomenon of the ghost-riding yesterday. And I was so fascinated with the story of the black rider that I almost forgot about other, no less important facts, such as traces of an outside presence in the main chambers of Privolnoye and the attack on me in the greenhouse ...

As I expected, Mr. Stukalin listened to the message about the riding ghost with great interest (by God, an arrogant judicial investigator would not hurt to learn from a police agent attention to people).

However, with all the attention paid to me, it was difficult to understand how seriously the syskar took my words - he was in a cheerful mood.

- What do you say, madam! - Stukalin was amazed. - Headquarters captain, it appears, his shovel grist! A demon of this black-skinned one! Who would have thought ... That is what front hardening means. Neither the devil nor the devil is not afraid! And the cocked hat from the head of the rider is therefore fyut! And he himself spurred his horse and dra-la-la ...

Chuckling and making notes in a notebook, he asked and asked questions, and then suddenly let down an unexpected summary:

"I suppose this is one of the Gireevsky guests on horseback riding a horse under your windows ... Officers are usually good riders, even if they are serving in infantry or artillery." In the garrisons without a riding horse, the officer will not get anywhere, but not in a cab, while riding maneuvers.

In response, I expressed surprise (but not because I did not believe the detective agent, but because I wanted to make him talk and share some of the conclusions that secretive Stukalin probably already made for himself).

- It can not be! Where did such a splendid horse come from the wounded of the Gireevsky? I understand that officers usually ride, but after all their horses remained in the disposition of units, here they arrived light, without horses, without batmen and without subordinate subaltern-officers.

- Without horses? Oh, my dear, do you really think that gentlemen officers are sitting in the hospital day and night, not sticking their noses out of the limits of Gireev? - smiled a police agent. "So they all would have long ago strangled out of boredom!" The officers had already trodden the paths into the nearby villages and found everything that could entertain them. These beauties know perfectly well where you can get a horse for riding, drink, and not only moonshine, but also good wine from previous stocks (I found out that the innkeeper in Mytnino trades little by little), and where to find a female society.

- Is there really a women's society? - I was surprised. It seemed to me that in these deaf places, besides nurses and Anna and me, officers do not see any women ...

"Women's society is everywhere," Stukalin strictly replied. - For undemanding taste and demanding - someone has something to do with it ... Someone will be satisfied with drinking with bored soldiers, and someone with a romantic date with a local teacher or young lady with a post office. By the way, all the dead girls were rumored to have romances with officers. In their own ways, each of the girls tried to keep the love story secret, but in the village, you know that ... You can't hide the awl in the bag, although I cannot disclose my sources of information.

At last, Stukalin allowed himself to slip a little. To find out anything else, I decided to support this topic.

- Of course, if you open the sources, they can quickly run out. But if you act skillfully, it is not difficult to collect all the rumors circulating in the district. In such places, any news spread extremely quickly. Even if you sing songs in your own bathroom, then fuck off the hemp in the surrounding villages will discuss your vocal abilities.

In the heat of the moment, I did not even have time to think a little about my own words, and only having stated this wonderful maxim, I understood what kind of nonsense I was carrying. It was necessary, though late, to bite the tongue.

"That's right," Stukalin agreed gallantly. - Except that the local public does not sing in the bathrooms for lack of such. The village, you know, the level of comfort is extremely low.

Then the doctor came up and we all three went to Privolnoe.

My dear, I devoted myself to instructive reflections on how to build a fool full of people is usually not difficult, but I should still sometimes refrain from such practices.

CHAPTER 21

Anna

Since the captain who was hit by a horse suffered the most on the
eve of everything, Anya decided that she should take care of him
like a real sister of mercy - Valentin Petrovich came to these places
to recover from front wounds, and not to get new injuries.

But Valentine for his part tried to surround Anna with such attention
that they had to argue for a long time who would do the next service
to whom.

In general, in the presence of Anna, Valentine was becoming strange
- he turned pale, was silent and looked into her face with a long, sad
look. With Leleu, he was different - funny, boyishly mischievous,
joking, fooling around, but, being alone with the young widow of his
colleague, he immediately changed.

At first, it seemed to Anna that she simply reminds Saltykov of her
deceased sister and awakens sad memories in him - after all,
everyone knows that he once was madly in love with Nina. But soon
Anya felt that Valentine's actions were guided by something else.
What exactly, she was afraid to say even to herself, but from these
vague guesses, her heart sank sweetly.

While sitting at the table, they both could not eat a single piece, but
tried not to betray excitement and had some kind of endless
meaningless conversation over cooled cups with tea ...

Anna spoke in a secular tone about something, internally wondering
if her heart was beating too loudly. To her, the frantic heartbeat
seemed simply deafening. Suddenly Saltykov will understand that
she is unable to cope with anxiety, and will draw some wrong
conclusions from this? Men have a habit of strange interpretations of
events ...

Anya even felt some relief when Lelia returned to Privolnoe,
accompanied by a doctor and a Moscow detective, breaking them
with Saltykov tête-à-tête.

"Well, my dear child, what are we complaining about?" - the elderly doctor boomed with his low baritone. - Let's, my dear, leave the guests, gentlemen will excuse us, and retire for a medical examination. I just grab my sac bag, there, my beauty, a lot of what is needed in the doctoral part ... I remember, dear one, you all asked everyone before me to listen to your dolls with a pipe to hear if they have, say, wheezing in my lungs. And we installed pneumonia in one pupa and assigned it to bed rest, - the doctor burst out laughing and continued: "Now, madam, you don't play with dolls?

The doctor spoke to Anna in a calm, kind voice that is usually spoken to with small children. Anya thought that the old doctor, who knew not only her father, but her grandmother, and maybe her grandfather, was probably difficult to perceive the current owner of the estate as an adult lady, and not as a capricious, sickly little one, whom she had recently .

He called Anya a child and could not believe that she not only managed to get married, but also became a widow ...

"Nerves, my dear child, nerves," the village doctor repeated, feeling for the pulse of Anya's pulse. - I understand everything, beauty, war, early widowhood, gloom, tears at night ... Sadly, what can I say, very sad. But you have to make an effort, you have to live ... Fruit, walking, sleeping at night - that's what you, my child, need. I give you a sleeping pill, light, based on bromine, and droplets from the nerves. Drink, my dear, three times a day, seventeen drops for a glass. And for God's sake, no more suffering in the wrong moonlight. No, no, no, it is contraindicated. In peacetime, I would send you, my child, somewhere to the resort, to the waters ... To Kislovodsk, or even to Karlsbad or to Baden-Baden. But now you will not go to Nemchur, and I don't risk sending you to the Caucasus, it's painful times of troubles ... I repeat, fresh air, sound sleep and, moreover, men's society ... Believe the old man, this is the best and proven tool. Receive guests, be in public more often, allow yourself some pleasures of everyday life, and remove all illnesses as if you take it away with your hand ... Look at me - I'm over sixty already, and at the same time I am full of energy, and all because alien Yes ... And now, darling, let me leave you - I will go and see our hero. Something the captain also ached.

While the doctor was engaged in patients, Elena Sergeevna took the detective agent into the abandoned wing of the estate, where she presented him with fresh traces of an unknown person discovered on the eve of the house.

Mr. Stukalin was extremely interested and looked not only at the ballroom and the portrait gallery, but also at all other rooms. Then the detective and Elena Sergeevna, with a view of the conspirators, produced some mysterious manipulations, in particular, interfered with the gypsum solution in order to make impressions of traces left under the windows at the Saltykov fight with the night visitor (oddly enough, the marks of the feet on the damp earth still retained clarity) , and sprinkled with some powder found in the ballroom prints of others' hands.

The doctor, having completed his medical affairs, gratefully accepted the offer of a nanny to eat and drink a glass or two - good wines have become uncommon in modern times.

But even after the meal, he did not hurry to leave, waiting for Mrs. Croatowa, who was unable to tear herself away from the exciting detective affairs.

Anna had to go to the park, where Elena Sergeevna and Stukalin were crawling on their knees, looking at the traces of horse hooves with a magnifying glass, and hurrying her friend.

- Lelia, forgive me for the sake of God, that I distract you from such a fascinating occupation, but the doctor wants to talk with you about something. It scares me! Has he really given Mr. Saltykov a difficult diagnosis and is going to inform us about this? Suddenly, Valentine's ribs are broken? Or has internal bleeding opened? From hitting the horse hoof can happen different troubles. I'm afraid we pulled the captain into dangerous games ...

As it turned out, the doctor did not find Saltykov's fractures, although he couldn't exclude the presence of a crack in the rib, and prescribed tight chest bandages.

"Well, we did everything right yesterday," Lelya nodded in satisfaction. "I knew the dressing wouldn't hurt." Now poor Valentin needs special care and a constant sister of mercy. Since tomorrow a new girl arrives in Gireyevo instead of the deceased sister Eugenia, you, Anya, I relieve you of all worries at the Gireyevo hospital and entrust you with the health of the staff captain. He deserved that we do not leave him in the lurch.

Anna nodded and for some reason burst into thick paint.

"N-yes, nice, nice," the doctor smiled. - Now for the life of the captain you can be absolutely calm. With such a charming sister of mercy, he will quickly recover. But I, dear Elena Sergeevna, would like to talk with you about another patient. I am very concerned about the lieutenant Stepanchikov, very ...

A strong surprise was reflected on Lelia's face.

- Stepanchikov? What about him, doctor? It seemed to me that the lieutenant had fully grown up after being wounded, and only a slight limp reminds of his illness. Did he start having complications? Or has the wound opened?

- My dear, Stepanchikov has no complications with the wound, I am even sure that the limp will become completely invisible with time. The organs of movement are usually well restored after similar injuries. The thing is different. You see ...

The doctor fell silent and carefully glanced at Anna. Elena Sergeevna caught his eye.

"There can be no secrets from Anna Afanasyevna in this matter," she said. - Do not forget that Anya took over the duties of your assistant to care for the patient's weight and was quite good at this matter.

According to a nod, the doctor continued:

- So, about Stepanchikov. Hmmm ... He never fully recovered, but, how to put it more clearly ... His illness is not a physical one, but rather a mental one. You see, the war did not pass for him without a trace, and the poor young man partly lost his mental clarity.

- Do you want to say a little moved? - Elena Sergeevna asked in surprise.

"In vulgar language, yes," the doctor replied sadly. - Psychiatry is too thin a sphere, a specialist is needed here, and I, as you know, a simple rural general practitioner. I have often been able to treat measles and scarlet fever in the local children ... Well, I can somehow cope with a gunshot wound, I have some surgical experience, but mental disorders are not in my competence, madam. Nevertheless, even I managed to notice in Mr. Stepanchikov certain oddities, some inadequacy, so to speak.

- Inadequacy? Unhappy Stepanchikov! - Elena Sergeevna exclaimed. - How sad that the war with its cruelty, blood and mud has a fatal effect on the nerves of the front-line soldiers. And it seemed to me that the lieutenant reasonably reasonably, just his character leaves much to be desired.

- Persons suffering from schizophrenia, often argue quite sensibly, and not even without intellectual brilliance, just to hear. And not all can be attributed to bad character traits. I repeat, Stepanchikov needs to be consulted by specialists in psychiatry, I will insist on this, "the doctor continued. - Since you, dear Elena Sergeevna, are currently replacing Varvara Filippovna and have taken upon yourself the entire burden of administrative issues relating to the Gireevsky hospital ...

- Excuse me, doctor, I'm not going to argue with you at all and refuse the lieutenant in the necessary help. The only question is how urgent this assistance should be. Do you think that the lieutenant should be sent to Moscow to the bodies of psychiatry today or the case can suffer at least a few days? Varvara Filippovna is about to return literally from day to day, I will hand over the hospital's affairs to her and take the lieutenant myself to Moscow to show the best professors. But if you insist on resolving the issue immediately, you should think to whom we will be able to entrust such a delicate mission, and this is not so simple ...

"No, no, nothing extraordinary is happening yet," the doctor hastened to reassure. - I'm not saying that this young man is crazy. He just lost some common sense. Apparently, the consequences of the shock experienced at the front. This happens - the fragile youthful psyche is not easy to cope with severe shocks. It is not at all about putting a straitjacket on him today and sending him to a yellow house. I personally do not see any particular reason for this. But do not delay with the consultation of a psychiatrist, listen to my words.

With this, the doctor, who considered his mission accomplished, found it possible to leave.

Chapter 22

Helena

I admit, the words of the doctor made a very heavy impression. In my soul, sympathy for the young man, who had only recently not seemed to me particularly sympathetic, immediately began to glow. Poor, poor lieutenant!

Alas, starting bloody military actions, the rulers always believe that the war will be short, victorious, will cost a little blood and will strengthen the pride of the fatherland in the winners.

In fact, wars are stretched for years, and not all the blooming young men who went to the front under the brave marches and patriotic speeches, in order to become heroes, are destined to return. And those that return, remind rather tired, disappointed, too many old people who survived, than former boys.

I'm not talking about the fact that the younger generation of men are taught only to kill, kill and kill again, not knowing pity, not paying attention to other people's moans and blood, and consider killing to be personal prowess.

And then, when the world comes and the soldiers do not need their rulers, a lot of strong men who can only bring death to people, do not find the strength to stop and continue to kill and kill ... But for society they are no longer heroes, but criminals and the fiend of hell!

Sometimes, when there are too many such people, whole nations seem to go crazy, and human life turns out to be cheaper than half a million, and blood flows like water, and great kingdoms die, the peoples of which destroy themselves ... God forbid Russia to live to such times!

Having got rid of these apocalyptic visions with difficulty, I decided to think about everyday things that worried us all. Perhaps mystical phenomena in Privolnoye were the work of a distracted lieutenant Stepanchikov? Even a black rider ... Why would a young man suffering from schizophrenia not imagine himself a knight of the eighteenth century, say the Most High Prince Potemkin-Tavricheskim or noble robber Rinaldo Rinaldino from cheap bazaar books?

Having entered the image, the lieutenant could dress up in a cloak and an ancient cocked hat, jump on a horse and rush to God knows where, frightening all those who came along ... Who knows what a madman would think?

But only this demonic coloring on the horse's face - burning circles around the eyes, shining mane ... Since Conan Doyle's books were translated in Russia, even the lazy one knows - in order to give an animal an eerily-demonic look, you should use paint with phosphorus. , and then release the painted monster at night, when the composition starts to glow.

In principle, a person familiar with crime novels can paint not only the Baskervilles dog with a phosphorescent paint, but also a horse, a cow, a cat, a canary, anyone. And here's a ready satanic brat, spewing hellfire in the night. Practical and inexpensive. Only hardly points to the mental imbalance of the offender, on the contrary, testifies to a sly, quirky mind.

No, with hasty conclusions about Stepanchikov's involvement in our theatrical nightmares, it's not worth it to hurry.

I decided that I had a couple of free hours, and wondered where else to dig the earth in search of treasure and how to provide my own protection in order to avoid new attacks when the nurse distracted me from practical thoughts, loudly announcing:

- Gentlemen officers have come! Will you have to go to the living room or take it to the dining room right away? The samovar is still hot. By the way, I made pyrozhochkov baked with fungi. There is something to greet guests ...

On the threshold stood Krivitsky and Stepanchikov. Seeing the unfortunate young man, who, according to the doctor, lost his common sense, my heart trembled in fright. It remained only to hope that today something inadequate would not occur to him.

- Elena Sergeevna, we took it upon ourselves to go into Privolnoe, visit Anna Afanasyevna and the staff captain. They are said to have ached and you even invited doctors to them, "said Krivitsky, apologetically, more than ever like a fallen angel. - Do not drive away? You almost never stayed with us today, and Anna Afanasyevna didn't come to Gireevo at all. Cruel to deprive us of your society.

Oddly enough, Lieutenant Krivitsky completely lost his usual self-confident-arrogant tone, disguised as fake romanticism. Moreover, his voice sounded nervously, as if he really was afraid that he would be chased away like a lousy cat, tossed after his boot.

"Come on, gentlemen, come in," I squeezed out of myself, trying to be kind and hospitable. - I am very glad to you. I'm sure, and Anna Afanasyevna your visit will take great pleasure. I ask to the table. I suppose you will not refuse tea with fresh pies?

I sincerely hope that my words sounded with secular ease. In any case, I tried to give my face a more ingenuous and friendly expression than ever. Since you are in the same company with the alleged killer and the madman, it is better not to annoy them once again. Whatever Agent Stukalin told me, Mr. Krivitsky continued to remain on suspicion of me, and with Stepanchikov, in the light of the circumstances that had opened up, a certain fear was needed.

Gentlemen sat down at the table, and Krivitsky, to whom self-confidence was gradually returning, began, in his usual manner, to talk about this subject, interspersing it with radical remarks of a political nature. Stepanchikov also tried to insert a word or two into the conversation, but his friend rather unceremoniously silenced him.

- Elena Sergeyevna, Boris doesn't say a word to me! It's outrageous! - Stepanchikov sulked in a boyish way. - I am surprised, Krivitsky, that you took me with you at all.

- You can attribute this to your personal charm and ability to persuade. But do not open your mouth, my friend, if you have nothing to say. Elena Sergeevna is an educated lady, true emancipe, and your nonsense is not at all interesting to her. Only a silly nurse, peace be upon her, could listen with delight to all your nonsense.

Lieutenant Stepanchikov, already looking rather dull, completely limp under the strict gaze of a friend. I, frankly, was crooked by such unceremoniousness of Krivitsky. There was not enough yet for the young man, whose nerves were already upset by the war, offended before my eyes. Even if his behavior, according to the doctor, is somewhat inadequate, this is not a reason to expose the unfortunate Stepanchikov to ridicule.

A hot wave of sympathy rose in my heart, making me give the poor man more attention.

The lieutenant melted in the rays of my spiritual warmth, immediately like a peacock, fluffed up all the feathers and, to my surprise, began to flirt.

Well, I, of course, are older than young officers, but, apparently, not so much that they no longer see me as an object worthy of male attention. Of course, sooner or later I will also start to appear to young people as a sweet aunt, like Mrs. Zdravomyslova, but with this I am not in a hurry.

Anna, referring to ill health, never left her room, and Valentine nevertheless went down to the guests and sat with everyone at the table. Tight bandage on the ribs deprived him of his previous mobility. He could either turn the whole body, or turned only the face to the interlocutor, remaining in the same position, so he seemed like an Egyptian pharaoh from the ancient frescoes - head in profile, and chest in full face.

I do not know why, but it seemed to me that the painful state of the captain pleased Krivitsky. Why would it if the lieutenant had nothing to do with it? Intuition sometimes sets such tasks that you have to mobilize all your logic in order to at least somehow explain them ...

However, as Agent Stukalin repeatedly asserted, I am generally inclined to suspect Krivitsky of all mortal sins, perhaps that's why my inner voice tried to give me a new one to write for reflection.

When the two lieutenants finally got ready to take their leave, I went to take them through the park to the edge of the forest.

(Oddly enough, both decided to return to Gireyevo on foot, along a forest road. It seemed strange to me because Stepanchik had recently complained of pain in his injured leg, was limping and even refused to participate in the search for the missing girl, referring to the impossibility for him personally long pedestrian crossings. And the road to Gireyevo is not that close, two versts with a hook ...)

So that I did not stumble in the dark on the running tracks, Stepanchikov offered me a hand and quite gallantly led me through the park. However, sometimes he covered my palm, which was lying on his sleeve, with his free hand and squeezed it somewhat stronger than they required decency. Fearing that these are the very manifestations of inadequacy, I pretended not to notice anything.

We were already approaching the old gate, and I was about to say goodbye to the gentlemen officers, when ahead the moonlit silhouette of a woman appeared, walking slowly towards us. It was amazing! Where would a stranger lady come from?

Peering, I realized that she was dressed in the fashion of forty years ago. It suddenly seemed to me that this is the former owner of the estate, the old countess, is walking along the alleys in the direction of her grave ... After all, the countess was depicted in portraits in similar outfits.

My heart pounded deafeningly, and my palm, covered by Stepanchikov's hand, instantly became icy and trembled like an aspen leaf. I was ready to read some prayer and only for a moment thought that in this case it would be more effective - a prayer to the Guardian Angel or "Our Father".

"Holy Angel, come to the damning of my soul and the passion of my life, do not leave a sinner to me," I managed to say to myself when the woman approached so much that it became possible to recognize her.

No, life in Privolnoy sooner or later will drive me crazy!

It was the sorceress Sychiha dressed up, probably in a dress, once presented to her by the hostess. There was no headscarf on her head this time, the old woman's gray hair was arranged in an elaborate old-fashioned hairstyle with a small laced headdress. However, there was nothing particularly strange in this, because Melanya, when she was young, served as a maid or as a maid at the Countess, and she was probably trained in quafer skills.

Sychiha came close to us and silently, with a withering gaze, began to drill our faces, turning her eyes from one to the other. In the hands of the old woman was some kind of dark object, which she tried to hide behind her back, covering the folds of a fluffy skirt.

- Swine, Satan! Sgin, Sgin! - she gave a hand to Stepanchikov and suddenly, staring into the eyes of Krivitsky, she extended her hand and gave her the load to him.

- Take, Iris, dropped! Said Melanya in an ominous tone.

I involuntarily looked down and realized that she was holding an old cocked hat. In this moth-eaten hat, our black ghost rode under the windows of the manor. After the clash with the captain, he dropped his exotic headdress, and I, no matter how hard I tried, could not find him later ... So, who picked up and kept an important piece of evidence - Sychikha's grandmother! Well, of course, we always forget about the old woman who lives in the park hut, and she probably sees and hears a lot of things.

But why did Sychiha bring her hat to the attacker, and not the policeman or the mistress of the estate?

Krivitsky, staring at Melanie in horror, did not answer or even move to take the three-cornered hat from her. Therefore, I had to take the hat out of the hands of the old healer, not waiting for the bewitched Boris to wake up. It's amazing how I could stand on my feet and move my hands, but my fingers dug into the evidence very tightly ...

- And you, child, remember about the water! - gently said, looking at me, Sychiha to the complete bewilderment of the officers. - And wait, as it was ordered to you. Soon you will wait. Come to me tomorrow, I'll whisper to you!

With these words, Melania turned and wandered to her gatehouse, in the window of which the faint light of the candle left on the window-sill flickered.

- Who is this crazy witch? - nervously asked Stepanchikov. "And what did she want from us?" What kind of shit did she give you, Elena Sergeevna? Old hat? And what water did she mumble about? Why do you have to remember about water? Does the old hag really want you to drown? You do not listen to her!

"Oh, lieutenant, you asked me too many questions at once." But I don't know what to answer them, "I sighed feignedly, although I understood much more than I wanted to show. As, however, and Krivitsky, judging by the expression of his face ...

We have already reached the old gate, and perhaps it was time to say goodbye.

"Well then, Honorable Lady, the audience is over?" - threw with ironic grin Krivitsky and intricately, in the old style bowed. A three-necked hat would have come to him for the sake of completeness, but it was already possible, but I had already managed to pull her closer to me and would not return Krivitsky for any price.

Stepanchikov, taking advantage of the fact that he had long since seized my hand, shook her goodbye. I flippantly responded to the shake, after which I couldn't release my hand from Stepanchikov's tenacious fingers for a long time. Fortunately, even the longest farewell cannot last indefinitely.

- See you tomorrow, gentlemen! - I waved after the officers with a cocked hat, which I was afraid to let go of. Surely, Krivitsky in his heart curses himself that he had missed such a valuable hat, and would have given dearly to take possession of it. - I hope, on the way to Gireyevo no more unpleasant incidents will happen to you. Bon Voyage!

The officers moved along the dark road to the edge of the forest, and Krivitsky suddenly dragged in an old army song, to which the military, especially the cadets, often march:
Hello, summer residents, Hello, summer women! Summer maneuvers have already begun long ago.
And Stepanchikov picked up:
Ley, my song, Beloved, Boule-Boule-Boule, Baklazhechka my marching.
I felt my heart clench. Again, a wave of memories flew and poured me from head to toe. And the dacha on the Khimka River, and dancing with the cadets, and Valechka Saltykov with his young tender face and girlish blush, and the laughing eyes of Ivan Malashevich - everything flickered before my mind's eye ...

Suddenly it seemed to me that the late Ivan marched alongside the lieutenants to the forest and, famously twisting his cap, sang along with his soft, hoarse voice:
Shaped boots, Asterisks, Three stars, As on the best cognac. Ley, my favorite song, Boules Boules Boules, Bottles of official wine ...
- Chur me, chur! - I whispered, crossing. - Forgive me, Vanechka, that she so rarely remembered you and that for a long time she held a grudge against you, at the deceased ... But please, I don't have to come to me at night! Forgive and sleep in peace!

And from afar still came the words of the cadet song:
Lysya, my beloved song, Tsok-tsok-tsok, Podkovochki knock on the pavement ...
Chapter 23

Anna

Anya barely waited until the annoying officers, who had sat up at a party until late in the evening, would leave her house. Thank God, Lelia kindly assumed the duties of a hostess, and Anya did not have to go down to the table, pour tea out of a samovar, and entertain Krivitsky and Stepanchikov.

But as soon as the door closed behind the guests, Anya, who had time to rest and even take a short nap, jumped out of bed and dressed, hoping that Valentine had not left the dining room. There was no time to do her hair. Anya simply combed her hair and tied it in a girlish way with a ribbon, knowing that it was her face (although for the widow, perhaps, it was somewhat defiant, but she's at home, so she combed her hair simply, at home ...).

Running down the stairs to the first floor, she, as expected, found Valentine in the dining room. He sat thoughtfully over a cup of cold tea and spattered a spoon in his fingers.

- Anna Afanasyevna! - At the sight of Ani, Valentina's gloomy face brightened and lit up with a gentle smile. - How glad I am that you feel better!

For some reason, Anna was ashamed to talk about herself and asked:

- And where is Lelya?

- Elena Sergeyevna escorted guests and went to her room. She had a hard day again. She works a lot here and gets very tired.

"But Lelya only considers such a life to be real," Anya retorted, and suddenly, unexpectedly for herself, said: "Valentin Petrovich, today I am terrified that I want to drink wine." I hope you do not find my desire completely wild and inappropriate?

Saltykov jumped up.

- What are you, Anna Afanasyevna! The desire of the ladies - the law. Just order! To get a good wine in this wilderness is a difficult task, but solvable. I will immediately go to the village, find the innkeeper and make him open the bins. I know that the old miser hides something.

- No, no, such difficulties are not needed at all. Just take a candle and take me to the cellar. In my bins, too, there is plenty to choose from.

In the company of captain Ania, it did not seem dangerous even to travel to the wine cellar. Although, remembering the mysterious story that happened here with Lelya, she still missed Valentine inside, giving him the right to choose, while she herself remained at the door. God forbid, the door will shut again, and the spare key will not be in a secret place - Anya did not want to sit all night in the cellar, even shoulder to shoulder with Saltykov.

Upon entering the door, Valentine whistled:

- Wow, Anna Afanasyevna, you have a real treasure hidden here! At the present time - just a treasure, Ali Baba's cave!

"Yes, there were much more hidden treasures in my house than I could have expected," Anna agreed. - Choose soon and go upstairs. It's dark and scary here.

"Next to me, you have nothing to fear, I will not allow anyone to offend you," Valentine answered gallantly, grabbing a bottle of light French wine for Ani and brandy for himself. - Well, now we drown your fear in the glass. Soothe my sorrows, so to speak ...

Then they sat at the table, put out the kerosene lamp and lit the candles, and talked, talked, talked ... Anya slowly shed a tart ruby liquid from her glass, admired the candlelight reflected in Saltykov's eyes and told him about the late father, about Nina, about childhood, about the almost forgotten high-school girlfriends and teachers.

She didn't want to talk about Alyosha for the first time. Strangely enough, but it seemed to Anya that the image of her husband, always invisibly hovering somewhere nearby, began to go farther and farther away and melt in the mist, taking her pain to the same ... And talking about other dear to the dead men did not cause pain.

Valentine was not a stranger, he perfectly remembered both Nina, and their Moscow home, and all of their surroundings. Ani's words found his most responsive response. Honestly speaking, no one ever treated her with such attention. For some reason, other people did not find anything particularly interesting in her stories.

- If you knew, Anya, with what warmth and tenderness I remember your family. This is one of the best and favorite memories of my youth. I then had little joy - the cadet school, the barracks, the drill, rough military manners ... And rare vacation days, when I could come to your house like a fairy tale. Until now, your cozy living room with a soft light of lamps, with a grand piano, with flowers, with pink curtains that close it from the weather and evil reigning outside the windows, and is before your eyes. In your house I was happy, I lived in hopes. Then it seemed that there was a lot of good, light, ahead, just to be patient to wait for it. And what awaited me was the officer's shoulder straps, service in a small dusty garrison with its stupefying boredom and the same drill ... That's just the memory of a distant sweet home in which lovely people live, warmed the soul. And everything

Anya wanted to ask: "Did you love Nina very much?", But she said nothing, feeling that this question could not be asked now. And Valentine, without looking into her eyes, continued:

- Then there was another garrison, and another, and then - war, trenches, exploding shells, bayonet attacks, splashes of someone's blood on the face, dead friends falling under your feet, making it difficult to run ... I dreamed of your pink curtains not letting House night dusk, how about a miracle. If you only knew what such visions of the past mean in the trenches, under enemy fire! Anya, my dear, I am talking nonsense, but you will understand what you cannot tell with words. You must understand me, I know. Now you for me are the personification of that beautiful and inaccessible dream.

Saltykov raised his eyes, and Anya noticed that there were tears in them. It was so amazing, like a piece of granite was crying. And the staff captain suddenly knelt down and began to cover Anina's hands with hurried gentle kisses.

Anya thought that Valentine's hands should be taken away from Valentine, he was too forgotten, but there was no strength to push him away. Yes, and the thought that she was a widow, who was in mourning for her dead husband and should not allow herself any liberties, seemed to her hypocritically out of place at such a moment.

It would be very cruel to offend a good, kind and unhappy person, making him even more unhappy. Anya was silent, feeling how her thoughts were confused in her head, and her heart was torn apart by tenderness towards this officer, whose existence in this world she did not even recall just a couple of months ago.

"Anya, I love you," Valentine whispered, buried his face in her palm. - I love to madness, if you forgive me so hackneyed expression. But now any words are empty words, they cannot convey my feelings. I would say that I am ready to throw everything at your feet if I did not understand how ridiculous the infantry officer is, saying that he can throw something at the feet of his beloved. But let me at least throw my life on your altar, my deity, without you, it is not my joy. Understand - my whole life belongs to you without reserve, my precious, beautiful ...

Anya was silent. Blood was pounding in her temples with heavy waves, and it was also difficult for her to find the right words. And really, what can be said with empty, worn out words? She just knelt beside Valentin and kissed his bowed head, feeling the faint smell of chypre from her hard hair. From this almost forgotten male smell, Ani's fingers trembled and her dizziness began.

"As if fainting happened again," she thought. - Fall on the floor, rolling his eyes, and Valentine will have to mess with me. What a shame! "

But Saltykov suddenly, despite the pain in the damaged ribs, easily lifted Anya up in his arms and carried him somewhere ...

Chapter 24

Helena

That night I could not fall asleep again for a long time, despite all my tiredness. Today I had something to think about - fate throws up such facts for reflection not every day. However, insomnia has become so familiar that I did not feel the same discomfort.

When at last the dorm almost overcame me, I suddenly heard careful steps in the corridor. Someone tried to go quietly, but my hearing now caught every sound with such sophistic suspiciousness that I immediately understood that there was someone in the corridor. Self-proclaimed ghosts never left us alone! Forgive me, Lord, but I will have to open fire!

Pulling the Browning out from under the pillow, I, also trying to be inaudible, slightly opened the door of my bedroom and looked out.

On the tiptoe, with a candle in his hand, a man walked ... I, perhaps, would have had time to be frightened, considering him to be another ghost or raider, and prepare to shoot or pray, but at that moment I recognized the stranger. It was Saltykov. I breathed a sigh of relief.

Well, no wonder that, taking us under the protection and protection, he goes around the house at night - quite a natural act for every sane person. But why did he drag a bottle of wine with him, which he carefully pinches under his arm? Probably incomprehensible to us, mere mortals, front-line manners ... And by the way, if you think about it with your mind, it's very understandable!

I decided to wait until it disappears, so as not to creak once again the door and not to give Valentine to understand that he is being watched. That would put both me and him in a very awkward position.

Meanwhile, the captain reached the room of Anna, without knocking, but observing the previous caution and trying not to make any noise, opened the door and disappeared behind it. Soon I heard a muffled laugh, not only male but also female.

Well, perhaps, and this night visitor is better to consider a ghost. As the nanny says, something was lashed about ... Yes, yes, exactly! Although I personally have nothing against ghosts that can make a grieving woman laugh. Moreover, it seems to me lately that in Anna it is again possible to discern the pretty girl who she was before, until grief overwhelmed her whole being. If this is the influence of some ghosts, then they honor and praise.

I hope only, by the way about the ghosts, that the late lieutenant Chigarev will not appear today in Privolnoye, like the Stone Guest in Donna Anna's house, and will not address the head captain with the words: "Give me your hand!" ...

The next morning I gathered in Gireyevo - today, perhaps more than ever, Anna herself is able to communicate with her spirits, and my help will be simply superfluous here.

But before plunging into the day-to-day cares of the hospital, you need to come to visit the old woman Sychihe, it's not for nothing that she called me. I wonder what kind of mot she is going to whisper to me? It was simply impossible to postpone the visit to the guardhouse for the evening and leave for Gireyevo, without knowing anything. By golly, I would not have waited for the evening, having died of curiosity at the hands of the nurses of Gireev ...

Heading through the park to the gatehouse, I ran into the alley with Saltykov, who was in some unexplainable circumstances of sleepy reverie. However, at the sight of me, he somewhat revived, but his very revival seemed gloomy to me.

- Helen, tell me, just be honest, hand on heart - you do not find my behavior the greatest folly? - he asked melancholy.

Valentine did not explain what exactly he means by stupidity, but he didn't need long explanations.

"Don't you think so yourself?" - I pushed him slightly to make it more talkative.

"I," Valentine hesitated a little, "I ... am afraid that this is exactly what I think." But I can't help it. Anna ... She is so dear to me ... And I was so selfish that ... Damn, how difficult it is to talk about it.

- You know, if we are talking about Anna, - I realized that for some reason it became difficult for me to speak, but I still tried to find words. "This young lady has never done anything stupid in her entire life, has always been too virtuous and reasonable, and maybe she should have done something like that." Stupidity so adorn life! And it depends on you that your stupidity does not turn out to be irreparably bitter for Ani, but, as far as I know you, you will never allow that to happen.

After such soul-saving words, having considered the mission of the resonator entrusted to me exhausted, I considered myself entitled to retire.

Now all my thoughts are focused on the park hut. I had literally two steps left, but I still puzzled over how to address the old healer, crossing the threshold of her house.

I thought that the nickname Sychiha was too rude and offensive, to call just by name a person who suits me almost as a grandmother, is also incongruous, Melanie's patronymic name was unknown to me. And an appeal like madam or madam with reference to the village would be very strange ...

Having decided, if possible, to do without any recourse, and in extreme cases, to name the healer with my aunt (the word grandmother would emphasize her age and could offend), I knocked on the door of the gatehouse.

"Come in openly," Melanie's cheerful voice came to me. I crossed the threshold.

Like all estate buildings, the gatehouse, built according to European architectural canons, did not look like an ordinary village hut, not only outside but also inside. Small but graceful windows and hearth, built in French style of rough stones and decorated with indispensable cast-iron curls, made the house look like a dwelling of wealthy peysan somewhere in the Marne or Loire Valley. The whole situation obviously got here from the manor house and even claimed some luxury.

(Especially when you consider that the furniture in the county estate, which had been standing for a long time without master's supervision, cracked, soaked with dust, rose, and the lacquer on it grew dull and peeling. And here everything was well matched, and each chest of drawers glittered with the brilliance of waxed sides and brass handles and was a complete contrast with the desolation in the master's chambers.)

Under the windows, a carved oak wooden bench stretched along the wall, obviously giving out foreign origin with its nobility, nadraen copper pots crowded on the kitchen shelf and there were plates of good porcelain with golden monograms, and the shelf over the hearth was decorated with Saxon dishes with a characteristic cobalt ornament. Yeah, the owners of the estate old Melania spoiled, do not say anything ...

On the hook above the fire was hung a pot in which something gurgled, spreading the pungent smell of spicy herbs. However, the countless bunches of dry plants and roots, suspended on beams under the ceiling, also filled the local atmosphere with unusual flavors.

A black cat, already familiar to me, sleeping peacefully on a bench, jumped to the floor when I appeared, stretched and began to look at me with unkind yellow eyes with interest. I'm afraid I did not cause him much sympathy.

"Hello," I greeted respectfully, laying out a box of chocolates from the Einem factory on the table in front of her. "I brought you some sweet tea."

The nanny, I remember, said that Melanya did not shrink from small gifts, so I did not dare to come to her empty-handed and picked up a present. But she waved chocolate away, grumbling:

- And, konfekty ... This is a masterly venture, empty! You, my dear, go here and sit down. Listen to me, old woman, I will tell you. Those two that were with you yesterday are dark people. Everyone has his own evil.

I did not doubt this without the warnings of old Melania.

"You don't make friendship with them," she continued. - Famously naklishish.

"But otherwise you will not understand what is on their mind," I replied to the healer. "If you know what the enemy is planning, you are already armed against his wiles."

"Well, it's your business," the old woman nodded her head. - But remember about the water. Will fit still.

This water was given to her! Did she call me today just to remind me of water again?

Melanya looked at me sternly from under a low-bound dark shawl. Today she was again in a peasant's headscarf and shapeless old clothes. And it's a pity - it occurred to me involuntarily that in the dresses of her deceased mistress she would be in harmony with the interior of this unusual place much better.

- You're a count treasure looking for? - asked suddenly after a long, sustained almost by Stanislavsky pause, Melania.

I flinched. All unimportant thoughts immediately flew out of my head. Amazing This ancient grandmother, who seated in her little house, is known more than anyone. Well, the conversation took such an interesting turn that I did not consider it necessary to reject it.

- Yes, I am looking for! I believe that the grandfather's treasure would be very helpful for a young widow, who was in a very deplorable situation. The late lieutenant Chigarev left almost nothing to Anna. The girl has nothing to live for!

- Well, I believe you don't see your self-interest in someone else's good.

Melanya continued to drill at me with a burning look, which made me uncomfortable. The cat also looked at me with a burning look, probably having adopted the skills of his mistress.

For a second I waver - I wanted to quickly leave this strange and slightly scary house. And yet my ineradicable curiosity did not allow to interrupt the conversation.

"The treasure of the count is conspiratorial," the healer finally whispered. - He would not give anyone hands. The fact that you have a storage room in your hands has not yet promised that you will easily find the treasure. Treasures, my mother, look for a head, not a shovel. And it is necessary to go to the cause, pray and help by asking our Father in heaven. Remember, another time you go to search for a treasure, take with you a white wax candle, spryn-grass and the grass "Petrov cross" so that the unclean harm will not cause ...

- "Petrov cross"? - I asked shakily.

Easy to say - take it ... Lord, where can I get such an exotic plant, if I don't even know what it looks like? My knowledge in the field of botany, learned in my native gymnasium, where I did not differ in particular diligence, helped me to distinguish plantain from dandelion and cornflower from chamomile, but "Petrov cross" ... And spryn-grass ... a natural scientist, and even then, it's not for everyone - the masters of scientists have a very narrow specialization, and the geologist botanist is not a colleague ...

The old woman looked at me indulgently and, climbing onto a bench, took two bunches of dry herbs tied with a hard thread from the ceiling. Throwing these little brooms in front of me on the table, she continued:

- Search for treasure is necessary only with good intention. Give a pledge to convey all that you find to the true owner, and take yourself only what Anna offers. Remember, taking the treasure, you can not talk and you can not look back. And never sleep where the treasure is buried, the unclean will blink ...

- Oh, aunty, you say so, as if I have already found this treasure, or at least I know exactly where it lies, - I could not resist a pragmatic remark, but immediately bit my tongue.

- And you will not know, orca, until you remove the spell. He was talking, treasure, it was said to you. Remember: put a knife in holy water, draw a circle, draw on all four sides of the world, and put four candles in it. You'll light the light on them, and every candle, like every side, bow to the belt and say the words cherished ... You take a pencil and write after me, it will fly out of memory. After the test, learn, and burn the paper at midnight and scatter the ashes in the water. On, write!

Melanya handed me a piece of thick yellowish paper and, bending low, whispered:

- "The four apostles of the Evangelist, guardians of God's secrets, Matthew, Mark, Luke, John, cleanse this place of the curse imposed on him." This prayer is eternal, and if you find treasure and get it from the earth, say above it: "The Lord God is ahead, the guardian angel is behind, the holy evangelists on the sides, I will repay you, Father of Heaven, glory! Protect me, name, with your power from the devil's wiles. Free this treasure from a heavy spell. " But before taking the treasure, read our Father over him forty more times.

- Is it really necessary to read a prayer forty times? - I was surprised.
- Maybe three times is enough?

"Forty," Melana snapped. - Do not be lazy, a servant of God, and not evil. And most importantly - do not look back! Do not look at what is behind your back!

"But I was attacked right from the back when I was searching for something," I could not help but tell Melanie what I was hiding from others. - Here, I still have not had a lump, they hit me so ...

Melanya disassembled the hair on the back of my head and applied a rag with a pungent-smelling liquid to the bruise. Maybe it seemed to me, but I felt the bump under the rag shrinking ...

- You listen to what I say! - strictly declared Melanya. - Do not stop! If you do everything according to your mind, no one can approach you with evil. Feet do not incur. The main thing is not to turn around, do not give strength to the enemy! And when you bring the treasure home, sprinkle it with holy water, hold each thing over the flame of a candle, and you will find gold there, so put it in running water for another day. So the treasure from the spell and filth will be cleansed. Voditsa evil wash away.

- But after all in flowing water gold things can carry away a current, - I was not kept.

"That's for you, darling, head, and given, so that you can think about it in advance," answered the old woman and made it clear that the audience was over.

I left the lodge with very strange feelings. Perhaps the only thing left for me, according to the testament of Anton Pavlovich Chekhov, is to rejoice in the consciousness that it could be worse.

Chapter 25

Anna

In the morning, Anna woke up late, unusually calm and peaceful. On the eve it cleared up again, and now a bright summer sun came through the curtains and leaves of trees growing under the windows into the room.

In bed, she was alone, but the pillows and a crumpled sheet kept the contours of the second body and the faint smell of male cologne. Anya buried her face in a pillowcase, catching that smell again and again, evoking so many memories.

She was with a man this night ... Forgetting about her mourning, about her late husband, who was going to keep her loyalty for the rest of her life. This is sin, sin! But does a sinner feel so good, so peaceful? Is the sun smiling at them?

Maybe the sin is not so painful, since the Lord, who knows all our actions and thoughts, let him go? And does pity and love have such sinful feelings?

Anya stretched lazily, then slowly got up, felt her shoes for her feet, went to the balcony door and flung open the doors. A light summer breeze blew into her face. The great sinner would have to be broken in place by the thunder of heaven, and on Ani, on her face, warm rays and tender blows play ...

No, nothing can be vicious in love!

Anya was standing in the doorway to the balcony, without risking to lean on the balcony lattice, - Lelya was right in asserting that this lattice was an unreliable and even dangerous thing because of decay. Suddenly, from somewhere below, a kind of shaggy object soared, flew over the railing and plopped down to Anya's legs. It was a bouquet of wild flowers, tightly tied with a long blade of grass. And it was easy to guess with whose hand the bouquet was thrown at Anya's feet. Picking up the flowers, she spun around the room with them, and then, casually grabbing her hair with a ribbon, went down to drink coffee, without letting go of the bouquet.

There was no large vase at the bottom, I had to use a broken-faced earthenware jug with forget-me-nots stuck from the kitchen. Typing in a barrel under the gutter, Anya arranged flowers on the table, and then sat down with her cup closer to them.

- Elena Sergeyevna got up? She asked the nanny, hiding her shining eyes.

- What about? "In the morning, I ate some coffee early, and for business, I suppose Giraevo has been in control for a long time," the nurse answered.

- And Valentin Petrovich? - Anya continued inquiries, feeling how her heart sank at the mention of Valentine's name.

- Also rose before dark. I fed him breakfast. He got hungry, hearty, for the night - he ate the egg, and the pies. It is a well-known business, a strong, healthy man, even on his face and wounded ... I cooked for him even cereals for satiety. The food is simple - it is always healthy, and it is more full in it. Now Valentine Petrovich is walking in the park. You, Nytochka, go to him?

- What for? - Anya asked carefully.

- Well, so why? - Nanny slyly squinted. - Maybe that will be done by you, God forbid. Not the same age you widow, orca.

Anya wanted to reply to the nanny something stern to suppress such hints, but she could not find an answer and only blushed deeply.

Before lunch, Anya did not see Valentina and was a little afraid of meeting him. How to know that she will now read in his eyes? Maybe a conviction?

But in the eyes of Saltykov she read only tenderness. Anne was again light and happy in her soul.

Elena Sergeevna returned from Gireevo tired, but, as always, active.

"Ah, gentlemen, I have completely forgotten about the counting of the laundry received from the laundresses. Today I did a spot check and missed two sheets, a tablecloth and three towels. Varvara Filippovna will be very unhappy, "she complained straight off. - But what to do, I have more important things to do today. Concerning the papers of your grandfather, Anyuta.

With this allegorical phrase, Elena Sergeevna was going to make it clear to Anna that she was going to look for treasure again. However, Saltykov, whom Anya talked about the found records of his grandfather and great-great-grandfather on the eve, could not restrain himself and asked directly:

- Will you be looking for a treasure hunt, Helen? Count treasures discover think?

- So you already know everything? - Elena Sergeevna glanced at Anya, however, without much reproach. "Well, well, maybe it's for the best." How much will we hide from you? Yes, gentlemen, I myself am surprised at my own stubbornness in this matter, but, speaking secretly, I am going to spend ... hmm ... how better to put it, some kind of mystical act.

- Mystical? - Anya was surprised. - You always stood on rational positions and was an ardent opponent of all mysticism.

"You see, I do not exclude that there can be some rational grain in mystical rites," Elena Sergeevna expressed an unexpected thought. - If you do not know where to start, you can start with mysticism, anyway. In extreme cases, we can consider it a fun game. This morning I was visiting your healer Melania Sychova. She thinks your grandfather's treasure is conspiratorial.

Anna and Valentine stared at her in all eyes. Yes, for a progressive-minded lady, Elena Sergeyevna spoke a little strangely today ...

"And you believe that the treasure is conspiratorial?" - Anya asked with surprise, hoping that Lelia is about to make the whole thing a joke, as usual.

"Who knows, maybe the one who has spoken, and yet, as it were, Melanya herself would not have spoken to him in her younger years," Elena Sergeevna continued to surprise everyone. - In any case, the old woman insists that you should read a certain spell, without which the treasure will not open. Well, I read it, I hope it will not be worse. Only, Valentine, please make sure that Lieutenant Stepanchikov does not hang around anywhere. He literally didn't give me a pass today in Gireyevo, dragged me like a tail and, I am afraid, wouldn't have decided to finally show up on Privolnoye with a friendly visit. It is very undesirable if he finds me behind the fortune-teller. And then try to attack from the back ...

With these mysterious words about the attack from behind, Elena Sergeevna extracted two bunches of dry herbs from somewhere and hooked them to her belt.

Anya and Valentine looked at each other. Lelia was clearly out of her mind. Well, also, that she does not want to demonstrate her mystical actions to her acquaintances, this is just explainable. But why is she afraid of being attacked from behind? All this is strange, strange! Probably, fatigue and chronic sleep deprivation affects.

Valentin, in order to calm her down, walked around the house with a watch and reported that Stepanchikov was not observed anywhere. That was the way.

Lelia asked the cook a large bread knife, sprinkled it from the bottle, drew a circle on the porch of the house with a knife, and asked Valentine to determine more precisely where it was north.

- It seems that in the forest you need to look at the moss covering the trunks of trees if you are looking for the north. But there's not much moss on the park lindens, "she said apologetically, standing with a knife in her hand above her circle.

Intrigued, Valentin drew a small compass in a suede case from his pocket and indicated where the cardinal points are located. Lelya put appropriate marks on the ground and placed four white candles, after which she entered the circle, began to beat bows and whisper the words of an unknown prayer that remembers the names of the holy evangelists.

- Helen, with such numbers you need to speak in front of the pilgrims in Sergiev Posad. If you ever, do not bring it, Lord, you will be ruined, "Saltykov chuckled," you can collect some good alms by presenting your mystical sketches on the square in front of the monastery.

"I would ask to keep such comments in the future," said Lelya. "If I've done it all, it's not at all to amuse anyone." Well, gentlemen, now we will wait for help from the guardians of the secrets of God, but for now I suggest we raise a glass for our luck.

"Oh, you need to go downstairs to the cellar for the wine," Anya blamed guiltily. - Everything that we brought yesterday is already over ...

"Nothing, I'll come down," Elena Sergeevna grabbed a candle and a bunch of keys. - Only if I stay there too long, go to my rescue. Suddenly the door will lock itself again or something else will happen ...

"Lelia, take the grass off your belt," Anya advised. - That you walk like a savage. They bother you.

- No, no, these are not simple herbs. This spryn-grass and "Petrov cross." Sychiha promised that I would receive help and protection from these herbs.

Anya and Saltykov looked after Lele with some regret. It simply could not fail to notice all the oddities that manifested themselves in her behavior.

"Lelia has always been so sensible, although she was considered somewhat eccentric," Anna finally spoke. - I do not understand what is happening to her now. She works too much here and gets very tired, she doesn't get enough sleep, and she was pretty nervous. But I did not think that it would all affect her mind so much ... How can we look into her husband's eyes if Lelya develops mental illness? And we will be guilty of this ...

While waiting for Elena Sergeevna, Anna and Saltykov went into the dining room and prepared glasses. But Lelia with the promised bottle of wine did not come and did not come.

"Perhaps I'll have to go down to the cellar and see what happened there," Valentine said. "It's time Elena has come back ..."

- I'm with you! - Anya exclaimed, not wanting to be alone. - Is there something happening again related to mysticism?

- Why is it necessarily related to mysticism? - Valentine shrugged. "Maybe Lena just twisted her leg." Or the flame of her candle was blown out by a draft, and she slowly, gropingly, looks for wine in the dark.

Chapter 26

Helena

I went down to the wine cellar, occupied with my thoughts - where could this damned treasure still be ... I never thought that treasure hunting, which before had seemed to me to be just a topic worthy of the pen of Stevenson, would be equally exciting in real life.

So, I did everything to break the spell's guarding treasure. If the old Sychiha's spell really works, the treasure should somehow open up to us ... But how? Well, yes, the higher forces will probably come up with something themselves.

Lord, what am I talking about? Did the strange places here have a detrimental effect on my psyche and I'm slowly losing my mind? And I, after all, had the nerve to be proud of my sanity!

Okay, now there is a small practical matter in turn - to choose from innumerable stocks a bottle with a suitable drink for our company, but you can poise your mysterious secrets with your mind and then, at your leisure.

Pinging a bunch of keys, I inserted a familiar key with a twisted head into the lock and opened the door. The flame of my candle wavered and stretched into the cellar. Just in case, I laid in the doorway, closer to the lintel, a bunch of keys - it will not let the door slam from the draft.

This time, the interior decoration of the cellar could have been considered much better - besides the light of a candle, which slightly dispersed the darkness, thin snaps of light from small vents under the ceiling also penetrated it. On the street, after all, a white day ...

I looked at the walls, lined with huge old barrels. They are probably installed here in ancient times. Probably the notorious Anin Schur remembers them, and even with his grandfather, the Balkan hero, they were definitely ... Oh, mummies, these barrels remind me something ... And I already understand what it is!

And here before my eyes, as if on the screen of a cinema, the drawing of the late graph, the one with the mysterious circles, turned around (I looked at this paper so often that I could reproduce it even with my eyes closed).

Well, of course, if these barrels were drawn on the diagram in the form of circles (and how else? Cylinders would have made the treasure's solution too obvious!), Then everything is the same! How many are there? One, two, three, fifth, eighth ... By God, if the count has not buried his grandfather's treasure in his own wine cellar, then I can be considered a complete idiot (and I want to believe that it is not so!).

However, perhaps some reason to suspect me of idiocy will still be found - otherwise such an obvious thing would have occurred to me earlier. Wow, look for treasure anywhere, not remembering what is literally under the very nose!

Feeling how my thoughts were tangled from feverish excitement, I rushed upstairs ...

- Lelia, we were already waiting! They wanted to go look for you in the cellar, they thought something happened again, "Anya said with a quiet reproach. - And where is the wine? Did you forget to take the bottle?

- What? Wine? To hell with the wine! - The confusion in my head was fraught with a fit of inert speech, and it took me a few seconds and two or three deep breaths to get myself together. - Valentine, take the spade. Let's go to the cellar, my dear. I think I know where Anin's grandfather had buried a casket with the gifts of the empress.

"God, Lenochka, did your mystical rites and prayers from north to south really work?" Did you manage to spell the conspired treasure? - Saltykov chuckled incredulously.

"Then, then, we will talk about everything afterwards," I interrupted rudely of an old friend, confident that now everything will be forgiven for me. - I myself am still not completely sure of anything, but let's still be naughty! So, I have a white candle, spryn-grass and "Petrov cross" with me ... Yes, remember, while we search for treasure, you cannot talk and look back. Anya, you hear, this is especially important - in no case do not look back and look at what is behind your back! And yet - do not be surprised if I suddenly begin to read long prayers. This is not at all because I'm going to fall into religious ecstasy. Just so necessary. This is a mandatory part of the ancient rite! Well, gentlemen, go ahead!

"As you say, Madame clairvoyant," Valentine bowed. - Is one shovel enough for us?

- I hope so.

In a string, one by one we went down to the basement. Knocking on the barrel, under which, as it seemed to me, the treasure should be hiding (on the plan there was a cross on the circle), I discovered that it was empty.

God, do my vague hopes start to come true? Together with Valentin, we moved the barrel. Being afraid to say at least one word, I signaled Saltykov to dig.

Anya, standing on the side, held a candle, but her hands were so trembling with excitement that our shadows darted along the walls like living ones. Besides, it constantly seemed to me that someone was breathing right in the back of his head, and chilling blows reached my skin ... Probably, these are nerves or just a draft. It was easier for me to think that way, because you can't look back anyway.

Valentine managed to dig only a dozen times, as a shovel hit something hard. It turned out to be the lid of an old oak chest, bound with strips of copper. Yes, this is not that pathetic, roughly cocked casket with coppers, the find of which almost cost me too much. This is something weighty, in every sense ...

At that moment my fingers shook as well, and Anya groaned with restraint, nearly dropping the candle. Valentine, hurrying, dug up the top of the chest, so that you can open the lid, and knocked the lock with a shovel.

Inside was a huge, almost on a par with the chest, an old casket, upholstered in morocco corrugated with age and dampness, with a faded gold embossing.

Valentin, wincing at the pain in the broken ribs, pulled the casket out and was already trying to crack the lock in the morocco lid with a penknife out of his pocket, but I silently stopped his hand and murmured the words of the "Lord God ..." prayer spell that Melanya had taught me. None of my companions in the search for treasure did not bother me - they, as if spellbound, were looking at the casket and, perhaps, they even didn't understand what I was mumbling.

So, now it was necessary to read "Our Father" forty more times, and this test was not an easy one ... First, it is difficult to pronounce the canonical text, trying not to lose, and at the same time counting how many times the prayer was read and how many ; and secondly, dear companions, waking up, still doubted my mental health (judging by the expressions of their faces), and I was afraid that some of them were about to start talking to bring me to mind and make me stop.

But, in spite of everything, I still persistently repeated the words of the Lord's prayer again and again.

For a moment, it seemed to me that someone was calling me in a thin, crying voice, almost childish, and I even almost looked back, but I just remembered the order of the old healer — not to look back. Whoever calls — whether her husband, a deceased mother, someone's child, beloved grandmother, who has long been sleeping forever in Donskoy Cemetery — will never turn around and not look back so as not to give the enemy strength.

However, that may happen to me personally if I still can not stand it and look around, Melanya did not warn me. But one must think that something is bad, since the enemy will gain new strength from it ...

It seems that Anya experienced similar torments because I could see with my lateral vision how she had stiffened, not allowing herself to turn her head.

"And lead us not into temptation, but deliver us from evil." Amen, - I completed the fortieth prayer, thereby fulfilling my arduous promise.

Both Anna and Saltykov continued to stand, completely numb and motionless, not realizing that their torture had come to an end. I raised my finger to my lips, just in case, never allowing anyone to speak, and with gestures I offered to take the casket out of the cellar. The chest was incredibly heavy. Or is it the evil forces who decided on the last attempt not to give the treasure to its rightful mistress?

Noticing how blood filled the veins on Saltykov's forehead, which had raised the casket, Anya and I together grabbed a heavy burden on the other side and helped get her out of the cellar. The gravity was incredible, but only when our trio climbed the stairs and left with their cargo in the upper hall, I risked breaking the vow of silence.

- Well, gentlemen, look for the key or still allow ourselves to take the help of a knife and spoil the family heirloom? - I asked, brushing sweat from my face and not knowing where the spider's web came from.

- Glory to you, Lord! - Valentine theatrically raised his hands to the sky. "I was afraid that we would no longer hear from you a single word of the world, and you will always whisper:" ... like that in heaven ... "

By God, the reproaches now were so irrelevant that I simply could not resist shouting at Saltykov, as at an unreasonable child:

- Shut up immediately, so it was necessary!

But he did not let up.

- Helen! Do you seriously think that we managed to dig out the grandfather's little trunk thanks to your candlelight, spryn-grass and all these religious rituals?

- Valentine, I ask you, do not scare away luck, - Anya whispered.

"That's it," I added. - I can not say with certainty that we have found the treasure precisely because I observed the ritual suggested to me by Melania. Maybe this is just a coincidence. But, on the other hand, the treasure was revealed to us only after the accomplishment of the corresponding, as you put it, religious ceremony. And if you say that it is not so, you will have to deny the obvious. Let me still do what was ordered to the end. I guess there will be no big trouble.

Valentine shrugged. He could have limited himself with this eloquent gesture, so no, he also mercilessly added:

"Why are all women so superstitious?" Okay, some other little malachol woman who is fond of spiritualism and pilgrim trips to ancient monasteries (many now manage to combine such hobbies) ... But such incarnations as an enlightened feminist and an archaic klikush will be combined in one person - this is beyond my understanding.

Yes, men are terrible skeptics, and the army service, as I have noticed, brings up in them some kind of special die-hardness, which is simply unshakable. Why can not just show leniency to someone else's weaknesses, it is quite harmless? This is easy. Or, gentlemen, officers give a special oath, obliging them to impose their opinion on everyone around them?

I decided to ignore the headquarters captain's insinuations and elegantly walked away from the discussion imposed on me, recalling:

"Gentlemen, let's finally open this casket!" If I do not immediately see with my own eyes what we have been able to acquire, most likely I will simply die of curiosity! "And, not restraining myself, she added, addressing her words to the captain:" And on my grave you can write: "The feminist rests here, the rest of which is an archaic clicker in her soul ... Peace be upon her."

Valentin again, this time without any sarcastic comments, pulled a folding knife out of his pocket and flipped it into a casket lock. The cover with a crunch lay back ...

Chapter 27

Anna

The lid fell back, and the whole company stared inward with tension, expecting the casket, as in pirate novels, to be filled to the brim with treasures piled up in a pile — precious stones and ancient coins entwined in huge bundles of pearls, gold chains and monists, various ornaments. , studded and trimmed with emeralds and diamonds.

But the contents of the casket were covered by a dilapidated canvas rag, which, having been thrown off, the treasure seekers discovered many more similar patches, in each of which something was wrapped. Yes, grandfather-count was, judging by these canvases, a very pedantic person - he had to tinker a lot, packing valuables for a long time.

Everyone was so overwhelmed with excitement that no one could decide first to deploy at least one of the convolutions.

- Well, with God, gentlemen! - Elena Sergeyevna finally found the strength to take one of the rag knots and unwind it.

The decayed fabric spread under her fingers, and Lely had a golden cup in her hands, the walls of which were decorated with twelve large rubies. Without a doubt, the treasure of the imperial favorite was hidden in the casket.

- We still did it, gentlemen! We found a treasure, found it! - Elena Sergeevna cried gleefully, raising the goblet up and shaking it like a banner in battle.

- Oh, mommy! - Anya squeaked, clutching at Saltykov's sleeve and not taking her eyes off the huge rubies that cast red reflections on the faces of people in a ray of light.

Holding the lady close to a swoon with one hand, with his other hand the head-captain reached for the casket and pulled out a long and narrow object wrapped with a strip of canvas.

"Girls, I swear, this is a weapon!" - Valentine whispered, tearing a canvas from his find.

And indeed, it turned out to be an old dagger in a silver sheath, encrusted with a rich scattering of large amethysts.

Here, too, Anya ventured to take the smallest convolutions. Two diamond rings were hidden in it.

- My God, how many carats are there? She whispered dazedly, admiring the clear edges of the transparent stones. - I've never seen anything like it!

Clear blue water diamonds were really beautiful, and the decoration of the rings that framed the stones rose to real heights of jewelery.

"For evaluation, you will have to turn to a knowledgeable jeweler," remarked Elena Sergeyevna, to whom, it seems, her usual rationality and composure returned. - But the fact that not three carats, as in my ring, I'll tell you myself with a great deal of confidence. This is, after all, a gift from the empress, not the merchant Likhoveev, my second husband ... At least eight carats, if not all ten, and the antique value is unquestionable.

Treasure hunters bent over a diamond ring, admiring their find. It was like a dream.

"Well, gentlemen," Elena Sergeevna finally spoke, "now we have a real reason to bring a bottle from the cellar and raise a glass for good luck!" By God, very few people are so lucky!

Elena Sergeyevna kept silent about the fact that you should go to the cellar not only for wine ... In the happy turmoil you need to remember to abandon the hole left and put at least some order, otherwise anyone will understand that the treasure has already been found. And hunting for a treasure that has already been found is much simpler than for treasures hidden from the eyes of men and where ...

"However, any such can be in a locked wine cellar? She thought. - Yes, but after all, someone is scampering through the rooms of Privolny as at home! He will not get around the cellar ... "

Lely's thoughts were about to return to mysterious ghosts ... It's good that Saltykov distracted Elena Sergeyevna from these thoughts.

- To raise a glass is a good thing! But first, let's get the casket into the rooms, Valentin suggested. - Do not leave the same incalculable values in the hallway? Especially, Lenochka, you seem to be afraid of the late visit of Lieutenant Stepanchikov? I somehow reluctant to show our finds to the persistent youth. Alas, for understandable reasons, I would not risk inviting men from the village for carrying, so sorry, dear ladies, but I have to call on you again for help ... So, we raise the casket and carry it to the living room. Come on, girls, they took!

- Wait! - Elena Sergeevna cried suddenly. "There is still something to be done with the treasure before you can bring it into the house and use these things in any way." Otherwise they will not bring happiness!

- Good God! - Valentine again jokingly raised his hands to the sky. - Did "Our Father" have to be read over the treasure five hundred and fifty times, and you, being too lazy, read only one hundred and twenty?

- "Our Father" I read as many times as required, namely forty. And this is not my whim! And now you should sprinkle the treasure with holy water, and then hold each item found above the flame of a candle. And yet - all gold items must be left in running water for the whole day ... Only after that they will be completely cleansed from the influence of black forces.

- It was all in the instructions received from the old healer? - Valentine asked. - Who would have thought that the use of old treasures is such a complicated thing. To overseas cars and the instruction easier. And that is characteristic - it is not necessary to withstand a car even in running water.

But here, Anna, as a hostess, stood up for Elena Sergeyevna and demanded that Saltykov stop jerking and better consider how to put gold into running water, since there is such a sign. And old woman Melanie should be given a gift in gratitude for her advice - who knows, maybe without them the treasure would never have been found.

And there is no reason to excel in wit, there is simply no, not the slightest. Unless, of course, a wit is not a complete cynic, unworthy to be accepted in a decent society.

Ashamed staff captain bit his tongue and even apologized to the ladies for their frivolous behavior in such dramatic circumstances. It seems that Anna's opinion was not indifferent to Saltykov.

In order to atone for sins, Valentine proposed the following method of washing gold with running water - a deep and fast stream flowed through the park, which, after artificial dams, turned into a chain of ponds, once beautiful, but now muddy, stagnant. Unfortunately, the duckweed ponds, alas, were not suitable for a magical purpose, but the trickle itself could well wash off the traces of the influence of dark forces from the treasure. It is only necessary to fold the gold into a strong bag and lower the stream into the water, securing it with a reliable rope.

The evening was spent in business and hassle, however, very pleasant - the whole company, sitting in the dining room, assorted acquired values. Saltykov removed from the casket and unwrapped the next thing he met with enthusiastic cries of the ladies, then the practical Elena Sergeevna entered it into the inventory, and Anna kept the subject above the candle flame out of superstitious considerations, after which she put all the golden things into a canvas sack from under the potatoes ...

Behind these classes, treasure hunters, completely unnoticed even by themselves, drank a couple of bottles of wine, paused and toasted to ensure that the treasure brought good luck. No one felt intoxicated, apparently because everyone without wine was pleasantly agitated.

- God, what a beauty! Did Catherine give all her favorites equally luxurious gifts? - Anya was surprised. - And how did the treasury withstand such agony?

"Oh, your ancestor was still not the most fortunate, and maybe not just the most greedy, because he blamed himself for his vicious connection with the empress and indulged in moral torments. And here, for example, one of his rivals, Count Dmitriev-Mamonov, over the years of his favor received Catherine gifts for 900 thousand rubles, - read the read Elena Elena. - And the then, Ekaterina 900 thousand now, I suppose, correspond to ten million. And besides, having learned that the count is in love with young maid of honor, Darya Shcherbatova, Catherine not only gave her unfaithful lover complete freedom, allowed her to marry the subject of his passion, but also presented him several villages and two thousand peasants in the form of severance pay ... , apparently, they did not offend, but he did not rise to the heights of Mamonov ... Just think, a bag of gold trinkets with stones. Trifle!

- Oh, Lelia, please, do not ... I am still ashamed of this shameful spot on my pedigree ...

- Anya, well, why be ashamed of your own ancestors, and even more so to condemn them? - Valentin gave voice. - They lived as best they could, according to their era, and played by the rules imposed on them by. One of my ancestors also had an affair with the sovereign Catherine, however, in those times when she was not yet sovereign. So now, to assume that he disgraced the entire Saltykov family?

The ladies stammered with amazement at Valentine. For some reason, it never occurred to anyone that the famous Sergei Saltykov, one of the first handsome court courtiers of the 18th century, could have at least something to do with the poor infantry staff captain, who miraculously escaped from the front-line trenches. It is not enough in Russia Saltykov, and not all of them are related.

Sergey Saltykov, to whom the all-powerful Elizabeth herself, the daughter of Petrova, was indifferent, preferred the unfortunate, unborn, useless and forgotten to all Anhalt-Cerbst princess married to the empress's nephew to the great displeasure of the latter.

At that time, nothing else foretold the fabulous gifts of Fortune that they would fall at the feet of Catherine II in the future, and the noble Saltykov in his love was not only disinterested, but even very, very risky. Fortunately, he paid for the love of Grand Duchess Catherine with only a brief reference to his own estate.

Many courtiers believed (and rightly so!) Precisely Sergei Saltykov father of the heir, Tsarevich Paul ... But if so, then the staff captain is distantly related to the reigning dynasty! Valentin Saltykov and Emperor Nikolai Alexandrovich have a common great grandfather ...

No, in such a jungle, perhaps, it is better not to climb!

"Gentlemen, how do we divide our discovery?" - Anya asked, when it was already coming to an end, and outside the window the twilight in her eyes turned into night.

Elena, who printed on a sheet of paper: "No. 78. Golden snuffbox with twenty-four emeralds. On the lid - a portrait of Empress Catherine, made by enamel ", was interrupted and raised her eyes to Anna.

- What are you talking about? - she did not understand.

"It will probably be fair to divide the treasure into three approximately equal parts," continued Anya. "But I would also like to make rich donations to the church, to the defense fund, and to allocate something for old Melania." Let's separate what goes on donations, and the rest ... Three beats ... For each of us ... After all, without your help, I would never ... This is just some kind of miracle!

Having finally become agitated, Anya began to falter - it was always too difficult for her to talk about money matters. The topic is ticklish!

But Valentine and Lelia understood her perfectly well and then categorically refused any shares in the found treasure, explaining that the true heir to these riches is one, namely Anna, her ancestors have her treasure and bequeathed. And for her volunteers, moral satisfaction from participating in such an exciting adventure is enough.

Anya thought that anyway she would somehow make her friends accept some of the found values, at least as a memory of an exciting adventure ... A male ring with the largest diamond, or perhaps a dagger in amethyst sheath, would have served Valentine -captain, men love weapons so much ... And Lelia would have looked nice in an old necklace with sapphires and massive earrings that added to it (and how did this lady's set go to the ancestor's chest - it wasn't Catherine who presented this favorite gift to her favorite?). In Moscow, Lelia happens to be at balls, at receptions and at the opera, and ancient jewels will fit perfectly well for evening and ballroom toilets ...

"Okay, gentlemen, we will come back to this issue," Anya promised, trying not to smoke the last item smoked over the flame of the candle, about which Lelia has already recorded: "No. 79. A cup made of ivory with a thread, in a gold frame".

- The cup also needs to be put in a bag, it has a lot of gold. One golden leg is worth something, "remarked Elena Sergeevna, admiring the fine bone carving — among the magnificent ornaments they soared, spreading wings, eagles, and each feather was carved so that it seemed that the birds were about to tear themselves away from the walls of the cup and soar up.

- And the ivory from the water will not be spoiled? - Anya asked.

- I hope not. - Lelia took the cup from her friend's hands and, wrapping the wings of the eagles with a rag, so as not to split off, carefully put the rare thing in the bag among other items. - Functionally, the cup is intended for drinking, so it is not afraid of moisture. But to wash the icon in a gold salary in the water is terrible - the face of the Virgin is painted, and they deteriorate from damp. I suppose it is better to consecrate the icon in the church. Girevsky father, we will not refuse.

- The icon is better to the church and donate, - Anya said thoughtfully. - It seems that such miraculously found images are called manifested. It would be a sin to keep the icon in the empty house, if it can become a comforter for all believers ...

After silver items were separated from the ancient legacy, stones devoid of gold rims, the icon of the Mother of God and marching in massive salary with amber, and the remaining gold objects were transferred from the heavy casket, bound with carved copper stripes to a canvas bag, Valentine was able to lift the gold part of the treasure and without the help of women.

Lelya and Anyuta walked along the stream and found a suitable place where the water was deep enough so that the bag lowered into it would not immediately catch the eye, if a stranger wandered into the park. A green meadow on the bank of the creek made it possible to get close to the golden bag and protect it with possible comfort. After all, do not throw the same values without supervision! It was here that the women brought Valentine, bending under heavy luggage.

Lowering the bag with the gold found in the water and tying the end of a strong hemp rope intercepting the neck of the bag to a peg driven into the stitch, the treasure hunters could take a breath.

Chapter 28

Helena

Well, today passed in all senses for good reason - it was possible to find the legendary ancestor's treasure and, I confess, the treasure surpassed all our expectations.

I have repeatedly had the opportunity to take part in various adventures, helping friends to gain a legitimate inheritance. The story with the grandchildren of Countess Terek alone is worth what — a fake testament, impostors, several murders, brutal attempts on legal heirs, chases and shootouts ... and my current husband, Mikhail Khorvatov ...

But the thing with the search for an old treasure in Privolnoye was out of the ordinary in its romantic color - these are not boring papers on inheritance rights, although it is also not so easy to get them ... This is a real old treasure, of fantastic value and beauty! Yes, today we managed to do something unthinkable. And I still can't believe myself that I had just held in my hands the valuables that once had been in the imperial chambers, the cup from which Catherine drank, or the ring that she wore on her pet's finger ...

True, and now, at the last stage of our adventure, we could not fully relax and with the consciousness of a fulfilled duty to indulge in carefree rest. There was still not enough for the imaginary ghost, who had clearly dreamed of clearing the count treasure, to steal our bag from the stream, not waiting for the flowing waters to wash gold according to all the rules of magical rites.

Maybe this washing in and of itself - just a tribute to old traditions and no particular practical benefit from it, we do it like that, more to clear our conscience ... And for the villain chasing a treasure, our old-fashioned loyalty to traditions will be a real gift ...

I, albeit with some delay, told about the attack on me in the greenhouse. Valentin and Anya, of course, reproached me for levity and it was not clear where their passion for concealing important facts came from, but what could I say now ... The past thing!

However, they agreed that a person who nearly killed me because of a handful of coppers can go to any length if he guesses that we have found the county treasure.

I had to put at the creek sentries. The first to enter the post were Anya and Saltykov, who took over the night duty, and the next morning I had to change them, calling for a nurse or someone else to help me ... I would have to watch on duty in pairs - once again, one could not notice the enemy sneaking up.

To be honest, today I was very tired and had long dreamed of getting to my pompous canopy to fall asleep under its shadow. But conscience persistently whispered to me about the cold night fog, about evil mosquitoes, about thieves hiding in the bushes and other misfortunes waiting for my friends at the stream, while I selfishly indulge in rest in warmth and comfort.

However, Valentine promised that he and Anya would not feel any special inconvenience. He undertook to make a fire, the smoke of which would scare away mosquitoes, bake potatoes, boil tea over the fire and tell the most interesting and exciting stories all night. On the damp grass covered with evening dew, you can spread the blankets, and the rain, it seems, should not be.

Besides, the captain, after all, is a front-line soldier, he is accustomed to danger, he knows how to handle, and he will not be caught off guard in the night.

I did not begin to object too long - in the end, Valentina and Anya, under such romantic circumstances, might be quite nice at a night fire ...

Returning to the house, I remembered that, being in a state of joyful euphoria, not only did not dine, but did not dine on time. And now the feeling of hunger drove me to the kitchen. The cook had already gone back home, the nurse seemed to be sick today and, contrary to her habits, was not sticking her nose out of the room.

I juggled among the pans, I found the soup from the dinner and pounced on him like a hungry refugee from the western provinces ... Sitting at an uncovered tablecloth over the pan from which I drew a cold brew with a spoon, I thought that rural life, cool, very much simplification of manners.

That way I will soon begin, like Leo Tolstoy, to walk barefoot through the cold dew and eat rye thures.

Having quenched my hunger and rising to my bedroom, I was ready to collapse on the Count's bed under a canopy, but still this evening required some kind of festive completion. Since it was already drunk a lot, and I didn't want to dance alone, I had to choose the most prosaic business - to twist the hair on papilotki. To commemorate the solemnity of the moment (the treasure was found, after all, not without my participation, and long live strength of mind, imagination and patience - virtues inherent in not every woman!) Next day I will appear before a society with a good haircut.

Now that we have found the treasures, it would not hurt to even figure out what kind of "ghost" came to us at night and on whose conscience the ruined lives of the unfortunate girls, and we can safely say that my trip to the wild forests of the Moscow province was completely successful. Varvara Filippovna is about to arrive, having completed her business, and I will return to Moscow - to the bath, to the hairdresser, to a comfortable bed with a modern spring mattress, to a telephone set, to friends who look into my house in the evenings at light, to the Arbat restaurants and fashion stores ...

If only the search for a criminal did not take too long. After all, not knowing the name of the killer and not contributing to his punishment, I cannot leave these places with a clear conscience and a calm soul ...

In order to fall asleep as soon as possible, I uncovered Shakespeare's volume that had been idle for a long time and was just reading it over, trying to finally determine behind what the hell the great playwright needed obvious excesses like Rosencrantz and Gildenshtern, who were confused under Hamlet's feet, how I was distracted by noise. It slammed the sash windows, dissolved by someone's hand. How did I manage to get bored with all these mysterious noises, who only knew!

If a ghost appears, I'll just ignore it! And if a person - will have to run a heavy volume into it, without having managed to solve all the riddles of the creative method of Shakespeare. Or maybe it's time to just shoot a night visitor? At trial, it will be easy for me to prove that I acted in a state of passion (even how much you can mock me with impunity!), And therefore, I have the right to rely on an acquittal.

I did not even have time to find Browning, which was hidden under a pillow, as usual, when none other than Lieutenant Stepanchikov climbed over the window sill.

Yeah, the night visits to the lady's bedroom without an invitation from her clearly indicate some inappropriate behavior (what a remarkable, capacious, explanatory word the doctor suggested to me!), But to shoot the unfortunate officer who is not okay with his head, I yet I will not.

- Good evening, Elena Sergeevna! - Stepanchikov quite courteously addressed me, inspecting my pompous bedroom. - And here you are very cute, although somewhat old-fashioned. Cupids, rosettes, canopy ... But this, too, has its own charm.

Trying not to anger or excite a person who is prone to unexpected actions, I pretended that I was not surprised at all, but on the contrary, I was very happy to see the lieutenant, and there was nothing special about his appearance through the window of the second floor, except for sweet friendly simplicity ...

And what could I do? Mad lieutenant was with me almost one on one. The nanny is fast asleep on the ground floor, and Valentine and Anya are guarding a bag of gold by the stream. In the park, behind the trees, their campfire gleamed.

Probably, if I start shouting loudly through the open window, they will hear me and come running, but until they reach me, I will be in full power of a mad lieutenant ... And what will come into his unhappy head? Especially after my wild cries? God knows!

Eh, how could I have imperceptibly attracted the attention of friends to what is happening in the house? Although, maybe, this is someone's devilish reckoning - having frightened Stepanchikov, I have to call for help Valentine and Anyuta, and someone in the meantime will steal a bag full of gold from a stream? If so, then I'd rather do it myself!

- How nice of you to visit me, Mr. Stepanchikov! Would you like to go to the dining room? - My voice would not allow to doubt that the night visit of the lieutenant is a great honor for me and the event in all respects is very pleasant. - The samovar is probably already cold, but it can be reheated. I will offer you a jam and a very good cheese from the center, in the morning from the shop delivered on my order. Like, you know, with tears and big holes ... Do you like Meshchersky cheese?

Now the main thing is to talk, talk and talk in order to talk the lieutenant to death. Strange, but everything in life is in the habit of repeating itself - once a young man had already entered my bedroom at night, inclined to inappropriate behavior and did not hide his purpose in killing me. Only a well-hung tongue helped me save my life. That's interesting, snake charmer people are born or become? Personally, these skills came to me with experience.

- Oh, thank you, Elena Sergeevna, but do not bother - I am full. God bless him, with cheese. Let's talk about this and that. Tell me, just frankly, do you find me attractive?

And why all the talk about this and that sooner or later relate to one topic - about yourself, beloved? There is nothing abnormal in the desire to hear a compliment in your address, except that usually a somewhat more veiled form is given to such vain desires.

Stepanchikov meanwhile went up to the mirror, admired himself, clicked on the nose of a gilded cupid, nestled on the carved frame, and turned to me, waiting for an answer.

I assured the unfortunate young man that he was just handsome and could be quite proud of himself.

"Oh, many ladies told me that," Stepanchikov said thoughtfully, and suddenly his expression began to change, and a strange feverish glow appeared in his eyes. - Yes, they find me attractive, although, strictly speaking, I am not handsome at all ... However, since the war began and most young men have been somewhere on the fronts, ladies have become less capricious and do not require every cavalier to be written handsome In addition, the uniform is driving almost all the women crazy. Once they see epaulets, even they are ready to forget about their own mother. But ultimately, all these stupid hens need only one thing ... And after being injured, I cannot meet their aspirations. Alas…

Stepanchikov faltered, sat down on the window sill, stretched his legs and began to swing the toe of his boot. Damn nasty habit! The shoe-smelling wax shoe flickered before my eyes - to and fro, to and fro ... But at the moment it seemed not the most terrible. Frankly, what was happening in general I liked less and less. I even began to internally doubt the correctness of the position I was taking, but I still tried to console the lieutenant as much as I could, explaining that the slight limp from a wounded leg was essentially nothing and would only give women more hearts to it. A courageous defender of the fatherland, who shed his blood in battle, every young girl dreams of such a bridegroom ...

Stepanchikov looked at me without answering anything, and only an evil grimace disfigured his good-natured, snub-nosed face. Just silently, he jumped off the window sill and began to measure the room with his steps, pacing diagonally from corner to corner ...

"It's not a limp at all," he hissed at last. "The war struck me the worst blow." All the ladies want to see in me a strong male and they need from me only what I can not give. I can not stand these pathetic little monkeys with their searching, evaluating glances!

From the expression on Stepanchikov's face, it was unclear whether he included me in this vicious category, but just in case I fell silent. In the spacious room only the voice of the lieutenant could be heard:

- Nasty lustful bitches! They spin around me only until they are convinced of my weakness, and then, you see, how they changed it. But I learned to take from them what they didn't intend to give me at all ... Yes, yes! Their rotten, worthless lives. Do you know, madam, how blood plays when you cut someone's throat?

He asked it in such a casual tone, as if he really wanted to ask something completely innocent, like, "Do you know, madam, what flavor does a real mocha coffee emit?" But I heard his question, literally numb. It was at this moment that I happened to realize that Stepanchikov was not just odd, but completely insane. It was enough to see the expression on his face ... It seemed so scary ...

An irrepressible desire to get somewhere far away seized me, but, alas, it was precisely this that was absolutely impossible. The lieutenant would hardly have let me out of the room, and I myself would not venture to throw out the window, without being sure of a successful outcome. Out of awareness of my own helplessness, I trembled, but not the right word — I trembled, shook my whole body, and the lieutenant, paying no attention to anything, said everything and spoke, looking somewhere in the space with whitened eyes:

- I first encountered this at the front, in hand-to-hand combat. We shot all the cartridges, and we had to use knives, bayonets and our own hands to cope with the German intelligence unit that had fallen upon us. We slaughtered Nemchur like pigs ... My comrades were then turned inside out due to the fact that they soiled their hands with fresh blood (and these are combat officers, not snotty high-school students who got out because of a mamma's skirt!), And I ... Oh, I felt the feeling close to ecstasy, cutting the throat of some thin Hans, sweaty, badly shaved, with a nasty caddy ... You press a little harder so that the knife cuts through the skin, and then it goes on its own. And you feel how your heart fills with a hot wave of excitement ... I think you perfectly understand everything I think about?

My tongue did not obey me too well, but still I squeezed out with difficulty:

"I assure you, Lieutenant, I cannot read the thoughts of others."

What else could I say? It was not easy for me to cope with my own thoughts, full of confusion reigned in my head, imagination helpfully shoved a picture to me - I, in a robe thrown open, in foolish papillotes lying on the floor at the antediluvian four-poster bed, and from my slit throat lashes blood ... What a terrible combination tragic and vulgar! And how, thinking about such things, you can shine with eloquence, leading small talk with the murderer?

But Stepanchikov at the moment, it seems, was not interested in anyone's words and thoughts, except for their own. He ignored my comment and, after a proper pause, continued:

- And if you spend with a knife on the female neck, tender, white, smelling clean skin, perfume, fresh herbs - oh! Words do not explain! Chick - and ready, and the blood flowed ... It's like a drug, I want to repeat it again and again! He said, starting to tremble with excitement.

I involuntarily felt how my own neck was covered with "goose bumps", and my throat spasm prevented me from squeezing out at least a word ... It seems I overestimated my ability to speak to any villain. And Browning, damn it, stayed under the pillow. Now the lieutenant, who was watching my movements, would not allow me to snatch a weapon. Although he is a psychopath, he has a frontal grip.

Stepanchikov continued to repeat some incoherent phrases of a completely wild and even perverted character, and I looked up to the icon of the Theotokos hung in the corner. What else could I do but ask for help from the Virgin Mary?

How many times in the most hopeless situations I turned to her for protection and help, and if it was not she who was so kind to me, then who?

While I was mumbling the words of a short prayer, trying at the same time to keep the lieutenant in sight, ready, as it seemed to me, to rush at me with a knife at any moment, my glance to and fro fell on a cup of conspired water.

Sychiha ordered to keep water near the icon and more than once for some reason reminded me of this water ... As she sees me, she also says: "Water, water!" Maybe she meant just such a case?

"When I see an attractive woman in front of me, I involuntarily begin to dream," the insane Stepanchikov muttered, "like a knife opening her throat and warm blood from the wound ... Oh, that wonderful smell of fresh blood!" Just come to the lady from the back, otherwise it will splash ... Blood is gushing with a fountain.

Oh my God! Needless to say, it is regrettable if the victims of crime have such an untidy habit of soiling the murderers with their blood. How not to sympathize with the cleanliness poor fellow, carnivorous glancing at my throat. But for me, therefore, the main task now is not to allow the lieutenant to come up behind me!

"And then, when you think about everything and look at the cooling body, it becomes bad," Stepanchikov suddenly declared. "I'm not a beast, Elena Sergeevna, not a monster, but I want to cut the neck." I want to kill and can't do anything with myself. And it happens to me badly, oh, how bad it is ... At least go to the noose!

Then the voice of an old healer sounded in my head: "And if someone next to you says that it's bad for him, sprinkle it with this water three times!"

I reached for the cup and, dipping my fingers into it, splashed into the face Stepanchikov, slowly approaching me.

He stopped, confused. I, taking advantage of a short pause, sprinkled it again and again. Groaning, Stepanchikov dropped the razor from his hands, which, as it turned out, managed to unnoticeably reach, open and hold ready in his hand. Clutching at her head, as if a sharp pain had pierced her, the lieutenant grated:

- Witch! What have you done?

And then a shot slammed from the window and there was a wild cry: "Stepanchikov, stand! Hands up, lieutenant! "- after which the detective agent Stukalin stumbled into the room through the windowsill, losing his hat on the fly. Lord, I have never been so happy in the life of a policeman! I didn't even have to think about the unnaturalness of the situation - I was in a dressing gown and dressing gowns, and the bedroom was filled with extraneous men ...

(By golly, today my bedroom is the most popular place in the local district, the guest just went in the cant ...)

The lieutenant reached for his holster to pull out a revolver, but the detective managed to roll Stepanchikov under his feet, knock the enemy on the floor, and soon a mad ball of two intertwined male bodies spun around my legs.

Alas, an elderly detective agent suffering from dyspnea was not so easy to cope with a strong lieutenant who had gone through a good front-line school, and I, recovering from the shock, began to worry about the fate of the fight. The lieutenant lieutenant had already dropped a long time ago, he did not have time to grab the revolver, but what if he could beat the detective with his bare hands? After all, he has military experience in such cases, he said ... And the detective did not deal with anyone except our own Russian gangsters and thieves. Probably, they are still not as obsessively resisting as soldiers of the hostile army, and lower police officers usually help detective agents during their arrest. Perhaps it will not hurt me to take a personal part in the fight.

It is a pity that browning is not reach! However, it is dangerous to shoot during a fight - there is a risk of getting into the wrong person. But with my bare hands, unlike the front-line soldiers, the enemy cannot be defeated.

The table in my bedroom was decorated with some intricate porcelain sculpture (to call it a statuette the language does not turn because of the very decent size of the artistic creation). This piece of fine art depicted an old trunk entwined with flowers and leaves (or maybe a rocky cliff), on the ledges of which six thick pink angels with lutes and pipes in their hands sat in picturesque poses.

I don't know how valuable this thing was for the housewife, but there was no time to choose, it was the angelic sixttes that caught my hand in the first place.

Having estimated the weight of the creation in my hands (and it was quite impressive), I waited until the fighting turned upside down in such a way that the lieutenant's head was on top, and with a sweep lowered a porcelain snag with angels on it. Something cracked under my hands (I hope the porcelain, not Stepanchikov's head), and the fragments of the creation scattered into different corners.

The lieutenant went limp in the unfriendly embrace of a police agent, and soon Mr. Stukalin, riding the fallen enemy, was already tying his hands with a strong silk belt from my dressing gown.

"Sorry for the late visit, darling Elena Sergeevna," muttered Stukalin, breathing a little. - Circumstances, sir!

"Nothing, nothing, I'm used to it," I said, quite sincerely.

"Here he is, the murderer of the wretched maidens," the detective, not restraining himself, kicked the lieutenant with his foot. - The doctor says, psychopathy ... But I thought so - maybe not psychopathy, but pure debauchery. Sadistic inclinations! To Moscow, the psychiatric professors are to be provided with a darling for examination, of course. Let them figure it out - psychopathy is worse or worse. Where is his place - in a lunatic asylum or in eternal penal servitude. And if everyone starts cutting girls, because, he says, is his psychopathic attraction so that it will come out? By the way, your doctor is there, in the courtyard by the porch. You click it, so kindly, let it rise, pull the lieutenant's shirt over the lieutenant while our psychopath subsides. And then he wakes up and again, you see, he will fall into a riot.

I looked out the window. At the porch, indeed, a man was trampling about, barely discernible in the dark.

- Mister doctor, is that you? - I called him. "I'll give you the door key now." Get up! Your patient was briefly calmed down.

Having tied the key head to a coil of harnesses taken from my sewing pouch, I began to unwind the hank by lowering the key down so that the doctor could open the door - now there was no question of keeping the spare key in the pot on the porch! But the nurse, who was picked up by the noise, herself let the doctor into the house and immediately attacked him with questions ...

While the esteemed doctor satisfied the curiosity of the persistent old woman, for my part I was able to ask a couple of questions to the detective agent.

- Terenty Ivanovich, it seems that you caught the criminal on live bait, and in the role of this live bait you had to perforce to speak to me. You were not afraid at all that before you have time to get into my room, I will already roll on the floor with my throat cut?

"Well, madam, I would never allow that to happen." I don't mean that the mad lieutenant scared you so much, but what to do - I had to take it red-handed.

Yes, it is quite a policeman! Detective agent - he is always detective agent, no matter what happens! Again, I felt something like throat spasms at the thought that Stukalin could have miscalculated - no one is immune from mistakes. And Terenty Ivanovich continued, as if nothing had happened:

- I have long been convinced that it is he who gives tickets to the other world to young ladies. Each of the deceased had a love affair with a young officer, who was rumored to have guessed Stepanchikov. True, all the girls hid it for various reasons. Mercy sister feared scandal from the hostess - Mrs. Zdravomyslova does not encourage the liberties of the staff with the patients of the hospital. The daughter of a blacksmith was afraid of her father, who dreamed of marrying her as a miller from a neighboring village (and what comparison can there be for a girl's heart between a widowed miller and an officer?). Malasha, a servant from a tavern, and so the local guys a couple of times smeared the gates with tar, and they would have known that she and the trickster officer had spun, they wouldn't give the passage ... Popovna was brought up in great severity, as it should be in the families of clergy, and proselytized in marriage with a graduate of the seminary.

The parochial school teacher feared accusations of immorality on the part of the diocesan authorities and the loss of her place, because school salary was her only income ... But in the village, you know, it's difficult to keep such secrets, I've told you more than once. By the grain, by the grain, but I collected the facts, not for the first time. Detective service on it and worth it. It turned out that Stepanchik was fooling around each of the maidens and was arranging secret dates. The girls never returned from these dates ...

"So if you all found out, why didn't you arrest him right away?" - I interrupted. - Why did you want to play my life?

- What to do, madam? Stepanchikov - officer. So just an officer can not be arrested on a suspicion. There are a lot of formalities - that, that, permission of the garrison authorities is required, again to place the arrested officer, even a retired one, not that a front-line soldier from the active army, put in a guardhouse, not in a police jail. Judge for yourself - where is Gireyevo, and where is the garrison guardhouse? Woe to one thing, and not arrest! And so I took my darling red-handed at the time of penetration into someone else's home and the attack on another victim. As a police officer, I have the right to act in accordance with the circumstances in order to prevent the commission of a criminal offense. I will now write down the report on the authorities, I will take your testimony according to the form - and the whole is short.

And the killer, in a straitjacket, will be taken to Moscow under guard, and there they will figure out without me where to find him - to penal servitude or to the yellow house.

"Did he also depict ghosts here?" - I could not resist the last question.

- It may well be, madam. What he knocked on his sore head is God himself will not understand. Well, if he was muttering and pretending to be empty, the more interesting it was to dress up in a ghost. Rather, you go crazy for a madman, if that. Do you remember the cigarettes? It is he, my dear, "Senatorial" smokes ... So draw your conclusions, madam.

Then at last the doctor approached, accompanied by a sobbing nurse, showered me with reproaches (after all, he warned that Stepanchikov was not in himself!) And gave the lieutenant some kind of injection from which Stepanchik, who had already begun to recover, fell asleep. Then the doctor, together with the detective agent, dressed his patient in a straitjacket, tightly tied his long sleeves behind Stepanchikov's back.

- I will accompany him to Moscow myself and take part in the consultation. My observations will surely interest my colleagues, although I have no honor to be an expert in the field of psychiatry itself, the doctor muttered, looking in my direction very unfriendly. - From a scientific point of view, the case is very interesting, quite. Batyushki, how did you smash his head, gentlemen! But where is your mercy? How can you afford it! In mental pathology, head injuries can provoke completely unpredictable consequences ...

I don't know, perhaps, if I didn't resist, showing mercy, and the bloodthirsty lieutenant, who is of considerable interest to science, managed to cut my throat, this case would have seemed more interesting to the doctor. But somehow I didn't want to expose my throat, so that later the doctors of academic interest would try another murder committed by the maniac Stepanchikov. With all due respect to science ...

When the doctor and the police agent laid the swaddled lieutenant on the blanket and, grabbing the blanket by the ends, dragged the murderer somewhere down the stairs, I suddenly asked Stukalin another question (yes, I shouldn't have enough praise at the moment):

- Terenty Ivanovich, and what - no one else from the local officers smokes Senator's?

"Why, then," muttered Stukalin, puffing and puffing, carefully dragging his heavy burden down the steps. - Someone else smokes ... But not all of those who smoke have a habit of cutting people ...

"My dear, Elena Sergeevna, do not distract the policeman with questions," asked the nurse, who was walking in front, lighting the ladder with a kerosene lamp. - It's not even an hour, Terenty Ivanovich will stumble, fall on us, so after all everything will go down the steps and roll up a lump. Hand-legs then do not count. Go to yourself, darling, take the droplets of valerian, lie down. It's no joke how this said said frightened you. I almost killed! Oh, the war, the damned war, that does - the officers and they are mad and they start to rush at people ... You go, Elena, get some rest, I will see the gentlemen myself! And then you will cook a linden brew for calming down. Sleep, killer whale, and feel better!

I obediently fell silent, leaving with me the information that every cigarette butt had individual traits, the characteristic "bite of a smoker" and the police could, with a high degree of accuracy, determine whose mouth squeezed it ... Maybe novels like always, lie ...

Well, Mr. Stukalin arrived here to look for the killer and coped with his task, he is no longer in the smallest detail. And I am staying with an unresolved riddle like this - who nevertheless threw a cigarette butt on the porch of the house that fateful night and who penetrated into the estate, portraying ghosts, and most importantly - for what purpose did he penetrate? Was it the very same Stepanchikov?

The inner voice stubbornly whispered to me that it was not so ... But can you fully rely on the words of the inner voice? Suddenly everything is a simple game of imagination?

After all the adventures, I naturally could not sleep. And even the nanny fake decoction and the light bromine-based sleeping pills that the doctor ordered for Anya did not help at all. As soon as I fell asleep for a short while, fragments of an experienced nightmare began to flash before my eyes — that Stepanchikov's insane face, then the back of his head, on which I carefully tried on, lowered the porcelain sculpture, the fight, the subsequent vanity with the removal of the neutralized killer ...

And I woke up screaming, as if a needle had been thrust into my soul, and for a long time I was looking into the darkness, in which vague delusional visions continued to curl. Maybe if I found the strength to analyze everything that happened, sort through, explain to myself the rationality and expediency of my own actions, it would be easier, but I am too tired today to indulge in philosophical understanding of recent events. This should be done with a fresh mind, after a sound sleep, which returns clarity to the head, and the saving dream did not go and did not go ...

It even occurred to me whether I should go to the creek in order to change Anya and Saltykov at their post, I still don't sleep. But then they will have to tell them about everything that happened in my bedroom, and about the unexpected completion of the case of the murders of young girls, and I need to properly gather my spirit before subjecting Ani's fragile psyche to a new ordeal.

I stayed in bed and at dawn I was overwhelmed by a heavy, painful dream. I saw Varvara Filippovna. She recounted the clothes in a clinic in the Grayevskaya hospital and grumbled:

- Not enough three pairs of underpants! As soon as I was away for a while, everything in the house went upside down. Well, surprise! That's what the return was waiting for me ...

And in a dream I was painfully ashamed of my oversight.

Chapter 29

Anna

Anya and Valentin sat next to the fire, covered with the night coolness of one overcoat, and had a leisurely conversation. I didn't want to sleep, I wanted this night to stretch for a long, long time.

Below under the shore, the stream surrounded by clear water hid incredible treasures that were miraculously found, but they seemed so elusive that they tried to avoid this topic in conversation. Suddenly, from the careless word the wraith will shatter and the bag will be empty? Yes, and now it was something completely different ...

Annie finally decided to ask Saltykov a question that had tormented her long ago, even though her heart sank from her own tactlessness. But you need to know everything about your beloved until the end ...

- Valya, promise that you will not be angry if I ask you one thing. Why are you still the captain? After all, it is time for you to have another rank.

- And what, I am not fit for you? - Valentine tried to laugh it off. "Well, forgive me, I have not yet reached the generals."

- Lord, what are you talking about? I just don't want you to hide your past from me. Tell me please! It is very important for me to know.

- Well, since you so want. I was demoted for a duel.

- Brother, avenging the honor of his sister. - Anya immediately remembered Valentine from "Faust", about which Lelya spoke.

Valentine frowned.

- Well, since you already know, why ask? Is Lena probably gossiping? In those circumstances, I just had to shoot. It was impossible to allow my sister to be insulted and humiliated with impunity ...

Anya sighed. Explain that no one knows anything and does not gossip about anything, and her guess was just a random association? Or just stop asking questions on this sore subject?

"By the way, the war writes off old sins ... I received news of the production of me for the rank of captain," Valentine said after some silence. - As soon as we can escape from your treasures, we will wash my new shoulder straps. I want to throw a real feast. And ten days later I have to go back to the position. I'm filthy here.

- And will you leave me alone?

- Anya, the war is not over yet, I am an officer and must return to my unit. Leave for injury can not be eternal. But I will never leave you. If you want, we can get married before my departure. Just think properly, why do you need an infantry captain, a middle-aged, wounded, disfigured ... You are now probably one of the richest women in the Moscow province and can choose the best suitors. I am just not a gift as a groom. A sensible lady would prefer a neighbor landowner or an intelligent rural doctor, live with him in her estate, grow dahlias and greenhouse cucumbers ...

- I, perhaps, will choose a rural doctor to be able to use medical consultations free of charge, - Anya laughed. "Only on the condition that it will not be as old as our local doctor." But even if a lot of young, handsome, funny people with medical diplomas ask for my hand, I still prefer to all the doctors in the world one infantry captain who is nonsense and cannot stop at all. And if you think that you have offered me your hand and heart in such a stupid way, and this is quite enough, then I must confess that I would like to hear a proposal clothed in a more romantic form.

Valentin had no choice but to add to his words a fair amount of romance, and after long kisses Anya finally whispered:

- Listen, one thought occurred to me - I, too, will go with you to the front, sister of mercy. After all, I studied at nursing courses. I hope the command will not put up obstacles and will send me to the very regiment where my deceased and my living husbands served.

Valentine started and spoke ardently that he could not approve such a decision. After all, Anya does not know what war is! It is only in the articles of front-line correspondents that the fighting seems like an exciting adventure, but in reality it is blood, dirt and constant closeness of the soul and the death of others ...

And someone else's death is even worse than his own. When your friend before your eyes turns into a corpse torn by a shell; when you hear the groans of people dying in terrible agony and begging to be shot; when the attack has to run through the bodies of the dead, but one thought is beating in your head - you need to destroy as many Germans as possible, turned into a gray crowd of opponents running towards Russian chains with bayonets at the ready ... deprived of human features ... Does a woman have a place in this hell?

He spoke for a long time, weightily, citing more and more new arguments ...

Anya listened attentively, but she seemed to adhere to the previous decision.

"You know," she said softly at last, "at one time my grandfather, the one buried here in the park, over there, behind the trees, you can see his tombstone, and so, my grandfather went to the Balkan war, and my grandmother decided to accompany him." And the war with the Turks is also not an easy matter, even judging by the pictures of Vereshchagin who has been there. And blood, and dirt, and death, and inhuman cruelty, and all the horrors of war were there, except that the gas attacks had not yet dabbled. So, grandfather wrote in his farewell letter about his wife's decision to go to the army with him: "I cannot approve of this, but I do not have the strength to prevent it. We will surrender into the hands of God, only He is the master of our destinies. " You do not find that the only way to act if you yourself are not able to forbid anything to anyone?

For some time they sat in silence, moving a coal in the fire with a branch, then Valentine quietly sang a stanza of a famous romance to the verses of Solovyov:

Death and Time reign on the earth, You do not call their masters;
Everything, whirling, disappears into the mist, Only the sun of love
is still.
- Why think about the bad? - Anya spoke again. - The war will ever
end.

"I'm afraid this will not happen soon," Valentine said bitterly.

- Well, let! Let not this year, even in the sixteenth, even in the
seventeenth! Nothing lasts forever. We will wait, all the same
because nothing else remains. But imagine what a beautiful peaceful
life will come then. We gave so much blood, so many young lives,
that we deserve peace and quiet!

"Peace and quiet ... Honestly, I don't know what I'll do then,"
Valentine shrugged. - I was tired of war, but, on the other hand, my
whole life was spent in the army. Just as a boy put on his cadet
uniform, he pulls his infantry strap. And I simply did not know any
other life.

- Especially since it will be interesting for you to live in a different
way. Thanks to the inheritance of ancestor, we can afford anything.
We can go on a trip, we can do business, and we can put this
property in order and live like landowners near Moscow, this too has
its own charm.

"What else was missing for me to squander your inheritance." We
will live in my house and on my salary, dear. However, the estate, of
course, ought to be put in order - you would come here for a summer
vacation ... With children.

Anya was just about to answer, as from the side of the house there
was heard some kind of strange noise and it seemed that even a
muffled shot.

- You heard? Shoot! There is something going on! - Anya
whispered.

Valentine jumped up, dropping his coat from his shoulder. But the noise had already subsided, and no matter how much they listened, they could not make out anything else.

"There are very strange places here — there are some mysterious sounds all the time," Anya said, calming down. "Sometimes it seems to me that not everything can be explained from rational positions, it also doesn't do without ghosts ..."

"Annie, there is no one in the house except for Elena and your old nanny," answered Valentin, who continued to catch every sound keenly. - I do not like the tricks of ghosts, the victims of which may be two weak women.

- But Lelia is not among the weak natures! - Anya objected.

"Oh, yes, she herself is sure of this and has repeatedly demonstrated her spiritual strength to others, but any brave feminist who tries to keep up with men in anything can sometimes be useful help. And I'm not used to leaving in a difficult moment without the help of not only women, but also just friends. I'll go to the house and check what happened there. The sound of the shot, I heard quite clearly ...

- Yes, of course, may be, Lele needs help. But what about me? I'm afraid to stay alone at night with this golden bag! - Anya exclaimed.

"And this woman was just going to the front!" Take my revolver, in case of danger, shoot and shout - I will hear and come running. And do not be afraid so - because so far no one knows that we have found the gold of your ancestors, so it is not necessary to wait for predatory raids.

Valentin gave Anya a weapon, kissed her temple, where the naughty curls had come out of her hair, and quickly disappeared into the dark.

Anya wrapped herself in his greatcoat and sat down again by the fire, clutching the cold steel of an officer's revolver. Everything around was again filled with alarming sounds, rustles and almost sighs ...

Anya rolled a wave of fear. Suddenly someone hiding in the bushes behind her back? And if Valentine was purposely lured to the house so that she would be face to face with an unknown enemy? And what's in the house? If shot, then at whom? Did something happen to Lely? Valentine ran to the rescue, but he left the weapon to Anna, and now, perhaps, with his bare hands confronts an armed opponent ... Lord, help!

Rustles were becoming clearer, it seems, someone was walking in the park. Anino's heart began to beat loudly, and her beads of sweat appeared on her forehead.

Valentine ordered to shoot in case of danger, but did not say how to shoot - in the air or to kill. And what? So take and shoot at a person, maybe quite accidentally strolling into the park? And become a killer? Or shoot in the air in the hope that Valentine will come to the rescue? And if the monster who kills women leaves the park and pounce on her? Before Valentine appears, everything will be over with her ... What should we do?

Anya did not have time to come to any conclusion when the lieutenant Krivitsky came out of the trees to the fire. Having sighed with relief at the sight of a familiar face, the young widow immediately began to tremble again with fear - after all, Lelya suspected of having committed cruel murders of Krivitsky. Why does he wander here alone in the dark?

- Oh, Anna Afanasyevna, good night! I will not disturb you? Allow to bask in your light?

And Krivitsky sang with his sweet voice:
My fire shines in the fog, Sparks are extinguished on the fly. Nobody will meet us in the night ...
And I could not understand who lit the fire in your park. Let me think, I'll come over and look. Are you guarding your property or are you fishing in a creek?

"Yes, I'm here ... somehow ... I'm out ... I don't know myself," Anya burst out talking, hiding the revolver under her coat, but not too far in any case.

"I, too, usually do not sleep at night, so I became addicted to late walks," Krivitsky continued in his most friendly tone. - And today, moreover, I noticed something that intrigued me greatly, so that I completely lost sleep. Imagine, at first, our dear Stepanchikov slipped out of the house in Grayevsky and headed towards Privolnoye, and then at his heels, trying to keep in the background, like a medieval assassin, the doctor and this foolish detective, discharged by Elena Sergeevna from Moscow, walked. I, too, went after them, hoping for an interesting spectacle, but my dear was behind ... Stepanchik, though wounded in the leg, and almost ran through the woods at a run. I even, in a sinful affair, thought that the lieutenant was in a hurry for a date, he seemed to be getting ready for your guest. As I noticed the fire from a distance, I decided

Anya, who completely refused the gift of speech, made a few muffled sounds in response.

- And where is the brave staff captain Saltykov, who assumed the duties of a Cerberus with your person? - impudently asked Krivitsky, as if he had not noticed the condition of the hostess of the manor.

- He briefly departed. Now will be back. - Anya was finally able to cope with so much excitement that she said it already quite articulately.

- Well, it remains only to be glad that I took a moment and found you alone. I have long wanted to talk to you heart to heart, dear Anna Afanasyevna. Your late husband, Lieutenant Chigarev, told me a lot about you. You know, in the front dugouts, over a glass of alcohol to the sounds of distant gaps, the conversations are not just frank, and I would even say, beyond ordinary frankness. Alexey often remembered you. Long before I met you, I had a certain image of the Beautiful Lady, akin to the Blok one ... But, I must admit, reality surpassed all my wildest fantasies. You are like a fairy-tale fairy living in an enchanted castle ... This is the first thing that occurred to me at our meeting.

Perhaps Krivitsky was in tune with a long conversation and many compliments were reserved for Anna, but Saltykov returned to the fire, as promised. The appearance of the lieutenant next to Anna, probably, was not a pleasant surprise for Valentine, but he quite kindly greeted Krivitsky and even exchanged a few phrases. Anya, looking into the face of the captain, realized that he was somehow madly upset.

- Valentine, what happened there? - she interrupted the secular exchange of courtesies. - Did you find out anything?

Saltykov sighed bitterly.

- Misfortune happened, gentlemen! Lieutenant Stepanchikov went mad and in a fit of madness attacked Elena Sergeyevna, trying to kill her.

- Oh my God! - Anya cried, instantly falling into despair. - What about Lely? She is alive? Or ... Don't be silent! Did he ruin her? I will never forgive myself ...

- Alive, live, do not worry. Oddly enough, the police this time was on top.

Mr. Stukalin tracked down Stepanchikov and managed to twist it at the time of the attack.

- Wow! - exclaimed Krivitsky. "So our Stepanchikov is the very bloody murderer of women?" Who would have thought? Crime drama in the woods near Moscow! And apparently Stepanchikov is so quiet, it seems, he will not hurt a fly. However, perhaps, I also noticed in him a certain abnormality, although I did not give myself the report to the end ... It turns out that the unfortunate girls with cut throats are his doing. Damn it

- Boris, could you help the detective agent and the doctor to take Stepanchikov away from here? I suppose such support will not seem to them superfluous. The crew is already preparing.

"Well, of course, let's go along with them," agreed Krivitsky. - Our two old men can not cope with riotous. They say that crazy people manifest incredible physical strength at such moments.

- Sorry, but I would prefer to stay in Privolny. I do not want to leave women without protection and help, - answered Saltykov.

- Understand. I understand and share ... - Krivitsky chuckled and added: - Even more so, you and cute Anna Afanasyevna seem to have already become friends. Okay, where is our mad fellow there? I'm going to give him all possible help.

And Krivitsky retired toward the house.

- I probably need to go to Lele? - asked Anna. "Valentine, will you mind if I leave you alone for a while now?"

- I will not object, but it is better not to disturb Lena. She, according to the nanny, returned to her room to rest and, perhaps, was already asleep.

- Did she really fall asleep immediately after that? - Anya was surprised. - I would not sleep at least a week.

- Helen is a sane person with strong nerves. She is well aware that sleep is the best medicine. Let him rest. Do not wake her. After all, she got cool.

Chapter 30

Helena

I can not say that my awakening was wonderful. My head ached from pain, my general weakness did not allow me to move a hand or foot, for all the limbs seemed to be filled with lead and in every possible way proved their foreignness to my body. In addition, nightmares did not have a good mood, and as soon as I just remember yesterday, before my eyes all the pictures flashed worse than the other.

Nerves to hell, which, however, is not surprising - this holiday in the village completely finished me off. Finding corpses is not a pleasant occupation, but I almost didn't act as a victim myself ... And this is not the role that I usually prefer!

God, how bad I feel today! It is just right to splash water over myself, but after those cramps in which Stepanchikov has clogged, I will not risk it.

Maybe it will be easier if something to eat? Food can brighten up the most bitter despair. In addition, you need to somehow get yourself together and go to replace Anya and Valentina by the stream. I sit on the grass near the water, it calms ...

Although, maybe it is generally a stupid idea - why keep gold in running water for some unknown reason? Mystical evil wash away? If you judge a cold head, there was no mysticism here - grandfather, going to war and leaving the estate to strangers, buried expensive things in her own cellar, and her granddaughter and friends found her grandfathers treasure. The story is quite everyday.

As for the ghosts - probably Stepanchikov with a sore head duril. You never know what a madman can throw out ... Well, thank God, everything fell into place and is again explainable from the standpoint of common sense.

I went downstairs, determined to have breakfast, before something again got in the way, such as a new attack by a psychopath or something else like that ...

- Elena, you are my sweetheart, what a joy! - the nanny, who fiddled with the samovar, greeted me with a smile. - So you waited!

Is it really a joy? I really do not remember when the new day promised me something pleasant.

The nurse wiped her hands on her apron and whispered hotly in my ear:

- Your hubby, Mikhail Pavlovich, arrived in the morning with the first train. The local mistress returned to Gireyevo, so she brought him. They are kind of related? He was away from the station in Gireyevo, he thought you were living there, but when he learned that you were here, immediately jumped into the crew and came to Privolnoye. To wake, however, did not order, said, wait until you get up. I took him into the room to Valentin Petrovich, let him also suck an hour or two off the road, he got lost. Valentin and Nytochka have been kicking all the same at the stream all night ...

Without listening, I ran upstairs. Having climbed into the bedroom of Valentina, I did find Misha there, who was not sleeping at all, but had already risen and was just about to start looking for a wife.

God, I hope that this is not a ghost, but the real Mikhail Pavlovich of flesh and blood.

To finally verify this, I hung on his neck and began to cover his face with kisses with such fervor, as if we had not seen each other for several centuries. What a wonderful moment! If only it had not been overshadowed by thoughts of yesterday's incident — after all, now Mikhail would have to be told about everything in hot pursuit, and such stories can poison any joy.

- Well, how do you rest here? - My beloved spouse inquired when we found the strength to briefly open our arms. "Sorry, but you look unimportant." Probably from an excess of free time?

Glancing in the mirror, I caught a reflection of my own face. Hmmm, really, a so-so little face, you should at least get a bit puffy. However, if we take into account all the preceding circumstances, everything could be much worse, and my appearance hardly deserves serious censure.

- In my opinion, you're wrong, - I could not resist. - For the woman who tried to kill tonight, I do not look bad at all. Just beautiful! Believe me, my throat cut would have gone much less.

"So," Michael said hopelessly. - You are in your repertoire as usual. Come on, tell me.

I proceeded to the story, but instead of words, suddenly, tears poured in an irresistible stream of words. Yes, a modern emancipated woman should be able to cope with such trifles as murder-another, and not relieve the soul with self-oblivious sobs on a man's shoulder, but everyone has the right to a moment's weakness, isn't it?

Even for a second, it seemed to me that I was finally thrown in a wave onto a hard coast after I had endured long wanderings, an attack by pirates, a shipwreck and a storm ...

"Several women have already been killed in the local district," I finally said, choking on tears. "And I didn't want to fill up the list of victims when the criminal was caught on me as bait…"

"Why didn't you try to keep away from the killings?" - Michael asked in a stern voice, not forgetting, however, soothingly patting me on the shoulder. - You always struggle for the honorable right to rake dirt behind others! It seems your nose just itches and itches , if you don't put it on any crime story ... No wonder you were called the Angel of Death - truly where you are, there are murders.

Well, this is too much! For any notation, you need to be able to find a place and time, and now such tactless statements did not at all fit the situation ...

- Maybe you still dare to say that I myself am to blame? I exclaimed indignantly, feeling the tears begin to dry by themselves. "This time I was just a good-looking sweetheart!" I engaged in charity, comforted as a poor widow as I did and did not give any reason to cut my throat ... And in general, let me notice, trying to moralize, you behave like a disgusting bore! If I had not missed you so much, I would have remembered that it was time to be offended.

And yet the insult poked into my heart, helping me to pull myself together, stop crying and continue the conversation with proud calmness. When I managed to take a hold of myself so much that even the story of the bloody crimes that took place in the local wilderness I was able to calmly bring to the final point, that is, to the distraught Stepanchikov attacking me, who wanted to slit my throat with a razor, Mikhail sighed bitterly.

"I understood that my presence was necessary here ..."

- How could you understand that? - I was surprised.

- According to your letter. Returning from the trip to the front back to Moscow, I found in Zemgor prepared to send a letter and managed to intercept those that were addressed to me. Otherwise, your letter would look for me another month on the fronts. And it is interesting! Here listen.

Mikhail pulled a crumpled piece of paper out of his pocket with his crooked hand and read it impressively:

"I believe that a couple of weeks spent in the village will benefit me. There is marvelous forest air, fresh milk, and the society has been extremely pleasant, so this place is quite suitable to hide from the bustle of Moscow life. I enjoy peace and must say - idleness has a great effect on the nervous system.

Here are just a constant lack of sleep, I endure hard. But what to do if we are disturbed by ghosts here at night. I, however, doubted that the ghosts were the messengers from the other world, rather, it was someone's mystification. One thing can be said with confidence - well, I grabbed the Browning ... I literally do not part with it for a minute, and at night I have to put it under the pillow. "

So what do you think of all this thinking, my dear?

- Damn it! - I could not resist. - It is not harmful sometimes to re-read what has crawled out from under your pen, before sending a letter to the post office. I thought that I was writing to you a joyful, cheerful letter, so that I would not worry about me on my trip to the front, which was already difficult, and now I was distracted by another problem and finished writing the letter, thinking of something completely different. And let it slip unintentionally. But what to do, lies have never been my forte. So you came to save me?

- It may be, and save. In any case, I had to figure out on the spot, for which you are so necessary to Browning under the pillow.

- Oh, by the way, about Browning ... You will not mind if we grab the Browning and have breakfast in the lap of nature, on the grass by the stream? Such an improvised picnic by the water. The weather today has this.

- Picnic in the morning early? This is very nice, but maybe we will postpone it a bit? There, come, and the dew has not dried yet, the water will be damp, do not you think?

"Alas, dear, you have to accept some inconveniences." We must change in the post the owner of the local estate and the staff captain Saltykov.

- God, the wave of militarism has covered even the deep rear. And what are they, I'm sorry, doing in this post? Is the estate protected from enemy sabotage groups dreaming of breaking through to Moscow province to get around the Mother See from the north? Vigilance, of course, is a great thing, but let me remind you - the fighting is conducted in the far western outskirts and our army will not allow itself to pass the Germans to Moscow under any circumstances! This can not be because this can never be. And imagine this is impossible!

I had to explain that the post on the estate was not at all put up for protection against the Germans, but for completely different purposes. In the creek, the treasure found by us is washed by the waters, which is of such obvious value that you will not throw it at the mercy of fate. Have to guard. And guarding the treasure together with my husband will be much more interesting to me than paired with an old woman nanny, so Misha arrived even by the way.

But since Michael was not familiar with the entire history of the treasure hunt, my story turned out to be short and inconclusive, and there was no time for a more detailed and detailed presentation.

Having promised that we still have many hours of sitting by the stream ahead of us and we will have time to talk about everything, I dragged Misha to the park.

- Lord, what a wonderful air here! What greens! What a silence! - admired the estate of Ani my husband. - You know, after the war, I would also gladly settle in some rural corner ... How do you look at it? We would enjoy the closeness of nature, rural simplicity, and maybe even be able to do ordinary physical labor ...

Since I have already fully enjoyed all of the above, I could not resist the remark, seasoned with a touch of sarcasm:

- Oh yes, waving a scythe in the meadows, you would be irresistible!

Anya and Valentin, showing the advantages of rural simplicity, wrapped themselves in a greatcoat and naively napped at an extinguished fire, clinging to each other. If desired, all imperial values could be fished out of the water and dragged off right under the guards' noses.

However, this impression was deceptive - as soon as I tried to get close, Valentine opened his eyes and even grabbed his weapon. This is what front hardening means!

I introduced Michael and Valentines to each other. Saltykov, being a close friend of the late Ivan Malashevich, it seemed to me, was experiencing difficult feelings, shaking hands with my current husband, but in any case he tried not to give it out.

Anya, who was half asleep, hardly recognized Misha, dressed in a military jacket.

The main thing on which she focused her efforts were attempts to question me about yesterday's incident with Stepanchikov in obscene language. I promised to tell her everything in detail as soon as she rested.

Having let go of Anya and Saltykov, Misha and I settled on the bank and lit the fire again - the smoke drove away the damned mosquitoes, who decided to join our meal, using me and my dear husband as a snack.

- Is it true that Varvara Filippovna returned to Gireyevo? - I asked, removing from the basket all that grabbed for our picnic.

Yes, for a cheese with a tear, which the naughty Stepanchikov had refused the day before, there was a better use. However, I would not regret a piece of cheese, even for a dangerous maniac - after all, in a psychiatric hospital, where he will now have to stay, good cheeses are most likely not served.

"Nanny said you came with your aunt."

- Yes, Aunt Varya is already in Gireyevo, and probably plunged into the usual hustle and bustle, - confirmed the good news Michael. "She was just eager to get on with the affairs of the hospital as soon as possible."

Sleep in your hand. God, what a blessing! Varvara Filippovna was already in Gireyevo and took up the affairs of the hospital ...
Therefore, I am free from them. At last I am a free bird again! The shackles of labor for the good of society have fallen, and I am free as the wind!

And Misha, of course, was most interested in the story of the Count's treasure. What can you do, I had to satisfy his curiosity.

- You see, it all started with the fact that I had a chance to find an old notebook with a recording of the confession of Anin's ancestor, who lived in the 18th century and used to be in great favor with the Empress Catherine ...

- And what, any old sins were revealed? - Michael asked with curiosity.

- Yes, not without it. - And I told everything in order: both about the casket is great, and about the Shlisselburg fortress, and about the puzzle plan of Anya's grandfather, who hid the treasure during the Balkan war, and about our unsuccessful searches, and about the help of the old healer Sychikha, who taught me how to handle old treasures ...

As soon as I reached Melanie's advice, a skeptical smile began to play on Mikhail's face. Oh, another Thomas the unbeliever! Men are such disgusting skeptics ...

"I personally have never heard of the treasures found soaked in streams," Misha grinned.

"But you have never been a treasure hunter before!" And every serious treasure hunter from birth is familiar with such elementary rules! You have not heard a lot of things and you do not even guess. I am sure that the name "Petrov Cross" does not tell you anything. And without this grass to search for treasures completely pointless!

It is not known where our discussion would lead us, but then bushes rustled behind my back and, to the disgust, a familiar voice said:

- Raise your hands up, gentlemen!

CHAPTER 31

Anna

After a sleepless night spent by the campfire on the beach, it was especially pleasant to stretch out on your bed under a warm blanket and close your eyes. The tired consciousness did not long resist the waves of sleep, and now Anya was already floating on these waves, among some vague, but at the same time sweet images.

Visions lounged her, carried away farther and farther into the dark depths, and quiet, gentle music was heard, and someone's native voices whispered something tender to her ... And suddenly a short unpleasant sound with a discord intertwined into this soothing symphony. It was so hard to emerge from the dream, but somewhere near the door I slammed the door, and along the corridor heavy steps of male legs shod in boots ran through.

Anya jumped in bed. Did she hear the shot or was it the sound of her sleep? Somewhere in the park they were shouting ... Shots and shouts became the usual background of the life here, but I so wanted to hope that it was in the past. After all, the psychopathic killer is arrested, what is happening again in Privolny?

She rushed to the window and threw back the curtain. In the park, where the screams were heard, Saltykov ran with a revolver in his hand. Turning into the linden alley, he became almost invisible, but nevertheless it was possible to trace his path - Valentine did not have time to throw on his tunic, and behind the trees a snow-white shirt flashed with a dotted line.

Anya grabbed a bathrobe and, dressing on the move and tangling excitement in her sleeves, ran down the stairs, onto the porch, and further into the park, into the alley where Saltykov disappeared. The alley led to the creek.

- Nytochka, baby, what happened there? What did you and Valentin Petrovich stir up? - the nanny shouted after her, but Anya had no time to answer.

At the creek she opened a terrible picture. Lieutenant Krivitsky stood right on a tablecloth spread over the grass with the remnants of trampled food. With one hand he held Lelya, and with the other he pressed the revolver to her temple. Woman Krivitsky shielded as a shield from a possible shot of Mikhail Pavlovich, who took the lieutenant to fly.

But from the back Saltykov, already close, approached Krivitsky, having sent the muzzle of his staff officer gun to the head of the lieutenant.

Krivitsky's beautiful face was distorted by a hideous grimace. Mikhail Pavlovich was pale to blue, and his hand, squeezing Browning, was trembling badly - he was probably afraid that, having decided to shoot, he would inevitably catch his wife. Saltykov's disfigured features seemed petrified, his profile again looked like a roughly hewn piece of granite ...

Each of the men shouted to the enemy that any attempt to move would be worth his life, but none of them started shooting.

- My God, Boris Vladimirovich, what are you doing? - confused asked Anna.

Lieutenant Krivitsky ignored her question, but Saltykov, without turning around, threw:

- Annie, get away!

Move away? No matter how wrong! But she doesn't have any weapons ñ neither Browning, nor Nagan, and everyone around is armed. Anya searched her eyes for anything that could have passed for a weapon, and her eyes fell on the heavy fragment of the trunk of an old apple tree, which Saltykov brought from somewhere at night as fuel for the fire.

A cudgel in women's hands is, of course, not the message of God, but it is still better than nothing. Armed, Anya settled closer to Valentin behind Krivitsky's back, trying on, like a lieutenant to hit the lieutenant, before he dares to shoot Lelya. Alas, the chances that the club hit will outrun the shot were slim.

Meanwhile, the men shouted again.

- Hey you, one-eyed lord! Shouted lieutenant Crovatow. "Immediately get a bag out of the water, or I'll blow your skull to your lady now!" Do you hear, shpak, that you were ordered?

"If even the hair falls from the head of my wife, I will not leave you even a wet place," answered Mikhail Pavlovich in a broken voice, trying in vain to temper the tremor. - I will have nothing to lose!

- Before you, Krivitsky, you have time to smash the skull lady, I'll smash your own! - Saltykov snapped at his side. - Lower the revolver, Boris! You, like no one, know that my hand does not tremble!

And here came Elena Sergeevna's completely calm voice:

- Gentlemen, stop screaming! You completely stunned me. It is always better to agree calmly.

All of a sudden silence. Anya remembered that Lelya has long applied such tactics at a time of danger — to talk to the enemy.

While the enemy is busy talking, he is not so dangerous, and winning minutes can lead to salvation.

- Boris Vladimirovich, - in a secular tone, as if it were a card dispute, Lelya turned to the lieutenant. - In my opinion, you are doing stupid, and even very big. You have still not done anything particularly criminal. Should I start? Think about it! Penetrating a house where you didn't steal anything, and scaring women with imaginary ghosts are not so serious offenses, you can count them as just bad sense jokes ...

"Well, you and Madame Chigareva brought me to the idea of ghosts — it was true for you to regard me as a ghost and fear until I lost consciousness!" - snapped Krivitsky.

"That's it," Elena Sergeevna happily supported. - We are to blame for this. And the treasure does not belong to you! This is the legal legacy of Anna Afanasyevna.

- Legitimate inheritance is a bank deposit transferred to the heirs according to the will. And the treasure is a treasure, with him too, as fate would dispose. In whose hands he falls, that is his master. And I think, imagine that I have many more rights to this treasure than Anna Afanasyevna!

- This is on what basis? - Saltykov asked sternly.

"And on the fact that my father is the illegitimate son of the old owner of this estate, the heroic count lying under the tombstone here in the park ... And in an amicable way, not only a treasure, but everything here should be mine!"

Anya almost dropped the bludgeon from her hands - did the grandfather cheat on her grandmother, defying all her romantic love? And even had a son on the side? It can not be! And if you can?

"The count paid off his illegal son's mother with money and forgot about him," continued the lieutenant. - But the truth is! There is truth in the world! Not long after that, the count lived, returned from the Balkans in a closed coffin ... paid for his sin. And my father lived all his life with this insult. When the legitimate heir of the count, father Anna Afanasyevna, was on the verge of ruin, his father bought out his ancestral home in St. Petersburg.

"In Petrograd," corrected Lelya for some reason.

In general, there were too many unnecessary words, and therefore everything that happened began to seem to Ana as a nightmare, where all actions stretch endlessly, endlessly and without beginning.

It can not be that people really had such long conversations, aiming at each other from revolvers?

"In those days, the capital was still called St. Petersburg, as I hope, it will also be called henceforth, when everyone forgets about its shameful renaming," snapped Krivitsky. - It was important to my father at least that way, but to return to his ancestral home. Family property passed into his hands. And I was still a child, playing in the attic among old things, found a secret box in my grandfather's bureau, and in it there were papers, from which it appeared that there was a fabulous treasure hidden in the estate near Moscow. True, the damned old man did not name the exact place where he had buried gold, but I still vowed that I would someday find the treasure of the ancestors. War prevented me. But what was my shock when I learned that my front-line friend Alyoshka Chigarev was married to the heir of the ducal estate, that he, too, from somewhere had visited about the treasures and intended, as soon as circumstances permit, to search for treasure in Privolnoye! I just could not cope with myself!

"So you killed Alexey with a shot in the back?" - squeezed Saltykov, and his voice, and so deaf, was like the gnash of old iron ...

- Well, that, you suppose, you will never prove it! - shrillly declared Krivitsky, nervously twitching his shoulder, causing his barrel of a revolt and danced at Lely's temple, which seemed, in spite of everything, as calm as the marble Venus sticking up over the pond. - Do not go into this business, the captain! I do not want anyone's death, but I do not advise anyone to stand in my way, the blood will not stop me!

- Me too. And it is harder for me to restrain myself so as not to put a bullet in the back of your head, "Saltykov answered dully.

And in Ani's brain, only one thing jumped: here he is, Lieutenant Krivitsky - the man who took Alyosha's life. And now he is aiming again at a living person, at a woman, and threatening to kill ... Here he is, here. And keeps his finger on the trigger. Killer!

These thoughts circled my head and stirred mind.

- And how did you find out that we found gold? And what is washing it here in the creek? - Lelia continued in such a tone, as if she hadn't been told anything particularly interesting yet and she had to continue questioning in the hope of at least finding out something.

"Village, sir, madam, rural morals," answered Krivitsky, squeezing her throat even more to say that Lele was not so comfortable. - I went to the shop for cigarettes today, and there the cook of Anna Afanasyevna grinds her tongue with a pomelo. The treasure, he says, was found by the gentlemen, but with joy, with his mind and started to move. One officer was brought to the yellow house, and those who remained stuck the gold in a bag and soaked in the creek ... It is a pity, the day before I did not know about it yet. What would have been easier - to spank Anya at night here by the fire, while the other gentlemen were busy catching the distraught Stepanchikov, pull the bag out of the water, and the whole thing was not long ... Okay, we got too carried away with the conversation, and time passes. Anna Afanasyevna, gentlemen are too intractable. You will have to work hard and take the bag out of the stream, since you have put it in there for some devil. Move, madam, or I'll make a bloody cutlet out of your girlfriend this second. You did not see how brains scatter from a punctured skull? Believe me, the spectacle will not be pleasant. And do not care if the noble gentlemen rush to avenge in the late track, I, too, have nothing to lose! And without gold, I would not leave, I had dreamed about it for too long, and it came to you by chance ...

At that moment, Mikhail Pavlovich, unable to control himself, inadvertently dropped the Browning dancing in his hand and bent down to raise his weapon. Krivitsky focused all his attention on Croatia, expecting some kind of dirty trick from his actions.

- Damned killer! - Anna cried suddenly, waking up, completely aware of everything Krivitsky said, and unexpectedly for everyone, even for herself, with a sweep of a cudgel on her head. Falling, Krivitsky involuntarily waved his hands. Elena Sergeyevna, feeling that the grip on her neck was weak, managed not only to take her hand with the revolver away from her temple, but also dug her teeth into the lieutenant's hand.

Having fallen to the ground, the lieutenant pulled Lelia behind him, but Saltykov immediately fell next to them, trying to simultaneously take away the weapons from Krivitsky and wrest a woman from his hands. A shot crashed, and Mikhail Pavlovich also fell on the grass away from the three winding bodies.

- Mr. Horvath! - Anya rushed to him. - What's wrong with you? Are you injured? It seems there is no blood ... Mikhail Pavlovich! Wake up!

In the meantime, Saltykov managed to snatch the revolver from the weakened Krivitsky and drag him away from him to Lelya, who barely opened her convulsively flattened teeth. Twisting the lieutenant's hands, Valentin tightly tied them with a belt.

"Ah, Boris, Boris," he said bitterly. "Before, I used to turn only Hans captives, but now I have to mine. Most of our people went crazy. If it goes on like this, in a year or two everyone will start to fight with their friends and brothers ...

But Krivitsky did not answer - his eyes rolled up, and pallor spread over his face - probably, the nervous tension and severe head bruising led to fainting.

Women tried to revive Mikhail Pavlovich, who also lost consciousness.

- Misha, wake up! - Lelia, disheveled, in a soiled and torn blouse, bent over her husband, slapping him on the cheeks.

Anya found among the scattered around picnic supplies an overturned and half-drained bottle of cognac and poured a few drops into Mr. Horvatov's open mouth. He finally flinched and opened a healthy eye.

- Lelia, you're alive! He whispered. - God, when the shot slammed, I thought that this bastard still shot at you.

"Well, I would never allow myself to kill myself!" - snickered Lelia, straightening a strand of hair out of her hairstyle. - True, I had to bite, but I do not like it so much! Inelegant occupation, quite unsuitable for a lady who received a decent upbringing. Although, what to say, the circumstances are excused! But in the mouth now such muck ... Well, at least, that I did not bite a bite from the bastard, it would be possible to get poisoned! Annie, there is no sip of brandy left? Let me rinse my mouth. Oh, something a picnic today is not my joy, gentlemen!

"It would be better to understand what you had in mind when you wrote that the local peace has a great effect on the nervous system," Mikhail grumbled, getting to his feet. - What exactly is called peace in these places?

CHAPTER 32

Helena

Thank God, my vacation in the village came to an end (fortunately, it all ends someday!), And I could safely go home, taking away the vivid impressions of everything experienced and the extraordinary beauty of the Catherine's times sapphire set, which Anya almost forced take me as a gift.

Now that my emotions have subsided a bit, I realized that I had the opportunity to participate in one of the most exciting adventures I've ever come across. All the attributes of the adventure novel were there - lost and newfound treasures, love stories, ancient secrets, ancestral nest, full of charm of bygone times, noble knights, treacherous villains and beautiful ladies. Yes, I seriously risked my life, I was very tired, I didn't sleep and I was worried a lot, but there's no real adventure without it! And without them, life seems so dull, even if you sleep all day, take no risks and no worries.

Anya and Valentin left Privolnoye with us. In their immediate plans was a modest wedding and a joint return to the front. Annie got her way - with all the softness she sometimes knew how to be adamant.

I was packing in my room when Anya came to me, who just radiated charm (she had recently become prettier), but wearing, as usual, a gloomy mourning dress.

- Annie, will you go to Moscow? - I was surprised.

For the bride, in whose role Anya turned out to be again, deep mourning was a completely inappropriate outfit. Especially Annie paid the debt to the memory of her deceased husband, having revenged his murderer, and now she had the right to open a new page in the book of her destiny, without looking back.

"And I have nothing but mourning dresses," Anya explained, pulling at the black frill on the sleeve. - When moving to Privolnoe, it seemed to me that now I am doomed to walk forever in mourning. I did not expect any changes in my fate and other outfits did not stock up.

"Well, the more pleasant these changes are," I said philosophically. - Let's start by picking up some of my things for you, and in Moscow, as we were going, we go to the best modest women and order a new wardrobe for you.

- Lelia, I will soon go to the army of the sister of mercy. Why do I need a new wardrobe at the front? - Anya objected. - In addition to the uniform sister's headscarf and robe, I will not need much.

But still the idea to try on some outfits, as it seemed to me, came to her liking.

After going through a few things, Anya chose a gray business suit, one of those in French magazines called "tailleur gris clair" - the model is impeccable in terms of good taste, but too strict.

To me, a narrow fitted suit became a bit cramped (the local pancakes here did!), And on Anna he sat flawlessly. I enjoyed giving it to Anyuta and added:

"You know, savory accessories are needed for such a dress to make it truly sophisticated." Try on this hat ... My modist called it "soupir cTautomnes" - "autumn rustles".

- Poetic name for the cap! However, it completely corresponds to the plan.

Anya put on her hat and spun around the mirror.

- God, how it suits you! - I was not able to hide my delight. - You are just made for each other with this hat. Never before met such complete harmony! What a pity that soon you will change it to a sisterly kerchief from a simple canvas ...

- Oh, Lelia, it's not forever! Here the war will end, and everything will change. I think that after we all suffered, the post-war life will seem to us especially bright and festive - people will learn to appreciate every moment! You know, I have so many different plans ... Since I inherited my grandfather's inheritance and I can no longer think about money, I dream of turning life into a real holiday. If only the war is over as soon as possible!

Anya paused and carefully asked:

- What do you think, is this Krivitsky really my grandfather's grandson?

For my part, I had already managed to ponder this question, and Anya did not take me by surprise.

- I would not believe his word. Krivitsky does not look like a man who always tells the truth. Perhaps his father just bought a house from yours, the usual deal. And Krivitsky invented the history of secret kinship after his grandfather's documents fell into his hands to somehow motivate his rights to the treasure. Valentine said that the lieutenant always had a strange reputation, even for a trench officer. People like him are cowards and liars, but you can't hide it at the front. He tried not to take risks, if possible to wriggle out of danger, to hide behind others' backs, in short, as the English say, he was playing a "mean game."

- But he went to kill Alexei! - Anya exclaimed and bit her lip with excitement.

- There always comes a day when such cautious gentlemen lose their heads and go too far. Undoubtedly, it happened in this case as well - Krivitsky was simply mad with greed. And chose the moment to his crime goes unpunished. Well, God bless him. Tell me better, what did you think of doing with the treasure? Leaving it in Privolnoy is dangerous. You see, the cook broke out, the rumor of gold has already gone around, and in your absence any other greedy types may attack the estate. On the front you are with you, too, the casket is not big drag. Here, except to hand over valuables to a bank, but since the beginning of the war, banks seem less and less reliable ...

Anya laughed and handed me a folder.

- Lelia, I went on the path of my grandfather and, too, going to war, I re-hid the treasure. Valentin and I buried him yesterday in a secret place. I ask you to keep these papers. Here is my testament. I leave my estate to Valentin, and if neither me nor he is destined to return from the front, then you. It so happened that closer than the two of you I have no one left. And here are my notes, in which a secret place is hidden that hides a treasure. Now I'm sure - if, God forbid, something happens to me, you will easily find grandfather's treasures ...

I have escaped only one completely inappropriate phrase:

- You are crazy!

- No, I'm just in my right mind and I have foreseen everything as it should ... Although, honestly, I confess, it wasn't that easy for me to keep my mind this summer!

When the old cart, in which Mikhail, Anyuta, and Saltykov were settled, drove away from the porch of the estate, accompanied by the sobbing of the nanny, I involuntarily looked around to look at the old house and park for the last time.

Oddly enough, I was sad to leave these places - yet here I experienced one of the most exciting adventures in my life ...

Suddenly I came across a male figure standing in a shady alley near the pond. I thought that it was some of the Gireevsky officers who came to say goodbye to me and wanted to ask the coachman to stop the crew, but the figure looming in the distance did not get closer, although we seemed to be approaching her ...

Looking more attentively, I felt my heart beating deafeningly - on a high military uniform was the white uniform of the times of the war in the Balkans.

I looked at the faces of my companions - everyone seemed calm, chatted nicely and not one of them paid exactly any attention to the stranger, as if he weren't there ...

And the officer in a white uniform stood a little under the lace shadow of the lime crowns, waved his hand goodbye and disappeared among the old trees.

And was there an officer? Maybe just sun glare played? Lord, it is the same!

epilogue

In September 1916, Lieutenant Colonel Saltykov was buried in the city's Bratskoye cemetery in Moscow. Two months later, his widow, Anna Chigareva-Saltykova, sister of mercy, who died from wounds received at the front, rested in his presence.

In the spring of 1917, two men, a man and a woman, stopped at the tomb of Saltykov and laid several branches of white lilac on the tombstone.

"You often come here, Lelya," the man said quietly.

"Yes," the woman replied, adjusting the flowers scattered on the granite of the gravestone. - And I will come here while I live. It seems to me that the souls of the dead need to be remembered about them ... It's not for nothing that we accompany them with the words: "Eternal memory." And when many, many years pass and no one of us is left in this world, anyway, someone's hand will put flowers on the grave. And the souls of ancestors, like the ancient Lares, will protect and protect their descendants.

- You're a fantasy! - the man said, he extended his hand to the lady, and they headed towards the nearby church ...

The Moscow Fraternal Cemetery was opened in November 1914 on the outskirts of Moscow in All Saints by decision of the City Duma. It is located in a huge old park. Here were buried the soldiers, officers and sisters of mercy who died in the fronts of world war. There were many victims and the cemetery-memorial, equipped with donations of Muscovites, quickly grew.

According to the project of the architect A. V. Shchusev, a memorial church was erected at Bratskoye Cemetery with galleries in which it was supposed to place documentary evidence of the course of hostilities and to leave for eternal storage war trophies. Consecrated a new temple in January 1917 ...

In the early 1930s, by the decision of the Soviet leadership, the church was destroyed, and the cemetery was destroyed. Just so that there was no ... In the 1950s, large-scale construction was carried out in the Sokol area (the former All-Saints). Part of the territory of the Brotherhood Cemetery Memorial was built up houses.

Land from construction pits, mixed with the ashes of the dead and fragments of coffins, dumped into trucks and taken to landfill. The rest of the cemetery was finally flattened to the ground and turned into a city square.

The current Muscovites, walking around the squares on the Sandy, no longer remember that under their feet are the graves of ancestors who died once for their homeland ...

However, on the site of the Brotherhood cemetery, one tombstone accidentally survived - a monument at the grave of a student at Moscow University, mortally wounded in a battle near Baranavichy in 1916. The last words of the young man, spoken to him before his death, are inscribed on the stone: "How good is life, how you want to live."

Forgive us, ancestors ... Eternal memory to you!

Made in the USA
Monee, IL
15 May 2020